Primula Bond is an Oxford-educated mother of three boys and has lived in London and Cairo. She currently lives in Hampshire with her husband and younger sons and works part-time as a legal secretary for criminal defence lawyers as well as writing freelance 'human interest' features for the national press. She has written erotic short stories and novels for various publishers and magazines for twenty years and this is her fourth erotic novel.

Primula also offers a critique service for aspiring erotic and romantic writers through the online Writers Workshop.

PRIMULA BOND

The Golden Locket

AVON

AVON

A division of HarperCollins*Publishers*
77–85 Fulham Palace Road,
London W6 8JB

www.harpercollins.co.uk

A Paperback Original 2013
1

A catalogue record for this book is
available from the British Library

ISBN 978-0-00-752414-3

Set in Sabon LT Std by Palimpsest Book Production Limited,
Falkirk, Stirlingshire

Printed bound in Great Britain by Clays Ltd, St Ives plc

MIX
Paper from
responsible sources
FSC C007454

Once again my heartfelt thanks to all at Avon Books: Adam Nevill, Helen Bolton and Cleo Little, and all my Avon Ladies, for welcoming me to the Avon family. Their enthusiasm for and intricate knowledge of my efforts spurred me on even when the thought of all those rewrites had me flagging.

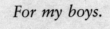

For my boys.

As I would not be a slave, so I would not be a master.
Abraham Lincoln

The pure and simple truth is rarely pure, and never simple.

Oscar Wilde

I can resist anything but temptation.

Oscar Wilde

CHAPTER ONE

I pinch myself. Hard. I still can't believe I'm finally here. I can't believe Serena Folkes has travelled halfway across the world and tonight has her face pressed against a triple-glazed window high above New York.

The distance between the cold cliffs of Devon where my journey began two months ago and these fiery, multi-coloured showers of New Year exploding over Central Park is, literally, an ocean. And just before Christmas I flew over that ocean with a one-way ticket in my hand, my mentor and lover Gustav Levi at my side, and the promise of a new life, a new home, awaiting us both.

A rocket shoots up into the air, level with where I'm standing. An umbrella of sparks spatters Manhattan as the rocket's discarded tail spirals away like a dead leaf into the boating lake. That papery shred could be the symbol of my unhappy childhood, adopted as a foundling by a neglectful, absent pair who every single day considered me a thorn in their flesh, never bringing themselves to touch me or love me, let alone call me their own.

Thanks to Gustav that past life finally nose-dived into the water two weeks ago. That's when he took me up in the London

Eye to toast the sell-out success of my debut photographic exhibition which he had helped to launch. Little did I know we were about to toast our future as well.

As the big wheel lifted us through the falling snow we glimpsed the gallery where he had showcased my work, and Gustav told me he was packing up the London house and moving to New York for a while, a year at least, to oversee his US businesses. For a moment there my heart did some plummeting of its own. A year might as well be forever. So much had happened between us in such a short time. The fighting, the making up, the silver bracelet he'd given me and the symbolic silver chain that bound us together. And then the sex, oh, the sex! That slow burn of passion had warmed us through the winter, but now I thought he was cutting loose. I thought he was telling me that our agreement, that I would be his until the last photograph in the exhibition was sold, was just that. An agreement.

But as the Eye spun slowly back to the ground Gustav Levi kissed me until our lips were swollen and told me just the opposite. He didn't want anything to end. His feelings for me were every bit as strong as mine were for him, despite, or because of, the weeks it had taken for me to win his trust. And then he gave me that plane ticket and asked me to come to New York City.

So now I'm up here in his stunning penthouse apartment on New Year's Eve watching these fireworks rain down on the city. Far below me festive cheers rise to hysteria and police sirens race each other up and down the streets whooping like arguing toddlers. I'm the luckiest girl in the world.

But there's one thing missing.

'Yes, ma'am, you have to be gold-plated to live up here.'

Gustav couldn't hide his satisfaction. We had abandoned

our suitcases and half-eaten pizzas and were wallowing in the huge oval Jacuzzi on our first night in the apartment. The sun was slow to set over the Hudson River and I was jet-lagged after the flight from London.

'And this is a gilded palace, that's for sure,' I murmured sleepily as he lifted my naked body, glistening like a seal.

The bubbles buffeted my skin, making me tingle. 'Who would have thought it? The urchin who ran away from the house by the sea, who even lived in a caravan for a while, now rescued by her handsome prince and installed in this beautiful tower.'

'That's why I call you my Rapunzel.' His laugh was low, stirring in his chest as his fingers trailed over me. 'And I might have to lock you in here to keep you safe.'

'I can always escape using this!' I flicked at his face with a twisted rope of my long hair. 'Oh, Gustav. I'm going to treasure every single moment of our adventure.'

He laughed softly again. He balanced me on the surface of the water with his strong arms and made me study myself in the mirror alongside. Made me watch as he pushed an egg-shaped soap slowly over my breasts so that the nipples pierced the caps of foam like raspberry icebergs. He moved it over my stomach and let his hand rest on my navel, rising and falling with my breath.

'If there was such a thing as a mermaid, this is how her top half would look.'

He pulled my legs apart, dangled my ankles over the sides of the tub, and stroked the egg of soap down, down into every nook and cranny.

I moaned sleepily and wriggled and slithered down his chest, my bottom bumping over the stiff jut between his legs. The physical desire sparking in response and unravelling inside me was arguing with the mental jumble in my head. After the last few tumultuous days my mind was like a snow shaker.

3

There was the pride and excitement of my first-ever exhibition selling out, then that trip in the London Eye when I had no idea what Gustav had planned for himself or for me. Then the euphoria when he asked me to fly away with him, the fantastic, blinding clarity that we were going to be together after all. Packing up the house in London, our faithful assistant Crystal helping to fold my new clothes, treating me to an expensive hair-do 'to tame that bird's nest', instructing the stylist to put in some golden highlights but not letting him take too much off the auburn tresses that tumble nearly to my waist.

Then Gustav's chauffeur Dickson speeding us to Heathrow airport, flying First Class, clinking champagne glasses as we hurtled through the skies before landing in an icy, glittering New York. The streets were bright with lights and decorations and shoppers as we motored up Broadway, hit the upper West Side. And arrived at our new home.

We had to stifle our giggles at the bowing doormen guarding the marble foyer of the condo. They looked like bouncers outside an East End gambling den. Their white gloves seemed too tight over their stubby boxers' fingers as they pushed the button to summon the lift to take us skywards. Then finally we were alone and Gustav was unlocking the heavy double doors to our new penthouse.

But there was a separate bass note beating beneath all this that could not be ignored. That was actually getting louder.

Something else had happened that snowy night in London. *Someone* else. We came off the London Eye with a bump, returned to the gallery to count our blessings, and a face from the past had appeared out of the blue and nearly stopped everything in its tracks.

Despite the warm water of the Jacuzzi a shiver ran through me. Because we might have crossed the Atlantic but there

4

were people demanding our attention, demanding answers, who were over here, too.

I rolled onto my front and stretched myself over Gustav's firm body. It was time to talk.

Gustav's quiet, dark face watched me, sharp cheeks and determined chin shadowed with the rarely fulfilled promise of beard that so turns me on. He was reading my mind. He knew what was unspooling inside my head. A hesitant smile nagged at his mouth, not quite flowering. His black hair was slicked back by the water, showing the sharp peak of his hairline and the perfect shape of his head.

'You look more chilled than I've ever seen you,' I murmured tenderly, smoothing my hand over his chest, keeping my eyes on his. Very calm, very quiet. 'Is it being here? Getting away from everything? I know you said we weren't going to be in New York forever. A year, maybe two. As long as it takes for me to make a name for myself, and for you to water your flowering empire. But it still feels like a new start, yes?'

'I'm relaxed because I'm alone with you. The more time we spend together, the more right it feels.' He played me over him, stomach to stomach, letting me slip between his fingers like an eel. 'What makes it even more special is that this is the first real home I've owned here in the States and I'm going to be sharing it with you. But I'm still a gypsy. I might take off at any moment. You know that, don't you?'

'Yes, but you have to take me with you next time.' I swayed in the water so that a warm wave lapped dangerously over the edge of the Jacuzzi and our limbs were tinged apricot from the sun's sudden surrender. 'I'll go anywhere, any time, so long as I'm with you.'

He grasped my hips and pressed me down on him. His hardness against my softness. 'So the world's our oyster. We're not shutting any doors. Only opening them.' His mouth settled into a serious line, the lower lip pushed out slightly as he pondered. His fingers ran down my spine, over my bottom. 'You're so good for me, Serena. I can't wait for our first Christmas together.'

'Me neither.' I paused. 'But I keep thinking about that showdown back in London just before we came out here. Your brother Pierre appearing at the gallery with no warning, all guns blazing. The terrible things he said.'

'The terrible things we both said.' Gustav grabbed at my wrists. 'Do you have to bring that up? Just when I was getting really, really horny?'

I resisted his grip with a couple of feeble tugs, his cue to pluck at the delicate bracelet glittering round my wrist. He locked on the silver chain that had been coiled neatly on the shelf amongst the bath oils, and looped it round the taps. I stretched my bound hands and, turning my head sideways on his chest, blew bubbles across his skin.

'It won't go away, Gustav. We have to talk about it. About him. It's all part of this new start. Ever since we first met, your five-year estrangement from Pierre has plagued you. And yet suddenly there he was, just when you least expected him. I'm only human, Gustav. I can't just make light of what happened any more than you can! I don't ever want to have something bothering me that I can't share with you. So. Don't you want to talk about it?'

Gustav sighed, tugged my wet hair back from my face and wound it tight around his knuckles.

I let my head fall back and waited, looking up at him through half-closed lids.

'How could I make light of that torrent of old grievances that poured out between us, all those painful reminders? I'm still processing it, I promise you. Pierre and I will talk more when he joins us for New Year.' Gustav rubbed his knuckles, gloved in my hair, thoughtfully across his mouth.

6

'But I'm glad he came to the gallery that day. Despite all that lip, I couldn't have gone to my grave without seeing him again.'

'You're centuries away from any grave,' I muttered, dipping my face into the warm water, briefly letting it filter into my nose, mouth, eyelids. 'But it was more than just lip, Gustav. He was getting off trying to make you squirm. He was vibrating with resentment, like a giant wasps' nest.'

Gustav shifted me a little to keep me half floating, half lying on top of him.

'It all needed saying. Like lancing a boil.' He kissed my hair away from my forehead. 'I'd forgotten how bitter his ranting could be. I wonder if it's only siblings who can twist the knife? We've both caused each other a lot of pain in the past, intentionally and unintentionally, and catching me off guard like that somehow cracked the ice. I know there's a hell of a lot still to say. We both have so much explaining and forgiving to do. But when we're through to clear water, Pierre and I can be brothers again.'

'I wouldn't know anything about brothers twisting knives. Or sisters for that matter. I don't have anyone except my cousin Polly. But I never want to see anyone attacking you like that again.' I pushed my face against him for another kiss as uneasiness still stirred inside me. 'And if they do, I'll defend you to the death!'

But we both knew there was something else we didn't dare touch on. We both knew there was a third person lurking at the centre of Pierre and Gustav's heartache. Gustav's ex-wife Margot. The woman who caused it all.

'I have to be big enough to apologise for all the pain. And I hope he will apologise to me too.' Gustav laid me more firmly on top of him so that his hardness was wedged between my thighs. 'But you know what's best of all? That, despite the foul things you heard, you're still here with me.'

I rested my cheek on his chest, and watched him in the mirror. The slow burn of arousal flamed inside me as he tugged at my hair. I didn't want to kill it with fretting. Every time he pushed his hardness between my thighs I burned with wanting.

'There's nowhere else for me to be. But I can't help feeling anxious that all you've achieved, after five long years, is that one awful row. I know you've made some tentative email contact with him, and he's confirmed the date, but New Year's Eve seems a long time to wait before you're face to face again, even though we're all in the same city now.'

'That's because his timing was terrible, as usual. I'm not going to be strong-armed into anything. I need time to gather my wits. And I want to be alone with you for Christmas.'

'Stubborn as a mule.' But I would store those lovely words up for later. 'Just make sure you fix this. He's your family. You don't want to lose him again.'

Gustav's eyes were tender as they returned my gaze in the mirror, his eyelashes misted with soapy water. He ran his hands over my bottom, grabbed the cheeks and pressed me harder down onto him. 'I will, my wise little peacemaker. But no more talking about it now. Just let me enjoy you.'

His long, lean body was beneath me. I pushed him by degrees, his muscular shoulders, his chest, smoothing my hand over his flat, taut stomach, down beneath the navel, tracing the central line of hair.

Gustav Levi sank beneath the bubbles until the only visible part of his physique, the part I wanted, was rearing like a mast out of the ocean. As he surfaced again, I hitched myself back, watching the brightness glaze over in his molasses eyes as I wound a strand of my hair several times round the stiffness, winching my face closer, smiling triumphantly as it strained towards my softly opening mouth.

'Now, let me remind you and that delectable mouth of

yours that to reside in this top-notch abode, you must toil and spin and be very grateful to me, *signorina*,' he groaned thickly as my lips closed round him. 'Bodily, spiritually, aesthetically, romantically, intellectually, carnally.'

'Orally,' I crooned, and nipped at him to shut him up. I grinned as a thought struck me. 'Ever noticed how the map of Manhattan resembles a dangling penis needing some attention?'

'Trust you to see the phallus in everything!' he said with a chuckle. 'Now suck me, girl, because there's a map of Manhattan right here needs some attention!'

To an outsider, I might look like a rich man's plaything, cavorting in his rooftop Jacuzzi, going down on him and sucking him close to climax, but this man is deadly serious about me and I am mad about him.

He waited until the last possible moment and then with a groan he quickly unwound my hair, prised my teeth and lips away, lifted me and grabbed my hips in his strong hands. He hitched me up easily, swayed and washed by the simmering water, so that I was free to ride him.

I tucked him inside me and slid slowly down, down, leaning over him, making him look at and touch all of me, my breasts, my nipples, my hair, my mouth, and I was setting the metronome of our rhythm, keeping it regular, changing gear, racking it up faster until we were bucking together in the bubbly water, causing first a high tide and then a near-flood in every sense as our new home grew dark around us.

Later I let him unwind the silver chain from my wrists and carry me, damp with scented water and heavy with satisfaction, to our huge new bed. I gazed out at the city spread below us as he padded through the huge apartment, turning the lights off in the guest rooms and arched corridors that were waiting to be filled with our new life.

'What have I done to deserve all this?' I murmured as he

slid beneath the feather-soft duvet beside me. 'I can't believe this nest in the clouds is where I'm going to come home every night!'

'You and the light in those emerald eyes are my Christmas present to myself,' he murmured into my hair. 'You will be my princess and I'm going to spoil you and spoil you until you beg me to stop.'

I pressed my face into his neck, licked at the pulse beating under his warm skin. 'I'm going to prove myself to you, though, Gustav. I'm happy to be your princess, but I want to earn my keep, too.'

He lifted my face and started to kiss me. 'Oh, I know you will, Serena. I have no worries on that score.'

I belong to him. But he belongs to me, too.

I'm jerked back to the present. Another burst of fireworks explodes over this side of the park. The display is so bright that I'm dazzled. My vision is streaked with silvery licks of fire and I have to rub them away.

Behind me, my own eyes gaze mournfully from the over-sized self-portrait Gustav has had flown over from London and hung on the wall. The girl escaping on the train from Devon the day that photograph was taken has become the girl on the plane. She's arrived. She's up on the wall, keeping watch as her first guests poke around, exploring the new flat. She's gazing at the fireworks flashing over New York City, gazing out from the top of the world, wondering what the next few months will bring.

It's New Year's Eve and the city is revelling. I was swimming against the tide as the Yellow Cab brought me slowly up Broadway just now after my fruitless trip to the airport, hoping that Gustav would be on the next plane. Everyone else was surging southwards, towards the overcrowded neon oblong of Times Square.

As the rockets explode like mortars above the building another reflection in the darkened window comes to stand beside mine.

Pierre presses his mouth against my ear. 'Such a pity Gustav isn't here.'

CHAPTER TWO

The Levi Gallery in central London, two weeks ago. The moment when Gustav Levi came face to face with his long-lost brother.

You could have heard a pin drop. The five of us were frozen in a tableau, our expressions ranging from bewilderment to shock. Gustav, me, Pierre, Polly, and Gustav's faithful assistant Crystal.

It was suddenly very dark in the huge space. The pool of light from the anglepoise lamp struggled against the encroaching shadows and the thick white snow falling over the Embankment outside, which blocked out the remains of the day, closed all escape routes and turned down the volume.

'Pierre! So let me get this straight. My cousin Polly's new boyfriend turns out to be Gustav's brother?' My voice, too shrill, was the first to shatter the silence. 'You were masked last time I saw you at the Halloween party. No wonder I never put two and two together, just the eyes – but my God, look how alike they are!'

Nobody replied. Nobody stirred.

'I'm – for once I'm lost for words,' Gustav stammered at

last, his voice creaking up from somewhere so deep inside it could have been buried in a coffin. He had taken one step, but he was still standing behind the gallery desk. I could see a dense stain of colour creeping up his jaw line. 'I never thought I'd see you again, Pierre. How did you find me?'

'I've always known where you were. After all, you haven't exactly ventured far in five years, have you, despite being an international man of mystery? I thought you might have started afresh, Paris, perhaps. Amsterdam. Tokyo. But I guess you've been keeping close to your assets.'

Pierre's voice was as deep and dark as his brother's. There was the same mesmeric, smooth texture to it, except that tonight it was pebble-dashed with bitterness and there was a transatlantic twang in his accent, contrasting with the clipped, European flavour of Gustav's.

'I'm just about to make a move to New York, as it happens,' replied Gustav. 'Various business projects over there need my attention for the next year or so. Another few days and you'd have missed me. But I'll admit it, a part of me always hoped you'd come back one day.' He leaned heavily on the desk, his dark hair falling over his face as he bit his lip, hard, in doubt. One hand was still poised over the sales figures we'd been congratulating ourselves on just a couple of minutes ago. 'So what are you doing here?'

Pierre gestured at the photograph *Stairway to Heaven*, depicting an empty escalator forever ascending in a shopping centre. The picture was now propped up against the desk, half wrapped in brown paper and gaffer tape. My self-portrait was still up on the wall, not yet destined for New York. All the other photographs had been shipped to their new owners.

'It appears that I'm a client. I've had a few hours to get my head round this unexpected reunion, so I'm better prepared than you, but until this morning, when Polly asked me to write a cheque to the Levi Gallery, I had no idea we had any connection.'

'No connection? No connection?' Gustav lifted both his hands and slammed them back on the desk, pushing it with a discordant scrape of wood and wheels across the concrete. We all flinched. 'We're brothers, you bastard!'

'Gustav! Stop it! He must be as anxious and wounded as you are, but he's here, isn't he?' I pressed close to make him hear me. My hand was still on my lover's arm. I locked my fingers hard even though I knew perfectly well he'd rather I backed off. 'I still don't know exactly what went so terribly wrong between you, but isn't this, deep down, precisely what you've longed for?'

'Serena, please,' Gustav hissed back at me. 'You don't know what he and that witch did.'

'They slept together. And left together. You and Crystal between you have told me that much. And I'm guessing it was extremely ugly – enough for you to stop speaking for five years.' I lifted my hand towards Pierre, still keeping my voice down. 'But he's stepped back into your life. Now's your chance to make up.'

Gustav shook his head impatiently, his eyes still lasering across the room at Pierre as if he couldn't bear the sight but could not tear himself away either. 'Pierre. First things first. You just said you found my business card in your car. How did it get there?'

'My driver gave it to me when he picked me up from the airport the other day. He'd cleared out the car immediately after my last trip to London and found it wedged beside the arm rest.' Pierre continued running the card across the dark bristles on his upper lip. 'Someone had left it there. It wasn't me, it wasn't Polly and it certainly wasn't you. So we had to recall who else had a ride in the limo when I was over here at Halloween.' Pierre flicked the card over in his fingers and tipped his head to one side. 'Which didn't take long. Because on the back, in your handwriting, it says, "Ring me, Serena." So it all started to fall into place.'

Now all four of us were looking at Gustav, waiting. He kept his black eyes fixed on his brother. So agonisingly similar. Same simmering, volcanic fury. Same height, same glossy black hair, although Pierre's is cut shorter and thicker, standing in rebellious boyish tufts on his head.

They were like a pair of matching stags about to rut in the gloaming.

Pierre cricked his neck and then waved his arm in a sweeping arc to encompass me and Polly. 'Looks like our lovely girl-friends have brought us together.'

'How did the business card I gave to *you*, Serena, end up in my estranged brother's car?' Gustav turned slowly and glared at me. I could see the muscle going in his jaw, the flicker of tension that I hadn't seen for weeks now. 'What the hell has been going on?'

I opened my mouth like a fish, closed it again. Kept my grip on his arm. He tried to shake me off, but I put my hand up to his face and turned it towards me, gripped his jaw in my fingers so I could feel the scrape of his teeth, see my own fingerprints going into his skin. The same gesture he uses to calm me down.

'Look at me, Gustav, and stop treating me like a jerk.' I kept my voice deadly calm. 'Nothing has been going on. I met Pierre on Halloween night. Just that once. I didn't know he was your brother. I didn't even know his surname. Only that he was Polly's new boyfriend and she'd met him through her work in New York. They are both in the entertainment industry. Polly's a fashion and personal stylist for magazine shoots. Pierre supplies wardrobe for film and theatre. He was throwing a Halloween party to launch his costume business in London.'

15

Gustav continued to stare at me. The veneer of anger was fading slightly but I couldn't be sure he was hearing me. I could see something else, confusion, fear, flickering behind his eyes. I put my finger on his mouth and pressed it hard.

'Go on,' he muttered hoarsely.

'That first night you and I met, we went to the Dukes Hotel bar, remember, and we had those Martinis. I was already hoping something would happen between us, but then I got that text from my cousin Polly saying she was over from New York and inviting me to a party, and I had to leave you. Turns out the party was Pierre's Halloween launch party. It was full of beautiful people in amazing clothes and masks, but I couldn't get into the spirit of it, I couldn't get you out of my head, I just wanted to be with you, Gustav. Even though we'd only just met, I wanted to get back to you somehow or at least speak to you. I was in a terrible rush to leave the party but I reckoned you would no longer be sitting in that bar so Pierre's driver took me home and that's when I lost your card. That's why I couldn't ring you.' I was gabbling now, aware that everyone was watching me.

'I was frantic, you had my cameras because I'd left them behind at the Dukes Hotel bar and in all the excitement I hoped you had them, but everything turned out fine because just when I was giving up hope of ever seeing you or my cameras again you phoned my mobile the next morning. Thanks to technology, you said. You'd put my number into your contacts so you obviously wanted to see me again, too. Oh, God, I wish I'd persuaded you to come with me to the party now.'

'Then all this drama could have been dealt with weeks ago. But how would that have played out, do you suppose?' murmured Pierre from behind me. His voice was very quiet, very low, as if he was feeling his way in the dark. 'Can you imagine the mushroom cloud going up over Aldwych if my beloved brother had sauntered unannounced into my London launch?'

'We were all in masks!' remarked Polly, finding her voice again and twisting her fingers in their sparkly fingerless mittens. Her elfin face with the ice-blonde crop and aquamarine eyes looked lost in the swathes of her purple suede and silver fur Afghan coat. 'You might not have known it was him.'

'I'd know my own brother! Gustav Levi is unmistakable, no matter how elaborate the disguise might be. He was always the one making the dramatic entrance, often with the sexiest woman on his arm.' Pierre glanced pointedly at me then lifted his hands as if belatedly greeting Gustav. 'But it's a good thing he didn't come that night, because neither of us likes surprises. We like to be prepared. And I've the advantage, Gustav. I've had time to mull over everything. Seeing that business card was a shock, but it was a kick up the butt, too. Did I want to pick up the phone and call you, put an end to these years of silence? I wasn't sure. I wasn't ready. In fact I nearly flew back to New York without seeing you. But then Polly needed my help to buy her cousin's photograph, and I realised it was hanging in the Levi Gallery, so there was your name cropping up twice in as many days, as if you were somehow waiting for me, and, well, everything was starting to feel like it was meant to be. Or maybe a conspiracy.'

'It wasn't a conspiracy!' Polly and I spoke in unison, our voices rising high like birds disturbed by gunshot.

We smiled at each other as I concluded the sentence. 'How could we possibly have plotted to get you together when we didn't even know you were brothers?'

'No need to squawk like a pair of hens!' Pierre put his hand on Polly's cheek. 'It was a figure of speech. Thinking of it as a conspiracy theory was the easy option, that's all. I could blame it on destiny rather than having to decide what to do. But in the end it seemed like utter madness not to take a chance on seeing my brother again. Not to grab such a golden opportunity to ' heal some wounds. Get some answers.' Pierre's hand remained on Polly's cheek as he turned to stare again at Gustav. This time it looked as if Polly was supporting him, not the other way round. 'And just think. I might have missed him anyway.'

Gustav couldn't seem to look at his brother, despite the fact that it was his turn to speak. Instead he kept his eyes on me. 'So you really had no idea who he was, Serena?'

'Don't take this out on her, Gustav. That would not be a pretty sight.' Pierre's voice grew deep and dark. Just like his brother's when roused. 'God knows I didn't expect you to roll out the red carpet, but ultimately you know that any hostility existing between us is almost entirely your fault.'

'No, no.' Gustav shook his head wearily. 'Not only mine.'

I took a chance and pulled him closer to me. To my relief he leaned his forehead against mine and closed his eyes. His thick eyelashes fanned out on his cheek.

Across Gustav's shoulder I saw Pierre frown. Was he surprised at our closeness, that I already knew how to calm Gustav when I needed to?

'An old head on pretty young shoulders, this one, and no wonder, from what Polly tells me about her appalling upbringing.'

Now it was my turn to flare up. 'Polly? What have you been saying?'

My cousin was still trying to take in what was going on. Her face went pink as she turned to me.

'Nothing awful! Just the truth. I love you, Serena. Of course I'm going to talk about you to my new man, tell him how we're like sisters rather than cousins, how I used to beg and plead to visit you in Devon because I knew how wretched you were, how we used to escape from your horrible parents and that horrible cold house on the cliffs and talk and smoke and sleep on the beach.'

She stopped, as if out of breath.

'I'm sorry, Polly. I didn't mean to snap at you.' I closed my eyes for a moment. 'For God's sake let's not you and me fall out as well!'

Gustav stroked my hair behind my ear and moved away. Pierre looked from him to me and back again.

'Just because you and I haven't spoken for five years, don't go driving a wedge through other people's lives, Pierre.' Gustav's voice was quiet, with a slight shiver to it. 'Not when we have a chance to talk this through.'

'You've obviously got a short memory, brother.' Pierre smiled, but now there was something mocking in his tone. 'You forget that I learned that kind of mischief-making from the mistress herself.'

Gustav stiffened beside me. I could feel the sharp hiss of his breath as if Pierre had slapped him. 'Don't you dare bring that woman into this discussion!'

'The road always winds back to Margot in the end, though, doesn't it?' Pierre lifted his chin, and his shoulders and fists rose with it. 'And by the way, you lost all rights to lecture me a long time ago.'

Gustav's jaw tightened. There was a tangible shift in the air, as if someone had opened a window to let an icy wind blow through the room. I could practically hear Gustav's muscles straining to control the fresh anger at the mention of Margot's name, straining to stop this pivotal moment from going horribly wrong.

'You came face to face with me tonight for a reason, Pierre. You could have just given the money to Polly and let her collect the picture on her own, but I'm glad you came. It's time we broke this stupid silence. So what is it you want from me? Revenge? Blood? I can do those.' Gustav clenched his fists, opened them again. Then patted his pockets with a harsh batting motion. 'Or is it money?'

'You're putting words into my mouth. What's wrong with cold hard curiosity? Seizing the moment?' Pierre was icily calm as if determined not to match Gustav's aggressive movements, but still he took a step closer. They were mirror images of each other. The uncanny likeness had been totally concealed by Pierre's Halloween mask when I first met him, otherwise it would have hit me like a truck. 'I could have ripped that business card into pieces. I could have left it five, ten years before giving you another thought. Maybe a lifetime.'

Any minute now their heads would butt, their antlers lock in battle. I fell away, powerless and frightened. The euphoria of an hour ago shrivelled like a bouquet of dead roses.

I watched Polly implode in the same way. She had even less idea of what this was about than I did. But we both wanted to avoid any conflict. We'd seen more than enough of that in the house on the cliffs.

'There is no way I would have wanted this estrangement to last a lifetime.' Gustav spoke through gritted teeth, as if the effort was hurting him. 'You said you wanted answers. As it happens, so do I. But go on. I'm listening.'

'What I did that night, screwing her then running off with your wife, I was driven to it. Because I was the one who was hurt and let down. And badly betrayed.' Pierre rubbed his chin with the card. His eyes blazed at Gustav, dark and direct. 'So I wanted to know how it would feel to be in the same room as you after all this time. After the disgusting scene I witnessed between you and Margot the last time I saw you. Maybe I wanted an explanation. Or, better still, an apology?'

Gustav spread his hands in the space between them, palms upwards.

'An explanation. I can give you that. I can run through every ghastly detail of my hideous marriage up until the day

Margot turned you against me. I can tell you that it was over, and she wouldn't accept it, which is why everything turned so ugly. But why should I apologise when I did nothing wrong? When what hurt me the most was losing the little boy I'd taken care of all his life?'

Gustav's voice was deadly quiet. I could see the very faint effect it was having on Pierre, despite his bravado. Blood flowing thicker than water. A slight softening around the eyebrows at the mention of his childhood.

'You were my rock.' Pierre's voice wavered. He cleared his throat. 'But don't you see? Rocks should never crack, and, when they do, there's no putting them back together.'

Polly and I pressed our hands over our mouths. My heart was sore in my chest.

Gustav closed his eyes as if stabbed by a sharp pain.

'I still am that person. Or could be, if you would let me. But I have nothing to apologise for. What Margot has no doubt told you about me, about our married life, that I was somehow the dominating bully forcing her into unspeakable practices and she was the cringing, unwilling submissive – it's all a tissue of lies.'

'Well, you certainly haven't forgotten what your wife is like. Because, yeah, she told me all that, and a whole lot more.' Pierre seemed to grow in stature the more Gustav struggled. There was a really black fire in his eyes now. 'But she didn't need to tell me what was going on that night. I can only work with what I've got. Which is the eyes in my head.'

Gustav stepped out from behind the desk, fists clenched, face thrust forward. I could see the tension in the sinews of his neck. Even his hair looked stiff with rage.

'I'm not the one who laughed in my face and told me I was scum! I'm not the one who ran off with his sister-in-law!'

'Whoa! Cutting to the chase!' yelled Pierre, stepping closer.

21

'I'm not the one who turned that *little boy*'s home into a sick torture chamber full of depraved losers, then kicked him out into the street when he caught you indulging your perverted fantasies. I'm not the one who changed the locks, physically and metaphorically.'

'None of it was intended to involve you. It was an accident! A mistake!' Gustav put his hand up to try to stop the flow of insults and injury. 'You asked for an explanation. So let me–'

'There have been too many accidents and mistakes, Gustav. So let *me* tell our audience what the butler saw.' Pierre interrupted, and gave a kind of maître d's bow, swinging stiffly from his waist. 'Gustav Levi giving his gorgeous wife Margot a sadistic hiding. The marvellous big brother who was so into his bondage and whipping that he couldn't do without it, even though I'd clearly left a message that I was coming home.'

'Don't make the mistake of defending that bitch.' Gustav's hands looked ready to wrap round his brother's neck. Their mouths opened simultaneously, teeth bared like wolves fighting over prey. 'I don't deny what I was doing, but everything was set up by her!'

'I saw everything solid and real being ripped away from me. That image still haunts me, Gustav, when I can bear to dwell on it. You brought me up to be a gentleman. The sun shone out of your arse. But that was all obliterated, up-ended, if you'll forgive the pun, in one fell swoop. There you were, bending over her, your arm raised in the air–' Pierre swallowed hard. 'If "that bitch" as you call her hadn't rushed upstairs and found me when she did, I can't answer for what I might have done to you. She distracted me, oh, in the nicest possible way! An image that haunts you, too, I bet? And thank God for her, because after that Margot was all I wanted. All I needed. Not the house. Not you. Her.'

Gustav staggered away from the skirmish, his hand over his mouth as Pierre flung the words out like stones. The fire drained away from his face. 'Hold on a minute. What message?'

'The message I left with Margot. I rang that morning and told her I'd be home early from uni. She swore she'd tell you to expect me, but no, you didn't give a toss. You were too busy forcing her onto her knees for her daily dose of dominance.'

Polly fell against the wall, looking exasperated. 'You didn't tackle this at the time? Don't you people ever communicate?'

'I never forced her to do anything, but there was no time to explain any of that to you!' Gustav shouted. 'Not once you'd vanished. Pierre, you have to listen, Margot never gave me any bloody message! She planned all this. Every single detail.'

'Always blaming Margot. Never yourself. You said yourself, you can't deny it. You probably even filmed it!' Pierre smirked and held an imaginary phone up to his ear. 'Or perhaps we should summon Margot. One call is all it would take–'

'Enough!' Crystal's voice was a thunderclap. Somehow she had materialised between them. Polly and I were on the edge of the dance now, and we drew close, our arms snaking round each other. Polly's eyes were bleached of colour as she glanced first at me, then at the curious Mary Poppins figure of Crystal. And then at the exit.

I knew what she was thinking. Should we just get the hell out of here? Let them slug it out?

Ramrod-straight, Crystal marched round the two men like a sergeant major as the two Levis squared up to each other again. She raised her hand like a headmistress calling for silence.

'Shame on you both! You're acting like a pair of common cage fighters. You are *brothers*!'

23

'So?' growled Pierre, bouncing slightly on his feet. 'Ever heard of Cain and Abel?'

Polly's face said it all. She'd never seen this aggression in her suave boyfriend before.

And what it showed me was that mirror image again, distorted. Pierre was a version of Gustav that was younger, stronger, angrier and resolved to see the bad in people. The version I never thought I would meet.

Crystal stood her ground. 'You first, Pierre. I'm ashamed of you, speaking this way. What has Margot done to that lovely polite boy?'

Pierre jabbed his finger rudely at her. 'Ah, dear faithful Crystal. You always did worship the ground Gustav walked on.'

'And so did you, Pierre Levi. Stamp and curse all you like, but you idolised him. Deep down, you still do.' Crystal seemed to be rising off the floor with the towering force of her presence. 'I'm not scared of you. Either of you. It's time this was out in the open. I was there that night, remember? I know exactly what happened. I didn't know about any phone call, but I still know who is right, and who is wrong. And I'm telling you, the person we should all be afraid of is Margot Levi.'

Crystal was magnificent. She was taller than ever, floating round the room, her arm up like Boadicea, a prophetess railing against the gods as we all waited for what she would say next.

'She's like a bad smell lingering under the floorboards. Still winning. Still wreaking havoc in this very room! She's the reason you boys are enemies, and if it all hinges on one missed phone call it can surely be resolved. You've never had a chance to explain what you were really trying to do that night, Gustav. Now's your chance. And then perhaps Pierre can man up and confess while he's here that not only should he not have been so ready to run off with his sister-in-law, it was he, not one of Margot's cronies as you suspected, who broke into your safe.'

Crystal was like the umpire in a boxing ring. The two men stared at her.

'It was you who took our parents' jewellery? His watch, her rings?' Gustav's voice was hoarse. His face furrowed into grooves of dismay. 'But it was all we had left!'

'And it was mine to take, just as much as it was yours. Margot picked the lock for me. When you chucked us out she said we'd need the jewellery to sell.' Pierre turned, walked over to the window and pressed his hands against the cold glass sprinkled with snow. 'See how upset he gets over a stash of trinkets. Metal and gems. Not flesh and blood. In the end we're all just trinkets to you.'

Another long silence dropped over us. The gallery was empty and cold. Lurking awkwardly round us were the humped shapes of the new sculpture exhibition waiting to be mounted, the pieces still shrouded in plastic body bags like mortuary victims.

And that portrait of me, the only one still hanging.

When I took that picture in a grimy station mirror back in October all I hoped was that the future would be a damn sight better than the first twenty years of my life.

I kept my arm around Polly, but really I wanted to be close to Gustav. I was frightened of the bleak distance in his eyes, the bristle in his stance. The only thread joining Gustav to anyone at this moment was the thin trail of gunpowder stretching between him and his brother.

The snow was faltering, the flakes still thick and fat but sporadic now. Somewhere out there across the river the Eye was turning, its lit-up pods of sightseers unaware of the drama unfolding in here.

Crystal started to back out of the room, towards the lift. 'Gustav. Pierre. Lose your pride.'

Don't go, Crystal, I begged her silently. We need you here.

Pierre thrust his hands into his pockets. His shoulders drooped slightly. Polly and I were still holding our breath.

'I took some precious jewellery from a man who already had more money than sense. *Mea culpa*. Now. Shall we go back to the reason I took it?' Pierre turned slowly from the window. 'It was far more than a missed phone message that drove me away. This lovely girl will run a mile now she's heard about your sick habits. As for me, I've changed beyond recognition since that night. I'm not that naïve, trusting young lad any more. Christ, I've even developed some pretty sick habits of my own! But where this is your fault, Gustav, is that everything I'd held dear about you, admired all my life, looked up to, was ripped away in that one hideous, graphic moment. Like someone smashing a mirror. No excuses. You were my big brother, for God's sake! Oh, I wasn't entirely ignorant. I was getting increasingly bad vibes from the goings on in the house. But you should have made certain that I would never see anything damaging – let alone *you* indulging in it as well!'

'And you should know, Pierre, that far from me being shocked and disgusted, Gustav's sick habits are old news,' I declared into the bitter silence, my voice louder than I meant it to be. 'Seen it. Done it. Got the whip. Supplied the weapon of choice, in fact.'

'So soon the sado-masochism?' Pierre flashed back. 'In a couple of months he's got you addicted, too?'

Gustav snagged his hand through his hair and glanced sharply at me. I smiled faintly back at him. Still Pierre studied us, every nuance. What was it? Jealousy of our silent communication? The pinching memory of their old closeness?

What were they like before their affection was shut off like a gas pipe? What impression did they make, the cool older brother and his young, eager sidekick hunting as a pair, ploughing their orphaned way in the world? These handsome men, their exotic black hair, tall, athletic bodies, demonic attraction radiating out of them. I really wanted to know.

Polly's eyes were huge with questions, too. I longed to take her by the hand, leave the brothers to it and run off to one of our childhood hideouts. But we weren't kids camping out on a windy Devon beach any more. We were involved in this fight between our men, whether we liked it or not.

'Leave Serena alone!' spluttered Gustav. 'This girl probably knows more about me than you do! I've told her about my past. But no, she didn't know the details of the night I lost you, because I forbade anyone to mention it and I hoped, stupidly, that I'd never have to relive it.' Gustav finally snapped out of his reverie and stepped towards the window. 'I've explained, Pierre, that I hadn't a clue you were arriving home from university. I was desperate to extricate myself from the marriage, what was going on, everything, because I realised it was only a matter of time before you witnessed something really bad. But Margot wouldn't have it. She clung on with her fingernails. I had always sworn that hell would freeze over before I let her anywhere near you, so that was her lever, her enduring threat. She swore in return that if I made her leave she would take you with her.'

For once Gustav had misjudged his timing and left it too late. Pierre suddenly barged up beside him, clamped his arm around Gustav's shoulders and pulled him roughly against him in a parody of an embrace.

'So you failed, yet again, to protect me. You were busted.'

'For God's sake, Pierre! What do you mean, "yet again"?' Polly jumped forwards and slapped at him. 'He's trying to hold out an olive branch, you dickhead!'

Pierre winced as her hand caught his free arm and he pushed her off. 'We were fine and dandy until Margot came along, and then Gustav changed. He was her lapdog. Worm.

27

Slave. I was fourteen, listening every night to them banging each other's brains out. Too much information? And when Margot was mistress of the house, I kept bumping into her creepy friends on the stairs when they came to the house for their perverted parlour games. The best thing my brother ever did was bundle me off to boarding school before I realised that he was in it up to his neck. But he failed in the end, because I saw it all when I came home that night. Gustav Levi trussed up in leather chaps and muzzle, bringing a horsewhip down on Margot's sweet little arse.'

'I don't want to hear any more,' Polly shouted. 'Rena, make it stop!'

I started moving towards the two men.

'You can't shock me, Pierre. When Gustav confided in me about the horror show his marriage, his *life,* had become, we were in the chalet in Lugano. I had already found Margot's punishment parlour or whatever she would call it, her room of pain, but it was mostly empty because all the equipment had been shipped to London. He told me he was obsessed with her from the moment they met, but once they were married that changed, because the rougher and more demeaning her demands became, the sicker he found her.'

'The effect on him was pretty sick, believe me,' Pierre growled, his teeth biting down into his dry lips. 'That wasn't my brother. It was a weak, addicted loser.'

I could feel Gustav's eyes boring into me, but I refused to look at him. He'd pitched me into the middle of a battlefield with no armour. He'd kept the details of that horrible night from me and I only had a few seconds to prove that I could handle it. If I couldn't, we were finished.

'I reckon that was Margot's handiwork. That's how he saw himself, too. But he's the old Gustav Levi again now. Your rock. *My* rock.' I took one more breath because any minute now the tears were going to take over. 'I look like the kind of woman who would be attracted to a weak, addicted loser?'

'Who knows? You could be as bad as he is.' Pierre's eyes, those dark lasers so like his brother's, were steadier now.

I decided to plough on until someone stopped me. 'Don't sneer as if I know nothing, Pierre. I've seen the dominatrix films in the old house in Baker Street.'

Pierre raised his hand in protest. 'That "old house in Baker Street" was my home! The place Gustav said I could always feel safe. I wasn't a baby, I didn't need to be wrapped in cotton wool, but I didn't deserve to feel threatened either. Everyone needs some kind of haven when they're a kid, don't they? Except he turned my haven into a knocking shop.'

A rush of familiar, icy helplessness swamped me. 'I know exactly what you're talking about, Pierre. I never had a haven when I was growing up. The only time I felt safe was when Polly was with me.' I paused. I had no idea if this was championing Gustav's cause or making everything ten times worse, but I couldn't stop myself now. 'So I understand why you thought your world had ended. But Gustav has just told you he was fighting for you. Fighting to put a stop to all the madness.'

Pierre was the first to speak, and it was as if he hadn't heard a word I was saying. 'Well, he fought so hard that Margot had to run to me for help.'

'Help?' I shook off a restraining gesture from Gustav. 'I bet it was *her* favourite horsewhip he was forced to use! The long black one? He was turning the tables on her. She'd been humiliating him beyond endurance and the last straw was–'

'When she threatened to involve you in her sordid games!' Gustav's voice as he interrupted was strangled with fury. 'She goaded and goaded until I lost it. I couldn't let her steal you from me. I had to show her, once and for all, who was boss.'

Pierre snorted. 'By whipping your wife to kingdom come?'

'Margot loved all that! The harder the better. She didn't need anyone's help. You're the lucky one, because you had a brother who tried to protect you from her!' I darted towards Pierre, my fingers out ready to scratch him.

'Protect me? Oh, he's good at that!'

'Serena. My warrior queen. This is my battle, not yours.' Gustav moved towards me. Letting me take the stage for a few moments seemed to have given him time to regroup.

'Serena is right. I was ending it that night, Pierre,' he continued quietly. 'I *had* ended it.' Gustav swiped his hand over his forehead. 'I'm desperately sorry you had to see that. But I'm even more sorry that she carried out her threat. Found you and fucked you, just like she promised.'

'Fucking, flagellating, what's the difference? You show me yours, I'll show you mine! Someone sits on your face, you're not going to turn her down, are you? Especially not someone you've secretly lusted after for years!' The expression on Pierre's face was a combination of smile and snarl. 'Oh, your wife was so hot, Gustav. Steaming. The sexiest thing I've ever had. Ever will have.'

Polly gasped. Her blue eyes were round and red. We were all trapped in this room, this snapping of words and images. I slammed my hand down on the desk. 'Would you listen to yourselves? Do you want a reconciliation or not?'

They weren't hearing me. They were being drawn back together by the images scrolling across the cine-screen of their shared memory.

'You're like Margot's ventriloquist!' Gustav was jabbing his finger now at Pierre. 'Your going with her was despicable, the worst call you ever made. You may have thought she was your new protector, but all she wanted was to break me. P, she took you and turned you into someone else.'

There was a brief, heavy pause. Surely Pierre would

respond to that heartfelt cry of love and despair? That unexpected use of a childhood nickname?

'She didn't change me. You're the one who changed from hero to bad guy.'

The massive building shook with a sudden gust of strong wind. A train rattled loudly over Hungerford Bridge and a series of sirens wailed up the Embankment towards some catastrophe.

'The worst thing I ever did was welcome Margot into our lives and I will never forgive myself for that. Or for letting you think of me as a villain.' Gustav walked stiffly back to the desk, all the while keeping his eyes on his brother. 'But take some of this on your shoulders, Pierre. You didn't have to fall so completely into Margot's trap, choose her over me without a second thought. Oh, I know how relentless she is when her claws are in, but you broke my heart.'

The brothers stared at each other across the abyss. Surely this was the moment to forge some kind of truce? Pierre followed his brother to the desk and leaned across it.

'I might have tried to resist her charms if she hadn't told me one more tiny fact about you. Every word of which made perfect sense.'

'That woman would swear day was night and people would believe her! Every word that comes out of her mouth is a lie, Pierre. I've tried to explain myself to you, but if her poison is still in your ears, what's the point? I can't take any more of this today.' Gustav looked down at the sales ledger and started, very slowly, to close it. 'You're still so damn prickly.'

'Is it any wonder I'm prickly, with my problem skin?' Pierre stroked his hand up the arm that Polly had slapped earlier. 'Remember that?'

'Of course I remember.' Gustav's eyes followed the curious gesture of his brother's hand as if he was being hypnotised. 'How is it? Still gives you grief?'

31

'What do you think? That's something else you have to answer for.'

'You're holding me to ransom. It's one-way traffic at the moment, and it's getting us nowhere.' Gustav shook his head. 'I've nothing to hide. I will do whatever it takes to fix this, Pierre. But I'm done for now.'

'You're ending the conversation? Just like that? Detaching yourself from me yet again?' Pierre went very white. Stretched out his hand as if to grasp something. Or to shake hands? But his hand remained empty. 'So cold, Gustav. So bloody cold.'

'Far from it. I'm deeply attached to you, Pierre, and I always will be. But for now I need to step away. I want to get this conversation right.' Gustav opened the desk drawer with unnecessary force and took out the gallery key. 'It took balls for you to come here today, and I salute you for that. We will talk again, and I promise I will listen too. So I'm suggesting we meet at my apartment when we're all back in New York. New Year's Eve. How about that for a symbolic date to start afresh?'

'You know what? For the first time in five years I agree with you.' Pierre's shoulders and fists dropped. The blaze of animosity was fading. 'But you're the one who's talking as if we're business associates scheduling a summit meeting.'

Gustav stared at Pierre for so long that I wondered if he had lost the power of speech. The physical resemblance of the brothers, yet contrasting fire and ice, was mind-blowing. I knew Gustav could be controlled, but this towering silence was something else. God, I still had so much to learn about my lover. Because Pierre, despite himself, was dwindling in front of Gustav's calm authority. The fight was seeping out of him.

'That's become my default position after losing the person I loved most in the world.' Gustav looked straight at his

32

brother as if he was relieved to be able to say the words at last. 'It may not look like it, but I'm struggling to keep it together.'

'I came here hoping to find something I'd lost.' Pierre's voice was barely audible now. 'So you promise? That we'll talk?'

At last. Some kind of fragile calm had come over the room. The first glimpse of what the brothers were like once upon a time. The younger pleading with, needing, the older.

'You have found it, P. I promise. New Year's Eve is when we'll continue this. But Serena and I have packing to do and a plane to catch, and I need to be alone with her.'

Gustav's voice regained its strength and clarity. He tossed the gallery key carefully in his hand. I wanted to run to him, wrap my arms around him, but I also wanted to drag him towards his brother, heal this debacle with some kind of initial touch, some kind of real contact that would mean a thousand words and keep us all going. But this was not the time. All those toxic words were still reverberating in the air.

Pierre nodded. 'Fine. But next time we meet I will tell everyone the final nugget Margot told me. Then we'll see whose side your lovely girlfriend will be on.'

'No more sabotage, P. No more!' Gustav raised his hands, both silencing and surrendering. 'Whatever happens next, remember that I am sorry, and that I love you.'

Gustav took my hand and to my astonishment lifted it to his mouth. Breathed in the scent of my skin. Had I given him this quiet strength?

'There is more to say, and you know it.' Pierre stared at his brother for a long moment. Something had been punctured. 'But I'll be there. New Year's Eve.'

'Good.' Gustav held my hand against his chest where his heart jumped and throbbed like a trapped animal. 'Now get out.'

When they'd gone, Polly rolling her eyes and making 'call me' gestures at me, Gustav walked slowly over to my self-portrait and gazed up at it. One hand flattened against the wall where the sepia shots of the French prostitutes used to hang in a previous exhibition. I came up behind him, hesitated, then leaned my head on his shoulder.

'I won't rest till my brother has forgiven me. I won't rest until he gets it all off his chest and makes some kind of sense, and then I can forgive him. But first let's make our own pact. A white Christmas in New York with you. Just you.'

Crystal's words to me, weeks ago, tinkled quietly in my ears.

The day he tells you about that saga is the day you'll know he's letting you right in.

Gustav walked towards the lift. I gazed once more at my self-portrait as the gallery emptied for the last time. For a second I envied the girl in that photograph: she hadn't been forced to listen as her lover's brother burst back into his life then tried, and failed, to reduce him to something beneath his shoe.

But the portrait's mournful gaze told me I was wrong to envy her. I was in the right place, with the right guy. His hand had just been forced. He hadn't chosen to reveal the saga to me this evening. His brother had made the choice for him. But at least now I knew what, or who, had wrecked Gustav's life.

I never wanted to be that girl again. I was never going back to a life without Gustav.

CHAPTER THREE

'No, Gustav isn't here,' I reply to Pierre's quiet taunt now as we stare out at the New Year fireworks. 'But he will be.'

I search the sky out east again, where the planes are taking off and landing. I rub at the blur of steam my breath has left on the glass. Oh, Gustav, where the hell are you? This is the night you promised to meet your brother. I'll do my best to keep things sweet until you get here but, like you said, this is your fight, not mine.

I move away from the window, away from Pierre's piercing eyes, and go to fill my glass. Right up to the brim. Polly is sprawled on one of the long, low sofas that are angled to get the best views from up here. She's already pretty drunk, but it's a kind of aggressive drunkenness I've never seen in her before.

'Why won't you come out with us? When did Serena Folkes become such a bore?' Her voice is a lazy slur. 'You're only just twenty-one. You've got a swanky new pad, photographic commissions to sink your teeth into, a new city to explore and a wardrobe full of Ralph Lauren for me to borrow, but you'd rather spend the evening hanging round at JFK arrivals lounge?'

I press my glass against my hot cheek. 'I'm just worried about Gustav, that's all. I won't relax until he's back here with me. I didn't want him flying at such short notice to the house on Lake Lugano just when we'd had such a lovely Christmas together. I hate the idea of him being there, full stop. He bought it with his ex-wife so there's all these ghosts from his past life, Polly. Without me he'll be surrounded by them.' I glance at Pierre, wonder if he'll pick up on what I've said about ghosts, but he's still over by the window, frowning at his mobile phone. I run the glass over my lips. 'I'm worried something has gone wrong. Why wasn't he on that flight back from Switzerland?'

'Worried his evil ex will have turned up to claim him? Oh, don't get all upset, Rena! There's bound to be a good reason why he's late. No need to fret. Especially as the cavalry has arrived! Your New Year wouldn't be complete without me, now would it?' Polly kicks her foot against the tawny, butter-soft suede cushions. 'If you'd been here last New Year you'd have been whirling like a dervish as they counted down. Probably wearing nothing but sparkly cheerleader hotpants and an Uncle Sam hat! You can be the life and soul when you're on form, girlie! How is it that you've changed so much?'

'I haven't changed, and I'm not a bore!' I take a long swallow of the vintage champagne that fills our fridge here and sit down in the sofa opposite, tucking my feet up under me in an effort to chill. 'If you weren't my beloved cousin you'd get a slap for a comment like that, the mood I'm in, so watch it. In any case, this time last year I was in Piazza San Marco, not Times Square.'

'Dressed as one of your masochistic Venetian nuns, no doubt!' Polly tips her head at Pierre as he comes across the room and flops down next to her. He drapes his arm closely around her neck and gives me an astonishing, broad grin as his hand lands on the swell of her breasts.

'Yeah. I wish I'd bought those kinky convent photographs I've heard about from your exhibition before they sold out. Think how educational they would have been for my popsicle here,' he smirks, fingering one of Polly's nipples through the delicate lace of her electric-blue dress. 'I could have organised a personal signing from you, Miss Folkes, dressed as a flagellating holy sister.'

'Everyone dresses up when there's a party in La Serenissima. That's what they call Venice when there's some kind of fiesta going on. It's the city of masks and costumes, after all.'

I shift in the blast of heat from Pierre's black eyes. So like his brother's, yet so different. While Gustav's eyes glow from deep within, Pierre's seem to flicker and change depending on what or who he's looking at. There's still a kind of vibration about him this evening, the impression that something is brewing, yet he's almost jaunty, too. I feebly try to move the spotlight and focus on him as Polly's boyfriend rather than Gustav's brother.

'You know, Pierre, as a costumier Venice would be a goldmine for your dress-supply business. You'd find a wealth of period outfits there!'

'I'm flattered you remember what I do for a living!'

'At least the two of *you* are communicating. God, it's been like pushing a boulder up a hill getting everyone here tonight. But you're being very restless and strange, Rena,' Polly complains, taking Pierre's chin and wrenching it round to get his eyes off me.

'That's because it doesn't feel right – talking to you, I mean. It's good that we're all jolly, drinking and chatting together, especially after the last time we met in London. But it would be better if Gustav was here. I feel as if we should be waiting for him!'

'It was his invitation, and we're not saying anything behind his back while we wait.' Pierre runs his finger across Polly's mouth. 'In any case you're allowed to have your special cousin to play for New Year's, aren't you? It's a great chance to get to know you better. But I'm disappointed Gustav can't be arsed to get here on time. You sure he's in Switzerland? He's not got cold feet about seeing me and done one of his midnight flits?'

His brittle words are like a slap in the face. I press myself back into the soft cushions as if they can somehow protect me. I can't bear the idea of Gustav running out on me.

'Give him time. I trust him.' The sudden fear nearly chokes me. 'Midnight flits aren't his style.'

'It's a shame when his emails over the last few days have built some bridges. They're a bit po-faced but conciliatory and, well, brotherly. I was warming to tonight's plan.' Pierre keeps his eyes on Polly, tweaks her nipple more blatantly. His eyes, even his actions, are oddly distant. As if he's tuning a radio. 'But hey, we can have a party here all by ourselves. Maybe we could get Tomas over, remember him? The guy in the toga whom you knocked back at my Halloween party? He hasn't forgotten you – he's still got the hots for you!'

Polly giggles. 'Yeah, how about it? Let's get Toga Tomas over!'

To my relief Pierre stops groping Polly and leans towards me. 'So tell me, Polly's cousin. How did my brother ensnare a Celtic beauty like you? Or has he got you locked into some confidentiality clause?'

I try to smother my shocked laughter by delving into the ice bucket. 'Yeah, it was business at first, but it's all pleasure now.'

'I knew it. You *did* have some kind of contract! God, he really has lost his *joie de vivre*. The eccentric millionaire, signing parchments in blood.' As he speaks I can see Polly's nipple perking through the lace and wish I couldn't. 'But, talking of business, why don't you tell me more about your beloved Venice? Your knowledge of the city could be invaluable if I decide to follow up your suggestion for sourcing period material.'

'Then you should go there some time, honey.' Polly nudges him. 'My cousin, as you insist on calling her, could show you round.'

Polly hitches her bottom across the soft seat. She hooks her leg over Pierre's to get his attention. Her lace skirt rides up to her tiny matching knickers. Ridiculously I worry that she'll smear something messy on the beautiful fabric.

I catch Pierre's eye over the top of Polly's white-blonde crop as if he can read my dirty mind. He picks up Gustav's cocktail shaker and tops up their glasses. He is still brazenly eyeballing me, but I can't look away. I can't ignore that what he also shares with his brother is the ability to render people speechless and immobile with just one smouldering glance.

'I'm not sure I'd be safe travelling on my own with your cousin, Pol,' he murmurs, watching me but tickling Polly as she protests weakly. 'She's always, I don't know, so jumpy.'

'That's because I'm missing Gustav and I wish he was safely back here with us. But you're jumpy too, admit it. Tonight is massive for you.' I swizzle the pale fizz in my glass. I can't shake off the feeling that he's playing me. I also can't help enjoying it, even though I know it's wrong.

Gustav's brother and I stare at each other. A blue vein has come up on his right temple.

'Yeah, you're right. I'm jumpy as hell. It's this place. All this opulence is unnerving,' he drawls, glancing round the apartment. 'I knew Gustav was rich, but since I last saw him he's moved up into another league altogether. Maybe we should have chosen neutral territory for this meet.'

I smooth my hand across the honey-soft suede sofa. 'He'd be here now if he hadn't had to fly off like that, straight after Christmas, but some problem arose with the sale of the

Lugano house and Dickson needed him there to sign some papers or something. The sooner that place is sold, with its past and its memories, the better. It's hanging over us like a guillotine.'

'Shame to sell the old place. There were a few wild parties there, I can tell you!' Pierre keeps his smile light. 'It's more of a shame that he stood me up, though.'

I let out a breath I didn't realise I'd been holding.

'He's stuck in the stratosphere, Pierre! He's not standing you up.' I'm damned if I'm going to tell him I'm also jumpy because that's the inexplicable effect he has on me. 'He wants to thrash this out once and for all.'

'"Thrash" being the operative word.'

Pierre's voice invades the low-lit, airy space of my new home. Polly is half asleep with the drink. Her head is back and she's jiggling her shoulders to a new track on the music system. It's not like her to zone out, but I'm glad. There's a ticker tape of questions and challenges clattering behind her boyfriend's eyes.

'Baiting me won't work, Pierre. I'm not going down that road again.'

He shrugs and falls back in the sofa, that broad smile disarming me again. 'Point taken. So. What about the house in Baker Street?'

'What about it?'

I'm glad he's changed the subject, but I don't like to think of the images Gustav showed me projecting across the old walls in that house, the whips and masks, the sick excitement that infected me and had me dragging him home and begging him to whip me too. The loop of video showing Crystal being whipped by a masked Margot. Gustav disguised and participating somewhere in that writhing orgy. The agonising knowledge that he lived and loved there with another woman.

'I sometimes walk past it when I'm in London.' Pierre

40

removes his hand abruptly from Polly's breast, and she curls away from him. 'It's looking pretty bleak now. Gone to rack and ruin.'

I cross my legs, too late aware, from the gleam in Pierre's eyes, that I may have given him a flash of my crotch. 'That's all part of the Gothic façade. It's still a functioning museum. The installations are still up and running. I think the exhibition earns him a fortune from collectors and visitors.'

'You mean he still owns it?'

Pierre's face goes still, watchful. I shift on the sofa opposite him, tug at the filmy white dress studded with tiny sequins that I'm wearing especially for Gustav. Pierre obviously appreciates it too, in all its see-through flimsiness. I bite my lip, sensing that as well as showing my knickers I'm probably giving away classified information that I didn't know was classified.

'He's getting rid of it. Crystal and I have finally persuaded him. It's an albatross. But there's been some kind of hold-up with the marketing, or the agents, that's all.'

Pierre rests his hand on the curve of Polly's haunch where it pushes up against his leg. Runs his fingers up under her skirt, just like he did at the Halloween party the very first time I met him and had no idea who he was.

Just then his mobile phone gives a series of insistent bleeps. Pierre glances at it, texts something, then gives me a long, slow wink. 'Don't tell the missus I'm getting mysterious calls.'

Above us, the twig-like silver hands on the huge white blank face of the clock show twenty to midnight.

'Go on, you can tell me.' I lean close again, trying to see a name or number on his phone. 'A bit on the side?'

'That would be telling!' Pierre hesitates, then transforms his expression into a sly grin. 'No. It's work. There was a show tonight. I made sure the wardrobe was ready, complete with extra costumes and seamstresses, and I told them I was

41

on important family business, but they insisted on keeping tabs on me and now they're telling me what a great night I missed. So. Baker Street. What kind of price is he asking? I suppose there are plenty of perverts out there interested in buying that sort of debauched, twisted crap.'

'Gustav is not proud of his past. He hates it. I hate it. God knows, my own story is pretty grim. But you can't turn me against him. I don't care about any of that. I love Gustav.'

'I can tell.' Pierre mirrors my actions, leaning towards me across the coffee table. 'You've got it real bad.'

I grab his collar before I can stop myself, pull his face right up to mine. 'We all know who caused this mess between you two. When Gustav ended it your cougar Margot needed easy meat to pay him back.'

'Easy meat, eh? What do you know about any of this?' Pierre flicks my hand off his shirt, his nails grazing my skin. He picks up a bowl of savouries, stirs them with the forefinger that has just been tickling Polly. 'You've known him five minutes.'

'That's all it took.'

'The old Levi charm. We both have it, you know. Just different shades.' Pierre unnerves me yet again with his smile. 'You'll soon be in a dilemma, wondering which one of us to pick!'

The sour taste of uncertainty taints me. Gustav has thrust me into this scenario, but he's also made me strong enough to withstand whatever history throws at us. And if Gustav has the urge to confess and make this right, then surely, somewhere behind that surly exterior, so does his baby brother?

I pick a nut out of the bowl, toss it neatly between my teeth. 'There will be no dilemma. I'll always be on his side. So grow up, and talk to him. Otherwise this will eat you up.'

Polly stretches, all white fur and blue eyes, like a Siamese cat.

'Message received, Fräulein Rottweiler. He has you well trained, I can see.' Pierre cocks his fingers in a duelling-pistol gesture and narrows his eyes as if taking aim. Then he sits back, pulls Polly roughly over his knee. 'My big brother is a lucky man. Even if he is a cradle-snatcher.'

I realise another difference between Gustav and Pierre. While Gustav is like an Easter Island statue, shadows and sunlight alternating over his hewn features, sometimes changing his stance and aspect but always rooted, Pierre is a shape-shifter. A series of masks, different voices, different gestures.

'You have a wonderful knack of putting your finger on it! Hmm, that sounded a bit naughty, didn't it?' he murmurs quietly so that I have to lean closer across the table. 'But you know what? It's not eating me up so much. Facing Gustav in London was a huge hurdle, but it wasn't as horrific as I thought it would be. And I'm no longer that scandalised spoilt brat, either. There's not much that would shock me now. Who knows? I may have seen and done far worse since then!'

I gape at him, fumbling for a reply. Now he's testing me in a different way. He's moved from taunting to teasing. Before I can think of a suitable retort he starts running his hands up Polly's slender thighs again, right in front of me, right there on Gustav's sofa.

Polly's long white legs are bare despite the season. Thick snow covers the streets outside and buries any carelessly parked vehicles. Sub-zero temperatures have New Yorkers swathed in long coats and fur hats, pushing their way aggressively along treacherous sidewalks, no matter who else is trying to get a foothold. Everyone is glued to their mobile phones even when waiting to cross busy intersections or refusing to make way for oncoming walkers.

'Making you horny, eh? Don't you wish my brother was

here running those clever hands of his over you to calm you down?'

They both chuckle. Polly's pale-blue eyes, as he gropes her, don't shine with embarrassment but are glassy with a wild kind of triumph. She's always enjoyed a drink, but she's more out of control than I've ever seen her. Maybe she's just crazy, in the true sense of the word, about this guy.

'You bet. He won't know what's hit him when he gets home.' I smile coolly. I stand to replenish the now melted ice in the bucket, aware of a hot stickiness between my legs. I try not to stare where Pierre's fingers are wandering, but a gremlin inside is imagining him fingering me.

'Gustav has you exactly where he wants you.' Pierre sits back, pulling Polly hard against his groin. Above us the clock is saying five to midnight.

'Wrong way round. He's where I want *him*.'

Pierre nods, the surliness finally lifting into straightforward youthful amusement. He lays his hands on Polly's legs and pulls her thighs open. She starts to grind against him. As I retreat to the kitchen for more ice I see her trying to keep a straight face. I can tell she is counting the minutes till she gets him into bed. I've never seen her so distracted. So giddy about a guy.

In the kitchen I lean against the massive fridge. Feel the cool flank of it hum and buzz quietly against my spine. This whole evening has been bizarre. Of all the men in all the world Polly ends up with Pierre Levi. I didn't expect to spend my New Year's Eve playing gooseberry with my cousin and Gustav's bellicose *doppelgänger*, but although he's tricky and difficult to work out I think I've laid some friendly ground. I hope Gustav will be pleased. But I've had enough now. I want to be with Gustav again, playing with him as he lies back in the bubbling Jacuzzi, taking him in my hands and then riding him like a cowgirl.

44

The little golden locket he gave me for Christmas taps at my clavicle as I take deep breaths. I touch its smooth oval shape, trace the tiny bumps made by the trim of seed pearls for comfort. It's already my talisman. The underside is engraved with an 'S' and is permanently heated by my skin.

'For the urchin who had no jewellery to her name when I met her, a second piece for her collection,' he murmured on Christmas morning as I took it out of its velvet box. 'Made by the same French craftsman. You'll see the tiny silver clasp that closes this has the same design as your bracelet.'

'So you could tether me by the neck as well as by the wrists. Then I'd never be able to escape.' We both shivered at the promise of kinkiness. How well I knew how to light his fire. Any minute now he'd be prowling round the apartment, choosing the place where he would next attach the silver chain.

I turned the locket and something weighted inside tipped and rattled. 'It looks like an heirloom.'

'I don't have any of those left, thanks to Pierre. So it's brand new. Yours and only yours.' He threaded the chain round my throat. 'And when people see it resting on your beautiful breast they will know that you are mine, and only mine.'

'Monsieur Gustav you are really spoiling me!' His fingers tickled my neck, my hair, as I sensed rather than heard the tiny click-lock of attachment. The chain was just too short for me to lift the locket over my head, even if I had wanted to. 'But what's that tapping inside?'

'My darling, another priceless symbol locked away, which you have yet to earn.'

I giggled and twisted myself quickly so that I was strad-dling his lap where he sat beneath the Christmas tree. I ran my tongue suggestively over my lips before biting his ear

45

lobe, hard. 'Show me how to earn it, then, lover. Tie me and take me.'

A tinny ringtone from the other room pierces my reverie and the sudden quiet space between music tracks. Pierre answers his phone and Polly makes some high-pitched complaint.

I curse under my breath and wrench open the huge fridge. Now it's my mobile phone as well clamouring for attention. I clutch a bag of ice and a new bottle of champagne and charge back out of the kitchen. Pierre has apparently finished his call and to my surprise he has risen from the sofa and is over by the windowsill, watching my phone singing and dancing with skittish energy on the ledge.

Pierre glances at the caller name and presses the decline button on my mobile, looking at me with an odd expression on his face. 'Big brother's too late. We're outta here.'

'I'll check my own phone, thanks!' I thump the ice bucket and the bottle down on the table. 'Let me call him back. You have to give him a chance, Pierre.'

'He could be calling from Switzerland! Who knows when he'll arrive! He gave me ten minutes back in London, and now he can't even be here on time. Oh, you've tried your best, girl. You're a real Trojan. Everything Polly has told me about you is true. But Gustav? He doesn't deserve you.'

Polly tugs at her skirt and sits on the edge of the seat. 'Pierre? What's got into you? You were perfectly chilled all evening. Something happened? Who was that calling you just now?'

He doesn't reply, but rudely starts texting. I pick up my mobile, but my fingers are trembling too much to press the recall button.

'Everything is Gustav's fault according to you. You'll never meet him halfway, will you? Just remember you were way out of order five years ago, too!' I stammer the words, trying

46

to work out what has shifted in the air. What has changed. 'He has said how sorry he is that you had to witness him whipping his ex-wife. He has told you he only ever wanted to keep you safe, and he's even admitted that he failed in that one simple task. But Margot wasn't innocent. She wasn't even unwilling. She was a professional dominatrix who punished people for money. It was all part of life's game to her, and you were the next prize.'

Pierre sends the text, taps the phone on his smiling mouth. 'And what a prize, eh? The young blood, snatched from the older brother.'

I lean back against the window. 'Don't you think you should at least apologise for that instead of crowing over it? Fucking his wife and running off with her?'

'If he hated her so much surely I was doing him a favour!'

My face heats up, throwing me off balance. 'If you won't back down, either of you, then let's hope focusing on the future will work. A light flicked on inside Gustav when you walked back into his life. Don't snuff it out.'

Pierre chuckles. 'It's you who has flicked his switch, I reckon.'

My grip on the windowsill tightens. My mobile starts vibrating. I don't recall putting it on silent. I grab the phone, but the voicemail has clicked in.

'We all want this resolved. But something's not right. You hinted at something back in London? "One more tiny fact", you said.'

I wait for Gustav's voice on the phone, have a fierce longing to hear him speaking, but there's only a kind of creaking and whirring as if he's walking round with me in his pocket. 'Is there more?'

Pierre Levi is so close that I notice his glowing black eyes don't have the unique crackle of gold round the iris that Gustav has. I can see the pulse above his collar, notice for

47

the first time a curious white bumpy scar winding up round his ear. The dark shadow of beard is coming through on the slightly thicker chin and cheeks.

He's the rough, uncut chip off the fine, faceted block of his brother.

'Very observant, Miss Folkes. Not that he picked up on it. Yes. There's more. Gustav asked me if I wanted blood. Remember?' Pierre starts to unbutton his shirt. 'This bloody enough, do you think?'

Polly and I gape at each other. 'Pierre, don't do this,' she mumbles, trying to stand. Her thin legs buckle under her and she falls back into the sofa.

'I know you can't bear the sight of me naked, Polly, but your cousin has to know what her boyfriend did to me.' Pierre undoes the final button, pulls his shirt open. 'I warned Gustav that Margot had the final word the night I left. And as he's not here to explain it, I'll just go ahead and throw my final grenade into the proceedings.'

He yanks his shirt off, tosses it at Polly and spreads his arms out like a martyr.

There, distorting his chest, carving ridges in his upper arms, slicing across his back, is a cobwebbing network of burns, puckering the red, raw, shiny skin. Polly crumples the shirt against her mouth.

I keep my eyes on Pierre's, reading the curious mixture of accusation and appeal burning there. I refuse to stare at the welts and grafts. I'm trying to find words that will comfort, spreading my fingers towards his scarred, burnt torso.

'This is how Gustav Levi protects his loved ones. This is the "tiny fact" that Margot told me when she saw me naked for the first time. How easy do you think it was to leave Baker Street after hearing – I'll phrase it in that gorgeous Germanic accent of hers – "Gustav Levi sets fire to your house, and then he lets you burn."'

We all stand there rigid, breathless. The silver hands on the clock join as if in prayer to mark midnight, and that is when Gustav opens the huge white door to the apartment with such force that it crashes back against the wall.

I swivel desperately round to stop him crying out in hearty greeting. I wonder what he sees, what terrible story this web of scars tells him. Somehow I fear that I've cocked up, that somehow I'm to blame for this unpeeling of yet another onion layer.

'What's going on?

Gustav clutches the back of the third sofa, the one where he always sits. The one with the best view over Central Park. The one I call the shagging seat, because – no. I can't think about the two of us entwined there. Not right now.

'I'm showing her what you did when I was a baby, Gustav. You started the fire in our house and you let us all burn. You were smoking in your room, and you dropped the cigarette carelessly and climbed out through the window to meet some girl. You kept this tiny fact from me all my life, too gutless to confess. So Gustav is the one who betrayed *me*, Serena. Not the other way round.' Pierre's use of my name for the first time is almost as shocking as the ruined state of his flesh. 'He's the one who disfigured me. Who robbed me of my parents. He's the reason I still have nightmares.'

Gustav has to speak now. If he doesn't speak within the next ten seconds, I'll never trust him again. I take one stumbling step towards him. I can't stand to hear Pierre's voice any more. Gustav forces his gaze from his brother's body and holds up one hand like a traffic policeman, shaking his head over and over again. When he focuses on me, the white-hot blankness in his eyes shades itself in. The deep blackness returns. The jagged lines of his face arrange themselves not into softness but at least into some kind of order.

'Lies, lies, Serena. Polly. Listen to me. It's all lies. I've never smoked a single cigarette in my life.' He turns back to his brother. 'Why here, Pierre? Why now?'

'I should have flown at you as soon as I heard the words but Margot stopped me.'

'Because it was a cheap shot,' says Gustav, deadly quiet. 'How could any of that possibly be true?'

Pierre takes the shirt from where it has fallen over Polly's legs, and holds it in front of him. I have the weirdest snapshot in my mind of him wearing a hospital gown, sitting on a narrow iron bed.

'She got me out of that house before she told me the full story, said I should save it for when it would hit you the hardest. How was I to know when that day would come? But it did, thanks to Serena. Thanks to that business card.'

Gustav's eyes are narrow slits of concentration, as if Pierre is speaking in tongues and he is simultaneously trying to translate. 'Ah, yes. There it is. The single knell of truth. That's exactly Margot's *modus operandi*. Plotting her chess moves, right down to the best time and place to accuse me of – what exactly are we saying here? Murder?'

As the word stabs through the air Pierre eases one sleeve back over his sore, scarred arm. I see now why he pushed Polly off so viciously the other day when she slapped it. What on earth can he say?

'I'll give you manslaughter. Would that be more accurate? You're looking me in the eye and denying it? You'd swear it? Because it all seems perfectly believable to me.'

'And perfectly preposterous to anyone else. It's not murder, and it's not manslaughter, purely a monumental accident which was not caused by me!' Gustav turns in a tight circle, looking up at the ceiling as he pulls in every ounce of control. 'I should be incandescent right now, but do you know? I look at you, and I can't possibly be angry.' Gustav speaks so slowly and quietly it's as if he's using his last breath.

'You've been walking around all that time thinking I'm a monster because of Margot. Yet again this comes down to her. I'm finding that so hard to bear. Look at me, P. Look at me very hard, and listen.'

Pierre reluctantly raises his eyes. He is still scowling. The anger isn't gone, but it's melting like wax into sullen defeat.

'Just make this all go away, G.'

Gustav keeps his eyes on his brother, makes a move towards him, then walks across to where I am still standing. His hand comes to rest just beside mine on the window ledge.

When he starts to speak again his voice is forced, as if he's using his last breath. Like Othello, more in sorrow than in anger. 'You wanted to cause a sensation just now. That's your prerogative, but you should have waited.'

Pierre's hands pause as he buttons his shirt.

'What difference would waiting around for you make? Miraculously absolve you? Cure these scars after twenty years? Put out the fire?'

'I meant stripping off like this, using your injuries as a shock tactic.' Gustav is choosing his words as carefully as if he is selecting surgical instruments. 'It's a stunt. Not even your own idea. It's got Margot written all over it. But she's excelled herself this time, using your disfigurement to torment me.'

'I'm no puppet, Gustav. This was my idea. But I'm tired. You're tired. Either admit it or tell me it's not true, make me and these girls believe you. Then maybe we have a chance.'

They stare at each other for a moment. Gustav nods. 'I swear on your life and my dead parents' memory that I did not start that fire.'

Another tripwire, another challenge overcome, and Gustav grows more impressive in my eyes, not less. With a few careful words he has defused the last bomb.

'So everything you told me then, when I was having

51

nightmares, when you used to put that special cream on my skin in the middle of the night, that was the true story?'

Gustav lifts his hands and runs them through his hair in that achingly familiar gesture. Then he does something I've never seen before. Crosses his fingers and lays them up against his heart.

'They were my parents too,' he says.

Pierre copies the gesture. 'That's exactly what I hoped you'd say.'

His shirt is buttoned up now, but the sight of his poor burnt skin is seared onto my mind. All that damage going on beneath that cocky exterior. For the first time I feel a genuine, spearing anguish for this scarred young man. For both these lost brothers.

There's an intense hush in the air.

'I should have been more understanding when you first showed me. I was useless,' Polly pipes up, dragging herself into an upright position and tugging at her skirt. 'That's why you won't let me into the shower with you, isn't it? You always wear something, a shirt, or–' Her white face is streaked with an uneven pink. 'We always do it in the dark.'

'What's the matter, Polly? Ashamed of your deformed boyfriend?' Pierre's fresh antagonism is this time aimed at her. There is a harsh wobble in his voice. 'Can you see now why I like to dress up? Why I have developed a fascination with masks and costumes? My life has had to be one long illusion. One long cover-up.'

Gustav rubs his chin. I can see a little nick of dried blood under his jaw where the black bristles have resisted his half-hearted attempts to shave on the journey over from Europe. That little sign of vulnerability makes me want to take his face in my hands and kiss him. Whether or not it's because he has an audience, Gustav is superb in the face of Pierre's raging self-pity.

52

'P, don't lash out at Polly. Maybe you need help with this.' Gustav's knuckles are white as he lowers his hand to grip the windowsill again. 'Maybe we both do.'

'It never goes away.' Pierre taps his temple, the one with the blue vein. 'I've only ever talked properly about the fire with you, Gustav. And Margot.' The two men stare at each other again. However hostile their earlier words, the way they hold each other's eyes in this moment still speaks of their old closeness, the direct link they used to share.

'I would take every one of those burns away if I could.' Gustav's eyes are shadowed as if he hasn't slept for centuries. As if he's been hollowed out.

'I believe you. You didn't start the fire. But you ran out on us.' Pierre has a fragile calm about him now, as if rocked by his brother's quiet gravity. 'You should have been there to stop it ever happening.'

'You and I know the truth and it isn't how you're painting it.'

Pierre's eyes flicker over to me. The scars near his collarbone and throat look like a vile red and white scarf trying to strangle him. I look back at him, still speechless, trying to communicate some kind of sympathy even while worrying how disloyal that might look to Gustav.

I think Pierre has interpreted my intention, because he clears his throat. 'I'm sorry for that display. It was clumsy, and it was unpleasant, and it nearly jeopardised everything we've come here for. I'm sure a psychologist would have a field day with me, but my simple diagnosis is that I still blame my brother for not being there when it mattered. I always will. But no. Gustav didn't start the fire.'

At last Pierre is calm, at least on the surface. Perhaps sensing that he's scored some kind of victory. Because Gustav, despite his poise, looks shattered.

Polly stands shakily and puts her arm around Pierre's waist, but already she's acting differently, gingerly, as if he's made of glass. As if she's scared. Pierre ignores her, a strange, sad smile playing around his lips. I can't quite articulate it, but it's as if he sucks strength from Gustav's dismay. Even at this fragile moment he still reminds me of one of those Roman emperors who threw Christians to the lions for a laugh.

The celebratory fireworks outside have long gone quiet. Gustav sits down and I follow him. He starts to speak.

'We were living in Paris, near Montmartre, down a dead-end street. I was fifteen. Pierre was a little toddler of three. I had sneaked out to see a girl when I was supposed to be studying. They were loving and decent, our parents, but they were heavy drinkers and, once they were asleep, that was it. Nothing would wake them. I thought I could get away with disobeying them this once.' Gustav watches Pierre, but Pierre's head is down as he tucks his shirt into his trousers. I'm astonished to see him checking his phone before putting it back into the pocket. 'Anyway, a fire broke out in our apartment on the top floor. It was a beautiful old building but decrepit. A tinderbox. The other residents had moved out. Something made me dash home earlier than I intended, otherwise – I should never have gone out. I should never have left him there.'

Gustav lifts his fist to his mouth and coughs, almost as if he's back in that smoke-filled house. I sit like a sentry beside him. Pierre's face has solidified into one of the masks he sells.

'I saw the flames. People panicking with buckets of water. Well, I rushed straight up, the fire hadn't spread beyond our apartment, and I found this one crying in the hall. It was like he was wearing an orange liquid cloak. Just his little face was clear of the flames.'

Polly grips Pierre's arm, her mouth open in horror, and this time he doesn't flinch as her nails dig in. As if she isn't there.

I slide my fingers over Gustav's thigh and lace them through his. He turns his head as if it weighs a ton. His lips move, but nothing comes out.

'Gustav rolled me in a rug and carried me down to the courtyard, but he couldn't get back up the stairs.' Pierre's voice has lost the transatlantic drawl. The faint European trace of an accent clips at some words, just like Gustav's. 'The only good thing is that Gustav escaped the flames unhurt – he had no long-lasting damage. No scars. The rug protected him.'

The images rip through our minds. The tall shuttered windows buckling, the grey Parisian stone starting to blacken, the tiles loosening like teeth and crashing onto the watching faces below.

Gustav clears his throat. His grip is so tight that my fingers have gone white. 'Do you see now why I cared so much about our parents' jewellery? They weren't trinkets. They were mementos.'

'But they were also life-savers. They fetched a lot of money when I sold them. Surely our parents wouldn't have begrudged me that?' Pierre shrugs on his jacket, keeping his eyes on his brother. 'Look. We've both done dreadful things. Made each other suffer. But don't you think it's time to call it even?'

I stiffen. None of this is even. But, as Gustav said, it's not my fight.

Gustav nods wearily. 'We could argue until the cows come home. But yes. Let's call it even, if we are ever going to move on.'

He stands as Pierre comes up to him and lays his hand awkwardly on Gustav's arm. They've sucked the life out of each other as only warring brothers can.

I wait for a moment, afraid to invade the space, then make a decision of my own. 'Do you mind if we say goodnight now, Pierre? Polly?' I murmur, turning to each of them as I say their name. 'I think tonight has knocked the stuffing out

55

of all of us, and in a way I'm glad. I don't know much about families, or brothers, but it had to come out at some stage, otherwise Margot's lie would have festered in there forever.'

'She's right, Pierre. Let's give these guys some space. And you and I need to talk about all this, too,' echoes Polly, tugging at Pierre. 'Maybe you two brothers should make a pact. The angry words end here. And next time you should meet up alone, without me and Serena getting in the way.'

'You two girls have been more help, more use, than you can imagine.'

Gustav answers her but it's me he is staring at, the dark fire glowing in his eyes and pulling me towards him. A secret flame ignites inside me.

'Yes. We need to be alone now,' I say quietly.

'Happy New Year, G,' Pierre says, and lifts his other arm to grasp Gustav. Gustav mirrors the gesture, his hands on Pierre's shoulders. Pierre has to look up slightly to meet Gustav's eyes. They stand for a long moment then stiffly move apart. 'I'll be the one to choose the next meeting. OK?'

Gustav goes to the door and murmurs something to Polly. I am about to sink back in the sofa with relief when I realise Pierre is still standing above me.

'Happy New Year, Serena, and here's my wish for you.' He bends down to me and whispers in my ear, so quietly I can barely make out his words. 'That you are still here to celebrate with us this time next year.'

I wait for the closing of the door. The chime of the lift. Wait till I know they will be at ground level and walking out on the pavement at this upper end of Broadway.

And then I push brother and cousin out of my head and take my man. I get up, coil my arm around his waist then hesitate, as if it's Gustav who has scars all over his skin. We stare for a long time out of the window, over the rooftops of Manhattan.

'I'm worried about what he said just then. That he confided in Margot about the fire, and his burns. That kind of tragedy is something she would use again and again, if she could.'

'Pierre is scarred inside and out. You're the only person who can help him.' I pause. 'We can't trace everything bad that happens back to her.'

'Can't we? Let's pray that you're right.' Gustav turns me so that I'm lined up against him, body to body. Groin to groin. He buries his face in my hair, takes the long strands in his hands and yanks my head back so that he can look down into my eyes.

I press against him, feel the hardness. He needs me badly. It's going to be rough, and hard, and I can't wait. The golden locket taps in time with my heartbeat.

'But I still don't like the way he gets a kick out of shocking people.'

Gustav sighs. 'I used to understand him so well. He was always troubled, and no wonder. That was my role in life, to clear his head, give him confidence, face the world. Can you see now why it was so catastrophic when Margot took him over?'

'Everything is so much clearer now, Gustav. You and he have a long road to travel. But it started here, and that has to be positive.' I aim the remote at the music player. 'But, as you said at Christmas, I wonder if we can just think about ourselves for a little while now?'

As the soft jazz croons through the room, I start to sway to the music. I let the white dress fall off my shoulders but when he starts to drag me down onto the sofa I shake my head and lead him out of the sitting room. Away from the arena of so much discord and into our bedroom, our glass-walled, starry-ceilinged eyrie.

He follows me, a dark shadow in his rumpled dark clothes, the lights of New York glittering like hot coals around us.

57

We don't even pull the blinds. As I walk to the huge bed I let the dress slip right off me, and the whisper of air over my skin distracts me at last. I glance over at him. He's stopped in the middle of the room, still watching me. I remember the first time I visited his town house in London, how he made me dance for him, how embarrassed I was to perform in front of that dark, watching face. But now he needs all that and more.

'You were too long in Lugano.'

I lie down on the bed, naked, stretched out before him, and extend my wrist where the bracelet glitters. Once the silver chain ensnares me everything else will disappear.

He groans and at last I see the rise in his cheeks as a long-lost smile opens his face. 'That sounds like a cruise-ship song.'

I laugh softly and he rips off his navy-blue pullover and his shirt. I can smell the musky sweat of him after his long journey, and I love it. I beckon to him like a true temptress. His eyes glitter in the strange light, their blackness reflecting the backdrop of night sky and relentless metropolis. He smiles wider, my wolf, his teeth white and glinting hungrily. He sits beside me and clips on the silver chain. Lets it fall onto the white sheet while he unzips his trousers, pulls them slowly down, teasing me. The stiffness of his arousal springs forward. It's like a spear, so big and hard, shaped so perfectly for me, and now the soft seduction I was planning flees, because I want him badly, quickly, now.

'You're even more special than I realised,' Gustav says quietly as we both stare at his hardness. 'The only person who could take my mind away from what just happened. Just for a few minutes.'

My body bothers me with its urgent lust. I open my legs, hook them round his slim hips. I run my hands over his smooth, warm, unblemished skin, so different from his brother's, but oh, God – suddenly Pierre is in my head, his black eyes blazing with all that wounded anger.

Gustav falls forward to hang over me. I pray he can't read my mind. I shove Pierre away, cling to Gustav, push my open, wet mouth and my breasts at him, my stomach heaving with catches of breath, and then he lifts my body and runs his tongue up me like a large black cat until I'm whimpering with wanting. But he's not licking for long, because he lets me drop onto the soft bed and roughly pushes himself into me, holds my arms down as he presses his still wet mouth down onto mine.

'My God, in all the rush to get here, all the furore that met me when I arrived,' he growls as he starts to move. I pull away, alert with anxiety, but his mouth, all of him, follows me to keep me still, his body possessing mine, locked inside me, his teeth nipping at my lower lip to keep me there. 'I never kissed you hello.'

CHAPTER FOUR

Focus, focus, focus. The photographer's mantra. It's been several luscious, lazy days since that traumatic New Year's Eve with Pierre and Polly. Apart from that tricky meeting and some tentative emails back and forth between the brothers, Gustav and I have been cocooned from the world since before Christmas, which is exactly what we needed. So, apart from a commission for a gaggle of Park Avenue princesses yesterday, I've had more than two weeks off. I have to get back to work. I have to put the Levi traumas out of my mind, just for today.

If I look behind me I can just make out our apartment amongst the phalanx of towering, tough buildings planted along Central Park West. Before I left this morning Gustav hung a Union Jack onto the end of his big new telescope bolted to the roof terrace. It's my Christmas present to him to improve on the spyglass he brought from Lugano, and the flag means I can always find my way home.

'Is that our code?' I asked, as I packed up my camera kit in the hallway. My hands were shaking as I fitted the lenses and tripod into their sections in the bags and tried to quell the butterflies flipping in my stomach. 'I mean, if the flag isn't there it means you're not at home, like the Queen? It will mean you've been called away on business?'

Gustav took my shoulders and stood me in front of him. Stroked my face. Untwisted the golden locket to rest at the base of my throat where it constantly quivers with my pulse. Tucked wisps of hair into the heavy plait hanging down my back. Wherever he touched or brushed, he sent a ripple of tiny shivers through my skin. Every muscle was stalling, refusing to let me leave.

'Too risky. Remember how Theseus forgot to hoist the white sail on his ship as the agreed sign that he had slain the Minotaur, and his father, seeing the black sail still up, thought his son was dead? I will never go anywhere without telling you face to face or at the very least using this marvellous contraption.' He tapped my nose with my little silver phone and dropped it into my pocket.

'Now, deep breaths. You're already back in the saddle with those débutante portraits you took yesterday. Today's assignment will be different, admittedly. But you'll do this job standing on your head. Which I would love to see, by the way.'

I stood on tiptoe and brushed my lips against his. Even now I half expect him to deflect me like he used to, turn his face and offer me his cheek instead, or move his mouth over my face, towards my throat, murmur in my ear, anything rather than actually allow himself full intimacy.

'I'd rather go back to bed.' I could hear the new huskiness my voice had acquired. The timbre of a happy, fulfilled, satisfied woman getting plenty. 'I missed you when you were away.'

'We've barely slept all week so you could show me how much you missed me!' His breath mingled with mine as he wrapped his arms tightly round me, padded jacket and all. He lifted me right off my feet. 'God, you're still so hot this morning.'

'All part of the service!' Then I frowned, leaned my forehead against his. Suddenly serious. 'I wanted you to forget all the things Pierre resurrected.'

'And I did. For a few glorious few days and nights.' Gustav squeezed me so tightly that I couldn't breathe. 'But it's my job, not yours, to put everything right.'

'By forgiving him everything, while he barely gives an inch?'

'I'm the oldest. If giving more ground heals us, that's the way it has to be.' Gustav lowered me to the floor again. 'But you are still my priority, Serena. It's you I need to keep close.'

I stared at him, at the pulse throbbing in his neck, the silky question mark of hair bouncing with it. 'I've never heard you talk like that.'

'And I've never felt like this. My bella donna, I don't want to let you out of my sight even for a day, in case you find someone else to tie up and tease.'

Every word he uttered made me shiver with desire. And then he kissed me, and all the shadows retreated once again. I was melting as he nudged my lips open, slid his tongue over the hypersensitive surface of my upper lip, then kissed my mouth closed again.

'Me be unfaithful to you? Never. This bod is for your eyes only.'

I started to unzip the jacket, slid my arms under his suit, spread my hands to squeeze his firm bottom. He watched my face, his dark eyes flashing with amusement, his hands resting lightly on my face as I touched him.

'You don't know how beautiful you are, Serena. That's the danger.'

I giggled softly, bringing my hands round to the front of his trousers. There it was, under the expensive fabric, straining against the zipper, always ready for me. 'I can always re-arrange this commission for later. Stay here with you for the morning and then go with you to your meeting about the new exhibition space you're developing under the High Line?'

He snatched at my wandering hands. He slid my soft green leather kid gloves over my fingers, one by one, pushing them snugly into the spaces, fastening the fiddly three buttons over each wrist.

'My darling girl, rookie's rule number one. You never postpone a commission. Rule number two, never stay home when your paramour suggests it. I'm rock hard just kissing you. I need to get my business head on. Go. This is a fantastic commission. The Weinmeyers are a real coup for your repertoire. If you hadn't spent all last night practising your Girl Guide knots on me I'd have talked you through this already. They're renowned for their art collections and fundraisers and general philanthropy. If you impress them your work will be plastered all over the walls of their mansion, and East Coast society will be flocking to see it.'

I picked up my kit reluctantly, then stopped. 'You didn't pull strings to get this job for me, did you? I'll be livid if you did.'

Gustav walked me to the giant wooden door of the apartment and heaved it open. He pulled me close to him, kissed me hard again, then ushered me out onto the landing.

'You impressed them with your talent at the London exhibition, Serena, but sometimes life is a system of favours, especially in business. You know how I like to make any working relationship official and documented at the earliest opportunity, and I suggest you do the same. Boil it down to I take, you take. I give, you give. And here you are, oh, yes, still giving. Still fulfilling your delicious part of our bargain! Your gorgeous body, that plump little ass, your mouth. Repaying me every night. Most mornings. And some afternoons when we have the time!'

'I just want to show you, them, the world, that I can do

this alone. I'm feeling a bit nervous, that's all.'

A slight shadow still stained his face. So long as I'm not the cause of it, the occasional sweep of darkness doesn't scare me any more, but it's a reminder of emotions and complexities still to be unravelled.

He tipped my face towards him. 'Look, I'll admit I have fingers and toes in every pie. Back in the day my ancestors were hawkers and travellers. I set out my market stall, display my protégée's wares and invite punters to roll up, roll up, take a look, buy it if they like it.' He rubbed his finger and thumb together with a sly grin. 'And give me my commission, of course. How else do you think we can afford this place?'

'I can see you as a gypsy, now you come to mention it.'

I just wanted to look at him all day. Tall, lounging in the doorway, his tie hanging loose around his unbuttoned neck, his black hair brushed back over his noble forehead. His eyes roving over my body even though I was swathed in winter clothes. He's the opposite of a chancer market trader. He's the epitome of suave, sorted entrepreneur, and I am the beneficiary of all that, and much, much more.

Reading my mind, Gustav murmured, 'Believe in yourself, Serena. A cliché, perhaps, but I mean it. The Weinmeyers flew all the way to London to see your show after your sensational private view. It's your talent they're after.'

'Nevertheless. I feel nervous.'

He stepped round me to call the lift, and then kissed me yet again.

'This is the first day of the rest of our lives, girl.'

The wind buffets me across the park now, past the cyclists and ice skaters and out by the Metropolitan Museum of Art onto Fifth Avenue. I'm too far south, so I turn north and the wind knocks me into a pile of snow banked under a starved-looking tree.

As I trudge my way between Park Avenue and Lexington, my kit is weighing me down. Where is Dickson the Driver when you need him? The surly chauffeur is locking up the holiday house in Lake Lugano for the last time. Goodbye to Switzerland. Goodbye to Margot and all that history.

Despite the weight on my shoulder, the weight in my heart starts to ease. All that remains is for Gustav and Pierre to neutralise the rest of the poison.

I walk right past the house at first, an old Upper East Side wooden mansion with curled wrought-iron balconies that looks as if it should be situated in New Orleans. The marble and limestone mansions all around here have long ago been split into apartments or donated to museums and schools, but this, I realise when the door opens, is still one complete town house.

The front door looks flimsy enough to kick in but it swings silently open as soon as I ring the bell. The petite façade hides an enormous wood-panelled hallway with black and white floor tiles and dominated by a staircase Scarlett O'Hara should be sweeping down. There's no butler or housekeeper bustling about. Just an elegant blonde woman around Gustav's age, maybe older, standing at the top of the stairs in a fuchsia-pink, diaphanous halterneck dress.

'Serena, come in. How lovely. Welcome!'

She is silhouetted by the huge arched window behind her. The low winter sun is a perfect backlight, shafting straight through the voile fabric of her dress and rendering it see-through. I step further inside and the door snaps quietly shut behind me. Mrs Weinmeyer rotates one foot in a gold Louboutin sandal and I can see that her incredibly slim thighs are slightly parted, flickering with impatient muscles. She raises her leg to take a step down the stairs and the slit cut into the dress makes it float open at the top of her legs.

I drop my bags and equipment on the floor and get out my bigger Canon. 'Hold it there!'

'Why, sugar, what's wrong?' Mrs Weinmeyer halts as instructed, one knee cocked in front of the other, her slim arms reaching to each banister in an angular, Cecil Beaton pose. Her face is in shadow, but as I adjust the exposure I can see through the viewfinder my subject's fuchsia-painted lips parting slightly in surprise, showing perfect American white teeth.

My finger slips on the shutter. 'I didn't mean to shout at you, Mrs Weinmeyer, but please could you hold that pose? Because I think I've got my Grace Kelly shot!'

'Your cute English accent.'

Mrs Weinmeyer shrugs one pale shoulder, glances over it deep into my lens, twists this way and that, then continues to descend the stairs as I click the shutter. She has the taut, toned body of all upmarket New Yorkers, which makes them look as if they never bite into a Krispy Kreme. Not ideal for a photographic subject, but who am I to comment? If anything, that makes my job all the more challenging. Finding the curves and angles, the planes and shadows, in a body with little substance.

As for her cool, pale face, I daren't speculate if she's had work done. The camera will tell me later. I remind myself to inform all my new clients that I discourage any form of post-production touching up, but if they insist then the charges will be suitably astronomical.

'Come along with me, sugar,' the lady of the house purrs into my thoughts. 'There will be many other shots, I can assure you. Just follow me round the domain and tell me where you want me.'

The reception rooms at the front are decorated with a mixture of old European grandeur, wooden cornices, comfortable chintzy soft furnishings, some exquisite rose- and cherrywood pieces that look as if they would splinter if you so much as brushed the dust off them, and an array of paintings and photographs on every available surface of wall. The effect is full but not cluttered, elegant but not spare. From the clear north light filtering through from the rear I'm guessing that the other half of the house has been extended and totally modernised.

I follow my client as room flows into room, watching the way Mrs Weinmeyer's bottom twitches under the fuchsia silk as she walks ahead. The way her little buttocks catch the material between the cheeks, then softly release it again. Every so often I take a shot as my hostess pauses casually by a sofa, a fireplace, a mirror.

'So, Serena, tell me how you want to play this. As the hookers say, I can be whatever you want me to be.'

Mrs Weinmeyer gives a girlish giggle. I know she's watching me as I pace round the wood-panelled drawing room she has finally led me into. Maybe she's wondering how such an ordinary-looking girl could have taken the erotic photographs she saw exhibited in London. Maybe she's doubting my ability to fulfil this commission.

I must keep my cool. The walls are crammed with paintings and photographs but what also catches my eye on a window shelf is a row of vases and goblets and delicate sea creatures all made of glass. The muted light filters through them, making them look as if they are filling with smoke.

'Ah, you're admiring my exquisite glass collection. Do you like it? It's from Murano, but a little-known, very specialised manufacturer.'

Her perfume reaches me before she does. Her slim arm winds round my waist as I finger the tail of a jade-green sea horse.

'I know the factories on Murano,' I say. 'I saw them blowing glass in Venice when I was there. Did you know that the glassmakers' craft was considered so valuable that they were kept prisoner on the island under pain of death, to stop them giving away the secrets of their skills?'

She inclines her head. 'Venice is the city of secrets, isn't it? Our palazzo on the Grand Canal is the perfect place to showcase them. One day I'd love you to come visit. Carnevale in February perhaps? But those naughty nuns in your photographs! You got right behind the grille when you were there, didn't you? I would love to prise open the hushed world of the convent like you did. You have a real watcher's skill there, Serena.'

I blush and step as politely as I can away from the array of glass before I break something. I open the French windows to let more of the clear but shaded north light flood in.

'Well, today I'd like to try something fairly formal, classic, you know, but using natural light? Just your face and shoulders, Mrs Weinmeyer, looking out from these shadows into the garden.'

'It's mighty chilly out there, sugar, but whatever you say.'

Mrs Weinmeyer does as she is told and leans dreamily in the doorway, resting her head on one upstretched arm. I remember reading somewhere that she used to be a model, or a dancer, which would explain the leopard-fit physique.

I step outside onto the terrace and try not to shiver as I set up my tripod, but the light today is perfect. There's a layer of snow-heavy cloud flattening the light so it's bright but matt. There's something of the Singer Sargent in Mrs Weinmeyer's Edwardian-lady persona. She keeps her eyes trained just past my ear as if she is staring out to sea, her pink lips parted, her pale limbs totally still.

'I must say, Mrs Weinmeyer, you're an incredibly easy subject.'

'And you're an incredibly easy artist.' She keeps her face still. 'We wouldn't rest until we had you over here to do these shots, Serena. We absolutely loved your work. See? We have a couple of your Paris shots right there.'

She tips her head slightly and sure enough hanging on the wall beside the fireplace, among an artfully crowded collection including several Hockneys and a Warhol, are three of my monochrome 'Lovers' series, an homage to Robert Doisneau but far more sexually graphic. In the first picture the couple seem to be the only people in the world, just the two of them kissing passionately, open-mouthed with greed, tongues pushing between each other's lips as they tangle on a bench beside the Seine.

I remember that hot day so well. I was crossing the Pont Neuf and saw the couple oblivious to the passing *bateaux mouches* full of gawping tourists. They had abandoned their half-eaten baguettes in ripped paper bags, put down their bottles of beer and were totally unaware of the tramp who was waking up from under a pile of newspapers in an alcove in the wall behind them.

In the second picture the boy has the girl on her back, her little floaty skirt up round her hips, and he's leaning over her, his leg pushing between her bare knees. Her blonde hair trails onto the dirty ground, catching in the litter, pecked at by passing pigeons.

I had to use my zoom, which is what gives the pair that distant, isolated air, but manages to pick out the tramp sitting bolt upright on his stone bed, greedily eyeing not the lovers but their abandoned picnic.

In the third picture another girl has approached. It looks as if the first girl hasn't noticed, because her arms are flung above her head as the boy opens her blouse, and her eyes are ecstatically closed. The boy has his free arm round the knees of the second girl, pulling her so that she is about to fall on top of the first, but the composition means that all three subjects are frozen in formation just before they meld into one.

69

And behind them the tramp stretches one grubby hand to snatch the baguette.

'You can sit for hours imagining what they did next, yes?' Mrs Weinmeyer's voice purrs into the quiet, and now I note her slight German or Dutch accent. Her royal-blue eyes remind me of a Dresden shepherdess. 'But that's why we hired you. The reviews described you as the innocent voyeur. You watch and catch people in the act of loving themselves, like the Venice nuns, or in the act of loving each other. Thanks to you my husband and I have decided to expand our collection of erotic pictures.'

'Well, I'm your girl,' I murmur, trying not to sound too eager. 'Tasteful voyeurism is my forte.'

'Well, we're already making enquiries. In fact we have a proxy buyer at an auction of photographs and films coming up in Baker Street, London. The Levi installations. Do you know them? An incredible series of images and films featuring Margot Levi. Your patron Gustav Levi curated it, I believe, and now he's finally selling. Your work might complement that rather well.'

'Yes, I know the collection.' Any mention of it by definition threatens and excludes me, representing as it does Gustav's life with his ex-wife. 'But with respect, Mrs Weinmeyer, that exhibition celebrates professional sado-masochistic porn. My work aims to be a study of human beings, and if artistic erotica is one way in which it evolves, well, that's a happy progression. But it's not how I would define myself.'

Mrs Weinmeyer tips her head admiringly.

'You're very sure of your genre, Serena, so I'll come clean. We know Gustav quite well. And he knows you pretty well, too. He's told us how you come aglow when you're asked about your work. But about Baker Street. I'm sensing I've touched a nerve?'

I step towards her, into the shelter of the pergola outside her window. 'It has bad vibes. And much as I would truly value your custom, Mrs Weinmeyer, perhaps I'm not the right artist for you. I wouldn't want my work hanging in the same venue as the Levi collection. It's skilful and beautifully shot, but it represents a period of ugliness in the participants' lives. There's a backstory there that I don't want to be linked with.'

There is only the rise and fall of her breasts as she breathes, making the silk shiver over her skin.

'I can see why you have your reservations, sugar. Margot Levi is about as far away from your wholesome charm as chalk is from cheese. Don't look so shocked. Like her husband, sorry, ex-husband, she's well known in certain circles. Or was, before she did her disappearing act. Anyhow, let's talk about you. You're far too young and sweet to engage with that kind of behaviour, even if you do get pretty close to the dark side in some of your pictures. But you have to leave each to their own. Take me, for instance. Do I look like the kind of girl who can only come if she's whipped to high heaven?'

I blush and shake my head.

'Well, appearances can be deceptive. That's for me to know and you to find out. Yes?'

I bow my head. I've backed myself into a corner now. I may have ballsed up the most prestigious commission I could have hoped for.

Her laugh is like wind chimes. 'Sugar, I admire you. Have no fear. We have plenty of different venues to exhibit our investments. We won't sully your work by mixing it up with anything that isn't perfectly matched. We intend today's commission to be very firmly placed in the personal "family album" category. Flattering, subtle, soft-focus if necessary.'

'Christ, isn't my wife just gorgeous?'

A chunky blond man appears, holding a cigar and speaking on a mobile phone.

Without apologising for interrupting, he clicks shut the phone and slips his hand through the slit in the fuchsia dress where it falls open across his wife's thigh.

'That was Gustav Levi on the phone, would you believe? Great to hear from him. Just wanted to know how his protégée was getting along. What kinky exploits she was goading us into!'

'He shouldn't have troubled you.' I can't help blushing with pleasure at the sound of Gustav's name, even though I thought I'd made it plain to him I needed to be left to my own devices. 'Or interfered.'

'Don't let me stop you, young lady.' Mr Weinmeyer slides his hand right up to the top of his wife's leg. 'You should feel how soft her skin is. How warm. Just up here, you know? Isn't that where every man wants to be? Just here where her body splits and gets all damp.'

'He gets so turned on by me, after all these years of marriage! Watch and learn, sugar!' Mrs Weinmeyer purrs, eyes half closed like a cat. 'Wanna see what he's getting so worked up about?'

'You look great as you are, Mrs Weinmeyer. Can you hold that pose for a while longer?'

I drag my tripod with unnecessary scraping to the garden table. The two of them are regarding me through the French window. They look like Si and Am, the evil cats in *Lady and the Tramp*. Both cool, polished, slanted blue eyes, blond, evidently charming. But there's still a hint of teasing menace flicking round them like a cat's tail.

I clear my throat. 'Just hold it like that, and then I'm going to have to come inside. I'm freezing my butt off out here.'

I jam the camera against my nose and keep shooting. They are consummate performers. As his hand disappears into her dress, Mrs Weinmeyer's head falls back, her blonde hair wisping out on the dark-grey shoulder of his business suit, her eyes fluttering closed, her lips parting wider. He wrinkles open the dress with his other hand, gathering the folds on her hip so as to expose her and running his finger down the slice of red just to make sure my camera has seen it. And yes, like all New Yorkers, she has the Hollywood wax.

'Serena has such a cute English accent, hasn't she? If she wasn't part of Gustav Levi's bevy of admirers I'd have her down as perfectly innocent, a little like your *Fräulein* cousins back in the old country.' Mrs Weinmeyer twines her arms round her husband's neck. 'No point looking all Bo Peep, sugar. Gustav has told us *everything* about you.'

Her dress is still open, the silk shifting across her thighs, catching in her crack, attracted perhaps by the wetness there.

I fuss around for another vantage point. The thought of Gustav telling them about me, maybe even boasting, actually makes me puff up with pride. But maybe Mrs Weinmeyer just means I'm one of Gustav's many projects.

My beret feels too hot on my head and I pull it off and stuff it into my kit bag.

Mrs Weinmeyer says softly, from somewhere nearby, 'And such beautiful Celtic hair. Like a mermaid.'

'I think maybe I should leave the two of you now? Looks like this is a private moment.' I fiddle with my camera to scroll through the images so far. 'But I've got some lovely shots. You are perfect subjects. Natural models. I've just concentrated on the head and shoulders, obviously.'

'You think I put on this expensive silky negligee just to show my top half?' Mrs Weinmeyer's tongue flickers over her mouth as she drifts across the thick Persian rug and brushes my hair off my hot face. 'We only just got started, sugar. And I think full frontal is what we're after, know what I mean? The whole body. We should have made it clearer. I

73

was just getting comfortable with you, I guess.' She pats her stiff yellow hair, pushes her gown a little off her shoulder, and floats out of the room towards the hallway. 'I'll go and make sure the bordello room is ready.'

'You look a little flustered. Why so coy, Serena?' Mr Weinmeyer puts his hand on mine as I'm about to pack up my equipment. 'The photographs in your exhibition were horny as hell. You hang out with Gustav Levi, and he knows a thing or two about the seamier side of life. You don't have me fooled, even if my wife thinks butter wouldn't melt in this tasty mouth of yours.'

I look at his hand resting lightly there. Asserting its authority. He is the customer, which ought to mean that he is always right.

I look him in the eye. He is like a Bond villain. Aryan, impenetrable, powerful. Probably armed. 'I get to choose what stance to take when viewing my subjects, and it's usually at a distance. I've never got up close and personal before.'

'Interacted with them, you mean? Well, there's always a first time. Now, you're perspiring, I can see it. Let's take this jacket off you. This scarf. I think this thick jumper, too?'

He tosses my outdoor garments onto a chair then leads me out to the hallway, past the stairs and round to another set of stairs descending into the basement. The first thrill of alarm shivers through me.

I steady my voice. 'Like I say. My speciality is watching, you know? Unobserved?'

'Ah yes. Gustav said. It's your USP, he reckons, for such a young pro. But we saw that for ourselves at the exhibition on London. The voyeur. Spying, in other words?'

'They don't know I'm watching. My subjects. That's the point. I catch them unawares. I can't direct them. I just let them get on with what they're doing.'

'I like it. Your *subjects*. Queen Serena.' He laughs, and

pushes me ahead of him down the stairs. 'That's exactly what we want you to do now.'

The stairwell is painted blood red and adorned with rich oil paintings full of plump, naked nymphs and goddesses by Titian and Tintoretto being ravished by swans and incubi and fauns. The stairs lead into a room with walls and low ceilings padded in red velvet and lit by the fractured glints from red glass chandeliers. My ribs contract for a moment. Something about it reminds me of Margot's room of pain in the chalet in Lugano. Perhaps it's just the fact that it's hidden away. Probably soundproof. Down here, nobody could hear you scream.

But where Margot's was designed for single-minded brutal punishment, all bare floors and walls, unforgiving lighting and an arsenal of weaponry with one intention in mind, this frilly bordello, as Mrs Weinmeyer called it, was designed for pleasure. It is all softness and comfort, seductive lighting. And sex.

Mrs Weinmeyer herself is already in position, reclining on a vast bed that takes up most of the room and could easily accommodate eight or ten participants. Her filmy dress has fallen away from her pert white body. I can't take my eyes off the small jut of her breasts, the flat stomach, the thighs loose and relaxed.

'We want you to portray us in a really sexy, edgy light so we have something to amuse us and our friends on these cold winter nights.'

Mr Weinmeyer laughs. 'It's not even mid-morning yet, cherie.'

She giggles and stretches one leg up in the air like a ballerina. 'So decadent, yes? Living a half-life under the ground when everyone else is rushing round the city, stressed, strained. Not us. We no longer have to stress and strain for what we want. Which reminds me. How about something punchy and potent to drink. Get us going, huh, sugar?'

She hands me a big glass Venetian goblet, red of course.

'Thank you. Perhaps when I've finished the shoot. Why don't you get comfortable?'

I unfold my tripod, pace round the room testing the very dim light with my meter, and then aim the camera at the bed. Mr and Mrs Weinmeyer are already arranged amongst the pillows, lying back, legs entwined, and gulping from their goblets. They are the epitome of elegance. Except that his muscular body is naked bar a pair of tight white boxers.

I bend to peer through my camera. 'Edgy,' I croak. 'Right.'

'And we thought mainly monochrome? Tasteful, but pushing the envelope to the limit.'

Mrs Weinmeyer has hooked one leg over Mr Weinmeyer's thigh, and they are kissing. Slowly, their tongues sliding in and out of each other's mouths like they are licking ice-cream. They pause, tongues curled at the tips, and glance at me, eyebrows raised. My God. They really are like Siamese cats. Polly with her white blonde crop and crystal eyes would match them perfectly.

My mind seems permanently anchored to this new, perverted train of thought. Polly really would think I'd taken leave of every last sense if she thought I was setting her up, even theoretically, in a threesome. She was the one who taught me the facts of life, huddled cross-legged on the cold Devon beach amongst the cigarette butts. She was the one who told me about blowjobs, demonstrating with her bananas. She was the one who let her new boyfriend feel her up in front of all her London friends just a few months ago. Yet she can't seem to cope with his scars.

And it's her ignorant little country cousin who's alone in a room with two of the richest, most debauched people in North America.

My finger trembles slightly. The meter is running. I charge by the hour, and then a further rate for the preparation and development of the pictures. So I start shooting, and once

I'm in my stride the rest of the world, already far away, recedes even further from this sumptuous room.

Above us Gotham City marches on, the thrusting metropolis that never sleeps. Somewhere out there Gustav has cut his call to Mr Weinmeyer. Is he wishing he was here at the Weinmeyers' house, watching? Has he been here before? Has he ever been into this boudoir of delight?

There is a murmur and a squeal from my clients, arousing each other on the bed. I try to drag my mind away from my lover. Not to picture the rickety girders of the High Line and Gustav at his meeting in the echoing space of a converted shed in the Meatpacking District. He hasn't told me what he's up to, but the fingertips that can make my nipples hard just by hovering over them will be drumming on the surface of the conference table as some cocky risk-taker outlines their plans for the future. Or a young, green hopeful like me. A twinge of jealousy pricks me. What if he happens upon another female ingénue in the course of his talent-spotting, ripe for the plucking?

I can't go for more than about ten minutes without thinking about him. I must learn to park him well away from my mind.

I can now hear soft piano music playing. Mozart or Chopin, I'm not sure which, but the notes ripple up and down the octaves and pause, wind around the room. Now piano, now forte. Actually, the sensual ambience in here is perfect, like some kind of drug, because I'm relaxing too.

Mr Weinmeyer's hand peels his wife's negligee over her bottom, showing me her ballerina's thighs and buttocks and the pinkness between. Then he stops kissing her, reclines against the huge pillows and lifts her easily on top of him.

I think of Gustav, lifting my naked, slippery body in the warm, bubbling water of our Jacuzzi. Tying me to our huge bed with the silver chain.

Mrs Weinmeyer strips off her flimsy garment, twists it

rapidly in the air as if she's making pizza dough and reduces it to a strip of cloth that she winds over Mr Weinmeyer's eyes and fastens in a big bow behind his head. A huge dirty grin spreads across his face, and his blinded fingers explore her dark crevices, fan over his wife's bottom. I slow the shutter speed to get some of this not only in soft focus but actually blurred, to reflect how sexy this is, and yet intensely, deeply loving.

I can feel dampness seeping into my knickers. My jeans feel too tight. Mrs Weinmeyer's white bottom opens slightly as her husband rocks her over his groin. My hands are sweaty, and I lower my camera for a moment.

'No, no, keep shooting.' Mrs Weinmeyer is breathless. She keeps her blue eyes fixed on me over her shoulder. Her thighs soften, open a little wider.

Mr Weinmeyer lifts his wife off him for a moment. In one clean movement she whips his shorts off and lands lightly down again, sliding straight onto the erection quivering in waiting. I take a fantastic shot of Mrs Weinmeyer's long white arm launching the white shorts into the air as if freeing a dove. She bangs herself hard down onto her husband, making his body jerk helplessly beneath her, but she's not ready to let go quite yet. She rummages under one of the enormous red cushions and flourishes a pair of leopardskin-covered handcuffs. Nestling down on him she snaps the cuffs around his wrists and fixes them to a discreet hook fixed to the wall behind his head.

Weird shocked laughter catches in my throat. Gustav should have hooks like that in the apartment to attach the silver chain.

Mrs Weinmeyer joins in my laughter. Now she's like a rider on a bucking bronco, a position I love, but these two are so quiet, so graceful, choreographed in slow motion like a dance. It's sexy as hell, but you couldn't exactly call it *dirty*.

It's so warm down here. Even my silk long-sleeved T-shirt is sticking to me. I roll the sleeves up, pull at the boat neck.

What would Polly say? For the first time ever the question stalls. Once she'd have been taking notes, demanded that I give her every gory detail, but something's changed in her. I have no idea what she'd say about this scenario. She'd either tell me to join in or get the hell out. There was something so contrived about the way she writhed on Pierre's lap and flashed her knickers the other night as he groped her.

What about Gustav? What would he say? Do the Weinmeyers have a reputation for kidnapping new talent for sexual slavery? Did he know when he waved goodbye from the corner of the Dakota building that I was wandering into a den of debauchery? Is that why he called Mr Weinmeyer just now? Is this another test to open my mind, hold my nerve?

Mrs Weinmeyer rocks faster, her body sliding easily as Mr Weinmeyer enters her. I step round them as quietly as I can, seeing, catching, shooting. This is my job. Gustav will have to accept it. My body is tight with excitement at the sight of this elegant, white-limbed couple entwining in front of me, to be forever frozen in the act of riding each other on the big red bed deep beneath Manhattan.

Her bottom gyrates over him. His hands pull half-heartedly against the handcuffs but he doesn't want to escape. I take a close-up of his hands, clawed, the tendons in his wrists standing out from the tender underside as if he's being tortured, but straining as if that gives him leverage and rhythm as his wife works her thighs and butt. I squeeze my legs together as the pair accelerate their pace, the little muscles flexing in her slim back, his legs lifting and falling, his toes curling in response as the two of them move soundlessly.

Mrs Weinmeyer waves her hands wildly in the air and although they're making no sound I realise from the way her head is falling back and his legs are bending and kicking up under her that they're coming in perfect harmony. I rub up between my legs, I can't help it. I tremble in the corner, biting my lip to keep from moaning out loud, until they've stopped moving. They remain totally still. The porcelain shepherd and his shepherdess enacting a scene from the Kama Sutra.

'Hey, sugar,' coos Mrs Weinmeyer after a few moments, flicking her hair away from her face. 'Come over here. All this lovin' making you horny?'

'Ingrid,' growls Mr Weinmeyer, 'you're coming on all southern belle. You were born in Vienna, for God's sake!'

She sniggers, her pink lips curling back over sharp little teeth like a yawning cat. 'And I prefer it when you come on all silent Aryan beefcake. Hey, Serena. Come round this side of the camera, why don't you? Come sit with us.'

I don't move for a moment.

'I'd like to see the images so far,' she soothes. 'See how well they've come out.'

She's the client. Remember that, Folkes. Remember that they are certainly going to report back to Gustav. I'm sure that's what he's requested, no matter how vehemently he denies having anything to do with this commission. Rule number three. Never disobey or displease the client. Especially a very rich, well-connected client whose home you are in.

Mrs Weinmeyer casually unclips her husband from the handcuffs and unties the scarf from around his head. His eyes are closed as he lies quietly beneath her. He looks asleep. She pats the bed. I can't refuse. I take a slug of the red liquid from the Venetian goblet and it is such a rich, herbal wine punch that it goes straight to my head and I topple slightly onto the deep cushions, falling onto my side.

Mr Weinmeyer grunts and rolls away, leaving Mrs Weinmeyer lying where he was. Letting me fall on top of her.

Before I can right myself Mrs Weinmeyer has pulled me

closer to her, and now we're lying side by side like a couple of girlfriends at a sleepover. She takes the camera and scrolls through the images on the screen.

'These are great, honey. I could come all over again, just looking at them.' She hands the camera back to me and I take a look. Clicking through them rapidly makes them into a stream of moving images and yes, it's very sexy to see the two of them, so white against the red bedding, rapidly humping.

'Oh, you spilled some punch on your cool top.' Mrs Weinmeyer takes the camera off me, slips my T-shirt over my shoulders and while she's at it unclips my bra too, and throws both items across the room. I'm dizzy with the drink and the heat, and before I can move or cover myself she is pulling me down, brushing my bare breasts across her closed eyelids.

'Mrs Weinmeyer, what are you – what do you want me to—?'

'Just relax, sugar. Just playing with you a little. Indulge us. Indulge yourself. You're so gorgeous, don't you know it? Gustav knows it, that's for dang sure. The reputation he has. No one really knows him, but everyone wants to. I'm guessing he's a wild one, isn't he? What will he say, I wonder, when you tell him all about this job? Because you must tell him, sugar. Never have secrets. Mr Weinmeyer and I have no secrets. This was his fantasy, two girls, and now it's mine. So we are always looking for lovely young women to join us.' She smiles, seeing how her voice is hypnotising me. 'Ever done this before? Ever been *paid* for it?'

'No, not for this. You're not paying me for sex. You're paying me for my work!'

'Absolutely, and marvellous work it is, too, darling. We'll want all the shots. They're fantastic. But right now? We want your cute little ass.'

I'm losing my willpower. I'm so warm and dozy. I wonder

if Gustav knows exactly how far the Weinmeyers are trying to take me? I try to twist round to see what Mr Weinmeyer is doing, but Mrs Weinmeyer's hands are on my back and she's pulling me down, her lips nibbling the round flesh of my breasts with the merest touch of a butterfly, tickling with her fingertips, her eyelashes, even her hair. I'm holding my breath. I'm also thrusting myself towards Mrs Weinmeyer's mouth. My nipples are dark points in the dim light. I like them to be sucked. Gustav never does it enough. Mrs Weinmeyer's lips are running over them as if she knows. She's about to take one into her mouth.

But I pull away frantically. I want her to do it, more than anything. But how can I? It's kinky, and naughty. Unprofessional at best, unfaithful at worst.

'I'm sorry, Mrs Weinmeyer. I can't do this. I've never done this. With a woman. With strangers.'

'Strangers? We're not strangers any more!'

Mrs Weinmeyer stares up at me as if I'm a tasty morsel, and then her tongue flicks out, just touching one burning nipple before flicking in again. I moan out loud before I can stop myself. Embarrassed? I should co-co. But incredibly turned on.

Behind me Mr Weinmeyer plants his hands on my bottom and cups the cheeks and then I feel him reaching round to undo the top button of my jeans. I'm burning up with humiliation, but I can't get away from him because now Mrs Weinmeyer is drawing my nipple into her lovely pink mouth. Mr Weinmeyer pauses, as if for permission.

Mrs Weinmeyer gives one sharp nod, nipping me and making me squeal. So the big blond tycoon has to ask his wife first? What about *my* permission? Her husband starts to lower the zip, ease my jeans over my hips. I want to jerk away from him, but I can't move.

Mrs Weinmeyer senses my unease and massages my breasts

a little harder, sucks very gently now on one aching bud, then the other.

My jeans are halfway down my buttocks. I'm hanging between them, their easy plaything. Enough of me is exposed now, because Mr Weinmeyer starts to rub himself against my soft butt. His penis is long, and slim, already hard. And it's the alien feel of his manhood that finally brings me properly to my senses. I don't want it. I don't want any other man. I *can't* have any other man.

'Stop, please. I can't do this. This isn't why I'm here.' I pull away abruptly, feel Mrs Weinmeyer's teeth still nipping sharply at me. 'Gustav would kill me if he found out.'

I fall off the edge of the bed, stand up swiftly, buttoning my jeans. I stand for a moment, staring down at their calm, watching faces. My breasts are bare, bouncing frantically with my breath, my nipples taut and sore, shining with her saliva. I scuttle about, locating my discarded clothes and holding them in a bunch in front of me. I can't find my bra, but I don't want to fuss about that now. I fumble for my camera. Not so cool and professional now, eh, Folkes. What now? How do I leave? How do I make this polite yet firm?

They have moved back into each other's arms, lying calmly on the bed watching me.

'*Au contraire*, sugar. Gustav will be proud of you when we report back. You've passed the test with flying colours. He dismissed any idea of you succumbing when I ran the idea past him, and he was right. You've learned from the master.' Mrs Weinmeyer laughs, licking her lips one more time as I pull the T-shirt over my head. 'Not even *he* would let his libido get in the way of a good deal.'

'This is my commission, not Gustav's, and it's important to me, Mrs Weinmeyer, but I'll understand if you want to cancel our association because I've rejected your advances. I can give you the prints of today's shoot for free, or I can wipe them from the memory if you prefer,' I stammer, realising that I've forgotten where the door is. 'You're lovely, both of you, and I admit it felt a little thrilling, but I can't have sex with you. I've never–'

'Tried it girl-on-girl? Or in a threesome?'

'Both. Neither.'

They both tip their heads back and laugh, shake their heads, and to my astonishment give each other a hearty high-five.

Mr Weinmeyer pulls his boxers on and stands up. Once more he's the towering businessman. 'You are lovely, too, and we wouldn't change a thing. Relax, *Fräulein*. No harm in trying it on with you, was there? I hope you'll forgive us, but you must accept the lion's share of the blame because you really are good enough to eat, and you looked, deep down, as if you knew exactly what you were doing. Mr Levi was right to snap you up in those wolfish jaws of his.'

'I suppose it's common knowledge that we're an item?'

They nod, still chuckling and nudging each other like a pair of kids. 'No way a cute piece of ass like you would pass by a connoisseur like him.'

I smile weakly even as my stomach lurches again. Of course he's had other women. Lots of them. Maybe even Mrs Weinmeyer herself! 'Right. But what matters now is my behaviour towards you. Please tell me there's no harm done!' I can feel the sweat pouring down my back. My neck under the long thick plait is sticky. 'You won't think me insolent or unprofessional?'

'You are a consummate professional as well as consummately faithful, and don't worry that pretty English head of yours. We have every intention of singing your praises to all our friends!'

They are both beside me now, guiding me up the stairs. There is no door, after all, just the staircase gliding up through the red walls out of the dungeon towards the surprising daylight. Of course. It must be about midday by now, yet it feels like the middle of the night.

'Ernst, what we should be asking the girl is, does she want anything more to do with *us*? Depraved creatures that we are. We might have scared her witless down there.'

They both stand at the bottom of the *Gone With The Wind* stairs as I collect my other clothes from the drawing room. They match the dark-pink walls and the gilt furnishings. She is wrapped loosely in her pink chiffon again. He is in his boxers. They look as if they're posing for a lingerie shoot.

'She's like one of our tasty Titians. We can't help wanting a piece of that.'

'A little crude, Ingrid. But I agree. It's her fault for being so beautiful.'

I gasp with laughter. 'That's what Gustav said to me this morning!'

'He's so right,' nods Mr Weinmeyer. 'But then, he always had impeccable taste.

'We're teasing you, Serena.' Ingrid runs her baby-pink fingernail down her husband's cheek. 'It doesn't matter what you think of us, or who you tell, because no one will be shocked. Everyone knows we like a threesome and we'll chance it whenever we find new blood. Usually money talks, but not in your case, evidently.'

Mr Weinmeyer glances up at the golden sunburst art deco clock above the mantelpiece. 'The only downside is that you are forced to see us again, Miss Folkes, because we'll need another meeting when you have the proofs. Would you prefer to come here with Gustav as your chaperone next time?'

Mrs Weinmeyer checks her reflection in the mirror, patting her blonde helmet. 'Oh, please do! I'd be the envy of the ladies who lunch. Probably a fair share of their pretty young lovers too. Everyone longs to know what he's like between the sheets. Please bring him! It would be like taking tea with Dracula.'

Mr Weinmeyer lifts his eyes heavenwards as if to say, *these girls are a lost cause.* 'Or you could come to my office if that makes you feel safer?'

His elbow is on the newel of the banister. Hers is draped up the handrail. Another perfect composition of limbs. The tilt of their chins, their quiet demeanour, makes it impossible to remember what they did downstairs. I can't take seriously the implications of what she is saying. That she wants to get my boyfriend naked in her 'bordello room'.

I zip up my jacket. It's not until I shove the beret down that I feel secure, and clothed, although the swing of my bra-less, unsupported breasts and the resulting rub of my tingling nipples against the fabric is disconcerting. I pick up my camera bags, and look them both calmly in the eye.

'I'd be delighted to see you again as soon as I've edited the proofs. Gustav can come if he likes. He's obviously in demand, but I think I have the advantage for once.' I smile, turning to the door. 'I'm the one who knows you both a whole lot better after today!'

They clap their hands and laugh again.

'Indeed you do. This is the start of a wonderful partnership.'

I catch a wink passing between them before Mr Weinmeyer steps away from his wife and comes to open the front door for me. As the light floods in I fill my lungs properly for the first time since I entered this mansion.

'That locket,' Mr Weinmeyer says. 'Come and see this, Ingrid. It's exquisite. Like something your grandmother would wear before the First World War.'

Mrs Weinmeyer moves to stand next to him again. She lifts the golden locket, turns it, sees the silver clasp, the little S inscribed. Hears the mysterious rattle of the object inside, tapping its golden prison as if asking to come out. 'How much?'

I smile generously, let her touch it for a moment. 'It's not for sale. It's a present from Gustav, and it's mine for life.'

Mr Weinmeyer puts his arm around his wife's waist to protect her from the elements as he opens the front door wider. A cold blast of air invades the hallway, along with a flurry of wet snow.

I step onto the doorstep, the air rushing over my skin.

'It must be serious,' both Weinmeyers murmur with one accord. 'And who can blame him?'

I feel like flinging my arms out to embrace the city. 'What can I say? I'm a lucky girl.'

'And he's a lucky man. Don't ever forget that.'

I grin at them. 'That's a lovely thing to say. I've really enjoyed today. And thank you for this opportunity, because it has been the next step on a very long ladder.'

'Believe me, honey,' smiles Mrs Weinmeyer, showing her expensively perfected teeth. 'The pleasure will be all ours.'

They each lift their right hand to wave from the doorstep. Despite their kinky tastes they are the perfect couple, an advertisement for matrimony, sturdy yet fragile.

I retrace my steps across Fifth Avenue to Central Park. I have a spring in my step, like Zebedee from *The Magic Roundabout*. And no wonder. I'm in New York. I've just finished my first commission with the smartest, naughtiest, richest couple in town. My cousin Polly and I are on the same continent and in the same city, at least for a while. My gorgeous rich lover is taking me out to a posh dinner later.

My mobile phone rings. Another commission comes my way, booked in a few days' time with a family who live in a Chelsea brownstone and have the very English name of Robinson. The father wants me to take some group portraits of the clan before his kids all leave home.

'Sounds an interesting challenge,' I remark as I take down the address. 'What made you choose me for the job?'

'Your range. Your classic way with composition and lighting.' Mr Robinson gives a low, surprisingly sexy chuckle. 'I've seen one of your, ah, more tasteful Italian photographs at my friend's house. The one with the girls on the beach? But I'm after something nice and wholesome as a family memento, if you get my meaning.'

I am trying, and failing, to picture this family. Respectable and preppy in chinos and tea dresses is what I'm coming up with, arranged on the stairs or grouped round the piano like the von Trapps. One or two tasteful nudes on the walls. Mr Robinson going to the house next door, trying not to ogle his friend's newest acquisition, my photograph of topless bathers smoothing themselves and each other with suncream on the island of Capri.

I giggle out loud as I hurry down the east side of the park. I circle the open-air ice rink and then my footsteps slow as I reach the zoo. A clutch of penguins pace fretfully on a big grey rock and in another enclosure a polar bear bats gloomily at a blue plastic bag. There are very few visitors today, probably because the wind is icy. As I come through the gate to the south-east side a strong corner wind blows me back against the railings.

I have a weird feeling of hands on me, pinning me there as I watch the smart shoppers on Fifth Avenue for a moment. Straight down there is the towering Empire State Building, still iconic enough to make you catch your breath even though it's no longer the tallest building in the world. In 1931 it took 3,400 workers 410 days to build it. Four and a half storeys a day. Imagine constructing something as fast as that now.

My mobile phone sings with the arrival of a text from Gustav.

Change of plan. Meet me at the restaurant an hour earlier. Developments with Pierre today – it's all good.

I shiver with excitement as I reply *yes, yes, yes* to him, then I zip my jacket up against the Atlantic cold, cover my face with my scarf and hurry south to explore my new city.

CHAPTER FIVE

'Christ! What's he doing to her in this one? They were touching each other up in front of you?' Gustav is trying, and failing, to keep the disapproval out of his voice. 'I never thought they'd go right ahead and try it on with you after I'd warned them off.'

Gustav's face is illuminated by my camera as he scrolls through the Weinmeyer images. The initial deceptively formal poses in the drawing-room window. Mr Weinmeyer's hand slipping inside Mrs Weinmeyer's dress. Gustav zooms in until the only part of Mr Weinmeyer in the frame is his long, clean, white fingers, prising his wife open like a conch shell.

'Luckily for you I'm going to forgive you for discussing my commissions with my clients. But just this once. They took your dismissal of the idea as a challenge. You probably made it worse, because there was much more than touching going on, it transpired.'

I reach over and transform the image to monochrome: monochrome fingers, monochrome lips, Mrs Weinmeyer's white bottom with the darker grey flash between her cheeks.

'Get in any closer and these would be like that 2003 Bailey exhibition of all those vaginas. Pussy pictures he called them.'

'You wait until you see the Weinmeyers migrating to the dungeon of delight.'

I wriggle on the banquette as Gustav studies my camera. I twist my empty plate and nibble on a leftover green bean. I'm unaccountably nervous all of a sudden. He's seen my work before. He's seen equally if not far more graphic images. He looks up at me, apparently not yet understanding what dungeon I'm referring to.

Gustav and I are in a cosy, intimate and very select restaurant in the West Village, tucked below street level. It's so discreet it looks like a kind of muted tavern and only has a small sign outside the glowing windows. I feel really special sitting here. I've seen one or two celebrities schmoozing in corners and a group of beautiful people who look like they must be models or the cast of a play carousing genteelly, if that isn't a contradiction in terms, in the glass garden room at the back. For a brief, blinding second I wonder if they are actors from Pierre's show.

'No need to obsess about the detail. They said it was for their private collection so I don't know if they'll want me to crop the pictures quite so brutally down to her private parts,' I murmur hurriedly as Gustav stares at the next picture. 'They were asking me to capture the moment. It's just that the moment they were referring to was when the two of them decided to get seriously naked.'

'You're telling me!' he splutters, bringing the camera close to his eyes. 'I knew the Weinmeyers were experimental exhibitionists, but these are practically pornographic, Serena! You're only just starting out in this business. What were they thinking of, dragging you into their dungeon and making you do this?'

'Teaching you a lesson, I reckon. Not to discuss me and my working methods behind my back, and not to dictate what goes on during a commission they're paying good money for!'

I try to take the camera off him, but he snatches it back and puts it on the red leather seat by him, out of my reach. His mouth has drawn into a line and a muscle flashes in his cheek. He sits back, loosening his tie still further. His stretches his arms out in an effort to look nonchalant, but I can tell from the way his fingers are drumming that he's agitated.

'So, after all that, you didn't entirely pass the resistance test, did you, Miss Folkes? You let them have their little feel.'

I start to shrink back in my own banquette. The leather squeaks under my bare thighs. I dressed up especially tonight. I'm wearing a very flimsy mint-green silk dress and some heels, and I'm not wearing any knickers. The leather is hot and sticky beneath me.

I'm caught on the hop by Gustav's sharp questioning. He's wearing his authoritarian, headmaster face. I know it's a thin skin over the bubbling passion beneath, but it still unsettles me. Makes me eager to please.

His frown furrows deeper when he sees a smile creeping round my mouth.

'You going to cane me for my misdemeanour, Gustav?'

He shakes his head slightly. His features are still carved in granite. 'It's not your fault for getting into a dodgy situation, Serena. I'm blaming them. They should have known better than to ask you to undertake a task like that.'

I part my legs slightly on the seat while I think how best to reply to him without wrecking the atmosphere. I allow the leather to rub against my tender private flesh until the friction starts to work on me and I have to stop.

'Give me some credit, Gustav. They asked me because I was the right person for the job. As you know, they saw my London exhibition and liked it. They've got my Paris lovers series on their wall. I'm a big girl. Just like you said this morning. I fulfilled my commission to order. Yes, I was embarrassed at first, and then I admit I was downright shocked when they enticed me down these stairs into this red room and started writhing around on a gigantic bed and all that, but hey! Two consenting adults pleasuring each other under the watchful gaze of Venus in a sexy cosy nest, plying me with delicious punch. A little slap and tickle, maybe. As Mrs Weinmeyer herself said, what's not to like?'

His fingers stop tapping. I see his mouth twitching then with a hint of amusement but there's a tinge of sadness in his eyes. 'My country bumpkin. What's happened to her?'

'She's still here. But I was always a voyeur, Gustav. That's the first thing you noticed and liked about me.'

I put my hand on his leg, and when he doesn't move I start to slide it up his thigh, squeezing the muscle which is all the sexier for being hidden under his formal business trousers. He shifts in his seat, his eyes half closing. 'Hey, baby. Let's not fall out,' he murmurs.

I move my hand into the warm fold of his groin, lean closer to whisper. 'I don't ever want to argue with you. But you've got to get this into your handsome head, Gustav. I want to be a famous photographer. And that means never saying never. To anything.'

The waiter approaches to take our plates and refill our glasses. He hesitates, eyes flickering over where my hand is massaging my man's thigh. I give him my best seductress stare back, followed by a deliberate flutter of the eyelashes. Lower my left eyelid in a slow wink and see the flush creep up his thin neck.

Then I take a real twisted delight in pressing my hand against Gustav's zipper, showing the waiter how my elbow and arm are moving while he tries to clear the plates and lay spoons without dropping anything in his eagerness to see. I rub my palm between Gustav's legs and feel the hardness growing.

The plates rattle as the waiter balances them up his arm.

He backs away, and I see him retreat to the corner of the room where he nudges a fellow waiter and jerks his head over towards us.

Gustav is in my thrall now. He presses his hand on top of mine, moving it faster and harder over him. The calmer he remains, the more determined I am to break his cool. If I take him all the way to the edge there will be the jump of his Adam's apple, the black-molasses glaze in his eyes that tells me he's about to come.

His voice is husky now. '"Never say never" could be a risky adage.'

'Risky is where the fun is, don't you agree?' Under the table I continue to massage him until he starts to buck gently against my hand. I glance over at the waiter. He's still staring at me, his hand moving in his trouser pocket. I twiddle innocently with my wineglass before lifting it, puckering my mouth slowly, and taking a long sip.

'Oh, you're transforming before my very eyes, Serena,' Gustav murmurs as I fondle and drive him to the point of no return. 'What have I done to you?'

I laugh softly as he bucks against me one more time then slumps back. I remove my hand, tuck it under my chin thoughtfully. Glance over at the waiter and mouth at him, 'Show's over.'

'I was already a twisted little thing when we first met, but you've taught me everything you know. Take another look at these pictures, Mr Levi. They turned you on, didn't they? And that reaction made you cross with yourself. Hopefully you feel better now.'

'I was cross because I was jealous. The thought of someone else touching you, their hands on you.'

'Even if it's a female?'

'I could get my head round that, I suppose. But only if I was there to watch. Get myself the best seat in the house and see all the action up close.' He shakes his head, a smile spreading over his face, softening the edges, giving a new sparkle to his eyes. 'You're an incorrigible little madam.'

'And you're a nosy devil.' I laugh softly and tap my fingertips together. 'But I may as well confess that it made me a little horny when I was down there with them. It's hard to disconnect, you know? I hope that will be a good thing, photographically. Look at the way Mr Weinmeyer is feeling his way. He's blindfolded, you see. Not that he has to do much, just lie back. And she handcuffed him, too.'

Gustav groans and forces himself to sit up. Adjusts his trousers, biting his lip with discomfort. 'Don't talk to me about handcuffs.'

I stroke my hand down his crotch. 'It was all very laidback and gentle, Gustav. No whips. No punishment. Just her being assertive, and him giving her what she wanted. Do you want to see how it makes me feel even now, just talking about it?'

His eyes flicker back into focus. He watches my hand as if it's a scorpion about to strike. I laugh again, take his hand prisoner and nestle it between my legs.

'Whatever went down in that dungeon of theirs, it's put the very devil into you, young lady.'

I see him bite his lip as he touches me there, see the flare of his nostrils as he realises I've gone commando under my pretty dress this evening. I push his fingers firmly into me and close my thighs to trap his hand. All this is going on under the white tablecloth as the snooty waiter comes up with the dessert menu and when he sees what is happening this time he nearly swerves away like a horse refusing a jump.

'Oh, don't go away, we'll take a look at the sweet things now, thank you.'

Gustav fixes the waiter with a steely gaze, all the while

hooking his other fingers into me under the table as I have instructed him. He is openly challenging the waiter, who has a visible bulge through his white apron. I struggle not to snort as he hands over the menu twixt finger and thumb as if it, or Gustav, might bite.

'The sweet things. Right,' he stammers.

'Thank you.'

Gustav nods, still keeping the waiter's gaze, and in the same way as I did he lets his arm speak for him, pumping up and down as he strokes me. I look at the two men, the waiter stumbling backwards to fetch the order and the haughty customer revelling in the idea that he can touch me when the waiter can't. The hushed, candlelit room full of adultery and secrets wavers slightly as Gustav's expert fingers set alight the embers of desire that have been glowing quietly all day. I fall against the seat, tip up against his fingers, an invitation for him to go further, push deeper, harder into the wetness.

'Oh God, I've been keeping this lust inside me all day. Can't we just go home?'

I lean close to him, impaling myself more fully by the movement, and make sure he can hear me amongst the buzz of other voices. I lift the menu to hide us so that I can run my mouth over his.

'Absolutely not. Have you any idea how exclusive this place is? We're staying here until I say so.'

I sigh. 'Mr and Mrs Weinmeyer. It's their fault I'm so wet. They were all over each other like a couple of teenagers.'

Gustav chuckles quietly. It's a private chuckle, just for me. 'Teenagers who play with blindfolds and handcuffs, and have Picasso hanging on their walls?'

'OK, not teenagers. A very kinky middle-aged billionaire couple.' I chuckle back, pushing him harder into me. My tongue runs across my mouth as the sensations intensify. 'Who knows? Maybe they've got one or two of those Bailey pussy pictures tucked away somewhere as another sex aid. In the bathroom perhaps or above the marital bed.'

'Not that you need anything like that to spark you off. You're insatiable. I'm definitely beginning to think I should keep a closer eye on you.' He leans closer and takes my face in his free hand, smiles roguishly as he fingers me harder and faster until my body clenches round him and reaches its little zenith, too short, so sharp, so sweet, and I moan into his neck as it happens, shivering and trembling. Tit for tat. Both goaded and reduced to jelly in the space of ten minutes. We're becoming specialists.

He withdraws his hand slowly, wipes its wetness back over my thigh, and then makes me squeal with shocked laughter as he runs one glistening finger down over the menu, leaving a snail's trail of my juice down the list of sorbets.

'What were you going to tell me, Gustav?' My voice is a tiny mew as I try to gather my wits around me like shredded lace. 'You wanted me here early to tell me something?'

'I didn't want to be apart from you longer than necessary.'

'My poor baby. Pull the other one.' I flick at him with my napkin, and a couple of pairs of famous eyes glance at me, then rest on Gustav. Pride swells inside me. He's well-known here as well as in London, and I'm going to bask in it. 'You said in your text something about "developments". So what did you want to tell me?'

He orders our puddings. It's a different waiter now. This one looks even more wary than the last. Gustav dismisses him and takes my hands. His face goes still, and pale, and serious.

'I spoke to Pierre this morning.'

'That's good. That's really good.' My voice is wooden and my hand feels cold even inside his warm grasp. I should have known we couldn't hold him at arm's length for long.

He nods gravely. A lock of black hair falls into his eyes.

'He phoned me just as I was watching you walking away through the Strawberry Fields bit of the park. He wanted to apologise for the shock tactics on New Year's Eve.' He smiles, a slightly grim smile which doesn't reach his eyes. 'But he couldn't stop talking about you, either. He thinks you're a bit of a harridan.'

'Charming!' My head swings up. Unease stirs in the pit of my stomach. It seems to be an automatic response whenever Pierre's name is mentioned. 'What makes him say that?'

He brings my hand up to his lips and kisses the thin skin on the back. It still makes me shiver. His eyes are watchful between the thick lashes as he plays my fingers across his lips.

'You gave him a piece of your mind when you were all waiting for me to get home from the airport.'

'He needed to know that I'm on your side, Gustav. No matter what.'

'He heard you loud and clear, it seems.' He continues to rub my hand across his mouth, his dark eyes surveying me as if he's seeing me in a new light. 'You seem to understand each other.'

'Not difficult to understand my message to him. I told him to man up and talk to you.' I can't help trembling. My body is still tight and hot from Gustav's fingers, but my head and heart are cold. I hold my hands up. 'Look, I'm shaking. Why does this stress me out? Making up with your brother is a good thing, right?'

Gustav sits back and studies me. I want him to take my hands and comfort me. I want him to put his arm around me. A long black shadow has sidled in between us. Two shadows, actually.

'You're stressed because of Margot. Because Pierre coming back is optimistic and positive, he and I agreed on that this morning, but he drags after him all that shit, the past, that part of my life you don't belong to. And you're stressed because I haven't done a good enough job of reassuring you.'

I nod. 'You're right, as always. That connection he has with her – it flaps around him like a shroud. And how do we know she's really gone? Where is she now?'

'It seems she eventually chewed him up and spat him out. That's all he will say for now. God, if only I could have spared him all that humiliation. She managed to wreak even more havoc on him than she did me, because he was more vulnerable.' He nods, as if confirming something to himself. 'I let him down. I've done it too many times. I've got to be here for him, whenever, wherever.'

I try to smile, but I can't quite manage it. 'You said all that in one phone call?'

'We've spoken a couple of times, actually.' He is silent for a moment. I hear the waiter putting down two bowls on the table with the tiniest of clunks.

A weak, addicted loser. Pierre's bitter words echo distantly in my ears.

'We've already come a long way, partly thanks to you, *signorina*. Look at me.' He pulls my hands away from my eyes. He kisses the tip of my nose. 'He can't hurt you or shut you out, OK? This is between him and me.'

I nod wearily. Pierre is a shifting tectonic plate under our feet. I pick up my spoon and press it into the fragile hillock of meringue on my plate. I tap it and thin cracks spider down it, like Humpty Dumpty's head. Raspberry mess spills out of it. Me and my big mouth.

'I don't think he likes me.'

Gustav's chocolate mousse is halfway to his mouth but to my astonishment he starts laughing.

'Funny girl. Sometimes you get it so wrong. The most brilliant thing is he's grudgingly admitted that he does like you. Admires you, even. And if he wasn't with Polly now, which incidentally makes him doubly family, who could blame him if he was half in love with you?'

I inhale sugary crumbs of meringue. 'That's the craziest thing I ever heard!'

'Yes, because who could ever do anything by halves when it came to you?'

Gustav pats me between the shoulder blades as I start to cough.

'Anyway, enough about that. We're going to meet at the Library Hotel's rooftop bar next week.'

I shove too much gooey meringue into my mouth and it sticks to the palate, even the insides of my teeth.

'That's great. Just the two of you. You need to have a heart-to-heart.'

'Oh, no, he wants you there, Serena. He has a proposal for you.'

I can only grimace awkwardly as I try to chew through the sugar, glad of the excuse to say nothing. I down an entire glass of wine in one gulp to wash away the meringue. Gustav's face is so open just now, his black eyes so bright. He spoons in his pudding like a little boy at a birthday party, happy that he has taken big strikes towards his long-lost brother.

'Come on, let's get out of here.' He beckons to the waiter, leans across and kisses me lingeringly, a new and precious habit of his. 'I want to get home and celebrate my girlfriend's burgeoning successes. This is going to be a fabulous year, Serena Folkes.'

It would take a heart of stone not to enter into the spirit of it. The other diners watch us through the flickering candle-light as we stand up. Gustav takes my leather jacket from the waiter and helps me into it, first one bare arm, then the other, zipping me up tight, buttoning the fiddly buttons on my green leather gloves, which match my filmy green dress. Running his hands round my hips and bottom to smooth down my skirt. Finally curling the wispy tendrils of hair that have fallen from the loose knot at the back of my head and brushing them away from my hot face.

'Perfect,' he says, leading me proudly out of the restaurant.

We must have broken a record for getting through New York traffic. The hired limousine bounced and weaved on its cushiony suspension up Amsterdam Avenue and Broadway, the driver's screen closed by Gustav as soon as we got into the car so that the invisible chauffeur couldn't see him running his hands up my bare legs, under my skirt, teasing the uncertainty out of me with his warm, wandering fingers until I was putty in his hands once again.

'I'll ravish you right here on this seat if he doesn't hurry up,' he muttered, his breath hot and harsh in my hair.

At last we're back at the apartment building, galloping through the revolving glass doors into the lobby, past the Mount-Rushmore-faced doormen, into the lift, kissing breathlessly, nearly doing it in there, tempted to shock whoever is paid to stare at the CCTV all day, but the lift is too quick so we crash against the huge wooden door of the flat, where's the key, his hands are still up my dress, somehow we're getting through the door, putting my camera kit carefully down before falling half on, half off the massive sofa in front of the window.

Gustav rips his jacket and tie off, half unbuttons his shirt, panting hard, spins me round so that I'm facing out of the window, looking down over the waving treetops of Central Park. I think of the enormous chalet back in Lake Lugano, the place where we first had sex. The big sofa in front of the fire, the picture window with its panorama over the flat lake and the craggy mountains, Gustav bending me over the back of the sofa so I could hardly breathe and taking me from behind.

My back is to him now. I want him to take me, any way he wants, but it must be now.

I know Gustav is hard, because I made sure of it in the cab. With superhuman control he is slowing the pace, unpinning my hair first of all so that it falls over my shoulders and back, tickling my skin as it tumbles. He scoops it up in handfuls and buries his nose in it, twisting and curling it round his fingers like a knuckleduster and tugging my head hard so that he can nibble at my bare neck.

His mouth moves over the top of my spine, still tugging at my hair to keep me still, kissing the ladder of vertebrae while his fingers fumble for the zip.

'Just pull it off, Gustav,' I hiss over my shoulder, trying to wriggle out of the dress. 'It's more of a petticoat. It will just fall away.'

His fingers stop on the zip. My hair is wrapped tight round his knuckles.

'Did they ask you to join in?'

His voice is low and guttural, like a growl.

'What? Who?' For a mad, crazy moment I think he's referring to Pierre and my cousin Polly. Pulling me into their tangle of limbs, his hands, her hands, his mouth, his hands on me. The picture, and the knowledge I can never confide it to Gustav, gives me an evil kick inside.

Gustav becomes rougher, circles his hands round my neck, up my face, claws his fingers through my hair.

'The Weinmeyers. In that red dungeon of theirs. Did they want you to come right into the bed with them, make up a full-on threesome?'

'They're clients, Gustav.' I shrug as carelessly as I can. Feel the dress slipping further down. Try to force the other images to slip away with it. 'I was working, for goodness' sake. Just like you told me to.'

'Nobody dares say no to them.'

'I did. I said no.'

My voice is a kitten's mew and he doesn't hear me.

'Did they want you to join in their sordid little scenario? Tell me!'

'Yes, they were screwing each other and having a whale of a time doing it. But you've shown me worse, remember? The dominatrix videos at your old house in London? Which they intend to bid for, by the way.'

Back he comes, uninvited. Pierre, with his black eyes, his unkind mouth. Asking about the house. Calling me a Rottweiler, a harridan, doubly family. Doubly his.

'They can have the Baker Street collection for free if that's what they want!' Gustav's voice is a low hiss in my ear. 'Those films were all artifice. The situation you were in this morning was a real live couple cavorting in their own home!'

'And how much healthier does that seem, compared with all that other pervy stuff? You told me yourself you hated it!'

His face goes dark. His body goes dead still behind me. I push against it, and he doesn't move. I clench my fists. This is good. Talking is good. Fantasising is bad.

'You're not listening to me, Gustav. There was no danger. No threat, to me or to you for that matter. Yes, they went all the way, but you know something? I was fascinated by it. Like observing animals in the wild. Mrs Weinmeyer may look as if she's made of porcelain, but she was on top today. She was in charge.'

He winds my hair tight round his fingers again as if it's a lifeline. 'And Mrs Weinmeyer's influence will have made its mark on you, however much you try to deny it.'

I lean back against him. 'Maybe it's not such a bad influence. Remember I don't have any other female role models in my life. Polly hardly counts. She was my partner in crime

103

when we were kids. God, how I used to look forward to her visits to Devon. I used to cry for hours when she'd gone back to London. When she was on a visit we were let loose, we could do whatever we wanted, go to the pub, camp on the beach, hang out with boys, because nobody wanted us in the house.' I stop for a moment, remembering the crazed look blurring Polly's lovely blue eyes on New Year's Eve, the way she clung to Pierre as if he might slither out of reach. 'I used to think she was the mature one, teaching me the facts of life, but I've caught up with her now. And she's a bit off kilter at the moment.'

'Well, you know her better than anyone, and I doubt Pierre can sort her out. He's way too wrapped up in himself at the moment. You'll have to go out with her, see what's up.' He holds me so tight I can't breathe. 'I want to be sure you're not drawn into anything you can't get out of. People like the Weinmeyers have your reputation in their hands.'

'I love that you worry about me. But it was fine, really. Harmless.' I attempt a careless laugh, but I'm not feeling careless now. Pierre is in my head, in the room again. Giving me that same lascivious look as when I was trying to make diplomatic overtures on New Year's Eve.

'The Weinmeyers could make you or break you.'

'You know that they will make me. You were practically in the room with us!' I decide to brazen this out for the moment. 'I know you called when I was working at their house, Gustav. So either stalk me or send me out with a minder every day, or let me go about my business.'

'I know you wouldn't lie to me. You're useless at it. There's this funny kind of grimace that passes over your lovely face when you lie. Even so, I think I'll come with you in future. It'll be fun! And if you get into any other kind of trouble, or get sucked in to the point of no return, well, I'll be there to watch!' Gustav's grip on me relaxes very slightly. 'So. Let's get into the imagined scenario. Tell me some more about the kinky Weinmeyers.'

I try to face him, but he pushes me against the back of the sofa. I let myself go limp, relish the relief of it. 'You won't like it, master. They asked me to sit on the bed.'

'Go on.' He waits. He still has my hair tangled in his hand, but he has stopped stroking me. The dress is half unzipped, slipping off my arms. 'Did they touch you?'

I stretch my arms along the back of the sofa but my fingernails are digging into the palms of my hands. 'I was kind of off balance and when I toppled onto her she got my top off and she kissed my – she kissed my nipples.'

'That must be how they get their kicks. Reeling in an innocent bystander.' He lets out a long, juddering sigh. But when he shifts on his knees behind me on the sofa I feel the unmistakeable shape of his arousal jamming into my lower back.

'Not bystander exactly. I was a guest in their home. Anyway, Gustav, enough talking. I want to forget about my day.'

He slaps my hands away. 'What about him? Ernst Weinmeyer. The big I-am. Did he touch you?'

At least he's unzipping my dress again, and it slithers all the way down my body in a pool of green silk.

'He tried to. He was still naked on the bed, and he was still hard. I was bent over her, my bottom was up like this.' I show him, wriggle my now bare bottom at him. 'He got my jeans halfway down, but he couldn't get at me. And then I felt his erection and that's when I felt sick at what was happening and jumped off the bed and told them no dice.'

There's a pause, and then Gustav loosens his grip on my shoulders. My hair unravels from his fists, and clothes me instead of the dress.

'That was too close, Serena. And they accepted your rejection? It didn't blow your commission?'

I shake my head. 'They assured me they still liked me, still wanted my pictures, still wanted to meet me again to go through the proofs.'

'Good. Because you're part of me now. So your success is my success. And vice versa.'

I twist round to face him. He's grinning at me. Interrogation over. He really does look like king of the heap. I grin back at him, put one finger on his chest and push him down on the sofa. My power is growing.

'With you by my side nothing's going to stop me.'

He sighs deeply and falls back against the arm of the sofa, pulling me down with him. 'You know? Despite all their wealth and power I feel sorry for those Weinmeyers. I feel sorry for anyone who can't have you like I can.'

We haven't turned the lights on inside the apartment, but enough light floods in from the city sky to outline his beautiful carved features, calm and relieved again. Life with him really is like battling over a stormy ocean. Gustav and me, one at each end of a boat, sometimes a battleship, sometimes a life-raft, but always tipping, one up, one down.

No. No one else is going to have me.

I see the silver chain hanging out of his pocket and I snatch it up. Something heats up inside me like a filament. The desire to work off this toxic steam. My lover's dark, chiselled face is in repose. The black hair falling across his eyes as he lies back, his hands resting on my bare legs now, the fight gone out of him.

'So cocksure, aren't you, Levi? Shall I rock your world for a moment and stop being a good girl?'

He pushes his hair out of his eyes and gives me one of his straight, arrowing stares. 'Go on. I dare you.'

I crawl over him like a lizard. He lifts his hands to take

my breasts as they dangle above him, but quick as a flash I wrap the silver chain tightly round his wrists, pull his arms up over his head and attach the end of the silver chain to the log-like legs of the coffee table.

'Silly girl. Think you're stronger than me?' But he makes no effort to struggle. Just watches me, in that way that makes me want to dance for him.

'I'm showing you what Mrs Weinmeyer did to her big strong tycoon of a husband. She handcuffed him, and then she mounted him.'

'Can a female mount a male?'

His black eyes are glinting but he's biting down hard on his lower lip to hide the grin. He tugs at the silver chain, but the heavy table doesn't budge and he's still attached.

'Oh, yes, she can. Just like this.'

My voice is soft, mesmeric, as I unbutton the rest of his shirt and yank it down his arms so that his elbows are trapped. I tickle the ends of my hair over his chest, over his stomach, see him shiver in response. Then I undo his trousers, as slowly as I can bear. They rip down along with his boxers and I shudder with glee, my body warming in response as he springs free.

Again I tickle him with my hair, brushing it around the shaft, running the circle of hair up and down until I see his Adam's apple jumping frantically in his throat. When he's rock-hard I brush over his balls, already shrinking as his desire increases, and then it's time.

I straddle him, hold myself up on my knees above him as if praying. 'I wonder how a threesome would have worked, technically? What do you think, Gustav?'

'Am I not enough for you, you little slut? You bored with me already? Maybe it was a mistake bringing you across the Pond. Too many new experiences. Too many new people.'

'Don't answer back, boy.' I slap his buttock. I catch his chin in my hand, just like he does to me, and grip it tight.

I don't want to think about anyone else.

'You're a man of the world. Which bit goes where? One man. Two women. Where does the man fit into the ménage, do you suppose? I mean, I've never been with a woman, let alone *à trois*.'

'If I told you I know exactly how it works, it would be your turn to be jealous.'

'You're right. I'd rather be the one making you jealous. So if you're going to accompany me on future shoots, then I'll have to teach you to be a voyeur just like me.'

Gustav nips my finger, worrying at it in his mouth, still tugging at the silver chain. I see it biting into the crease of his wrist.

'That doesn't sound remotely fair. What if I don't want to share you? Or I want to join in?'

'You'll do as you're told.' I slap his buttock again, a satisfying sound. I sit back on his thighs and fold my green silk dress into a strip. I hesitate before I tie it over his eyes. I love his eyes. Despite his best efforts to be unreadable, I am learning to translate each and every one of his expressions. Tonight's expression is ferocious, surprised lust.

I kiss him roughly on the mouth. Then I tie the blindfold, oh, so lightly, he could shake it off if he wanted. Then I ease myself onto him, oh, so slowly, run my hands over his body, see his nipples prick up, feel the jump of him nearly inside me. He groans quietly as I lower myself inch by inch. My breasts brush over his mouth and he catches one, licks at it, then bites it, hard. Still fighting me. My body clenches tight with excitement, sucks him in, all the way to the hilt. It's so tempting to rush, but this is me. I'm in charge.

Now we have a sweet rhythm. He's with me, we're rocking together, and all the talk, all the input of today is fizzing through my head. I get an overwhelming vision of him in another life, cavorting with other women, maybe two at once, the jealousy mingling with a contrary lust, an urge to see it, to watch, to try something new, a woman, a threesome, whatever.

I grind myself over him, the flicker of the forbidden there again, another pair of black eyes staring at me, goading me from the sidelines.

I push myself at Gustav's mouth so that the pain will eradicate that other face. The jealousy is good, we can keep that, I can risk imagining those other bodies, because Gustav is mine, I'm the only one riding him, jacking up the rhythm. I need to ease these urges because it's too soon, too soon, but it's so intense now, my lover pulling against the silver chain as I grip him tighter inside and he thrusts so hard that I bounce off him.

'Tell me I'm the best you ever had,' I suddenly growl, leaning close to him. 'I want to hear you say it.'

He shakes his head. 'You're a bitch on heat.'

I lift myself right up so that I'm just balancing on the tip. 'You want this or not?'

He lies still. I can't see him under the blindfold. I need his eyes on me, urgently, but I can't stop this, I flick myself so that he slips inside again and the pressure builds inside me, it feels so good to be on top. He draws back, tenses and pushes hard and doesn't stop until we can both hear my ragged gasps of pleasure, but as soon as I start to shudder and scream he untwists his wrists from the silver chain, shakes off the blindfold and, still inside me, hurls us both off the sofa.

Now he's hanging over me. 'Not so fast, young lady. And I'm going to do you right down here, my little slattern, because today you deserve an unforgiving surface.'

He pushes me across the cold floor and I relish the strength

109

of him as my skin scrapes and squeaks and then he's coming too and the sound and the fury are over.

We roll over and I rest my head on his chest, listen to the drumming of his heart. His arms are tight around me, our legs splayed on the rug. I kiss his throat and can't resist one last jibe.

'All we're missing is someone else to join in. What would you say, master? Would you allow me to try it?'

Oh, God. Why did I say that? Who am I talking about?

'Maybe. If I could vet who it was. And then watch.'

There's one person we could never allow. What is the matter with me? I have to hound Pierre out of my mind before he does any more damage.

'And if I am there to keep an eye. Make sure you don't get too sharp a taste for it.' Gustav brings his hands down with a harsh slap on my bottom. 'But, as the Miss Folkes Journal of How to Live says: Never say never.'

CHAPTER SIX

The family Robinson are grouped around the grand piano like the von Trapps. I catch Gustav's eye in the hope that I won't burst out laughing at the accuracy of my prediction. It's not just the chinos, preppy button-down shirts and tea dresses that are so funny. What's making me laugh is Gustav lurking in the corner behind the light box, dressed down in jeans, biker jacket and indie beard, posing as my assistant.

Mr Robinson and his two huge, lumbering sons break free from the tableau.

'I think that completes the family shots, Serena.' The pater-familias shakes my hand. His hands are enormous and powerful. I can imagine them wielding an axe to chop down a tree, or aiming a hunting rifle to shoot a grizzly bear. 'But I'd like to pay for some extra time to take some pre-wedding shots of my daughter Emilia with her maid of honour? The big day is fast approaching, and she wanted something – a little different. Scenes from her bachelor days, she says, before she becomes a wife. You know, trying on the dresses, doing their hair, what have you. More girly and fun than the wedding photographer could provide.' Mr Robinson rolls his eyes and pats his pocket to indicate the drain his family are on his finances. 'That bridesmaid will have to go once Emilia's hitched, of course. No more sleepovers.'

Gustav looks ostentatiously at his watch, and again I struggle to keep a straight face. No mere photographer's assistant would be wearing a Patek like that. And what's more, I'm certain Mr Robinson has spotted the discrepancy. I hope he thinks I'm prosperous enough to give my sexy assistants expensive gifts and even naughtier rewards.

'Oh, please, Serena?' pleads Emilia, shooting a poisonous look at her father behind his back. 'My best friend Rosaria is already waiting upstairs. Pop promised we could have a photographic session all to ourselves.'

'And what my princess wants, my princess gets.'

Mr Robinson puts his arm round his wife's shoulder but the look in his eye is of a hard-nosed senator who, when he isn't directing the country's fortunes, always gets his way.

Princess Emilia sidles up beside me and I am nearly knocked sideways by the strength of her floral perfume. She is demure yet curvy, her mousy hair drawn into a French plait, and her tea dress, busy with almost exactly the same splashy design of roses as her demure, curvy mother's, is too tight. I can see the cream lace bra peaking between the straining mother-of-pearl buttons.

'I would love to, Emilia, Mr Robinson, but this is a little short notice.' I dare Gustav to return my glance. 'My assistant has to be somewhere else and I really need him here to hump the heavy equipment, especially if we have to go upstairs.'

Emilia giggles prettily and marches straight over to Gustav, kicking off her kitten heels as she goes. She lays her hands on his arm, and I can see his elbow stiffen slightly beneath the leather sleeve. 'You don't mind, do you, Serena's assistant? You could just "hump" those big old cameras upstairs and then leave her to it, perhaps? It's just going to be us girls posing in my bedroom, after all?' She lowers her voice so her father can't hear, but I can. 'Scenes from a virginal girlhood!'

Gustav rubs his chin, tugs the beanie low over his forehead. God, I could rip those filthy jeans off his long legs and sit on him right now. He looks absolutely gorgeous. Dirty, mean, rough. I want to feel that beard scratching my face and other parts of me until they're raw.

'I stay with *Signorina* Folkes. But just a few minute.' He has exaggerated his foreign accent and hearing him mangling the language like that makes me want to giggle until wetness springs inside my knickers. I groan inwardly and twist on the lens cap. I want him to speak to me like that when we're in bed tonight.

'Yes, just a few minute,' Mrs Robinson sighs, ducking out of her husband's grip and sweeping out of the room after her enormous sons. 'I have a roast chicken just about to come out of the oven and I don't want it resting for too long.'

'You'll do it, Miss Folkes,' mutters Mr Robinson, flexing his arms in readiness for the carving knife. 'And I'll pay you triple time.'

I give a silly curtsy and follow the slow, strangely sensuous pace of Emilia Robinson's wide bottom up the white painted stairs that lead several storeys to the top of the narrow house. I deliberately imitate her swaying gait for Gustav's benefit, stopping short every so often in front of him so that he bangs, at eye level, into my own butt.

The daughter of the house has a thickly carpeted and curtained bedroom that is a riot of pastel femininity, just as I imagined. The curtains are half closed so that we are bathed in a kind of rosy twilight. The bed is festooned with chintz curtains and fairy lights, and hanging from the wardrobe door is a huge white wedding dress, crackling in cellophane as if it already has a body inside it, breathing.

Emilia calls a name softly and pads over to the bathroom. I lean close to Gustav as he erects the tripod and studio lights, running my hands over the front of his jeans.

'I know it's a pain, but it was your idea to accompany me on as many future assignments as possible, so you're working to my schedule now. I'll make it up to you, honey,' I murmur, pressing the growing shape of him under his button flies. 'Or I could dismiss you from your duties?'

'I stay right here,' he answers through gritted teeth, holding my hand hard on him before opening up the white umbrella to diffuse the already dreamy ambience and handing me the light meter. 'I'm getting huge pleasure, also erection, when rich powerful Robinson dynasty think sun shine out of your sweet ass.'

The ham Latino accent nearly has me coming on the spot. But before I can say anything the bathroom door opens, and a petite girl with raven ringlets framing her round face steps out on bare feet. She rushes over to Emilia, who is arranging herself on her bed.

'My maid of honour. Rosaria.'

Emilia giggles and bats her eyelashes at her friend, who crawls onto the bed and kneels up behind the bride-to-be. She hooks her fingers into Emilia's prim plait and pulls it apart, so that Emilia's thick tawny hair is released in waves.

The girls go into action, posing demurely, one brushing the other's hair, one arranging a necklace round the other's throat, both going to stand by the window in their pretty see-through petticoats, then Rosaria buttoning Emilia into the wedding dress, admiring yet envious, while Emilia smiles smugly at her own reflection in the mirror. Soft-focus photographs that could advertise expensive French scent or bedroom interiors.

'Those shots will do for Momma and Poppa. Keep them thinking I'm their innocent daughter all pure for her arranged

114

marriage with Mr Perfect,' says Emilia, giggling, as she takes off the jewellery, unpins the veil and hangs up the gown before slipping back into her tea dress. 'Now for *my* private collection.'

Rosaria, evidently the mistress of the scene, pulls Emilia over to the bed again and fondles her friend's loosened tresses for a moment, transforming Emilia from teen into temptress. Then she brings her hands round to the front of Emilia's dress, her fingers working quickly to unfasten all those over-exercised buttons.

Gustav glances at me, then at the door as if considering his escape, then at the least obvious place to sit. Which is in the corner furthest from the bed, on a vast, white-painted rocking chair.

The girls notice him moving, and their eyes glance up sleepily. 'Oh, he can come, go, we don't really care,' Emilia says, stroking her maid of honour's dark hands as they rest on her big white breasts. 'An audience might be fun.'

'I'll make myself as invisible as possible, too. Just need to take a light reading,' I murmur, leaning towards the girls and holding the meter up.

Something clicks in their eyes. The black Mexican eyes and the forget-me-not WASP ones. Rosaria pulls sharply on Emilia's flowery dress, and it rips. They both smile innocently at me, and rip it again, so that it falls in flowery strips on the bed.

What will Mother Robinson say? Not just about the torn dress. The girls are running their hands over each other, now wearing their old-fashioned satin petticoats, and Rosaria, who I realise has nothing on under her slip, suddenly yanks Emilia's petticoat down and unclips her bra.

Behind me I hear the creak of the rocking chair and Gustav swearing under his breath.

'We don't want you to be invisible. We want you to sit

over here, Serena,' Emilia orders, sublimely comfortable in her state of *déshabille* and patting the puffy duvet.

'Well, a few close-ups, if that's what you want?'

I glance over at Gustav, but he is looking straight at the girls, and not at me. I feel a stab of competition as I see the gleam of amused lust in his eyes. I'm fully clothed in my working gear, unwinding cables and setting up cameras, my hair twisted up in a messy knot on my head, and these two are an abundance of semi-naked plump flesh, female aromas, round shoulders and strong bare legs.

'Yes, it's what we want. Pop said I could ask you, tell you actually, to do whatever I want. You know he has friends in the White House?'

I can't look at Gustav now. I can just imagine the look of derision on his face at such rank-pulling, and in any case I'm distracted by the way Rosaria is kneeling up behind Emilia, cradling her heavy white breasts as she starts to kiss the bride's neck.

Gustav leans back in the creaking rocking chair. His lovely long legs are spread akimbo as if he's relaxing on his own front porch. He winks roguishly at me. I frown back, hooking the meter onto my belt and fussing with the aperture settings on my Lumix camera. What does he want? Not to leave, obviously, otherwise he would be on his feet by now, making our excuses. Maybe he'll think twice about escorting me to my next assignment unless it's guaranteed to be girl-on-girl. Or girl-on-me. Surreptitiously he runs his hand over his groin and my stomach lurches with an answering leap of desire.

But I also want to show him the way I work, no matter what clients throw at me.

I take some shots, tiptoeing round the thick carpet close to the bed. Through my viewfinder the girls start to play with each other, stroking, kissing, squeezing, going further

116

and pinching each other's nipples so that they pucker to sharp points. The shutter snaps.

Rosaria suddenly shoots out her hand and pulls me down beside them.

'Emilia asked you to sit close by,' she whispers, pushing me down on to my back, into the soft pillows. She sits on my legs. 'And you have to do what she says.'

Emilia leans over me and picks up the golden locket. 'What a pretty necklace. Your rich lover give it to you? A grateful client?' she croons, turning it this way and that. 'I recognise the design of the initial. This is one of the top designers in the world. Paris, I think he's based.'

We all hear the sliding rattle of the mysterious object as she lets it fall back onto my throat.

Rosaria runs her fingers under the chain, across my collar bone. 'What's that inside?'

I shake my head, flatten my hand over the locket to hide it from their prying eyes. 'Secret. I'm not allowed to see until he decides the time is right.'

'You have to pass a series of tasks, you mean? Like in a fairy tale? Well, how about me and Rosaria here give you a new task? Very simple really. We just want to fool around for a while.'

I try to struggle up on my elbows, but Emilia pushes me back down. She's very strong, and very heavy. 'Triple time, my daddy said. So. I've got the pictures I wanted but they're just for me to frisk myself over when Rosaria's not here. My future hubby will just have to keep on going to that club of his for kicks because he ain't coming anywhere near me till the wedding night.'

Rosaria runs her hands up my legs. 'Cos I'll be keeping the bride warm until then, eh, Emilia? And maybe there'll be three in the marriage after that!'

'Yes, ma'am. My Rosaria ain't going nowhere!' Emilia

giggles, taking my camera off me and putting it on the bedside table. 'But now I want the photographer.'

Rosaria whips off my T-shirt and jeans. So she's succeeded where Mr Weinmeyer failed. I squeal helplessly, try to push her off, but Emilia holds my arms, smoothing back my hair, kissing me while Rosaria pulls down my knickers. Her fingers are insistent, tracing and teasing, while the other girl moves her lips across my cheek and starts to nibble at my mouth.

The creaking of the watching rocking chair stops.

The dual sensation of a girl's soft lips on my mouth and another girl's fingers wandering between my legs is electrifying. I have no time to think about it or question it. Gustav is watching this, but he's not stopping it. Is he too good at playing the role of subservient scruffy assistant, or is this exactly what he hoped would happen when he accompanied me here today?

Female fingers push at me, other slim fingers pinch my nipples. Emilia kisses me full on the mouth as she pushes me against her best friend. I'm sandwiched between the two.

The rocking chair gives a little creak, and starts to move again.

My cue to perform. Emilia responds as I tentatively kiss her back. Her lips are wet, greedy, pillowy but determined. So different from the firm, rough feel of my man's. As she eagerly devours me she plants my hands on her breasts, pressing my fingers, inviting them to squeeze, and I do it, because I've gone too far now, and I want more than anything to try this, to see if it feels as good to touch as it does to have someone else touching. Her breasts look and feel big and warm and oh, so soft and her nipples poke hard into my hands and so I start to fondle her as in return she prises open my mouth with her tongue.

Behind me Rosaria rubs herself and her breasts against my back, and to make sure she's fully participating here she pushes one long slender finger up me. I clamp my legs together, trying to hide what she's doing, but that just traps her inside me all the more tightly and despite my shame I feel my body clenching tight to hold her finger there as ripples of dark excitement make me moan and tremble.

Creak, thump, goes the chair in the corner. Creak. A long pause. Creak.

Watch me, Gustav. Watch me!

Emilia pulls away from me as her friend gets to work. Her big mouth is wet with my saliva as she grins, and then she starts to wriggle about, fondling her own breasts, dancing in front of me, offering her nipples to me to kiss. I resist for a moment, crane my head to catch what Gustav is seeing or thinking. All I can make out is one biker boot, lifting rhythmically, and I think I can hear the soft whir of my other camera's shutter.

'Hey, eyes this way, missie. My daddy's paying you to pleasure me.'

Rosaria explodes into throaty laughter. 'You wanna bet? He'd have a heart attack if he knew what we were doing up here with the pretty English girl!'

These spoilt little madams have lived their lives getting exactly what they want, and they have obviously been experimenting on each other for years. As Emilia's tongue flicks over my nipple I wonder what kind of sex life she and hubby will have. Does he already know that Rosaria will always be a part of it?

What would Polly say? *Nothing like this ever happened in Devon.*

As I sink into a kind of reverie beneath the weight of the girls' bare bodies, I realise that they are turning their attentions away from me. Rosaria, her finger still inside, sways about on top of me but thrusts her velvety brown breasts at Emilia.

119

'Go on, cutie, you wanna know how to do it? Suck me.' Emilia croons. The chair has stopped rocking.

Rosaria pushes Emilia at me, her white breast squashing up against my face, and I feel the nub in my teeth as I start to suck. Emilia squirms against me and her friend speeds up the thrust of her finger inside me, and I suck harder, wrap my arms round Emilia and pull her closer, and we're a trio of writhing, excited female bodies and all at once the tiny sensations knit together. My body contracts round Rosaria's finger and I come, falling onto the broderie anglaise pillows with Emilia on top of me, wriggling against me and screeching in frustration because I've got there first.

I struggle weakly. I can't breathe. I've got not one but two hefty girls lying on top of me, continuing their work on each other, Rosaria crooning in Spanish as she gets the bride to the climax on time.

When finally they roll away, they practically kick me off the bed. I fall obediently to the floor, hitch my jeans up my damp legs, leave my knickers goodness knows where in the tangle of cushions and toys and writing girls. It's time to face the music.

The white painted chair is rocking silently, but it's unoccupied. Gustav has gone.

'I was upstairs being fingered by his precious daughter and you were busy networking with Daddy Robinson?'

I refuse to sit down when I finally get back to the apartment. In a Yellow Cab. I snatch the glass of wine Gustav hands me and pace up and down in front of the window. Manhattan is dark and smug down there, laughing at me.

'Actually I was doing no such thing. I remained totally in character.' Gustav pulls off the leather jacket. 'You are a big girl, as you never tire of telling me. You were in pretty safe, if greedy, hands. And the more those lesbian wenches wound you up, the harder I was getting, believe me.'

Dirty excitement kicks in my gut. 'You liked what you saw, master? You didn't get jealous of those game gals groping me like that?'

'My darling girl. I was so into it I was on the point of stage-directing it myself. *Mon dieu*. That was one hell of a sexy floor show. I even took the liberty of taking some tasteful shots of my own, since you weren't using your camera.' Gustav waggles a new memory stick. 'But then I heard Pa Robinson stamping up the stairs with his stopwatch to check we weren't going over our allotted time, so I had to head him off at the pass before he discovered what his little princess really gets up to in there.'

He swaggers into the bedroom. I hear the wardrobe opening and closing. He'll be turning himself back into Gustav Levi. Dragon, not dogsbody.

I sink down onto my favourite spot on the wide windowsill overlooking Central Park. The place where I stood watching the fireworks on New Year's Eve.

'How did you stop the daddy bursting in on us?'

'I pushed him downstairs to show him some of the initial respectable shots on my camera, then got him to help me lug your kit out to the car. Forgot we had a new one. So then had the task of explaining how a young photographer could afford such a thumping great Hummer.' Gustav pokes his head round the door. His black silky hair is ruffled where he has been pulling off the ragged jumper, and the belt is hanging off his jeans. 'All the while hoping he wouldn't hear all that snickering and moaning from his daughter's bedroom.'

'He hasn't a clue about his little precious? I bet his wife does. I bet she was getting suspicious about why Emilia didn't have a boyfriend, and persuaded Poppa to choose a groom for her. Arranged marriage, New York style.' I bite my finger, cross my legs suggestively, swing my foot up and down. 'You didn't speak to the hunky brothers, then?'

Gustav goes still, leans up against the doorway. Honestly, he's like a hound on the scent. 'No. Just a brief chat with Robinson Senior. I could have dished the dirt on several of his political running mates, but who am I? Just the photographer's assistant! Then I decided to teach you a lesson and leave you there.'

'Well, they collared me in the hall to pay me and then when Pops was out of the way they offered me another commission.' I examine my nails. 'They want me to go to their club and take some informal shots of the groom and his mates at the start of their stag day. It's downtown somewhere. A branch of some establishment in London where men go to get away from their women. The Club Crème.'

Gustav is in front of me before the cackle is out of my mouth. Something glitters in the air. He catches my gesticulating wrist and snaps the silver chain around it.

'I know exactly where it is. Getting a gig there would be a massive coup. You would make a name for yourself simply by stepping inside. It's the second home to every swinging dick in this town. It's so select, elite, hand-picked, Miss Folkes, that I, and even Ernst Weinmeyer, are members. Pa Robinson, too.'

'So he's not such a good, clean-living family guy after all, and nor is the groom, even though both deluded fools think Princess Emilia is pure as the driven snow?' I chortle, remembering Miss Robinson's insistent, powerful hands on me. 'Talk about double standards!'

'But you females will always run rings round us guys in the end. And what about the mother? What do you think she gets up to in her parlour when the menfolk are out hunting and gathering!' Gustav slaps his leg as he laughs with me. 'Even so, it's a good thing I was in disguise today at Chateau

Robinson. Our paths will be crossing again over a business deal sometime, I'm sure.' He saunters away from me, letting the silver chain follow him as he chooses where to fix it. 'As for the Club commission, you'll have to turn that one down, *cara*. It's men only.'

I notice that he has rearranged the sofas around the suspended fire, which is burning briskly. The mercury has dropped to below freezing since we set out this afternoon.

'What you mean is that female partners aren't allowed in to spoil their men's fun,' I murmur, letting the chain go slack and sinking down onto some oversize cushions. I rake my fingers through my hair, lifting it away from my scalp. 'But all the staff at the club are women, right?'

'I should have been there to explain to those Robinson boys why this won't happen,' Gustav snaps back. He halts on the other side of the room, beneath my self-portrait. He turns his head so that I can just see the angular planes of his noble profile. 'That club, to use an old-fashioned phrase, is a den of iniquity. It's swimming with booze, narcotics, gambling, loose ladies of the night. And testosterone. Although fetishes such as domination and punishment are banned, which is why I agreed to join. They like their sex straightforward, even if they sometimes multiply the participants. You'd be out of your depth.'

'You know an awful lot about it, Gustav. Care to tell me what exactly you have *participated in* when you've been down the dastardly Club Crème?'

'Sure you won't be jealous? Because it involves women. Lots of them.'

I stare at him. Heat coils between my legs and I run my hands down my thighs to touch myself. I'm repelled, yet somehow intrigued, by the thought of my Gustav losing control with someone else, with a group of people, maybe. Preferably people with no names. No faces. Grainy images

123

rather like the films in Baker Street play through my mind, but there aren't whips or masks involved here. Just bodies. Plural. If there's more than one, he can't get attached, and so the jealousy is less keen.

'The men. They go there expecting certain – services. They pay astronomical subscriptions to get high-class service, total discretion and total freedom.'

I kneel up on the cushions, reach for the bottle of wine and tip it into my glass.

'I'm not talking about men in general. I want to hear about you. Go on. My imagination is running riot, so go ahead and shock me.'

He runs his finger along the photograph frame, still looking sideways out of the window.

'You remember the exhibition in my London gallery the first time you came there? The sepia images of the French prostitutes waiting to be chosen by their punters?'

'Vividly. They were beautiful, and sad, and you said one of them looked like me, and her name was Rapunzel, just like the Rossetti painting you have above your bed in Mayfair.' I sink back on the cushions, swilling the wine around my mouth. 'So you picked just one? A favourite?'

'Never the same one twice. Danger of attachment.' He smiles over at me, and the mischievous heat from his eyes matches the intensifying heat inside me. 'The Club in its eccentric way aims to protect matrimony, not destroy it!'

'So did you go along to their orgies when you were married?'

'Before, and during. Not after.' The smile fades.

'Will you go while we're together?'

'Oh, Serena. I only spent time there back in the day because I was nominated and it's an incredibly prestigious member-ship. When I was later specifically invited, I took part a handful of times to obliterate what was going on at home.

124

There was nothing worth saving there, believe me. But now? Why would I go out for gourmet burger when I can have fillet steak at home?'

I kick my feet at him with a snort of satisfaction and arrange myself more decorously on the cushions.

He crosses his arms, well into the subject now. 'And do you remember those other images I had exhibited at the London gallery, the terracotta and black paintings from the *lupanare* walls in Pompeii? The figures looked as if they were dancing or praying at first but in fact they were whores and punters in a brothel going at it like there was no tomorrow? There was a man taking a slender girl from behind? An elegant woman straddling her client?'

Gustav bites back a really evil grin.

I giggle and wriggle on the pile of Moroccan cushions. These have come from the chalet in Lugano. The only objects I allowed in here, because they have no Margot connection. 'I remember. So horny. The man with a thumping erection. That girl giving her punter a blowjob. You telling me all that happened to you? You saying the Club Crème is like the *lupanare*?'

'That's exactly what I'm saying. Except instead of those stone shelves they do run to luxurious beds and couches and bar stools. And instead of a hot, dusty brothel the punters are shown into sumptuous bedrooms, libraries or the bar. But if you think of those pictures, and superimpose my face on any of those lovers, any position, any combination of participants you can think of, then you'll get the gist.' He shakes his head. 'But my darling girl, you'll never know for sure what goes on there, because you're not going.'

I hurl one of the cushions across the room at him, and he catches it easily in one hand.

'You want a fight, you've got one, lover!' I growl at him. 'Because I am doing this whether you like it or not. It would

125

zoom me straight to the top of the charts if I got this commission right. And then you'd be proud of me.'

He runs his hand over the black beard peppering his chin and cheeks that he hasn't had time to shave. 'I am proud of you anyway, Serena. But I would never forgive myself if I let you go into that place.'

I drain my glass. 'You're just making it sound more intriguing, Gustav.'

'What I've sketched out for you is just the initiation ceremony for the younger members. No wonder there's a waiting list as long as your arm!' He laughs out loud now. 'Imagine being surrounded by beautiful women who are employed to meet your every whim. A cross between a housekeeper and a hooker.'

I lift my hair up with my hands, turn myself this way and that coquettishly. 'Won't I cut the mustard, master?'

Gustav hitches down his jeans and wraps the chain several times round his own waist. I watch the delicate silver strands snag on the hair on his stomach, the angle of his hips. The beautiful bulge pushing out in front.

'My God, Serena, that's the whole bloody problem! You'd shatter the Louis XIV mirrors in their elegant dining room with your gorgeousness! You'd rattle the silverware out of their walnut cabinets. You just don't get the effect you are beginning to have on people!'

'Take those jeans right off then, and show me the effect I'm having on you,' I croon, pulling my T-shirt slowly up my stomach. 'And then show me what you've been doing in that club, you naughty boy.'

He kicks his jeans off and now he's only covered by his tight-fitting black boxers. He kneels down on the cushions near me, tugging on the silver chain so that I come closer.

'They have a basement bar where the word cocktail takes on a whole new meaning. Men can choose their tipple, and have their way with the hired help right there in front of the others.'

'So far, so kinky.' I wriggle up to him, hook my fingers in the waistband of his boxers. 'Do the women have any say in who chooses them?'

'Absolutely not. They are totally subservient. Unless they are told to pick another woman, in which case yes, they can take whoever tickles their fancy. Oh, my God,' he groans suddenly as my fingers touch his warm skin and start to pull at his boxers. 'They would all want you, Serena. In the bar, in the party room, in the smoking den. You'd never get out of there alive!'

I straddle his lap so that his erection jabs into my stomach. 'So what do you suggest I do about it, master? Strap on a chastity belt? A suit of armour? Go dressed as a man? Because you are not going to stop me.'

I grind against him. I take his face in my hands as I move, keeping my eyes on his until he calms a little, comes to heel.

'OK, I surrender. Photographing inside the Club Crème will be your most prestigious commission yet, and I can't deny you this chance to prove your mettle. We're partners, remember?' He leans towards me, and runs his tongue across my mouth. 'So you can go, you wicked little witch, but I will most definitely be accompanying you.'

'As my green-card-faking assistant with the awful Spanish accent?' I rub against his body. 'Or as my tooled-up minder?'

'As a fully paid-up member. In every sense of the word.' He winds my hair round his fist. 'And as your secret consort.'

'Right. Talking of members,' I whisper, running the hand tied with the silver chain idly over his warm, flat stomach. 'All this horny talk is doing it for you, I can see.'

He laughs softly. His shorts are straining to contain his arousal, but he pushes me onto my back and with one deft yank he removes my jeans and knickers. Excitement quickens inside me as he pulls off my socks so that I am naked from the waist down. Then he starts to lick his way up the inside of my legs, blowing hot breath onto my cold skin. He stops just above my knees, pushing my legs further open.

'I think I could handle seeing that again. You with a girl. Or two.' His fingers continue their way upwards, and I squeal and wriggle as they reach their target.

'That's called having your cake and eating it. How would you feel about seeing me with another man? Like we discussed before?' I bite my lip. 'I mean, in a controlled situation. Like with the Weinmeyers, but probably not the Weinmeyers.'

'You're not making sense, Serena.'

I close my thighs over his stroking fingers. 'I mean if you were there with me. Watching, maybe even participating. We're in this great big dirty city, Gustav. We can do whatever the hell we like! But I never want to hurt you. Would playing with fire like that count as infidelity?'

Gustav's dark hair falls over his face as he leans over me in his wolf pose, on all fours, his shoulders hunched into hackles, his mouth slightly open but the lips drawn tight, white teeth trapping his tongue. He wrenches my legs further open, hands clamped down on me, thumbs running up and down my skin as if he's both imprisoning and tuning a harp.

'I'm just putting it out there. Just playing with the idea. I don't mean to make you angry,' I pretend to whimper, trying to catch his hands. 'I don't know how these things, these clubs, work. I'm just talking about assignments that I can control.'

He cups my softness for a moment, not speaking, still running his finger up and down possessively until I can feel the spring of wetness, and then he removes his hand, strokes it over my stomach, my breasts, pushes my arms down, frames my face.

128

'I'll do anything to keep you happy and by my side, Serena. You're beautiful and smart, and you're mine. I'm reluctant to share you, God knows, but you are so young. If you really want some adventure, some experiment, then I have to allow it.'

I lie very still as his fingers work on me. I don't want to distract or divert him while his mind is working like this. 'But you got so upset and jealous when I told you about my little session with the Weinmeyers.'

'Yes I did, but now I'm asking myself why I was surprised. Everyone in Manhattan, in London, Paris, Amsterdam, Venice, knows exactly what those two are like. And since then, and since your girlie session with Princess Emilia and her consort, I've had time to think. And what I realise is how seriously I underestimated you. My God, the Weinmeyers must have been so impressed that you resisted them, not to mention frustrated! You were being faithful to me, weren't you, my angel? Really I should reward you for being true to me. I should show you how much I trust you. But I have to be there. I have to know everything that happens to you.'

He is deadly serious, and I love knowing that he wants to watch over me all the time, but he can't hide a tinge of dark sadness in his eyes.

'Forget it, Gustav. I'll cancel the commission at the Club Crème.'

'You'll do no such thing!'

'So what do you want me to do? You want me to be faithful, but you want me to do things that might hurt you. I don't even know what I want to try. Girls? Boys?' I murmur in confusion. 'You're my man, Gustav. I will always want you by my side. Watching over me. Even if I do something like that, go off-piste, I will never lie to you.'

He regards me for a long moment, his face very pale in the flickering firelight. Then he bends over me. I arch upwards for a kiss, but he slowly pushes up my T-shirt, unclips my bra, lets my breasts rise up into the flickering firelight.

'No. I owe it to you to allow you more freedom, so long as I can handle it. So long as whatever happens is within certain boundaries.'

I yank at the silver chain to bring him closer to me. 'And those are?'

'We'll make that up as we go along. A tweak on the chain every so often will keep you in check. But it might surprise you to know that the idea of watching you discovering yourself is making me hard.' He chuckles, relaxing at last. 'But I think you'll know if you've gone too far when the time comes. Because it will either feel right or it will feel very, very wrong. And when that happens, you will be punished.'

I squirm with pleasure and push my breasts up at him. 'Promise?'

He kneels over me, runs the palms of his hands over my hardening nipples. I push harder, waiting for him to touch them or kiss them. But abruptly he flicks his fingers, shows me something shiny and glinting in his hand, and all at once there's a stinging bite on each little bud.

Gustav puts his hand over my mouth.

'Nipple clamps, darling. Just to give you a taste of what to expect. If you ever do come across the more dominating female of the species in the club or in other little games, she may want to play with these. But I want to be the first one to use them on you. See? Painful, aren't they? Think of them as Princess Robinson's little teeth taking a bite.'

The sting eases into a deep, red-hot throbbing. Gustav watches me for what seems like ages, and then I hear the smooth slide of his shorts and the warm thump landing on my thigh. I arch myself harder, hook at him with my legs, and he kisses me at last, his mouth warm and wet on mine, his tongue pushing in deep as his body echoes that and he groans before entering me with one hard thrust.

The nipple clamps are more like terrier's teeth than any girl's, worrying at me with exquisite pain that radiates from my nipples through my breasts into my ribs and bones, growing duller but no less insistent the further inside me it reaches. I lift beneath my lover, embracing him as he presses deeper inside me and swift climax starts to wash towards me.

'Not so fast, young lady. You must wait for me.'

I reach for him blindly, my mouth seeking his. His warm skin is slippery on mine as he pushes harder, faster, his hands roving over me to keep me in the position he wants me, and he's huge now, and as I cling to him he draws back, his hips slowly rocking back and forth, and at last we are in harmony again, two parts of the same machine, his dark, solemn head steady above mine as his black eyes own me and he increases his speed.

I feast my eyes on the muscles rippling in his arms, his neck, his eyes as they glaze over, and then we're slamming into each other, he is moaning my name, my body filled, his face dark with the effort of holding on, and then he makes a soft low groan as he lets loose and my climax meets his.

I let him sleep for a while. I would love to sleep too, but my nipples are in agony now. I slide out from under him and pull the clamps off, watching the tortured points subside gratefully from heated scarlet back to pale pink, from stiff to soft. My thighs are sticky with mingled juices as I trail the silver chain after me and step into the shower to douse myself for a long time in warm water, flinching as the soap touches the sore parts of me.

I smile at my reflection as I think over the day. Over the promise of the days ahead. The potential of the Club Crème for all kinds of wickedness, all under the watching eyes of my Gustav. Time to remind him that if he wants to accompany me on future assignments, then I need free rein. He can watch. And I'll make sure he's turned on by what he sees. I will be the voyeur, viewed.

And I chuckle to think of Emilia Robinson, soon to be a married woman, carrying all that fake innocence, all those hidden lusts, bringing Rosaria to her marital bed. All the people in this dirty old town, up to no good. There's no such thing as virtue here, it seems.

Virginal girlhood, my ass.

CHAPTER SEVEN

It's next to impossible to tear myself away from this place. I glance at my watch. I've been here since the doors opened but there's still so much I want to see. Polly probably won't mind if I keep her waiting but I don't like being late for anyone. And I can always come back another day. This city is my home for now. The International Center of Photography isn't going anywhere.

The permanent collections here make my current crop of portraits look like holiday snaps, but that's not going to defeat me. It's galvanising me all the more. My first exhibition in London has been a sell-out, after all. The Park Avenue princesses and the Robinsons have already referred me to new clients here in Manhattan and others as far away as Paris. The assignment at Club Crème is coming up in a few days.

And the Weinmeyers have been in touch just this morning to arrange a meeting to go through the proofs of our session. And to offer me a new commission.

Little do they know that Weinmeyer has swiftly become a code word for me and Gustav to instigate particularly rough, argumentative sex spiced up by a running commentary.

He figures that if we talk enough about the Weinmeyer predilection for one-man-two-women threesomes, I won't be tempted to try it. But he's the one who sowed the seed. And the idea is sticking. Something to save up for.

I dance a little jig on the spot. This evening he wants me to dress in a crinkled silk chiffon dress from Ralph Lauren that's hanging in my wardrobe. Then he's taking me across the park to the jazz bar in the Carlyle Hotel to listen to Woody Allen playing the clarinet with his band.

I push out into the cold white midday light and hurry up Sixth Avenue to the Rockefeller Center. Today I'm wearing the Dr Zhivago white hat and white jacket that Crystal kitted me out in when I went to Lugano last November, because Polly and I have decided to behave like tourists and go up to the top of the Rock before hitting the ice rink.

She's standing by the ticket kiosk and I see her before she sees me. It's only been a couple of weeks since New Year's Eve, but I'm taken aback. She's wearing a neon-pink bobble hat with matching jacket, her legs skinny as sticks in a pair of white jeans exactly like mine. But contrasting with, or maybe because of, those jolly bright colours she looks haggard and pale. She is flipping the tickets in her hand as she waits for me, and as she stares into space there is a fractured look of dejection.

'Hey, babes, sorry I'm late!'

I rush to hug her. I can feel her shoulder blades poking through the padded pink jacket. She clings onto me, her cold cheek pressed against mine. I recall the Halloween party back in London when she was in her element, dressed up to the nines and pirouetting through the racks of lacy dresses and feather boas in Pierre's new London outlet. She was the hostess with the mostest that night. Now she won't let me go. We stand there, buffeted by the crowds, her thin arms twined round my neck.

134

'Hey, move along there, sisters!' someone yells at us, and finally we break apart.

We join the queue to get up to the top of the Rockefeller Center, and I feel her staring at me.

'You OK, Pol?' I ask, surprised at the nervous quiver in my voice. 'I'm worried about you. I wondered if everything was all right with you on New Year's Eve, actually. You don't seem yourself.'

She shakes her head but we are then marshalled into the crowded lift before she can reply. We shoot upwards as if we're in a rocket going to the stars.

'Don't bother about me. We were all a bit on edge that night. A lot to get our heads round. But forget all that. You're on top of the world up here. Come and see!' she cries, grabbing my arm.

For the next half hour we are buffeted by the high winds circling the viewing platform. You can see it all from here. The impressive, solid Empire State Building may be fifteen or so blocks away but it looks close enough to touch. Below us the New York cabs scuttle up and down the straight lines of the city streets like yellow bugs, while planted at the mouth of the harbour the Statue of Liberty waving on her plinth looks like a tiny jade Thumbelina.

'If I screw my eyes up I reckon I can see our apartment from here.' I point to the west side of Central Park, and glance at Polly to see if she's following my finger. 'Maybe even Gustav's telescope!'

'Oh, change the record! All that domestic bliss gives me vertigo.' Polly turns her back on the stunning vista laid out at our feet and stares at me. 'But Gustav is doing something right. The change in you is phenomenal. I love your hair grown so long. It's like golden syrup. All those years when my aunt and uncle used to sit you in the kitchen with a pudding bowl and hack it all off as soon as it reached your collar. They hated it, didn't they? Called you an ugly ginger.'

I clutch onto one of the eyeglasses set along the parapet. I attempt to peer through it, to see if I can spy our flag. But all I can see is a circle of blackness. I swallow to try and keep calm. 'Why bring that up?'

'Just the contrast between then and now.' She reaches out and touches a strand of my hair. 'You look as if you're lit up from within, you know. Your eyes are sparkling. Your skin is peachy.'

I flinch away. Not so much from her hand, but the jarring note in her voice. 'You make me sound like a prize springer spaniel!'

'I'm a stylist. I advise on beauty for a living, remember? My job is about people's looks. Styling them, improving them so they look good for their public. I'm paid to transform them into the person they want to be. But that involves lashings of make-up, expensive hairdressers, and combing Saks, Bloomingdale's, Bergdorf Goodman for suitable clothes. It creates an illusion so far removed from the original that they end up looking like someone else. But you? You still look like the Serena Folkes I know and love, but with knobs on, and all with minimum effort.'

'That's because I'm happy to be here, I'm happy to be with Gustav. Hey, and most importantly of all, I'm happy to be with you! We're in the same city at long last! All those shops and bars and clubs you frequent, all the people you've met! First you were in London then over here becoming worldly and sophisticated when I was doing my best to get away from Devon. Did you know I nearly got on a plane and came over here to surprise you last year instead of travelling round Europe? But then I'd never have gone to Venice and those nuns would never – are you OK, Polly?'

She nods sharply, grabs at my sleeve as if she's about to faint. 'Sure. Cold, that's all.'

I put my arm round her, pull her close, rub her arms to warm her up. 'And now I'm here for the foreseeable future. I haven't even got a ticket out of New York because our stay is open-ended! So I can spend lots of time with you, meet your friends, see what you do every day, maybe even come and work with you if you can pull some strings?'

'It's been more than two weeks since New Year's Eve, Rena. I was beginning to think you'd forgotten me.' Polly pushes her cold face up against mine. But it feels more like a knock than a hug. Her cheeks are so bony. 'But I guess I should forgive you. You're head over heels. That bloom. Is that what love is supposed to look like?'

'Honestly, Pol, you make it sound as if I've got it all sorted, but I'll never take any of this for granted. Not for a second. I worked hard to get here. Gustav and I had a business arrangement and I had to prove myself. Anything could happen in the future, but I'm going to do everything I can not to jinx this.' I pull my white hat down over my hair to stop it whipping into my eyes. I'm aware she's studying me closely, as if she can't work me out, and the blue light of her gaze is unnerving.

'You've got it so right. And I think I've got it so wrong,' she murmurs so quietly that I'm not sure I've heard right.

'It was a rocky path for me and Gustav, Polly. If you can call eggshells rocky. We started out so incredibly wary. Trust, intimacy – some seriously thorny issues to deal with. It was supposed to be all about my photographs and the exhibition, and physical companionship from me in return, all very clinical, but who were we kidding? It was lust at first sight! Seriously, Pol. We were horribly mixed up, both of us. You know all about my past, you were the only good thing in it, but that Margot, and Pierre, they nearly destroyed Gustav's ability to get close to anyone ever again.'

'You could have called me. I would have come to you, wherever you were. I could have helped. Or I could have advised you to steer well clear. You've had enough horrors in your own life, Rena, abandoned as a newborn, taken in by those evil people who never showed you a moment's kindness, you've struggled enough to emerge from that life as beautifully as you have without being troubled by someone else's problems!'

'I know, hon, and thank God you were there when we were kids, but I don't think you could have helped me when I met Gustav. His problems are my problems now. I didn't want to steer anywhere that wasn't towards him, but it was still a journey I had to navigate on my own.'

She pulls away, but our arms are still linked. 'It's that ex-wife that worries me. You don't need that kind of grief.'

I can't hide my reaction. I realise I've dropped her arm. 'Margot is long gone, Polly. The boys have got better things to talk about now, and they're emailing each other every day. Come on. Lighten up! You and I have got so much to look forward to.'

'Look at you. All grown up.' Her bright-blue eyes are fixed on a point just past my shoulder. I can tell she's only half-listening to me and I can't understand it. I dig my elbow into her ribs.

'Well, I'm being rewarded now! Frequent filthy sex with a hunky, rich, adoring, imaginative male? What's not to like?'

She doesn't cave in and snigger as I expect. Instead her eyes remain fixedly open and staring away from me, as if she's forcing the tears away. 'Stop boring on about your perfect love life, Rena!'

My mouth drops open. She may as well have slapped me across the face.

'I wasn't just talking about me, Pol! I meant that another thing that feels so great right now is that we've both got lovely men – and they're related! So you'd know all about hot sex when you're dating Gustav's brother!'

But Polly's face snaps closed and she pulls me back inside. 'Let's just get on with the tourist bit!'

I drag my feet, prickling with annoyance as she harangues me into the queue to have our photograph taken. When it's developed it creates the illusion that we're perched precariously on a girder as in the 1931 Charles Ebbets photo of a row of construction workers having 'Lunch Atop a Skycraper'.

'I thought we would skate first, then eat? I haven't tried out any of the rinks since I moved here, and I could really do with the exercise,' she declares briskly when we're back on the ground.

I follow her mutely, allow her to take on the role of leader. After all, it's her traditional role when we're together, and it'll stop us having to talk. Her strange, abrupt behaviour is totally out of character, especially when we've got so much to look forward to. My insides churn with anxiety. She's always been my anchor in life, but today she seems to have drifted away from me, as if she's storing up something unpleasant or difficult to say. I feel as if I've upset her. But I can't think what I've done wrong. I glance at my watch, wondering if I can make my excuses instead of having lunch as we'd arranged.

But now we're at the ice rink, catching it when it's almost empty. As we're lacing up our boots my golden locket falls out of my collar.

'Pretty necklace,' Polly remarks, in an oddly cold voice that jerks as she loops the laces tightly round her ankles. 'Pure gold?'

I hold up the little locket, watching the light catch on the golden surface. 'It was a Christmas present from Gustav.'

'He has good taste. Come on, let's get going before the hordes arrive.'

I tuck the locket safely back inside my jacket. We skate out and, after some slow swizzles to get into our stride, soon we're twirling in the middle of the Rockefeller ice rink, smirking at the handful of stumblers clutching the sides while we glide and turn effortlessly in the very small space. Polly was right. Fresh air, clean exercise, the lovely speed of skating that gives you an elegance you never achieve on two flat feet.

When the rink clears for lunchtime, Polly bats her eyelashes at some officials so we're allowed to stay on while they brush the ice. We float round in silence, soothed by the goldfish repetition of our circuit, but her preoccupation is still hard to ignore. My chest starts to feel tight. Polly is the closest thing I have to a relative, and yet there's a force field around her today that I've never sensed before, made all the weirder by the high, feverish colour in her cheeks.

'Polly! Spill! Is everything OK?' I venture at last as the stars and stripes of several American flags and bright lights of the Rockefeller Center circle around us. 'Something's up, I can tell. You look more glum than glam. You look, really, well, you look–'

'Like shit? That all you can say when you deign to tear yourself away from your sugar daddy?' She skates away, scooting up a shower of ice. 'Thanks a bunch.'

'Hey, cool it, hon! I just meant you look like you need some TLC. A square meal and a big hug.' I catch up with her, grab her and shake her. 'You've always looked out for me. Let me worry about you for a change. I reckon you're too thin, for a start. Pierre's obviously not taking care of you, but then I get the impression he isn't exactly the nurturing type, is he, especially as he and Gustav are so preoccupied with getting things back on track. I'm here now. So talk to me.'

'All the women in Manhattan look like this,' she snorts, bending her knees and swooping low. 'By the way, Tomas has been asking after you. He's never gotten over meeting you at the Halloween party in Covent Garden, how you wandered out onto the patio like a vision in virginal white. I don't know what you did or said to him, but he thinks you're hot enough to scorch.'

I blush uncomfortably. 'He wanted me to go down on him, but I blew him out. As it were. I'd just met Gustav, and he was all I could think about.

'But I don't want to talk about him. Answer my question, Polly.' I pull my hat further over my eyes. The cold noon is being spattered by tiny specks of gritty rain. 'What's wrong with you?'

She shoots over to the edge and sprays up a hockey stop.

'If you really want to know, it's Margot.'

My toe pick catches and I topple hard, falling upon her and bashing us both against the barrier. The breath is knocked out of me as I struggle to get upright. I realise I've bitten my lower lip and can taste blood.

'Well, Margot *and* Pierre, to be precise.' Polly's voice is brittle, and strange, and she doesn't rush to help me. Her face has become a white mask. 'Which means your precious Gustav is also part of the problem.'

'What problem?' I try to keep it light even while I'm dabbing blood off my mouth. 'Please don't tell me that witch has flown back on her broomstick?'

Polly looks away over the plaza where the crowds are queuing to join us on the ice.

'Not literally, no. But since Pierre met Gustav again it's like he's been to confession or something. He can't seem to get Margot out of his head. She's everywhere. In New York. In my apartment. He won't stop talking about her, what she was like in bed, what she did to him.' Polly looks down, kicking her skate into the ice. 'I can't cope, Serena. I'm being a total cow, but I can't separate you from all this. Seeing you today just twists the knife!'

Polly yanks off her bobble hat and throws it onto the ice. I barely recognise her. I recall her and Pierre groping each other at the Halloween party. The first flush of their romance. And then New Year's Eve, when he was touching her up in our apartment, Polly so eager, so responsive, yet Pierre already different, such an odd, detached look in his eye. Or was he so different? How did I know the real Pierre, when until then I'd only ever seen him that once, in his Halloween mask?

The snow is thicker now and lands without melting on my cousin's white-blonde hair, cropped so close that I can see every plane of her narrow skull. My heart is skittering in my chest, my breath puffing out in uneven clouds as I clutch the barrier. *She* can't cope?

I suspect she thinks the buzz cut is rocking a *Star Trek* vibe, but the shaven head and angular cheekbones make her look more like the beautiful but doomed inmate of a labour camp.

'I've got nothing to do with Margot!' My voice is thick with dismay when I manage to speak. 'Don't give that woman oxygen, Polly.'

'It's too late. I have to tell someone, otherwise I'm going to go mad. And that someone has to be you.' My cousin flattens her pink mittens over her ears and screws her eyes shut. 'I know I shouldn't be taking this out on you, I know you're not directly responsible, but I can't help it. I'm jealous, OK? And I'm distraught. Everything's going right for you, but it's killing me, because the happier you and Gustav are, the more Pierre withdraws from me.'

I put my arm around her shoulders and pull her close. I need some comfort, too, but she's rigid against me, her elbow bent sharply into my ribs as if ready to jab me away. So this is what's happening. From whatever planet she squats on, Margot is stirring up trouble between me and my cousin. All the joy has been shaken out of me, as if I'm a pepper pot turned upside down.

'Pol. That isn't fair, and you know it. You can't blame me or Gustav if things are going wrong with you and Pierre!

'I know it's unreasonable, but I blame this rapprochement between the brothers for spoiling everything.' Her eyes, when she opens them, are red with unshed tears. 'Margot's breaking us up!'

She bends her leading knee and skates out from under my arm to the centre of the rink. I stare at her as she spins on one foot.

'She's nothing. A ghost. Powerless. Don't let her ruin your life. And don't let her come between us!' I yell from the side of the rink. Our breath hangs in raggy clouds behind us. 'Just calm down and tell me what has happened.'

She skates backwards so she's facing me. 'Here's the thing. Pierre was a normal guy when I met him last autumn. He was partying hard, working hard, hitting the big time, but he started to change after that confrontation in London, and then on New Year's Eve he refused to come home with me after we left your place. But he rocked up later, very drunk. He rampaged round my apartment and threatened to tie my wrists with his belt. I kicked him out, and now he won't return my calls. I'm terrified I've lost him.'

I'm shaking now. My ankles won't hold me up. A riptide, sucking me back just when I was sailing into calm waters.

'He wasn't a normal guy when you met him. Underneath he was the same bitter, scarred young man, estranged from his brother. You've only been together a short while. Maybe you don't really know him at all,' I say quietly.

'What makes you the expert?' Her voice cuts across the ice. 'Oh, I wish you'd never met Gustav Levi. Then this explosive reunion would never have happened.'

A handful of skaters swerve to avoid her and an ice warden is beckoning to tell us our session is over.

'This rapprochement would have happened one day, whether you or I were around or not. But I'm not discussing this here.' I jerk my thumb towards the exit. 'And I'm not having lunch with you either if you don't stop with this accusatory tone. I've done nothing wrong, Polly.'

She skims into a final hockey stop.

'I was really into him. I suspected he was a player when it came to women, that was part of his attraction, the bad boy, but I thought I could change him once we became an item. But no. Because no sooner has he walked out on me than he spends his time hooking up with those lissome dancers he works with.'

'So he's a philanderer and a cheat, he's left you and he's sniffing round other girls?' I wait for her to step up onto the rubber matting, trying to keep the tremble out of my voice. 'How am I to blame for that?'

'That theatre. It's like a candy store.' She stumps dejectedly over to the benches. 'Those girls are drop-dead gorgeous.'

'So none of us are to blame. Not even Margot. This has nothing to do with her, and everything to do with Pierre's sexual incontinence.' I hesitate, kneel down and take her boots off for her partly to hide my confusion. Is this the moment to mention that text Pierre received on New Year's Eve? His sly look when I asked him who it was from? It was to do with work, all right, just as he said. But it must have been from one of those dancers.

'Margot's still messing with Pierre's head. So she's involved, even by remote control.'

'We can't know any of that for sure.' I sigh. 'OK. Let's get warm and you can start from the very beginning, as Julie Andrews would say.'

She takes my arm with the ghost of the cousinly giggle I

remember of old. But the very pavements feel uneven, the world tilting slightly as she leads me round the block to our next destination and I pray that what she's about to get off her chest isn't going to blow everything apart.

The Bar American is warm, busy, full of food and drink, and I take comfort from the hustle and bustle of the other people. We sit up on the mezzanine level, staring down at the hungry diners chattering on their semi-circular Hollywood banquettes and the thirsty drinkers lined up on the bar stools downing cocktails even at this hour. We have two enormous beers in front of us and we order an equally enormous lunch.

'Strip steak pour moi,' Polly orders.

'Hot smoked salmon and sweet potato hash pour moi,' I echo faintly.

Polly plunges straight in, eager to get her problems off her chest.

'Margot Levi was, is, stunning, apparently. A tough act to follow. Like one of those avatars. All flashing black oriental eyes, glossy black hair, curves in all the right places, acrobatic, fearless, dynamite in bed.'

I snort. 'Jessica Rabbit, more like.'

'She's no cartoon, Rena.'

'I know exactly what she looks like. Gustav had portraits of her plastered all over an entire room in his chalet in Switzerland.'

Polly is regarding me cynically. 'And you're cool with that?'

'Not at the time, no! I couldn't handle it. Was convinced it was some sort of shrine to her and ran away, but Gustav followed me down to Devon and swore he had ordered those pictures to be destroyed years ago, so together we burned them, and all my childhood diaries, on the beach at Burgh Island. It helped me to move out of her shadow.' I sigh. 'You need to get past this, too.'

'I can't. Not yet. I'm going to do the bunny boiler thing and confront him at the theatre.'

Polly takes a long sip of beer, wipes her mouth. She still looks washed out, but so young, suddenly, now that she's pulled off her hat and jacket. Her unique style. She's wearing a blue cardigan the same colour as her swimming-pool eyes, buttoned up the back, and, unusually for someone who flaunts an ultra-modern style, some yellowing antique freshwater pearls.

'Pierre admits he had a bit of a crush on Margot when she came on the scene. Had the hots for her, actually. So this is a Biblical jealousy, too. That's my diagnosis. Evil temptress comes between two brothers.'

'Steals one, then the other.' I arrange some peanuts in a triangle on the table. My hands are shaking. 'But ultimately fails.'

'At first Margot treated Pierre like an annoying brat.' Polly pours olive oil onto some bread. 'Until she got too busy with her fetish club to notice him. All that sick bondage and whipping. That's when Gustav decided to send him away to boarding school, all these sailing and skiing camps in the holidays. Mr and Mrs Levi started off being careful about their "seasons", apparently, and they scheduled those films to avoid Pierre witnessing anything. He never even went inside the punishment rooms. They had these mediaeval locks to bolt them. But Margot started to get sloppy. Deliberately, I reckon. Occasionally when he was home Pierre heard the whipping sounds, saw her friends, or rather punters, leaving the house with welts across their backs. And then the whole shebang became crystal-clear when he caught Gustav at it.'

Just then the waitress comes to our table with enormous platefuls of food and I realise that the nausea churning in my stomach is mixed with hunger. I try to work out what to say as I fork salmon hash into my mouth, washed down with cold beer.

'I know it sounds pervy, Polly, but you need to know. That scene in your flat, with the belt, sounds as if Pierre is still obsessing about it. Somewhere along the line, despite his revulsion when he was younger, now he's got the taste for it, too. If you really want to fight for him, perhaps you should show willing, try some bondage or punishment to please him? Don't look at me as if I've just suggested you cut your arm off. These Levi brothers are complex. But you're the one starting to look like the wide-eyed ingénue.'

'I'm pretty experimental, thank you very much. Just not into weapons, and sex aids, and pain.' Polly holds her fork in midair. 'I – God, Serena, I didn't think you were totally serious when you said that you'd tried the whipping.'

'I stole a whip from that convent in Venice and yes, Gustav and I have tried it. And we have our own silver chain. It joins us and it's dead kinky, being tied up, unable to get free. Not scary. Liberating, in the right hands.' I hold up my wrist, showing her the bracelet. 'OK. I can see you think I'm mad. So start at the bit where Pierre has caught them at it. Margot on all fours and Gustav in a leather muzzle.'

Polly gulps at her beer, shaking her head and gazing at me over the froth.

'That didn't shock you either?'

'Of course I didn't like hearing about it, but I wasn't entirely unprepared for Pierre's so-called revelations in the gallery last Christmas. Gustav had already showed me the exhibition at the Baker Street house, the films and pictures of Margot and her clients in action, and told me he'd participated. But what Pierre stumbled into in that house was a set-up, Polly. It was Margot who was the dominant, not Gustav.'

'So everyone keeps saying. Well, Pierre couldn't hack it when he saw it right under his nose.' She starts to speak slowly, as if in a trance. 'He is horrified. He tears upstairs, swearing blue murder. Gustav doesn't come after him, that makes Pierre even more wild. There's silence, then Margot's rushing in, stark naked except for a ripped shirt.'

I lift up a gleaming sliver of salmon and force my hand to remain steady as I stuff it in. At the next door table a group of guys are glancing across at Polly and me. They must be able to hear what we're saying, especially the words 'naked' and 'ripped', because they keep whispering amongst themselves.

'She's taken off her leather gear so as not so scare him, that's all. All the better to seduce little brother,' I scoff through my mouthful of salmon. 'No great shakes. That's what she's good at. Pierre's a good-looking boy. You know what they're like at that age. Always hard, and always grateful.'

She manages a sad smile. 'Maybe. But you're missing the point, Rena. He was trying to explain it when he surprised Gustav that night at the gallery. His was a lad's world of pubs and rugby and his home, his haven, as he put it, was full of strangers filming each other copulating behind closed doors. Can you imagine? Makes the house on the cliffs look like a playgroup! Not only that but his adored big brother had lost the plot, allowing all this sado-masochistic bondage or whatever you call it to go on, joining in with it to please Margot and presumably himself until it got seriously out of hand. Gustav may have wanted it to stop. But it's too late, really. Pierre doesn't realise Gustav is trying to clean up his act. He just feels contaminated when he sees that final ugly whipping scenario, orchestrated or not. And then Margot's flinging herself at him, begging Pierre to rescue her, and he's putty in her hands.'

Polly stops then, goes very pale again.

'Don't tell me any more if it upsets you.' I push her plate closer. 'You need to eat.'

'And you need to listen.' She chews obediently on a piece of steak, and then another. Then she lays her fork down. In unison we drain our beer and she signals for more. The guys at the next table nudge each other and smirk.

'What did she do to Pierre that was so sexy?'

Polly's face is stricken as she speaks. The guys at the neighbouring table are agog. My throat has gone dry.

'That's the weird thing. Nothing special, at least not then. Just the trauma, the timing, the fact that it was forbidden. His brother's wife. A winning formula. Here's this femme fatale living under the same roof and here's Pierre, a red-blooded bloke who's feeling left out. He drives himself mad, jealous of his brother, wanting to see Margot naked, fanta-sising about colliding with her coming out of the shower, all wet and slippery, the towel unravelling to show him that amazing body. Yep. He told me all this.'

We stare at each other for a moment. We are both holding our knives and forks in the air like spears, the food not quite reaching our lips.

I gulp. 'God, this really is too much information.'

She jabs her steak at me before popping it into her mouth. 'He used to hear her moaning in Gustav's bed and it drove him up the wall with frustration.'

My sweet salmon hash threatens to find its way back up my throat. She might as well have stabbed me with her knife and fork. Cold sweat prickles under my hair. 'Stick to the night in question. Please.'

'Yes, your honour. So now the tables have turned, she's the damsel in distress, crying and sobbing on his bed, tearing off her shirt, terrified of big bad Gustav, and Pierre goes to comfort her, and she pulls him down on top, and Pierre's burning for her because just the sight of her in the doorway, her long bare legs, everything sweaty and ripped and dishev-elled, has turned him on and she wastes no time, she's got

149

his trousers off, the story about how he got those burns on his skin comes later, when they've finished, so her hand is wrapped round him, she's wriggling about on top of him like an eel and bingo!' She slaps her hand down on the table, making the cutlery rattle and our earwigging neighbours spill their drinks. 'She's banging him senseless.'

'Bingo!' I repeat faintly. My mouth has dropped open. It seems that half the diner is now listening in, but perhaps that's just my heightened sensitivity. I try to cough, but my throat is blocked. 'Pierre fell for the oldest trick in the book. Ever heard of Delilah?'

Polly stabs another piece of steak with her fork, and a little blood runs out of it. She lifts it up in front of her mouth and studies it. Her eyes are chips of blue glass arrowing at me.

'He was shagging his brother's wife. Graphic enough for you?' she hisses quietly. We all, me, the guys at the next table, the waitress bringing their check, we all watch Polly as she pops the steak into her mouth, the flexing of the muscles in her jaw as she chews. 'And the *coup de grâce* is your Gustav, walking in on them. The rest you know.'

I smash the remains of the salmon hash on my plate. Our new beers arrive, droplets of condensation running down their smooth glass sides. I lift the glass and lick moisture off the side.

'The only good thing is it's all out in the open now.'

Polly wipes a chip round the bloody gravy on her plate. As she nibbles it she notices our audience at the next table, who are very quietly counting out dollar bills. She turns and realises they're all listening to her. She frowns for a moment. The old Polly would have started flirting outrageously.

'Serena, there's nothing good about any of this. Everything's trashed. Pierre and I were only together a bit longer than you and Gustav, but things were going great. We were even talking about moving in together.'

'So soon? Polly, stop torturing yourself! You can't blame Gustav or me. You can't pin this all on Margot, either. Pierre's acting of his own accord now. She's history!'

'I know. Deep down I know that. I've spent all afternoon lashing out at you, all of you, but I'm not being totally honest. Pierre was already acting weird before we all collided in the gallery in London. Before any mention of Margot.' Polly slumps down in her seat, turning her glass so roughly that the beer spills on to the table. 'Truth is, I can't face up to the real reason he doesn't want me any more.'

Her eyes are hard and fixed on me, filled with tears. The tallest of the guys at the next table slips her his business card. She picks it up without glancing at him and he stumbles out awkwardly after his mates. Once she would have called out something witty.

'There's something else?'

'Some*one* else. He was getting the odd text and phone call in December around the time we met you in the gallery. He started being off with me on occasion, then being really apologetic, all passionate and loving, but around Christmas it got manic. Calls and texts at all hours. When we were having dinner. The cinema. The middle of the night. You can't have missed his phone going off when we were at your pad? He kept telling me it was work, you know, the time difference with the West Coast or Europe. But it's as if we were being watched. As if she knew exactly what he was doing and she wanted him to stop it.'

'She? Oh, God, you're scaring me now, Polly.'

Polly wipes her napkin across her mouth, several times, rubbing harder, harder, as if she's trying to rub the lipstick off. Rub the blood out of her lips.

'Not Margot. I told you. Someone else. I guess now I'm out of the way he's at liberty to answer these calls. But whenever I was present he never spoke. Just listened. Then he'd get all hyper, get rough with me. Apologetic. The usual cycle. Rena, I'm certain he's got another woman.'

I lean across the table, take her hands and crush them in mine. I am wrestling with pity for her and relief that we have finally dropped the subject of Margot. 'What are you going to do?'

'Not me. You, Serena.' She tangles her fingers with mine. 'I want you to speak to him for me.'

'Who? Gustav?'

'No. I want you to speak to Pierre. You had your heads together thick as thieves the other night at your place. He likes you. He said so when we left, and it wasn't just to please me. You're the one person he seems to respect at the moment.'

I try to keep my gaze calm, even while my face is heating up. Pierre said as much to Gustav, too. I try to ignore the unexpected tingle of pleasure this flattery gives me. 'Well, I've got a commission coming up at the Club Crème, then, as it happens, we're meeting him to discuss some proposal he has for me. But I'm not sure that's the appropriate time to probe him . . .'

'That will be the perfect time! I need you to do this, Rena.' Polly pulls me towards her across the table so that we are nose to nose. 'I want you to help me get him back.'

CHAPTER EIGHT

Gustav and I are staring at each other across the vast space of the apartment, the afternoon light blinding my tired eyes.

'I came. I saw. I conquered. And I came out nearly a hundred grand richer.'

I'm drunk, and it shows. It's only teatime, but it's all the fine wines they plied me with at the Club Crème. And I'm also drunk on my success.

'You excelled yourself today, Serena. Really. I'm proud of you. You got all the shots those Robinson boys wanted, which incidentally will be resurrected for blackmail one day if they ever run for Senate, but you know the club director asked to acquire copies? For the first time in the club's history he's thinking of replacing those antiquated oil paintings of founder members with photographs of the new generation. And they are going to be *your* photographs!'

Gustav undoes his bow tie and lets the black tails dangle onto the snow-white pleats of his dress shirt. He is moving very slowly and deliberately, and his eyes are glittering dangerously. Even through my alcohol haze I sense that a second commentary is undercutting his quiet words.

'Well, you're not my agent and manager and benefactor

and patron for nothing!' I give a little snigger, which turns into a hiccup. 'You are the man who made this all possible!'

'Don't you forget it. We are a team. Inextricably linked. That piece of paper still exists, you know.'

I frown woozily. 'Why are you bringing that up?'

I hear the echo of Pierre's voice, in this very room on New Year's Eve. *He got you locked into some confidentiality clause?*

'Just . . . your success is my success. There is not one without the other. I'm not merely your shadow, Folkes. I have big plans in the pipeline.' His voice is a quiet hiss, but I'm too drunk to process that at the time. 'So let's not do anything to blow this partnership. Or your career.'

'Why you being all grim and scary, Gustav?'

He takes a breath, irons out the lines in his face. Waves his hand carelessly in the air and goes to flick on the kettle. 'Sorry. Don't mean to rain on your parade.'

'Let's talk some more about the Club Crème. Did you know it's a rule that members are masked when they are up to no good to protect their identities? Which must be pretty much all the time! It made my job easier, actually, but it was like watching a lot of marionettes. And those barmaids, when they revealed themselves as strippers. The poor bridegroom!' I am burbling now but I don't care. 'They left his tackle in such a state that Princess Emilia might get out of her wedding night after all!'

I try to look carefree and confident but the hiccup spoils the effect. I giggle and turn to follow him into the kitchen for a glass of water.

'Those barmaids were professional sex workers, Serena. But you are not, which is why I have to punish you for what happened when everyone adjourned to the private smoking den afterwards.'

I stop by the big white counter, fold my arms to hug the

154

burgundy velvet of my cocktail dress. Now we get to it. What's really bothering him. Fear rushes up from my feet in a cold wave, and I have to flatten my hand out on the wall to steady myself.

'Thank God it was almost totally dark in there, even though it was broad daylight outside. It's like being a hobbit, or a mole. But I still don't know why you're being so grouchy. You've said I'm allowed adventures and experiments, so long as you are there.' I toss my head, relish the thick tickle as my hair drops slowly out of the pins and trails down my bare spine. 'I've not stepped over any lines.'

Gustav's black hair falls over his eyes as he shakes coffee into the cafetière. His teeth bite down into his lower lip. 'I know I said that. And I meant it.'

'Why didn't you stop me if it was upsetting you? Actually, I thought it might turn you on. You're giving me mixed messages, Gustav.' I persist. 'Oh, sod this. I need to take a nap.'

'You had them eating out of your hand, Serena. I couldn't spoil your moment.' Gustav hesitates, then produces the silver chain. He twists it round his knuckles like a cowboy winding in a lasso. 'I would never go back on my word. In any case, protesting would have made me look a jealous fool as well as going against the ethos of the club. To be honest, I'm confused myself. Which is a first. I can't say I enjoyed watching you cavorting in front of a bunch of drooling strangers. But it did turn me on, because you were sexy as hell.'

'I've hurt you, Gustav, and I'm sorry.' I bow my head, feel the blush rising, heating my cheeks. 'I'm a very naughty girl.'

'And? What else is going on in that beautiful head of yours?' Gustav stops a few feet away from me, the silver chain drawn taut between his hands. 'Are you plotting some other wickedness? Because it seems that, no matter how wicked you are, I want you all the more.'

I smile up at him, but I can't bring myself to admit what's bothering me about those so-called strangers. One in particular. I hold my wrists out so he can tie them with the silver chain, and I say the first thing that comes to my head. 'You know, I might have gone further if you hadn't been there to save me. Do your worst to me, Gustav. I deserve it.'

His dark face finally relaxes, and he comes towards me, the glitter of lust in his eyes. I shiver with excitement, but also a tiny nag of dread.

Because it's true that most of the men in that smoking den were strangers. But there was one man I think I recognised.

I behaved badly today, no question. But it felt good, too. I worked hard on the Robinson brothers' commission, and then I got drunk, because everything was crowding in on me. Polly's request for my help. Gustav's troublesome brother. Gustav's bloody ex-wife.

What I did was, I danced, dirtily, for a bunch of members at the Club Crème. If I hadn't danced, I would have let one or more of them have me. Gustav was there, and maybe he would have stepped in, but I wasn't dancing just for him. I think the devil was driving me.

We had all adjourned to the tartan-decorated smoking den, me, the Robinson brothers, the groom, and various stags, for some 'after' photographs. Gustav went to speak to the director about the photographs he wanted to buy and I was left alone with several horny men. Anything could happen. They sat about the smoking den on sofas, chairs and window seats, and two of them had come to lean against the mantelpiece on either side of me. One was the groom, the other had thick blond curls, and they were still masked from their earlier shenanigans.

We were all exhausted, even though it was a dark, wintry mid-afternoon. The high-class strip show and audience participation in the bar just now had made my viewfinder steam up. The stunning six-foot females stripping off their barmaid uniforms to reveal nothing but leopard-spot body paint and sequins had given us a very slow, very detailed introduction to full-on lesbian sex, and I had produced a fantastic series of arty photographs. They were jungle animals prowling through a sophisticated city bar. Jungle animals devouring sophisticated city boys.

Accompanied by a low, throbbing bass beat they had mimed a story about five girlfriends with the dynamic of a ringleader, followers and shy hanger-on. They started off admiring, teasing and flirting with each other before kissing experimentally. The ringleader picked the two she fancied the most, lying back on the bar while they serviced her with tongues and teeth on her nipples, fingers between her legs, leaving the other two to vie for her attention with their own increasingly raunchy dance on the sidelines.

When one of these two produced a couple of huge white dildos and tested them with an explosively sexy dance that ended with them using the toys on each other, and then the shy one, all inhibitions shed, started to edge with her dildo towards the boss girl's open legs, the effect on the men was exactly as intended. The stags pushed forward the feebly protesting groom and the two Robinson brothers, yanked their trousers down and guffawed uproariously when the girls compared their erections with the now glistening dildos, apparently found them wanting, and turned their backs to use the dildos on each other again.

The men – all mouth, no trousers – thought they were off the hook but the girls then became the leopards they were painted as and took a man each, so acrobatically that the other girls were 'forced' to abandon their display and join in.

In the den, where all was quiet, I took some close-ups of the strangers, now fully dressed again in their masks and dinner jackets, sitting in various haughty attitudes around the room, holding up glasses of blood-red ruby port, the scene lit only by the flickering light of the fire. It felt like the middle of the night. I kicked off my shoes and sat down. It had been a fantastic lunch and my working day was over before teatime – I felt totally relaxed. All I wanted was for Gustav to come back for me so we could wander home and chuckle over my success.

'None of us stags is going home until tomorrow. So how about a nightcap for the lady snapper?' The groom took a small, bulbous bottle of golden liquid and filled three glasses.

'In the middle of the afternoon?' I asked drowsily.

'There are no clocks in Club Crème. Haven't you noticed? *Prost!*' the blond one said with a grin, holding up his drink. He turned to his friend the groom. 'How was it for you in the bar just now? That hooker's mouth wrapped round your cock to show whose was biggest while the other girl took her from behind with the dildo?'

The others all roared with ribald laughter. I choked as the brandy went down the wrong way.

I was also blushing. I fiddled with the CD player on the table beside me, and some soft piano music filled the room.

'You thought those strippers were hot, didn't you?' The blond one topped up my glass. 'You thought the camera was hiding you, but I could see it in your face. You wanted a piece of that action.'

'They were gorgeous, sure, high-class, but that's what you guys pay for at the Club Crème.' I shifted on my chair. 'I just had a job to do.'

'Anyone with eyes and a pulse would fancy those girls,' the blond man said. 'They were worth every penny. Pity they had another gig to go to. I reckon we should fetch them back here.'

'I have a great set of photographs to keep you going,

though,' I reminded them. 'Bet I could turn you on every bit as well as they can.'

I couldn't believe I'd just said that.

They were all staring at me. Tall, well-built men. Still masked, but Gustav had told me you had to be good-looking to get into this club, and he wasn't joking. The blond man closest to me was unsettling me. Everything was unsettling me. It was the middle of the day, yet we were underground and the room was in semi-darkness. There was barely any light in any area of the club. Another club rule. But this guy was starting to look familiar.

'Your photographs, or you?' The groom had a boyish laugh. 'Oh, I have no doubt you could make us hard all over again. As you say, only top-quality pussy is permitted through these portals.'

I thought I could hear Gustav's voice speaking somewhere along the corridor. He'd be back in a moment. I needed him here. Now. The alcohol was turning my brain to couscous. It felt too damn good, these gorgeous young men preening themselves like the principals in an Oscar Wilde play. Lust scrawled all over their masculine features.

I responded in the best way I know. By raising my camera. They all started clowning around again, arranging themselves into dissolute Byronic poses around the central figure of the groom, all arrogant profiles and languid limbs, half lit by the dying fire. And when they flung their dinner jackets back to put their hands on their hips I could see the hard outlines pushing inside their black suit trousers.

I put down the camera. My head swam as the brandy warmed my veins and the men grew silent. Their eyes glittered through the plain black Batman-style masks.

I walked unsteadily back to the fireplace, pushed in between the two guys who had resumed their positions there, and stared at myself in the gilt mirror. My hair was still pinned

159

up, just, but my cheeks were flushed, my heavily mascara'd eyes huge and wild, and my lips were smudged and parted as if I was out of breath. I was the only one unmasked.

'Come on. Admit you fancied a little bit of girl-on-girl action yourself? Just hearing you say it would make me hard.' The blond man glanced at me sideways, and through my tipsiness his deep American drawl nagged at me. 'This club is all about hedonism, after all.'

'God, man, you're like a dog with a bone!' The groom wagged his finger. 'Can't you see how uncomfortable she's getting?'

'I am a little tired, boys,' I murmured, clutching at the mantelpiece as the room shifted in the mirror behind me. 'And I have another meeting tonight.'

'Lucky client, whoever he is. Hey. You're free to leave, whenever you like,' one of the Robinsons remarked.

'Except you have a bone that needs relieving, Robinson,' the blond one chuckled, running his hand over his own crotch. 'We all do.'

The room went quiet. They were well-bred men prepared to act like a pack of dogs at a given signal but, as with any dog, that signal would have to come from me. Two of them were standing possessively on either side of me. I was so hyped up now that even the slightly rough fabric of their black dinner jackets rubbing on my bare arms aroused me. Or maybe it was the visual proof that they were all hard. I felt sexy and naughty, and drunk.

Hurry up, Gustav, before I do something stupid.

As I stood there with my mouth still open, the blond one suddenly took my head in his hands and pressed his lips on my mouth. I could feel how smooth and boyish his skin was compared to the rough bristles on Gustav's chin. As his mouth opened to push in his tongue I pulled away.

'You frigid or something?'

160

That was the word my oafish ex from Devon, Jake, had used to taunt me when I finished with him. Something red and raw flared up inside me. I lifted my chin. 'You couldn't be more wrong. Just ask Mr Levi.'

'We would if he was in here, but the poor fool thinks it's safe to leave you alone with us. So, if you're not frigid, show us what you can do in front of the camera.'

'You bastard,' breathed the groom, watching us. 'You know I had my eye on her.'

I kept my eyes on my own reflection. If only he knew what his future bride Emilia was really like. I smiled at myself in the mirror, a very wide, wet smile, and fanned out my fingers to cup my breasts over the luxurious red velvet. I felt the bounce of my heartbeat as I started to squeeze.

The men's tongues were running across their mouths. The two spokesmen moved away from the fire, went to sit on two armchairs.

'That's the idea,' one of them growled. 'We knew you were a dirty little ho!'

I hesitated, looking down at the flushed faces reflected behind me, the bulges in their trousers, and here it came, the coiling naughtiness between my legs.

I started to push the red dress off my shoulder, relishing the embrace of its soft rich fabric upon my pale skin. I pulled it down to the matching red bra, aware that my heavy breathing was making my breasts swell out of the red lace.

The men were obviously excited now. It occurred to me that they could have any woman they wanted. A phone could be picked up and a high-class hooker could be here within minutes, but Serena Folkes wasn't one of those. She was just a respectable girl like their sister, or girlfriend, or wife.

Except the sisters, wives and girlfriends were tucked away at home.

I unfastened the one hook that held the dress together,

161

cocking my leg so that the dress fell open. Then I wriggled a little, freed my breasts from the lacy cups. They fell heavily forward. I unclipped the bra and flung it across the room as the red dress slithered right down to the thick carpet.

The stags were openly massaging their crotches now.

My breasts were jutting forward, wobbling with my rapid heartbeat, bare and full and swollen with excitement.

I started to stroke and knead, gently at first, then more firmly. My hands were all that covered them. The men swore crudely, bodies rigid with expectation. I could make them fight over me. I didn't care which one of them had me first. All I wanted was something big and hard very, very soon.

'Do you think she'll let us?' the groom whined. He sounded as if he was far away, and his voice had descended several octaves. 'Do you think that sergeant-major she brought with her will mind?'

The others guffawed. I had started something I couldn't possibly wriggle out of now. Where was Gustav, for goodness' sake? And what would he say when he came back? I flicked at my nipples, moaning out loud at the sudden quick burn.

'God, I'd heard that you were not only talented but sensational-looking, too. That amazing hair. That skin! So fuckable! So *not* a vestal virgin!' The blond man ran his fingers through his curls, now tight with sweat. Of course. The words 'vestal virgin' were a deliberate jarring reference to the last time we met. He knew exactly who I was. And I knew exactly who he was, too, but it was too late to back out and certainly too late to give in to the shock. All I could do was pretend that I had no idea who he was. That he was faceless, like everyone in this room.

The others were muttering to each other now. 'I'm going to explode if I don't do something with this boner!'

162

A surge of panic mingled with excitement pounded through me as the men nudged each other. Piano music wound around the room from the CD player as I swayed and caressed my breasts more seductively, and then as the blond guy surreptitiously unzipped his flies I saw the door opening.

Gustav's black eyes caught mine through the fire-flickered gloom. He paused and sussed the situation. My hands stopped. The guys pressed their crotches.

And then Gustav gave one quick nod.

I turned slowly from the mirror. I needed to face him while I did this. The men were perfectly aware of the new voyeur, but they were too far gone to pay attention. They were expecting me to behave like a stripper, and that's what I was going to do. I was going to be someone else, just for tonight.

I walked across to the middle of the small room, bent my knee and kicked off my knickers. I had bare legs and a shiny new Brazilian.

A low, guttural stream of obscenities flowed from everyone, but it was the blond guy who leaned forward, took me by the hips and pulled me towards him. My crotch was in his face now. His hands stroked up the back of my legs. I pushed and felt his breath blow across the bare skin. I started to sway my hips, desire pulsating through me, but I kept my eyes on Gustav.

The blond guy grasped my buttocks, pulling me right to his mouth. Gustav leaned against the bookcase full of leather-bound books, his features etched in stone.

The blond man's tongue touched me. My knees started to buckle as I tipped myself against his face. Ripples of pleasure matched the flicking of his tongue. Then I moaned and pulled away.

I was bottling it. I couldn't let him lick me with Gustav watching. But I couldn't stop the mounting excitement either. So I played it up, wagged my finger – 'no, no, no' – then

163

swiped that same finger where the blond man's tongue had been, and danced for my boys instead.

Gustav's mouth was partly open, his teeth clenched. I knew what that meant. He was disturbed, but that very disturbance was turning him on. I'd danced for him just like this once, the first time I ever went to his house.

'Just watch me. I'll be as good as any tart,' I crooned from my trance, running my hands up the inside of my thighs to open them a little more, and then I started to pleasure myself. The men's eyes glazed as I worked with my fingers, swayed my naked body, showed them glimpses of what I was doing, and then just as they started to fall back in their seats, their hands working furiously on themselves, someone else pushed into the crowded room.

Gustav glanced sideways, and we both recognised the newcomer at the same time

Mr Weinmeyer looked me up and down and grinned like the Cheshire Cat, and as he raised and drained his full glass of tawny port I made myself come.

There was a stifling silence, punctuated only by the zipping up of flies. The younger men shuffled about and tried to rearrange themselves into some kind of order as I turned my back and walked calmly towards the fireplace to study myself, and them, in the mirror. Any of them who hadn't come just then would just have to wait until they were alone.

'What a stunner. She's come a long way in just a few short weeks.' Mr Weinmeyer gave a long low whistle as if summoning a sheepdog, and clapped his hand on Gustav's shoulder. 'Shame Ingrid and I couldn't have got there first. You're even more of a man than I thought you were, Levi.'

Gustav's eyes bore into me through the mirror's glass. I returned his gaze, shaking now as the reality of what I'd just done sank in. I raised my arms and pinned one or two loose tendrils of hair.

'I can't lock her away, much as I'd like to. She's so young, and she needs to learn. I'm enjoying watching her, and I'm discovering it's the best way to keep her happy. Even if she runs away I know she'll come back to me. She always comes back.'

I smiled at him in the mirror, and to my relief he returned my smile.

'You struck gold when you found this one, Levi. And don't forget the rule that what happens at Club Crème stays at Club Crème.' Mr Weinmeyer chinked his glass against Gustav's. 'Actually, Mr Levi, Miss Serena, I'm glad I've caught you both, especially at such a dazzling moment. Let me just feast my eyes for a moment longer before I go over this new commission Ingrid and I have for you.'

I realised how pissed I was now, and turned carefully towards the two older men. Gustav picked up the discarded dress, came over to me, eased it on over my arms and shoulders and hooked it gently back into place. The golden locket had somehow slipped back out of sight, and he pressed it back into place before kissing me on the lips. The younger men had retreated to the corner of the room, where they were drinking and muttering and texting on their mobiles.

'What do you have in mind, Ernst?'

'My wife and I would like Serena to come to Venice. We have some business there, and we also have a whole lot of pleasure planned for all concerned.' Mr Weinmeyer's laugh was deep, booming and self-assured. 'I promise we'll send her safely home, Levi. Just like a pigeon.'

My legs won't hold me up any more. The scene of my strip-tease at the Club Crème fades into my tired, pissed mind now that Gustav has brought me home. But there's one detail I can't avoid. The blond guy who nearly got a taste of me back there is Toga Tomas. He was at Pierre's Halloween party in London. He asked me to give him a blowjob and I refused. He's the one Pierre and Polly keep teasing me about.

I slide along the wall towards the wide arched corridor and into our bedroom, collapse onto the bed face down.

Gustav sits beside me, winds the silver chain round my wrists and very carefully ties the end of it to the curved pole of the bedhead.

'Maybe I still need a little time.' He tests the silver chain unnecessarily. 'Maybe I'm not as cool as I thought with this setting-free idea. Maybe I think your head will puff up with all this success, and you'll fly away. Like Weinmeyer's pigeon,' he murmurs, stroking my hair back from my hot face. 'Hey, don't go to sleep, *signorina*. We're meeting Pierre tonight, when he's finished at the theatre.

'That's not till nearly midnight. Can't I just have a little nap?' I moan and shake my head. 'Pierre Levi is the last person on earth I want to see!'

'You don't expect me to cancel our rendezvous, do you? Every time I see him we become closer to one another again – back to the good old days when nothing could break the Levi brothers apart. I'd forgotten how much I really missed him. There are already moments when it feels like the week-ends when we used to drive out of London on our motorbikes. We had these helmet-mikes so we could talk as we drove. Sometimes we'd be on the motorway, heading to Brighton maybe, and we'd just decide on the spur of the moment to go to France or Holland, and divert to Dover!' Gustav stops stroking my hair and laughs softly. 'No women ordering us about then! But tonight he wants to see you, too.'

'And what Pierre wants, Pierre gets. Prince Pierre.'

'You are an essential part of this process, Serena. You kept your head when all around were losing theirs on New Year's Eve. This reconciliation would have fallen apart without you.' Gustav's hands pause on my hair. He starts to tug at it so that

I have to lift my head. 'I have another way to wake you up. My punishment. You came close to having someone else inside you today, but since I can't let that happen for the moment, I'm going to introduce you to an acceptable alternative.'

'You may as well be speaking Greek, Gustav. I don't have a clue what you're talking about. And I don't want to go out tonight.'

'Tough. Because after you have taken what's coming to you, you will freshen up, look beautiful again and attend this rendezvous. Partly because it concerns you. Mostly because I want you by my side.'

I turn my face sideways. I can see two people sitting there, sliding apart and merging. In my drunkenness I think it's Pierre on the bed, stroking my hair, now bending down and fiddling with something on the floor. It's Pierre's black eyes glaring at me from beneath glowering brows, so like Gustav's, the sweep of the forehead, the creases beside the eyes when they smile. Instead of Gustav's glossy hair falling over his eyes, though, I think I can see Pierre's stiff black hair standing up in spikes, his thick neck with that snaky scar bulging over his collar. His mouth tilting into a smile that I can't decipher. The blue vein in his temple going.

He looks so like Gustav. And he respects me. Polly said so. Which feels good, coming from someone as contrary and difficult as him. It's flattering. It's making me feel things I shouldn't. Making me see Pierre when he isn't here. I'm just pissed. But Polly said I'm the only one he'll listen to. She asked me to help her get him back. I need to speak to him.

'Pierre,' I murmur.

'That's right. We're seeing him at the Library Bar tonight.'

I squeeze my eyes shut, twist away and bury my head under the pillow.

Gustav shakes me, and the chill of sobriety nags me, because what my lover has produced from under the bed is a big, thick leather phallus, exaggerated in size but exact in anatomical detail, and curved slightly like a scimitar. This is a weapon, not a toy. He holds it up in the air between us like some kind of talisman, turns it so we can see it from every angle, then brings out a tiny jar of amber liquid.

'What are you doing?' I croak. I strain against the silver chain. 'That looks like honey.'

'Lubrication,' Gustav mutters in a deep, guttural voice, dipping his fingers into the pot and running the honey over the leather. 'To anoint my little sinner.'

I whimper and wriggle as he runs the tip of the now dripping dildo under my nose, pushes it across my upper lip, between my teeth so that I'm forced to suck it like a lollipop, then he hitches up my velvet dress and draws the thing slowly and deliberately up and down my spine, over my bottom, painting me with a languid trail of amber that is already turning from warm liquid to prickling stickiness as it dries on my skin.

'Don't resist, Serena. I saw your eyes watering with desire when those strippers played with their dildos in the club earlier. So I asked them if I could have one for my girl to take home. I actually wanted one of the white ones they'd used, but they said this one was brand new and we could have it as a gift.' He laughs so boyishly just then that it infects me, too. 'They were all for coming home with us to demonstrate how best to use it, but I said no, I wanted you to myself. But I took their number. For future reference!'

I giggle helplessly and feel my body going all soft and willing as he bends to his gentle task and runs the blunt end down between the cheeks of my bottom and burrows underneath me, pushing open my resisting body, nosing towards the centre. Those strippers oiled up their phalluses with something good enough to lick and then buckled on special belts and aimed them at each other, suggestively at first and then thrusting their pelvises like men, pushing in and penetrating each other, long and slow.

A little scream bunches in my throat as my legs come up to squeeze it away, but it's like a missile, what do they call it, heat-seeking, because the dildo pushes blindly against this different part of me, against the tightness, burrows in forcefully and pushes until there's a little pop.

The resistance gives way to melting acceptance, and I revel in the fact that this is Gustav, my lover, who asked those scary strippers if he could have their dildo to take home and is wielding this thing and invading my most private part with it. I don't want anyone else to do this to me, not even some domineering woman I might play with in the future. I have a vision of Mrs Weinmeyer locking those fur handcuffs and using a white dildo on her chunky husband, and it's that awful, naughty thought that makes my legs stop kicking against the soft white duvet, my wrist ensnared with the silver chain go limp.

'Trust me. I'm your teacher. Although this is a first for me, I have to admit. We're experimenting together, remember? So think of this not as punishment but as another pleasurable lesson. For both of us.'

I have managed to push away Pierre's presence at last, but I can't look at Gustav while this is happening. Now his other hand is lifting me, to get a better angle, I suppose. His long warm fingers are wandering over my bottom, following the path of the dildo, and the combination of sensations is emptying my mind of all thought, filling my body with a riot of responses. His fingers find another way in. How dirty can this get?

He seems detached from me, perhaps torturing himself with thoughts of me dancing in front of those grinning men. He'd be more tortured if he knew I'd just imagined his brother sitting on my bed, but I can't focus on that now, all I know is that several fingers and a dildo are working in tandem, tips inside me now, pushing on and up. My heart starts to beat thickly and fast. I'm not afraid, but I feel vulnerable, cracked open like a shell, my tender insides exposed to a new, brutal battering.

'I'm here, Serena,' Gustav grunts, reading my mind as always. 'I'll always be here. You're perfectly safe. Give in to it. Go on. See how good it can feel.'

I grapple for the remnants of my senses and he gives a low, throaty laugh, pushing the dildo harder so that I squeal and jump, but my body is letting it right in now, and the combination of the two, the leather phallus and the strong, gorgeous man holding it, the bulky weight of his body behind each thrust, the knowledge that I deserve this, is beginning to have its effect. If this is a new lesson, then I'm learning fast.

'You're so wet now, Folkes, you little slut,' Gustav mutters as I start to buck against the leather dildo, squeeze my thighs round it, round his hand and arm, to keep it there. He matches the buck of my body with an answering thrust. He runs his free fingers up me, out again, over me, making me wetter still, everything tight and sore and throbbing now, gripping what's inside me, keeping it there, my body scraping back and forth over the bed as Gustav watches and manipulates.

Above my head the sun sinks rapidly over the Hudson River. Around us the city hums and sings.

The brute hardness of the dildo is almost visual, sparks coming off it, off me. I don't care that it's false. It's big and hard, warmed by my body, and with a sudden rush the phallus speeds up inside me, making me arch upwards in shock.

And then it's him, of course it's him, Gustav is inside me now, his fingers fanning under me as he pulls out the weapon of punishment and enters me to show me that in the end it's always him.

'I feel like a cowboy. I can barely walk after that, ah, initiation.'

'No more than you deserve, *cara*. I was only doing what we both wanted to try out in the safety of our own home, but I never dreamed a well-endowed dildo like that would fit so snugly into your dainty little ass. And if you can't walk then it means you have to stay close to me, yes?'

Gustav kisses my hair as we step out of the lift into the cute rooftop bar of the Library Hotel on Madison Avenue. It's so intimate in here that it's impossible to miss Pierre. He's sitting out on the glass-roofed terrace with a bottle chilling in an ice bucket.

He stands and spreads his arms as soon as he sees us. I feel Gustav stiffen slightly. He takes my arm as if it's he who needs support. I totter beside him towards his brother. The high red heels I stupidly decided to wear to show Pierre I was not to be messed with were a bad choice. The unnatural gait makes my calves cramp, and the tendons at the tops of my legs, where they were wrenched open by my lover and his brutal toy, are twanging like a Spanish guitar.

The men stop in front of each other, study each other's faces for a drawn-out moment. It must be strange, I think, standing aside, to see another's visage so like your own. With a pang that nearly doubles me over with its acuity I realise how important it is that these brothers forgive each other.

I will never look into the face of someone who shares my blood, and the thought of two brothers turning their backs on one another breaks my heart.

They finally make an awkward, back-slapping embrace, and just before they separate I catch Pierre's eye over Gustav's

171

shoulder. The eyes are black and innocent, the mouth curled in a half smile of – what? Approval? Admiration? Thanks?

Instantly I realise what, or rather who, is absent. I sidestep round Pierre before he gets a chance to greet or kiss me, and sit down on the chair opposite him. I guess he's given up even going through the motions of treating my cousin like a girlfriend.

'Polly not joining us?' asks Gustav, glancing round, raising one eyebrow at me.

'Er, no. She's out of town tonight, some big casting she really couldn't miss. Didn't she tell you, Serena? Up Boston way.'

She told me no such thing. The poor girl doesn't even have an assignment at the moment. She's right here in New York, waiting for me to call her after tonight's meeting. She's either hunched in her flat or down at the gym riding an exercise bike furiously to burn off all her frustration and her few remaining ounces of weight. This is not going to be the moment to tackle Pierre about Polly, though. I promised her I'd try, but it doesn't look as if I'm going to get the chance, especially if I make sure I'm never alone with him. I'm beginning to doubt whether I *can* help her.

I keep my face averted from Gustav, try to alert Pierre to the fact that I know he's only pretending to care about Polly. But when he lifts his glass and we chink cheers he returns my look so easily, an attentive, waiting smile transforming his face with such open, boyish enthusiasm that I falter. There's little doubt that he is, or has been, cheating on her. But this handsome, groomed young man doesn't look anything like the deranged bully Polly described to me. Or the sexy, threatening face that hovered in my drunken imagination earlier.

I feel like a traitor, but I can't help being warmed by his smile. He has shaved closely. Even his hair looks calmer, the thick black tufts parted to one side like a schoolboy's and

172

brushed close to his head. He looks totally sorted. Totally together. In comparison it's my poor cousin who is sliding downhill. If Pierre Levi has broken her heart I have to tell him what I think of him. It's a terrible way to treat her. But for the sake of the peace these brothers are after, tonight is not the time.

Dare I say it, Pierre looks even smarter than Gustav tonight. Fair enough, we're all off-duty, but Pierre has really made an effort in a blue and white checked shirt and navy-blue blazer with the correctly folded handkerchief in the breast pocket, even crisp well-tailored trousers. Gustav on the other hand is taking more and more of his dress code from his role as my pretend Hispanic assistant.

I glance at my lover, though, as I always do for strength, and my stomach gives a sleepy kick. He looks gorgeous, like a bandit. Silky hair half falling over his brow, evening bristles hollowing his cheeks, an eager sparkle in his black eyes as he rests his hands between his knees.

'Yes. Of course she told me,' I lie sweetly. But the fear that I'm letting Polly down tastes sour. 'I've been so busy I forgot to mention it.'

Pierre pours out the wine. The body language of the two brothers would be funny if it wasn't so tense. They are leaning towards each other like two condemned buildings that if not shored up will be demolished.

'Busy at Club Crème today, I gather. The Robinson stag do. A really prestigious commission.'

Gustav and I exchange glances. Gustav pauses as he's about to sip his wine, keeps the glass in front of his mouth as if to hide what he really wants to say.

'And one we thought was highly confidential.'

He rests his hand on my chair, just beside my arm in some kind of protective code. I glance up through the glass canopy. To the left of the building I can just make out, if I crane my neck, the ice-cream-layered elegance of the Chrysler Building. Then the arches of Grand Central Station. Above us, the trail of a jet plane, heading east.

'Tomas will have to be blackballed, then. He's the one who told me.'

Pierre lifts his glass in another toast and smiles steadily at me, his tongue flicking quickly across his teeth as if removing a foreign object. I think I am going to pass out. Tomas isn't just the man I rejected at Pierre's Halloween party in London who still has the hots for me. He has broken every code in the book and told Pierre *exactly* what happened at the club, no doubt every slavering detail. I daren't look at Gustav. He must be recalling the same scenario. Those thick golden curls buried between my thighs just a few hours ago.

Gustav puts his glass down on the table. I notice his hand is shaking very slightly. 'Let's leave it there, shall we? Discretion being the better part of valour, and all that?'

Pierre grins and sits back in his chair. It honestly feels as if he's interviewing us for a job.

'Absolutely. But you know that Club Crème is the pinnacle of every man's desires. I know, I know. You're wondering why I want to belong to a den of iniquity like that when I've made such a big deal about what was going down in Baker Street. But this is different. Five years ago I was a clueless, cosseted young man who was genuinely shocked by what he saw and heard, partly because he was so green, but mostly because it involved you, Gustav. I'm still getting over that, to some extent.' He glances across the table, but Gustav is looking down, biting his lip, trying to keep calm. 'But I've learned a lot since then, and Club Crème is for grown-ups. It has a gloss on it that no other club in New York or London has. Everyone is panting to join. Its members are men of the world who know their own mind, and what they want is

174

pure, unpoliced hedonism. There's no other darkness involved. Just escapism. Extreme fetishes like whips and racks are banned, isn't that right, G?'

'You've done your research.' Gustav looks up. 'That's right. It's why I accepted the nomination to join.'

Pierre leans forward eagerly. 'The bottom line is, guys, that a lot of my friends and business associates are members, or on the list to be voted in. You're a nobody if you haven't at least been along as a guest. But my own brother is a member, which would have a lot more clout than one of my mates. How about voting me in, G? Put the seal of validation on this reconciliation?'

'I would love you to be a member, P, but it doesn't work like that.' Gustav isn't looking at Pierre but at his glass of wine, perhaps trying to defuse any slight tension with a small laugh and a shake of the head. 'For a start, you have to have a million in the bank.'

Pierre's expression barely changes, but I notice an intensifying of the blackness in his eyes. Just like Gustav's, when he's displeased.

'Of course. Money talks. I guess what you need is an inheritance, handed to you on a plate.'

Gustav turns the stem round and round in his long, strong fingers. Keeps turning it. The wine barely moves in the glass. I would not blame him for rising to that, but he keeps it very calm. Very low.

'Anything handed to me on a plate was used to look after you, Pierre. A home, school fees. Any fortune I have accumulated since you left came to me through hard graft. You're making big strides in your own work and I'm proud of you. So let's give it six months. If you can show me where you are with your current project, that midtown theatre and your costume business, how you've publicised it, who's taking it up, giving it their patronage, then of course I'd be glad not only to sponsor you for the Club Crème but more than that. I'd finance a business project for us to do together. I can see you doing something theatrical with these industrial spaces I'm viewing up and down North America over the next few months. My plan is to turn them all into venues for the arts. Something creative that interests us both.'

Pierre's face darkens slightly. He leans forward in his seat, frowning at his brother. 'You'd only give me a leg-up on the basis of a deal? Does everything work like that in your life?'

I shrink away from what could be a gathering storm.

'Honestly?' Gustav leans forward, too, so that their hands are nearly touching. 'Yes. That's how I've got where I am. You have to have concrete proven talent to go with. Not just someone's word. And I think you and I could work together, your design eye and my business brain. Serena came to me on that basis, and look at us now! You're my brother, and together we could be a force to be reckoned with. But first, show me your cards, yes?'

'Fair enough. It's why you're such a great example, and I'm a fool ever to have thought otherwise.' To my relief Pierre smiles ruefully and sits back in his chair. He spreads a hand towards Gustav as if presenting him to an audience. 'Don't look askance like that! I mean it! I'm going to work like a dog to prove myself to you. Let's forget everything else, all the other influences. All the bad stuff, the mistakes, the betrayals. If we can do that, all we need to focus on is the positive. And the positive is you, Gustav. You are an incredible success story!'

Gustav's mouth remains slightly open, as if he's trying to get his breath.

'Thank you, P. And I agree. That we need to jettison everything negative from this drama, like a splinter. You remember when you fell through the beams of the attic playing hide

176

and seek? I had to take out about ten wooden splinters from your knees and fingers with an ice cube and a sewing needle.'

'I should have known coming to you cap in hand wouldn't do the trick!' Pierre lifts his glass again. 'I could do with a few quid, who couldn't? It's just that some things aren't going so great. The business in London hasn't really taken off, despite my Halloween launch. In fact, the only punters who have been into the premises since then have been pantomime dames.'

There's a brief pause where we all look at each other. I can't blame Pierre for being anxious and embarrassed about that, especially after all the fanfare. But the vision of these grotesque comedy figures with deep voices and false bosoms barging through that little shop looking for Widow Twanky crinolines makes me giggle, then splutter into my wine glass. The brothers stare at me for a moment then start to laugh, too.

'You may have to cut your losses with that one, P. Close the shop or let it out, but keep grafting, build on what you're doing here in NY, and I have every faith in you.' Gustav shakes his head with amusement and takes another drink. 'And that neatly segues, does it not, into the other reason we're here?'

I realise that I've been staring so hard into the pale primrose of my Sauvignon that it is blurring. I am so, so tired.

'Serena, yes. I want to put some business your way.'

Gustav laughs again. 'You sound like a car dealer!'

Pierre laughs, too. I'm happy to hear their laughter. It sounds comfortable, like some kind of in-joke they share. I take another sip of wine. If I get much more relaxed I'll nod off.

Gustav reaches over to me and tucks a strand of hair behind my ear. His way of getting my attention. I blink and yawn. As his fingers trail down my neck, pluck gently at the chain holding the golden locket, the sliding rattle inside rouses me and I look up. Just in time to see Pierre's eyes wandering over my body. Up my legs, long and lean in the burgundy leather trousers I've chosen. Taking in the smoky grey silk T-shirt clinging to my breasts.

'You up for another commission, Serena?' he asks, lifting the wine from the ice bucket. I keep my eyes not on his face, which is unsettling me more than ever this evening, but on his hands as they tip the bottle to pour. The fingers are thicker than Gustav's. More powerful. Seem more capable of causing harm. I can see them snapping the belt from round his waist and flicking it in the air, frightening the living daylights out of Polly.

'Sure. I'm always up for more work.' I cross my legs calmly and hold out my glass for more wine. 'Tell me more.'

I'm too tired or too pissed to take anything seriously. Despite everything I'm enjoying myself. I'm with two gorgeous, hot-headed brothers. I'm the envy of several of the other women in this bar. I try to compose how I will excuse myself to Polly when she asks how I got on.

Pierre is either a consummate actor concealing a committed philanderer, in which case she needs to let him go, just like the failing little shop in Covent Garden – or the wide-boy charm she fell for in the first place, flawed as it is, is worth fighting for.

'I want you to come down to this theatre in Gramercy Park Gustav just mentioned. It's where I'm working at the moment, supplying wardrobe for a new off-Broadway musical show that's rehearsing there. I'm dressing the cast and I'd like you to come down and take some photographs. A day in the life. The dancers dressing. Dancing. Undressing . . .'

I nod briskly. *That theatre where he works. It's like a candy store.*

'They're a burlesque troupe who have come out of nowhere

but are already attracting attention. Possibly from Hollywood. I'd like you to take the publicity and fashion stills as part of a kind of photographic storyboard.'

'No pantomime dames involved?' I ask slyly.

'Absolutely not. These are stunning professional dancers. This could take me places.' Pierre grins at both of us. 'This could be the success story I bring to you in six months' time.'

We talk a little more, and make an appointment for me to come along to the theatre for the press show, which will give me some exposure, too. The conversation becomes practical and detailed and so interesting that before I know it it's the early hours.

I stand up, and the men stand with me.

'I'm bushed now, boys. I'm going to leave you to talk,' I say, stepping back from the table. Pierre takes me firmly by both arms, and kisses me on first one cheek, then the other.

'Very French,' I smile, feeling the smooth wetness on my face.

'I'll walk you to the lift, *cara*.' Gustav curls his arm round my waist.

Pierre watches as Gustav escorts me to the lift and folds me into his arms.

'Thank you, my darling,' he murmurs, his breath hot in my hair. I lean against his chest and listen to the deep thump of his heart. 'You're a kind of balm, soothing everyone.'

'You make me sound like a hand cream!' I laugh softly. I could stand here forever. 'Why are you thanking me?'

'For being here. Making tonight feel as close to a normal family get-together as possible. For being in demand as a clever young photographer going places. And while I've been listening to you and him chatting on, I've made my mind up about one more thing.'

I look up at him. I have to crick my neck back to meet his eyes. He bunches my hair up in his hand.

'There's something I haven't told him. I thought the time would come eventually but no. There might never be the right time. Not when his happiness means more than mine.'

'Gustav?' I say, letting him pull me close to him. 'What is it?'

He leans his chin on the top of my head. 'I swore to him, to you, that I would be honest and open about everything. So I thought that would include, eventually, the devastating truth about the fire. But I realise, especially now you and he are building such a rapport, that I can't risk it. It would bring down the house of cards. I'll just have to accept that part of him will always blame me for everything, for robbing him of our parents before he got a chance to remember them. But I'm big enough to take it. We have to cut him some slack.'

'We?' I reach up and stroke his dark, troubled face. Feel the scrape of bristle under my fingers. 'What is this devastating truth, honey?'

Gustav catches my hand and kisses it, pressing the palm against his face like a mask.

'I've never told him – how could I? – but that night in Paris when our family home was burned to a cinder and we'd got him to the hospital, the doctors found matches and a lighter in Pierre's little pyjama pockets when they cut his clothes off. He was only three years old. He had no idea what devastation he had caused. The lift comes up with a little ding and the doors shiver open. 'How can I ever tell him that he started the fire?'

CHAPTER NINE

The roar of the greasepaint. The smell of the crowd. The dusty choke of hairspray, the stale whiff of caked lipstick and powdery make-up and strong, cheap perfume hanging like mist over a swamp. The velveteen wallpaper has come away in chunks, leaving crimson-painted bricks exposed. Starkly lit mirrors nailed along each crumbling wall add to the confusion, repeating the scene over and over again.

Setting up the dressing room as part of the scenery makes for a surreal mix. It brings the back stage to the front, and mixes period with modern-day. The music stands, a broken violin that looks as if it has been snapped over a starlet's head, tailor's dummies draped with corsets, beads and cloaks are all vintage, but there are also contemporary touches such as trailing wires, hair tongs, curlers, ironing boards and a huge ghetto-blaster.

It all makes for a clever contrast between the grandeur of the proscenium arch, the stage and stalls, the music, costumes, laughter and applause, and the cramped accommodation normally concealed beneath the stage, the scruffy brickwork, the twittering, gossiping and pale nakedness of the actors and dancers as they prepare – all symbolic of the illusion that is showbiz.

A few minutes ago Gustav crooked his finger to summon the car, which was hovering a few yards behind us like a respectful courtier. We're both inordinately pleased that he ditched that lazy limo and replaced it with this bright-red fire-engine-like Hummer with blacked-out windows and a series of burly drivers. All we're missing now is Dickson to drive it.

I have plans for that car. The back seat is as big as a double bed. How sexy would it be to order the burly driver to take us wherever we wanted to go around town so that we could tear each other's clothes off and make out, shielded by a few millimetres of blacked-out bulletproof glass from the eyes of all those unsuspecting passers-by? But so far there has not been the time.

'Before we get to the theatre, I need to talk to you about Polly.' I shook Gustav's arm as he read a message on his phone. 'Did Pierre say anything in the Library Bar the other night?

'No. He was too busy filling me in on the last five years. But if there's some hiatus going on between them, that explains why she wasn't there. I suspect my brother is a pretty lousy boyfriend.' Finally he glanced at me. '*Cara*, if Polly has asked you to talk to him, be my guest, but leave me out of it.'

I fiddled with the sleeve of his coat. 'Oh, I might leave it. He won't want me butting into his private life just when things are going so smoothly between you.'

'She's your nearest and dearest, Serena. You should help her, but be diplomatic about it. Now, I'm going to have to drop you at the theatre.' He waggled his phone at me. 'Something has come up. An iron in the fire that involves you, *signorina*, so don't look so suspicious. And talking of

182

fires, remember. You must *never* tell Pierre what I told you about him starting the Paris fire.'

'My lips are sealed. But I want you there with me, Gustav. I'm getting used to you being my minder. My watcher, watching.' I pushed my face into his shoulder, breathing in his fresh scent. Tweaking the red scarf to kiss the pulse beating beneath.

He held my face tight between his hands as he kissed me back, pushing the tip of his tongue, running it behind my teeth, just enough to tickle and turn me on, just enough to make me impatient for tonight to come.

'Not this time. You and Pierre need to talk business, and get to know each other better. I'd far rather be with you today. But unfortunately the dull world of commercial property deals, especially when I'm trying to sprinkle a little creative magic over them, won't wait, even for my girl.'

The car stopped in a tiny street just set back from the enclosed garden square of Gramercy Park and before we had time for a proper kiss he drove off.

At first I thought they'd left me in the wrong place, because all I could see was a small yellowish building tucked between two elegant black-painted town houses. It was very shabby. Not the grand structure I was expecting from Pierre's descriptions. This tumbledown place was all shuttered windows, ripped posters flapping in the cold breeze, and peeling paintwork. Not even the double entrance doors were functioning. There was a set of worn stone steps, a snapped handrail and a small sign tacked to the door saying 'Please use back entrance'.

I was a couple of minutes early. I didn't want to look too keen. I walked to the end of the street, took a couple of shots of the extraordinary angles of the Flatiron Building, dragged my feet back to the theatre and bumped straight into someone just coming down the steps.

'Hey, watch where you're – hi, Serena! You're on the dot!'

I spun round, nearly tripping over my own feet, and found myself staring up into the now familiar face of Gustav's younger brother. It was a strange, suspended moment. The two men, so alike. I'd only seen Pierre at night, but now, lit by the harsh daylight, he looked, despite the technical differences of height, hair and age, even more like Gustav.

Since we'd met in the Library Bar the other night he'd cut his hair even shorter, almost aggressively so. I wondered if he knew Polly had also shaved off her hair, her own declaration of his rejection. Either way he had changed his image yet again. The stiff black quiff jutting above his eyebrows and longish sideburns, along with the scuffed leather jacket, made him look like a rakish rocker.

'Good day, Pierre.'

'Are you all right, Serena? You look as if you've seen a ghost. Well, I guess it's weird, being alone with me like this at last? Not as handsome as my brother, eh?'

I managed a weak smile. 'No chance.'

Where Gustav's face is angular with Nureyev cheekbones and a strong nose tapering to a narrow chin and strong yet full lips, Pierre's features are broader yet meaner. Why couldn't I look away? Because it was the eyes. Whatever their setting of bone and sinew, the daylight accentuated the same dark, glittering, questioning eyes. Black enough to drown in. Expressions shifting beneath the surface like sand and pebbles being washed beneath the tide.

'The apple doesn't fall far from the tree, though, eh?'

We laughed awkwardly, still staring at each other. Pierre Levi, just like his brother, is devastatingly attractive. They have the same blood. The same history, even though they still keep massive secrets from one another. The same magnetic air that pins you like a butterfly in a display case, draws you in, whether you like it or not. And the answer to the evil, forbidden question clamouring at the back of my mind was that yes, I daresay I would have fancied him if he wasn't Polly's boyfriend. And if I hadn't met Gustav first.

'Being an orphan myself, I guess I'm still getting used to all these brotherly developments. Don't get me wrong. It's good. It's like the jigsaw is piecing together again,' I murmured faintly, sitting down with a thump on the steps. Damp seeped through my jeans. 'Gustav is so happy about it. Here you are, back in his life. Large as life.'

'And twice as ugly!' He sat down on the step next to me. He was wearing a blue scarf knotted round his neck in the same way as Gustav wears his red one, and ripped blue jeans. His long leg brushed against mine, and he made no attempt to move it. I shivered in the cold, but I didn't move mine either. I didn't want to look petty. 'Look. We got off on the wrong foot those first two times we met. I was oafish, and defensive.'

I glanced up at him. To an observer we could look like two mates having a heart-to-heart. 'And I was rude, too. A Rottweiler, you said.'

'We all have a quagmire to cross. It's like recovering from a long illness.' He kept his smiling eyes on me, drummed his fingers on his knees. 'You still feel feverish and shaky. Definitely unreal. But I shouldn't have spoken to you like that. You are my brother's girlfriend, after all, and he's mad about you.'

The blood rushed through my body. 'He told you that?'

'My God. Talk about an open book. Your face has literally lit up like a beacon. You've really got it bad!' I caught a strange look in Pierre's eye. Although he accompanied it with a chuckle, I wondered: if it wasn't jealousy, was it envy? If so, he had only himself to blame for wrecking his chances of similar happiness with Polly. 'I'm happy for him. For you both. God knows he could use the love of a good woman.'

I gaped at him, blushing scarlet. 'I never expected such nice words from you.'

'Like I said. Wrong foot earlier. Right footing now. Yes?' Pierre's soft growling laugh was like his brother's. 'And you will find me just as charming as my brother when I pull my finger out.'

'Not to everyone.' I stood up abruptly. I so didn't want to have a conversation about Polly, even though she'd called me twice this morning, urging me to try again. 'Shall we get on with the job in hand?'

He stood up with me, took hold of my arms. 'That lioness look in your eye. I saw it in the gallery in London. I saw it on New Year's Eve, too. You really would defend your nearest and dearest to the death. But this isn't about Gustav, is it? So it must be about Polly.'

I gripped the handle of my camera case. Tried to ignore the heat transmitting from his hands. 'Where do you Levi boys get this mind-reading skill from? Yes, I am worried sick about her, since you ask. I meant to tackle you about it the other night. She says you've had some terrible rows and you've simply walked out. First she blamed Margot, and now she's certain there is someone else. But you haven't told her where she stands, and she's devastated. She's lost the plot, Pierre.'

Pierre let go of my arms and leaned against one of the pillars at the bottom of the theatre steps. 'She's great, your cousin, feisty, cute, sexy, but it's all become too heavy. So I admit I've taken the coward's way out. Instead of being straight with her and finishing it face to face, I've gone off the radar as far as she's concerned.' He suddenly reached out and tipped my chin in his fingers, turned my face towards him. 'I thought she might be enough for me, but the world has tilted on its axis in the last month or so. Certain people have come bursting into my life and thrown me out of kilter.'

186

I gaped back at him, felt the pull of his black eyes. Tried to read what, or who, he meant. Was he trying to say that yes, he had behaved badly? That Polly wasn't exaggerating? And if so, who did he mean by certain people? I couldn't look down. It was like teetering on the edge of a steep staircase.

'You're not talking about Gustav now, are you? It's another woman. So who is it? One of your dancers? The one who texted you on New Year's Eve?' My voice came out in a croak. 'Polly asked me to find out from you what's going on, so why can't you be straight with me?'

'God knows I would love to confide what's going on in this tormented heart of mine. I could tell you exactly who it is I'm pining for. She could even be standing right here in front of me.' His eyes rested on me, for one brief second totally serious, before his face split into a grin. 'But we're not here to gossip. What would Gustav have to say about that? We're here to do business. And this is one path you really don't want to venture down. Because if I told you who I'm lusting after now, the balloon would go up. Believe me, sis. This person is out of bounds. It would be catastrophic.'

I decided to ignore the ill-judged familiarity and looked away from him. It was time to do my own detective work. Assuming Pierre wasn't talking about me when he'd hinted that the object of his desire was right here, then it must be one of the dancers, maybe a married one, and it would become obvious as soon as I got inside the theatre.

He started to lead me round to the back of the building.

One minute charming the birds off the trees, next minute dropping hints about something truly transgressive going on in his head.

If the old Polly was here, and obviously not involved, she'd say, *Duh. You're standing in front of a theatre full of lissome dancers. What makes you think he'd give you a second glance?*

The plates shifting beneath my feet again. That was Pierre's special trick, I was learning. But he was right. It was time to get on with the job in hand. Weighted down with my equipment I followed Pierre's rapid pace round the corner.

'You look a bit dubious, Serena.' Pierre had stopped by the back door. 'You're wondering what this dump I've brought you to is.'

He followed my gaze as I stared at the walls and windows, which were even scruffier round here than at the front. The door was falling off its hinges, there was a dumpster full of old scenery studded with rusty nails, and a pile of mossy roof tiles had cracked and smashed onto the paving around us.

'Very atmospheric, I'll say that about the place. It feels as if it could be haunted!'

He wrenched open the door, widening the crack that was running through the panelling.

'Oh, it looks shabby, I know, a few cracks here and there, but we've only just occupied it and appearances can be deceptive. A bit like the house in Baker Street in that respect. Part of the effect is deliberate downbeat chic, or will be when I've finished designing the refurbishment. The other point is that it was easy for my backers to acquire the premises.'

'I'll take your word for it,' I muttered, lugging my kit through the door.

Pierre took one of my cases. 'Look. I really want to work with you. You've got this energy about you, Serena. I've seen that with my own eyes but I've also done some research, and you're getting a great rap from clients already. Best of all, Gustav would be over the moon if we could collaborate harmoniously. But if you're not happy with the idea of working with me, or working here, because of Polly, I can offer this gig to any number of aspiring photographers.'

'And I could be offering my services to any number of

clients, but you should know that I never turn down a decent commission.'

He grinned approvingly and gave a slight bow as he held the door open for me.

'In that case I'll walk you through what I'm after. It could be exciting, Serena. But I'll understand if what I just said about Polly has unnerved you. If you want to jack it in.' He led me into a large, bare lobby lit by high arched windows. There was a makeshift box office in one corner and a pile of programme proofs on the table. He picked one up and tapped it against his mouth. 'I certainly don't want it coming between us.'

'Jacking it in is not part of my vocabulary. Let's get started,' I sighed, putting my bags down and getting out my iPad to make notes. 'But I'll not let Polly be the elephant in the room. You have to tell her it's over, otherwise she'll make herself sick with hoping.'

'Message received! I might need your help with how best to do it, though. Maybe you can advise me over a drink later?' When I shrugged without responding he perched one buttock on the edge of the table, swinging his long leg. 'OK. On with the dance. Well, as you know, I want you to create a pictorial storyboard observing what we do here, impressions, moments, vignettes, the raw materials of our work, which I can then edit and collate, but there have been some approaches in the last couple of days since I outlined it to Gustav. He doesn't know anything about this new angle, and I don't want him to know. Not until I've got something concrete to show him.'

I noticed that someone had drawn elaborate sketches of a series of dance moves directly onto the whitewashed walls of the lobby.

'I'm not sure I'm comfortable sharing a secret with you and excluding him.'

189

'I admire your dogged loyalty, but I don't want to big it up if it's not going to come to fruition. All I'm talking about is a proposal I don't want to jinx. Not some dastardly deal with the devil.' He slapped his hands down on his legs. 'No one outside these walls can know about this until the Hollywood moguls have stumped up the contracts and the cash.'

'Hollywood?' I typed in the heading *Pierre*. I glanced up at him. 'I'm listening, Mr Levi.'

The ground stopped tipping at last. We were a couple of acquaintances or colleagues. People who knew far too much about each other but were still treading uncharted territory.

'So. The additional input is, they want me to direct a kind of video short, a record of a day in the life of this theatre, if you will, which will expand into – well, let's see how this pans out first. You'll shoot the girls dressing, and then the rehearsal, with particular emphasis on the splendour and theatricality of my costumes. The twist is that the performers think they're preparing for a press run but it will actually be filmed, without their knowing, as a pilot for a reality show. Also, as you can see, the publicity material isn't complete.' He handed the programmes to me. 'We need your stills before we can go to print.'

He watched as I typed in a couple more bullet points, then jabbed his thumb in the direction of a wooden staircase lit by flickering bulbs, which looked as if it led to a torture chamber. 'Just one thing. A couple of our prima donnas will be arriving in a minute to prepare. Down there is the divas' dungeon. So, no entry.'

I laughed, a little more at ease and eager to get cracking. Poor Polly would be so disappointed in me, but I had to be single-minded about this and ignore her request. Just for today. 'You make it sound like the wicked witch lives down there.'

He laughs too, points his fingers at me in that pistol gesture again, makes it look jovial and cocky. 'You better believe it, sis. You better believe it.'

So I've picked my way round the props, listened to the discordant sounds of the orchestra tuning up in the pit, interspersed with some wild percussion and a hysterical high-pitched trumpet having its say, and now a crackly recording of a Viennese waltz trails from the music machine in the pretend dressing room.

As I pause to drink strong coffee from the cafetière that never gets cold, the mirrors start undulating and shimmering with restless reflections. One or two unearthly creatures float into the room, become a huddle, then a group, until the stage is an aviary full of twittering, fluttering birds.

They may be gossiping and texting, and they may initially be clothed in the universal youthful uniform of jeans and sweat tops, hair (both girls and boys) pulled into scruffy topknots, yet you can instantly tell by the straight-backed way they walk with their toes turned out, the erect posture of their heads, the twitch of their hips and pelvis, that they're not just any kid off the street. And once they sit down on the shabby stools here in midtown New York, their dreary uniform is quickly shed. They strip down to their underwear, baring their white, brown, black skin, their lean, supple bodies. And when they click their necks and wrap their ankles behind their heads to warm up and stretch, that's when I and my camera move into action.

'You'll need to blend in a little more if you want to catch them uninhibited.'

A large black woman with hair plaited in snaky piles on top of her head like Medusa pulls up a tiny three-legged stool behind me and plants her huge bottom. She takes my camera and puts it carefully down on my upturned case, then starts to pin up my hair.

'Excuse me? I'm the photographer, not one of the cast.' I try to turn round on the crate I'm sitting on, but she simply plants her heavy hands on my shoulders. 'And if Pierre catches me not working–'

'You *are* working! Participating. He's asked me to put you into a costume to make you less conspicuous. I'm gonna make you look like the madame of a brothel, and what will happen when Pierre Levi sees you is that he'll get a massive boner like he always does when he sets eyes on a new girl!'

'He can leave me well alone,' I say, blushing, as she drags over a long rail of clothes. The garments swaying and jangling are the same as, or similar to, the antique ball dresses that were hanging on rails and hooks all over the hopeful little boutique in Covent Garden last Halloween when the old, triumphant Polly laced me into a diaphanous white dress, calling me her vestal virgin. The reference that Toga Tomas used in the Club Crème to alert me that he knew exactly who I was.

'Pierre Levi's signature. His travelling fayre of costume and illusion. He's perfecting the spaced-out, Marie-Antoinette-meets-Twilight look, if that makes sense.'

'Perfect sense.'

The lady picks out a crimson corset with a few gossamer rags hanging off it. The very opposite of the virginal look. The lacy sleeves and slashed skirt could have been fought over by a coven of toothsome lady vampires.

'Come on, lady, play the game,' she croons, hitching off my jacket and jumper. 'You want your pictures to be seen on billboards all over the Hollywood Hills, dontcha?'

'Yes, but not pictures of *me*! I've got a brief to fulfil, and I've got Pierre Levi breathing down my neck!' Nevertheless my T-shirt and bra are ripped off and folded neatly beside my camera cases before you can say 'birthday suit'.

The birds in the aviary continue twittering and fluttering

amongst themselves, a little quieter now, the stretches and lunges completed. They are hunched in pairs, either on the floor or perched on dressing tables or pouffes or even a couple of sagging chaise-longues, hands wandering over angular cheeks, slender arms and legs looped round each other so flexibly that it's hard to see where one dancer ends and the next begins.

'Mr Levi would call this a feast of fannies and femininity,' remarks the dresser, waving her arms around her little domain as they turn to listen. 'His birds of paradise. I wonder which little booty he'll pick today?'

They all start to laugh, big red mouths open as they point at me and each other, push their tongues into their cheeks suggestively. One or two of them give me a sly once-over with big dolly eyes beneath false eyelashes long as spiders' legs.

'He can do what the hell he likes, honey. He the boss,' the woman says with a chuckle, holding the red corset around my body to measure it. 'These pussy cats are queueing up to service him, believe me.'

I wish the splintered floorboards would swallow me up. My poor Polly. How do I tell her that she was right about the casting couch?

Could this *droit de seigneur* behaviour that I teased Gustav once about in Switzerland, when we were out horse-riding in the woods, be a Levi trait?

The dancers are nearly naked now, little lace vests straining, their modesty just about covered by identically designed tiny knickers in all the colours of the rainbow. Some girls are leaning into the mirrors, their voluptuous breasts, prerequisite for the burlesque, still bouncy yet pert even when they're bending. Others slink up behind them and run their hands over their bodies as if feeling the texture of their silky skin. At first it seems like a free-for-all as they move from one person to the next, taking turns. Young men sporting bushy stuck-on sideburns and tweed trousers held up by braces reach to fondle and pluck at the bare nipples of girls pinning their hair into extravagant coils. Other girls straddle other boys with stiff crotches, dipping their fingers into pots of pomade and slicking the guys' hair while they grind at each other.

As I wait for the dresser to come back with my garment I swivel my zoom to catch the constant shimmying movement between the mirrors and clothes rails. Now the dancers are discarding their knickers and pulling on costume underwear. Everything they do looks natural and impromptu. If this is choreographed it's with the grooming and mating rituals of the jungle in mind. Hands smooth sparkly thongs into place, fingers stroke breasts into tight corsets, tongues lick at a smear of too much rouge. Lipstick is unsheathed suggestively and after it's applied to mouths it's slicked up sex lips, dotted onto nipples. Dipped into navels.

All this tactile preparation is surely leading to a virtual sex show. As they shake out their slim brown legs and feet like show ponies I see some of them brazenly tweak each other's nipples one last time before they are dressed.

They are all stealing glances at me from time to time as I film them. I feel totally drawn into the scene, but it's a relief when the dresser drops the corset dress over my head.

I am momentarily blinded by shreds of crimson taffeta. She pushes my breasts together for a moment, creating a deep cleavage, allowing the nipples to scrape against her palms. Sensation swoons inside me. I feel warm, treacly. As if I belong here, even though I can't dance. Even though I have a little more flesh on me than these perfectly proportioned gazelles.

I wish Gustav could see me now.

Now the dresser's hands are busy lacing me up so tightly

that I can hardly breathe. My breasts swell desperately, just resting on concealed pads, thrust forward yet also squeezed tightly together. My nipples are only just covered, rubbed to aching point by the trim of scratchy lace.

And that's when I'm sharply reminded of the black whalebone basque I tried on at the chalet in Switzerland, when I dressed up in Margot's leather boots and strutted about like a dominatrix, flicking my whip. But this feels different. This dress-up of tight corset and raggedy skirt makes me feel like a sexy showgirl.

'You could almost be one of them.' The dresser twists my hair into tendrils and pushes me away. 'Let the show begin.'

I grab my camera again, cutting and framing to reflect a Degas style, sometimes showing just a leg coming down a spiral staircase or a foot pointing into the corner of the canvas. But I also compose the shots to reflect that the scene in front of me is a play as the dancers leave real life behind to transform themselves for the performance ahead.

As the orchestra tunes up discordantly beneath the stage the dresser lumbers about the pretend dressing room, selecting various garments to hold against up against the girls' cheeks to see which colour suits, and I realise that this is the intro to the show. She pins their hair into baroque, tumbling structures involving bows and butterflies' wings, even tiaras and crowns. She swivels each girl this way and that, and as their little bottoms jiggle excitedly my eyes are drawn to the waxed mounds tucked between their legs.

The troupe are clothed so that they really do look like tropical birds now, especially when they start fixing matching feathers to each other's hair. The dresser drifts amongst them, trailing her hands down their throats, fingering the young swell of their breasts, while I work, watching, my body prickling with self-consciousness.

Then there is a tinny crescendo of trumpets and drums, and

195

Pierre appears at the side of the stage, in *fin de siècle* costume. As the dancers assemble in a can-can formation he walks along the line blowing kisses and high-fiving. He looks like the cock of the walk. This is his show. His baby. He gets to the end of the line, slaps a couple of stragglers on the bottom as they skip past and waggle their fingers at him. Then he turns in a courtly manner and, to my embarrassment, extends his hand to where I am lurking in the wings. His black eyes under the shade of the old-fashioned hat drive into me.

As I move towards him, still shooting my pictures, I get an inkling of how this scarlet dress must look on me. Or would, if I had the grace of these dancers. The slashed material falls away, revealing the jut of their hips and the shadowy dip and cleft between their legs.

Pierre guides me down some steps at the side of the stage and into the auditorium. I try to walk elegantly ahead of him, concentrating on keeping hold of my skirt and one camera.

'This is dazzling, Pierre. You've got something really edgy and exciting here.'

His face lights up. I realise he was expecting me to be touchy still, no matter how impressed I was with his show.

'Wait till you see what we've done in the stalls, then,' he chuckles, pressing his hand into my back. 'We've tried to recreate a louche Parisian essence right here in the middle of twenty-first-century Manhattan.'

From here the stage is bright and starlit, the backdrop painted milk-chocolate brown, similar to the sepia colours of Degas's paintings. Behind the can-can line the other girls are positioned on their marks, lounging back in chairs, putting on make-up, or with legs cocked high on tables to adjust their stockings, the classic poses of Degas's ballerinas.

Around me the auditorium has been arranged to look like the Moulin Rouge, all red velvet booths and banquettes, crystal chandeliers hanging low over the seats, raised walkways between the tables so the girls can be seen more clearly as they pose and move and dance. The orchestra are seated on bentwood chairs around the front of the stage, with oiled black hair and moustaches, wearing the cropped bolero jackets and slim trousers of a flamenco or Argentine tango band.

'It's perfect! A living, breathing lithograph! Just like posters of the café-concerts of Montmartre!' I open my arms to take it all in. 'I'm impressed. Were you involved in the set design, as well as the costumes?'

'Paintbrush in every pot, but really it's been a team effort. Now, remember you're being watched as well as watching, so I'm only doing this because we're in character!'

Pierre takes my outstretched bare arm and holds my hand up to his lips. Although I'm aware he's overacting, I still flinch as his lips brush against my skin. That raw, bullish energy pulses out of him so much more blatantly than it does with Gustav. The grip of his fingers, the flare of his nostrils, the blue-black shadow on his chin, are all so agonisingly familiar.

Pierre presses his mouth up against my ear so that I can hear him against the music.

'So you see? We can get on, and not just for Gustav's sake. We're all making an effort here. And to prove it I promise I will give myself up to a good browbeating and let you harangue me about your cousin. So let me buy you that drink over at the Gramercy Hotel this evening when we wrap up here.' He draws away and taps his watch. 'Don't be put off by the big movie camera that's just arrived, by the way. That's what I meant when I said you were being watched, and they may be watching you all the way in Hollywood! Oh, and don't be mistaken for one of the girls and get dragged up on stage. You really look the part, Serena. The semi-clad streetwalker.'

I give a little curtsy, because I'm carried away with the

atmosphere and spirit of the spectacle, then I lift my camera and take one more shot of him.

'The Impresario!' I shout above the noise. 'All you need is an evil moustachio!'

'Bring that with you to the hotel after this! The camera, not the 'tache!' he replies with a laugh, before backing towards a row of people with clipboards and earphones who are clamouring for him. 'I don't just want to dissect my failed love life. I'd like to see today's proofs, too.'

There are mostly men in the audience wearing frock-coats and stiff-necked shirts, lounging back in their chairs. A few women in very low-cut gowns wear brassy red hair done up like mine, twisted and curled and adorned with jet beads and feathers. Black stockings and a stretch of white thigh glimmer as they cross their legs theatrically under their skirts. There's even a battered copper bar set up along the side, with a barman shaking cocktails. Every shot I take is already perfectly composed.

'Did you know the post-Impressionist painter Toulouse-Lautrec is supposed to have invented a drink called the *Tremblement de Terre*?'

A deep voice murmurs into the back of my neck. I freeze for a moment, the camera still in front of me. Pierre has taken me unawares. It seems I always have to be on my guard, on my marks like those dancers. As the girls start to screech and whoop on the stage, rotating their knees and flashing their knickers, I turn slowly round, my ragged skirt swirling round my bare legs.

And find myself in Gustav's arms.

I fling mine around his neck, practically in tears at what I might have, could have said, thinking he was Pierre. Gustav staggers with me towards one of the little tables.

'Hey! You been there all along?' I ask as we scoop up cocktails on our way past.

'Since you were grabbed by that dresser and she dolled you up in this gorgeous just-ravished-in-an-alleyway get-up.'

Gustav smiles at me, his eyes roving over my costume. Over my face, my pinned-up hair, as if he hasn't seen me for years. Or as if he doesn't recognise this painted creature. To add to the confusion, he is dressed in a frock-coat and top hat, just like his brother and all the other men in the place.

'I'm so happy to see you.' I tuck myself under his arm. 'That cocktail. It sounds like a knee trembler!'

'How about that? Up against the wall. Oh, I wish!' He kisses me again, sits on one of the bentwood chairs and pulls me onto his knee to merge with the seated, watching audience. 'But I can't stay long. I've been called up to Toronto for a couple of days. My gallery up there is being transformed into a circus arena for a new show, but they're arguing about health and safety, whether the girders are sturdy enough to take the weight of the trapeze. Or something like that. Anyhow, I dropped by to see what you and Pierre are up to before I fly off.'

The music suddenly increases in tempo, a contemporary backbeat to a fashion show, and a dazzle of very modern lights, pink, silver, blue, flash on and off, pulsate in time to the music.

'So long as they don't make you swallow swords or eat fire!' I laugh. 'Now stay right there, because I have to film this.'

The girls change their moves as if a puppeteer has jerked their strings. They gyrate on the stage and then like catwalk models they start to strut out along the runway into the body of the theatre, their hourglass figures sensational as their thighs flex and kick, the design of their corsets allowing a tiny velvet drape of material to cover their modesty.

'Those post-Impressionists were all sex-mad. They all seem to have lost their virginity with prostitutes, hence their

199

enthusiasm for tarts and showgirls.' Gustav twirls his false moustache. 'Pierre says that's why they've set this up for audience participation. Bit risky, I'd say.'

'Can't we go outside for a few minutes?' I wriggle my bottom against him, deep into his lap. 'If you're going all the way to Toronto, how about I get you alone in the car and show you what you will be missing?'

But something makes me turn towards the stage. Pierre is still up there. At first I think he's watching his girls, checking they are moving right, but then I see he is standing just over to the side, watching me and Gustav as we sit entwined on the rickety chair.

Gustav follows my eyes and lifts his hand to greet his brother.

'*Tremblement de Terre* means Earthquake. It was a lethal cocktail made from half absinthe, half cognac. And did you know that Toulouse-Lautrec was nicknamed the coffee pot?

I press myself up against him, hook my leg round one of his. 'Because he was short, but with a huge spout?'

Gustav really laughs. 'Now put your camera down for a moment and dance with me!' He picks me up to swing me round in the air. I catch Pierre's dark eyes on me. On both of us. And I realise, from the almost manic grin on Gustav's face, that he is showing Pierre something. Me. He's showing Pierre that I am his to dance with. No one else's.

Gustav licks my ear as he whispers. 'Pierre says they've had a lot of trouble casting someone well hung enough to be *le* coffee pot for the show!'

His arm tightens around me as we continue to spin. The pretend rapt audience of gentlemen around us crane forward in their chairs, adjusting their trousers, not watching us but reaching out to touch the girls' ankles as they high-kick down the walkways with their feathers and fans. I wriggle out of Gustav's arms to grab my camera again to catch an under-the-skirt view of the girls' impossibly long legs. And impossibly tiny thongs, sparkling in the shadows between their thighs.

One of the pirouetting girls reaches down, pushes me aside with a sharp elbow and a wink weighted with sparkling pink eye-shadow and false eyelashes, and pulls Gustav up onto the walkway. He shakes his head in protest as she starts to dance around him, gesturing and beckoning. Now the other men, actors, audience, members of the press, who knows, are being pulled on stage.

It's just a rehearsal. Any minute he'll bow apologetically and retreat to me.

I shift forward on the chair, thankful that my camera keeps me busy, but Gustav doesn't come back to me. Instead he stretches his arms and tries to take the girl into a waltz hold, but she laughs and turns her back, rubbing her backside against him as if he was a lap-dancing pole. Well, this *is* burlesque. As her arms and legs entwine around him like vines, dancing him away from me towards the stage, the music seems to flow into Gustav. As the girl shimmies at him, he shimmies back. When she bumps and grinds, he stamps his feet at her, his hips thrusting like a matador beneath the black trousers and frock-coat.

My chest goes tight with the unaccustomed sensation of jealousy. No other word for it. He's watched me behave like this with other people, do far worse things, and yet I'm furious with him for making me sit here like a wallflower while he cavorts with another girl. It's only play-acting, I know that, but these girls are trained not only to move and dance and strip but to focus your mind on one thing and one thing only, and that's the sex act. This girl is limbo-ing, wriggling and thrusting, pushing out her fanny and tits, her knees spread, showing us all exactly where she would like to be: in bed. With my man.

201

And all he has to do, oh, God, he's doing it, is one simple thrusting move, to show exactly what he would do to her.

I'm left on the chair as the other participants, planted or otherwise, dance around them, and Gustav is dragged further away from me. Up on the stage the bright coloured lights are slowly fading. I pan my camera round the theatre, focus for a moment on the swing doors at the side of the auditorium, which have been propped open. I can just see a black-haired woman dressed in bridal white emerging from what Pierre called the divas' dungeon, and slipping down the side aisle towards the stage.

No one, not even Gustav, is looking at me now. I can't do anything except go on taking photographs. The tables are being turned. I'm being forced to watch him cavorting with someone else. And despite fantasising about it, I don't think I like it when it's happening right in front of me. Or maybe I just don't like being left out.

Pierre catches my eye from up on the stage. He's been left out, too. We stare at each other a long time, the two of us isolated by dancers whirling like planets around us. Then the lights are all extinguished so that the theatre is buried in a thick blanket of blackness and silence. A slow, thick, heartbeat rhythm is tapped out on a single drum, actually the wooden flank of a guitar, and then the strings hum into a low, sensual Argentine tango.

The blackness is pierced by pin-sharp bright spotlights beaming on supposedly random markers on the stage. I can't see Gustav anywhere. He might be one of the couples who are now stalking, elbows out, heads averted, in stiff tango holds in and out of the beams of light. Or he might have been dragged backstage by that randy showgirl.

I stand up anxiously, kicking my chair back with a loud clatter. A pair of glittering black Levi eyes is staring at me, but it's Pierre. Still up on stage, still in costume. He takes a step towards me, and then a long white arm in a white satin opera glove reaches out of the shadows and grabs him.

The new dancer moves into the spotlight with Pierre, takes his jaw in her gloved fingers and turns him to face her. She is wearing the same costume as the others, low-cut whalebone, floaty tulle, ribbons and hooks, the whole designed to look as if it would fall off with one tug, but although there are slashes of cerise in the silk similar to my costume, hers is predominantly white. As is her face, which is so thickly painted and mask-like it's as if they've used lead to obliterate her features like Queen Elizabeth I.

To render her even more otherworldly a white lace mask casts delicate shadows, swirls and flowers over her features, making her skin almost lizard-like. Beneath it her eyelids and brows are painted black, the eye-liner sweeping out to the edges.

Through the lace her cheekbones are high and sharp, the mouth coloured bright pink. She has an hourglass figure, tiny pricked ears and raven-black hair falling in tendrils beneath a ripped bridal veil peppered with tiny white flowers.

Who is she? She's horribly familiar, but maybe that's because I caught a glimpse of her just now coming up from the basement. Is she the one whom Pierre has picked to pleasure him tonight?

I continue focusing on the dimly lit stage. A single violin picks up the tango and her eyes suddenly lock onto mine just before the spotlight above her and Pierre snaps out. And just as suddenly I am grabbed from behind, lifted off my feet and bent backwards in a low lunge. A strong pair of arms stops me from falling as a long, slow kiss takes possession of my mouth, a warm wet tongue pushing open my lips.

A few soft pinkish lights come on in the ceiling, lighting the auditorium slightly, and I squeal with delight that Gustav has reclaimed me. I suck at his tongue, desire mixed with relief surging through me, all stoked by the music and the darkness, and the figures flickering up on the stage. I don't want him catching sight of the woman dancing with Pierre, because there's no getting away from the unpleasant fact that she looks very much like the sketches and paintings I saw stuck all over the walls of the master bedroom in the chalet in Lugano – of Margot.

But just as I respond to Gustav, parting my lips for him, showing him I want him, and try to waltz him towards the exit, the pocket of his nineteenth-century frock-coat buzzes against my breast, glowing incongruously. He plants me on my feet to take the call.

'Don't go without me! Let me fetch my clothes from up there and pack up my cameras!' I yell into his ear, clinging onto his lapels.

'You are halfway through a commission, Serena. Much as I'd love to get my hands on you, it's impossible!' He jabs his finger at the phone to cut it off. 'I have to go. Stay here, finish the shoot and have that drink with Pierre.'

He unhooks me, kisses me again, then lifting his phone in farewell he backs across the room and out into the lobby.

I can't get my stuff from the wings because the show is drawing to a close. The woman and Pierre are still circling each other in the sensual moves of the dance of love. He is totally mesmerised. Their bodies dip in and out of the single spotlight, the other dancers reduced to prancing silhouettes in the shadows. I lift my camera, but instead of taking more shots I zoom in on the couple to get a better look. In the intermittent light it takes a while, the focus blurring then sharpening then blurring again, like eyes waking from a drugged sleep.

The small film crew on the other side of the auditorium barely glance at the engrossed couple on stage as they study their lighting and sound boards, but one of the cameramen, thinking I'm photographing him, lifts his camera to his shoulder to take a tit-for-tat shot of me.

Now Pierre and his partner are clear in my viewfinder. The woman's costume is deliberately bridal, I see that now, though ripped and ragged in the manner of Miss Havisham. The little flowers in her veil, threaded in her hair, are tiny and white, and the name comes to me. Edelweiss. The same Alpine flower that Margot held in her wedding bouquet in the most painful picture of all that I saw in Gustav's chalet.

Pierre looks lost as he and the woman turn sinuously in slow motion, their bodies locked together, her leg up round his hip. I lower the camera. I don't want to see any more. I shouldn't be here, because I'm certain now that she must be Pierre's new woman. I'm standing here looking at the cause of Polly's heartbreak.

I have to get out of here. The spectacle may declare itself as a show within a show, performers merging with punters, reality blurred.

But this is all too real to me.

To my relief more lights come on. The conductor makes a cutting motion and the music stutters to an unexpected finale. Everyone stops dancing, becoming mortal again as they turn to listen to directions.

The black-haired woman presses her palm on Pierre's chest to push him away. And as she spins into the shadows at the back of the stage I see that although she has the lithe, immortal body of a youthful goddess, her hand has the spindly fingers of an older woman.

CHAPTER TEN

It's nearly dark outside, and a freezing sleet is falling over Gramercy Square.

I'm late for my drink with Pierre but after the shock of seeing him up on stage earlier with someone so spookily resembling Margot, and the anxiety that Gustav might catch sight of her before leaving so rapidly, I'm actually glad of the delay. The crazy half-hour I've just spent, when I was pleasurably waylaid by two of the randy dancers, has helped take my mind off the whirl of the burlesque show, and I now have some extra footage in my camera as well as a guilty conscience.

I give a residuary shiver remembering what those naughty dancers did to me. Maybe it counts as going behind Gustav's back, but I only allowed them to seduce me and film it because I thought it would be a little visual treat to turn him on when he gets back from his trip.

The theatre cleared almost miraculously when the director called 'Cut'. The spectacle was extinguished, like a candle flame. The auditorium swifly emptied of orchestra and cameramen, the lights changed to flat, bright electricity. Pierre was gone, deep in conversation with his colleagues, and even the dancers, nimble at changing out of their costumes, had mostly melted away, swanning off the set in their wild combination of jeans, hoodies and full theatrical make-up.

As the performers bustled round me I tried to check today's shots, but it was no good. I'd have to wait till I could go over them with Pierre. So I went up on to the stage to find my clothes and other cameras, and without warning two girls pulled me behind a flimsy Japanese screen.

'Can we have some quick pictures with you, on self-timer? We want to celebrate being together a whole month! It would be so cool, the white, the black and the redhead!' One of them, an almost translucently pale girl with white-blonde hair and slanting grey eyes, was standing by my tripod, wearing nothing but her sparkly thong. Her friend, also in just her thong, was an Amazonian black girl with huge breasts and long, spindly legs like a gazelle. Their huge Bambi eyelashes, rouged cheeks and dolly-painted cheeks gave them the look of a cartoon.

I shrugged shyly, trying not to stare at their breasts. 'I prefer auburn, if you don't mind!'

'You're a trouper!' The pale girl expertly set up my camera and timer and pulled me over to a battered chaise longue beneath an old hatstand. The other girl draped a feather boa round my neck and then round her friend's throat, which brought our faces closer together, and as I heard the first whirring shots the pale girl framed my face with her white fingers to pull me close and flicked her tongue across my mouth.

The black girl cackled. 'I think I prefer the movie setting. That OK with you, madame photographer?'

As she took her turn to fiddle with my camera I wasn't able to reply because the other girl kissed me again, her hands stroking my breasts, which were still straining against the red corset. My mouth opened to the delicate flicking of her tongue.

'No. Keep the dress on her. I'm not having you going the whole way with her!' ordered the black girl, settling behind me so that I was sandwiched between the two beauties. She ran her long fingers up my legs and under the tattered red skirt of my costume while her pale girlfriend pushed herself closer to me, her white breasts rubbing against mine, her breath soft and scented as she moved her mouth down my throat and licked my cleavage, making my nipples perk up against the stiff whalebone.

The black girl had lifted my skirt and was grinding her crotch against my bottom. The scratching sensation of the tiny crystals of her thong against my bare crack made me wriggle. The thong slipped sideways so that I could feel her wetness against my skin, and at the same time her fingers hooked themselves inside me. She started to buck harder and pushed her finger in deeper, and as I began to gasp with surprise and pleasure the other girl cupped my breasts out of the corset and sucked them.

The camera whirred and filmed as the girls moaned and the first pulsating throbs reverberated through me, too quick, taking me by surprise. These girls knew what they were doing, and as I my head went loose with pleasure they withdrew their fingers and lips, leaned across me, squashing me between them, and proceeded to kiss each other's brightly painted lips as they fingered each other to climax.

'All on your one clever camera,' sniggered the black girl after a few moments. 'You'll email us a copy? How about a meal out with us one night, as payment?'

'Sure. I'd love to. I'll keep a copy for myself, obviously. All good for the portfolio!' I pulled my jeans on quickly under the dress, feeling the wetness snag on the denim as I buttoned them up. Yet another pair of knickers gone missing. 'Here's my card, girls, but I'll be seeing you again back here, I'm sure!'

'The boss man Levi said we could take the extra time with you after the show, but now he's waiting for you at the Gramercy. Don't want to keep him waiting. You can collect all your other stuff later, he said,' announced the pale girl, switching off all the lights. 'Hey, Miss Photographer. You sure you're not the sweet thing on his agenda for tonight?'

They laughed throatily, waiting for me to grab my coat and scarf before pushing me through the dark auditorium, out into the lobby. Then, leaving me on the theatre steps, they ran off down the street in the other direction.

Now I hurry round the garden square. No, I'm most certainly not Pierre Levi's after-hours pickings.

The fading winter light, the sharp edges and silhouettes of rooftops and trees, the railings, the dark clothes of the people hurrying past, all make me feel more dazed, not less. The throbbing behind my eyes speaks of the input from an extraordinary day spent in the midst of sumptuous, exquisitely organised chaos.

I don't realise until I step inside the grand hotel where we're to meet that my scarf is dangling round my neck and I haven't zipped up my green leather jacket. Even my hair is still coiled up as if I'm about to dance out in front of the footlights. I managed to take out the feathers before I left the theatre. But over my jeans I'm still wearing the ripped red dress.

I must look like Orphan Annie as I shuffle through the huge foyer, but the tall Scandi-guy behind the desk doesn't bat an eyelid that I seem to be wearing nothing but a red corset, my breasts barely concealed.

The butterflies doing somersaults in my stomach after my encounter with those girls should be for Gustav. I would much rather be meeting him here. I wish I could catch sight of him in a corner somewhere, see the amused arch of his eyebrows as his messy girlfriend tries to compose herself amongst the expensive, classy people mingling beneath the vast chandeliers. I wish his dark eyes were resting on me possessively like they did earlier, for Pierre's benefit. Most of all I wish I could just walk into his arms, continue with that long, wet kiss and forget everything else.

I pull my jacket round me to hide my theatrical costume, although it seems that anything goes in this bohemian haven. Anything goes even more when I tell the staff that I'm meeting Pierre Levi in the Rose Bar and they direct me knowingly.

I'm not going to get the few minutes I need to compose myself, because Pierre is already here, hitting some balls around the pool table. He doesn't see me at first. He looks slicker than ever. He's changed out of the period costume and into a dark-red shirt that sets off his dark Levi skin. The sleeves are rolled up and show the ripple of muscles in his forearms as he leans across the pool table and strikes a ball.

Pierre spots me and I shake my head when he holds the ball up for me to have a shot. I walk past him, past the dusty velvet chairs with the flickering candles, drawn by the flames in the old-fashioned grate at the far side of the room.

'Allow me,' he murmurs behind me, turning me by the shoulders. He knows those dancers were going to get their hands on me just now. I wonder if he can smell them? He reaches to take off my jacket, lifts the golden locket on the tip of one finger and presses it back against my throat. 'It's very warm in here.'

Pierre stares unashamedly at my revealed cleavage, pale and burgeoning out of the tight bodice, and I realise that several other people are staring at me too. No good wishing Gustav was here to see me. Best just to enter into the theatrical spirit. So I put my hand on my hip coquettishly, sweep my hand over my own contours as if this is exactly the effect I intended. Pierre nods approvingly as I sit down as elegantly as I can, arranging my scarf over my shoulders to cover the expanse of pale flesh.

'I ordered you a Watermelon Mint Martini, heavy on the Reyka vodka,' he says, flinging himself down in the velvet sofa next to me. He hitches his jeans up to get comfortable. 'The cocktails here are legendary, and very strong. You need it, after everything you've had thrown at you today!'

I raise the wafer-thin glass by its stem, letting the grassy pale liquid tip in the triangular cup. 'Thank you. Just one for the road, before I get on home. I could really use a long hot bath.'

'Oh, no rush, is there? Gustav's on his way to Canada, so there's no one waiting for you. As promised I am ready to face the firing squad regarding your cousin Polly. And I was hoping to take my time going over the shots you took today.'

'Couldn't I just send you the contact sheet? I can get it to you tomorrow morning when I've got all the cameras in one place.'

'You're very jumpy all of a sudden, Miss Folkes. I thought we were getting on like a house on fire earlier. Is jumpiness your default mode? Or is that the effect I have on you when we're alone together?'

'Not you. Your dancers,' I reply casually. 'They are a demanding lot, aren't they? The artistic temperament, I guess. I'm sorry I'm late, by the way.' I look down, switching on my camera. 'And I'm tired. It was a lot of input today. I just want to unwind.'

Pierre leans forward and takes the camera out of my hand.

'And what better place to unwind than here? And what better company than with me? So. I'd prefer to go over the images now, if that's OK. I want to see if you caught the essence of the show, my girls, the music, their costumes.'

'Any girl in particular? The one you were dancing with just now perhaps?' I ask quickly. 'I'm guessing dark and menacing leading lady is your type?'

'Ah, yes. The diva from the deep. I don't have a type actually, Serena. Anything with a pussy and a pulse will do. I mean, surely you can see that dark and menacing is the opposite of Polar Polly?' To my astonishment he is smiling, his tongue running lazily over his lower lip. 'Oh, loosen up, girl. I'm kidding!'

'You most certainly are not!' I stand up so quickly that some of the cocktail spills freezing vodka onto my chest. 'You really don't give a damn about my poor cousin, do you?'

'I just meant that when you're surrounded by gorgeous women it's impossible to choose. Black-haired temptresses, ice-white blondes, unruly redheads – someone has to come home with me tonight if I can't have the woman I really want.'

'Which isn't Polly. That's increasingly obvious. But she's had my back all my life. And now I've got hers. I promised her I would ask. Yes or no. Is your relationship definitely over?'

'A simple answer, for a simple question.' He keeps his eyes steady on me. 'The woman I want isn't Polly. And if she's asked you to see if there's any going back, the answer is no.' He looks down and starts to scrolls through my shots as if I'm suddenly invisible. 'Now, do you mind if I go back to the business in hand?'

'By all means take a look at the shots I've brought with me, but I think Polly deserves a little bit more of an explanation than that. I'm not done with you yet.'

I need to go to the bathroom all right, but not to freshen up. It's to stop me slapping his arrogant young face.

This guy is a monumental pain in the ass and the worst

thing of all is that just then he sounded like a cockier version of Gustav.

'Before you lay into me again, these are brilliant pictures, Serena. The management are going to love these.' Pierre stands up chivalrously as I return from the ladies and take my seat next to him – realising too late I should have sat down opposite him. 'You're hired.'

He holds his glass up, and reluctantly I chink mine against it. Reluctant, because I'm secretly pleased that the pictures have worked out. And there's a tiny flash of annoyance that Polly's upset is getting tangled with my work. Pierre sits down again, beside me but not touching me. I scroll silently back through the images, wonder if he's played the video of me and the dancers. But if he isn't going to mention it, nor will I for the moment. I take a deep breath, repeat the words 'focus, focus, focus', and decide to paddle to safer waters.

'Today got me thinking again. You remember we were talking about Venice at New Year's?' I remark as the sweet-sour liquid hits the back of my throat. 'Your theatre, the stage, the music, the costumes, the feathers, the girls, all reminded me of La Serenissima. The whole city as an operative back-drop. I can't wait to go back.'

'You have a trip planned?'

I take another sip. 'I've been asked to go over there for some clients called the Weinmeyers. Actually I have a meeting with them to discuss it tomorrow.'

'Ah yes. Ernst and Ingrid,' Pierre replies thoughtfully. 'Long-standing business acquaintances of my brother. I remember them in London. They're notorious in this town for being swingers, amongst other things. They make Gustav and Margot look like Hansel and Gretel. Not really suitable company. Maybe I should come with you. Keep you safe.'

'To the meeting?'

'To Venice. And source finery for my masquerades theme at the same time.'

'Oh, that would really thrill Polly, the way she's feeling at the moment.' My cocktail goes down the wrong way as I realise how quickly I've been steered off course, and I start to cough. 'She'd never forgive me.'

'I'm not talking about moving to the place. Just a short business trip.' Pierre thumps me between the shoulder blades, making my scarf slide off. He takes it with one hand and runs it under his nose. The way he's sniffing for my scent is an extraordinarily sexy, Levi thing to do. 'We could run the idea past Gustav, if that's what's worrying you. Make sure he's cool with the prodigal brother travelling to the most romantic city on earth with his girlfriend.'

I shake my head too sharply, and there's a nasty twang as a button on Pierre's sleeve catches my hair. 'Oh, no. I'll only go if Gustav comes with me!'

'Hold still.' Pierre laughs softly as he brings his arm down carefully and starts to pick at the strands stuck in the cotton thread. 'Your hair really is amazing. Sunset pouring over your shoulders.'

His face is unnervingly close. He has shaved again since we were at the theatre. Not a trace of the determined stubble that pushes through his brother's skin. And his cologne is very different, too. Heady, and musky, the kind that wraps around you like an embrace then gives you a headache.

We are so close that there's nowhere to look except straight back at him. 'Thank you,' I murmur.

The golden locket falls free. Pierre balances it on the pad of his little finger.

'From Gustav? Thought so. His own special method of branding you. This amazing hair of yours, though. Unbelievable what those bastards used to do, hacking it off when you were a kid.' He releases the locket, eyes raking over my face now.

The rescued strands of hair still curl round his fingers. 'Polly told me. Those people should have been lined up and shot.'

If this is a tentative rapport between me and Pierre, it's now or never. Polly has entered the conversation yet again, so it needs to be said. I sip my sharp citrus drink as a delaying tactic.

'Pierre. I know you keep trying to derail me, but I need to know that you'll do the right thing. She'll be on the phone as soon as I leave here, but please, don't make me be the messenger. Just be straight with her and tell her what you just told me. In a kinder way, if you can manage it.'

I sense rather than see his annoyance, the stubborn shift of his body on the seat, but I'm ready for it. I decide that sitting close like this is the best way to corner him.

'Will your desire to continue working for me be affected by my answer?'

I tilt my chin. My eyelashes are heavy with mascara still. My hair is sticky with hairspray, one or two pins still in place, but I have to get myself together now. Back into the character of Serena Folkes.

'It depends on the answer. I have to support my cousin so I'm going to have to work out how to balance this, but my ability to work for you remains the same.'

He laughs. He has the same wariness as Gustav, the same narrowing of the eyes as if there's a caveat to his laughter and he's not prepared to give himself up wholly to it. I realise I may have the upper hand. A horrible little voice inside me wonders if my straight-talking cousin Polly challenged him enough. Living with Pierre must be like living with a jumping jack.

'I don't want to say anything to jeopardise this reunion with Gustav', he mutters hoarsely after a pause, twisting the stem of his glass in those strong fingers. 'This could turn him against me again.'

'Why would issues with you and Polly have anything to do with Gustav?' I hitch myself a little, wallowing clumsily in the deep velvet sofa. 'Who is this other woman, Pierre?'

'That's where Gustav comes in. Because all roads lead back to him. And thence to Margot.'

Pierre looks steadily at me, but he's not smiling now. We're still too close. In fact, the sumptuous cushions seem to be tipping me back towards him, but I can't move. I don't want to break the fragile new confidence I feel we're approaching, but by forcing him to speak about Polly, and now Margot, we've veered into dangerous rapids.

'So Margot *is* still affecting you, just as Polly feared?' I keep my voice very low, unaware until too late that it sounds husky and seductive, too. 'Is that why you even have a dancer in your troupe who looks like her?'

'Be careful, Serena. You're imagining things. We don't want you becoming paranoid as well.' Pierre glances away from me just then. Lifts his hand in greeting to someone on the other side of the room who has hailed him. 'I thought you'd grasped what goes on in that theatre. Those dancers make a living out of assuming a false persona. They are painted, dressed, they move, they act, with the sole purpose of becoming someone else. So if by chance they resemble someone real, well, maybe I directed that girl to act that way, but ultimately that's all in the eyes of the beholder.'

He crosses one leg over the other and I glance down at the strong thighs, the way the fabric of his trousers is slightly stretched as he rocks his foot up and down.

'You can understand why I got that impression though, can't you? She was even wearing the same flowers in her hair as Margot carried in her wedding bouquet.' I hitch my dress up irritably. 'You're making me feel a fool.'

'The Miss Havisham look always makes for good drama. Look, we're all in a state of flux. Me, you, Gustav, Polly.'

Pierre shakes his head at me. 'Real life is tough enough, Serena, without superimposing things that aren't there. Why do you think I have loved theatre all my life? I told you before. And it's not just because of my scars. Because it's an escape. I can surround myself by fantasy, illusion.'

He waves his hand around in a florid, airy-fairy gesture and I have to snort at the pretension. 'I have to admit you were in your element on stage earlier. But don't dodge the issue. How has Margot ruined things with you and Polly?'

Pierre's hand slaps down on his leg. 'Polly went in head first, as soon as that awful showdown in the London gallery was over. Questions, questions – she could see how monumental that fight was. She thought I was behaving badly towards Gustav, which I was, you all know the reasons, but to understand what happened afterwards she wanted to know everything about Margot. And I mean everything.'

I frown, glance away from him towards the other guests milling about, chatting quietly. How many of them have a Margot haunting their lives, I wonder? 'Polly said it was the other way round. She said that it was you who went crazy, who brought Margot into every conversation. It was like she was in the room with you. In bed with you.'

Pierre starts shaking his head before I've finished. Puts his empty glass down on the carved wooden table in front of us. 'She shouldn't have started it. Because the more I told her about Margot Levi, the larger she loomed and the smaller Polly Folkes became. Polly's got it all going on, or she would if she wasn't getting so petty and tiresome, but Margot's a force of nature, Serena. She changed me from a boy to a man in just a few tumultuous months, however corny that sounds, and she could probably do it all over again. And what will really hurt you to know is that it was all the more intoxicating knowing that she'd come straight from my brother's bed to mine.'

He covers his eyes with his hand and is quiet for a moment. Every instinct I have at that moment makes me want to thump him, but I rein it in.

'That was more than five years ago. Polly is here now. Margot isn't.'

Pierre lowers his hand. I wonder what he was hiding just then, because there is only a curious blankness in his eyes. 'Polly has become invisible to me. Just like all the others, in the end. You see, there was something else unique about Margot.'

'I don't want to hear how phenomenal in bed she was.' I put my hand up like King Canute trying to stop the wave before it drowns me. 'Please, Pierre. Maybe that's enough.'

'Tough. You have to hear this. Margot is one of only two women in my life who hasn't recoiled at the sight of my burns.' Pierre picks up one of the tealights in its little crystal holder and holds it up very close to his face. 'You are the other.'

Is it my imagination, or has everyone suddenly left the room? The voices, the music, the chink of glasses from the bar, everything reduces to a low hum. Pierre looks at me, still holding the crystal holder, which casts flickering lights into his eyes.

'Me?' The word comes out in a long gasp. I swallow, and feel the sweat pricking under my hair. Under my arms. Inside the flimsy bodice of my dress. I shouldn't be sitting so close to this man.

'I'll never forget it, Serena. The look in your eyes when you saw my scars, or rather the *lack* of any reaction. The other women all try to hide the horror, to shrug it off, but by then it's too late. They can't hide the disgust, the regret. They're not sure how to handle me. I can see their eyes, casting about for the quickest way out. Any idea what that can do to a man's ego? Any surprise that I keep going through women like Chinese takeaways because I'm constantly looking for The One? Polly came closer, except that she failed that test the first time, too. I tried to get past that, make a go of it, but then there was you. You were so calm, and unfazed. You didn't know it, but that just highlighted how wrong Polly was for me. Unfair, but true. And you looked deeply, genuinely sorry.'

I take the crystal candle holder gently out of his hand and put it down on the table beside our empty glasses. I run my finger towards his neck, not quite touching the scar which snakes up out of his collar.

'You know why I understood something about the turmoil inside you, even though it's so different from my own? Because outward, physical scars are like the harm people can do to you inside.'

'Very philosophical. Very deep.' Pierre Levi catches my hand where it's hovering over his neck. His hands are big and warm and his fingers start to curl round mine. 'You mean your family?'

'They weren't my family. They were strangers who happened to find a baby abandoned on a doorstep, and were stupid and high-minded enough to take me in. But not sensible enough to give me up when they couldn't bond with me. But yes. They barely left a physical mark but sometimes I wish they had, instead of all the nastiness they left inside me.'

'I've touched a nerve. But I'm not sorry to discover a vulnerable petal beneath that stubborn exterior. We may be more alike than you think.' Pierre brings our joined hands to my mouth as if to hush me. 'No nastiness in there now, Serena. You're impossibly beautiful, inside and out.'

I blush as I feel my lips damp against his fingers, and, as the voices in the room start up again, grow louder and more insistent, I realise how this must look. Me being wooed in a deep velvet sofa by a devilishly handsome man who looks just like my boyfriend.

I push his hands away and reach for my scarf, trying to wind it round my neck as some kind of protection even though I'm too hot. I scrabble the scarf between my fingers like an old lady plucking at her shawl.

'And that's why Gustav is so lucky. His life, so different from mine. Not just because he gets to take you to bed every night.' Pierre keeps looking at me. 'Disrobing in front of a woman would never be a problem for him. He came out of that fire virtually unscathed, at least on the outside. Is it any wonder my admiration of him has always been tinged with jealousy?'

Pierre has triggered a longing for Gustav so physical it gives me a kick inside. I want to be lying on his chest, touching the torso tapering to that slim waist and sexy hips, stroking that line of black hair running from his solar plexus over his smooth, flat stomach, wandering like a tease down into his jeans.

It's a wake-up call, too.

'So Margot was unfazed by your scars, just like me, but surely that's because they gave her something to lie about, and helped her to steal you away?' I'm returning his stare as the images and scenes play out in my mind. 'And, scars or no scars, you are still the spitting image of Gustav, which must have made it easier for her.'

'To exchange one Levi for the other, you mean? So if she could do it in the blink of an eye, so could you, Serena. You like being with me. Come on. Relax. I won't bite. Unless you ask me to.' Pierre's voice is a soothing hiss, like the snake in *The Jungle Book*. His hands are round my neck to pull the scarf away again, brushing his fingers against my skin. 'I can see I'm going to have to work bloody hard to tempt you away from Gustav.'

'You won't ever succeed, Pierre Levi. So don't even try.' I try to wrench myself away, but he has me by the hair now, so subtly that no one else can see. I can't ignore the insistent tugging at the tiny sensitive roots. 'Let's get this conversation over with. What happened to you and Margot after Gustav chucked you out? And what did you mean, a few tumultuous months? I assumed, and I know Gustav did, that you were together virtually until you met Polly.'

Pierre lifts my hair away from the scarf and murmurs into my neck. 'It won't help you, and it won't help Polly.'

'Call it curiosity. And it may well kill the cat. But if I'm ever going to get the spectre of Margot out of my head maybe hearing this from you will be a start. I know I've replaced her in Gustav's life, but for Polly's sake I just want to know what she had that Polly and those other discarded women don't.'

'I think you know already. Margot had to be pretty sensational to keep a man like Gustav enthralled.' Pierre raises the menu to summon a waitress and orders two new cocktails. 'For me it was macho triumph that to pay him back I'd conquered my brother's wife, right under his nose. But she was the one who conquered *me*. I guess that's the effect she had on him, too, in the early days. Anyway, from that moment I was hers. Whether she intended that or not, she was stuck with me. Even in the cab careering down Baker Street, away from Gustav, she was straddling me. All over me like a wild cat. I was always hard when she was around. I'm hard now, talking about it.'

There's a sudden silence between us.

He shrugs. 'I told Gustav a slightly edited version of this when you left us in the bar the other night. Well, I didn't tell him that I still get hard talking about it, obviously. That's just for your benefit.'

'No wonder he didn't tell me much about your conversation.'

'So, the elopement. Well, there was me thinking she'd whisk me to Heathrow, perhaps fly to Lugano, but we went to a

221

hotel in Holland Park. Hardly the great escape, but the staff greeted her like an old friend. Certainly didn't blink when she dragged in this rumpled, overgrown schoolboy.'

'Another life she'd already set up,' I muse quietly, as the thought strikes me. 'She was already planning her escape.' Pierre rubs his hair into unruly tufts.

'She took me up to this room painted black, with a huge four-poster bed, all black satin sheets and drapes. She'd glimpsed my burns back at the house, told me that spectacular lie about Gustav starting the Paris fire, so I was already hers for the asking, but this was the first time she'd had the leisure to study them properly. I was young, Serena. Totally different from the man you see before you. I thought my brother was a monster. She was my world from then on. First love? I think so. Obsession? Certainly. I've never been able to put a label on my emotions, but I knew she was the woman for me when, like you the other night, she just studied my skin for a moment, and then kissed me. Every scarred inch.'

I bite my lip. The power of that gesture to a bitter kid like him isn't lost on me. Somewhere deep inside I'm wishing someone had done that for me a long time ago. Kissed away the scars.

'She kept me tied up in that room as her sex slave, basically, and I was more than willing. Because until her I was a virgin. Don't know if Gustav was aware of that little fact, love god that he is, but the burns, you know. Didn't give me a lot of confidence with the girls. Not until Margot. Anyway, she plied me with all this drink and drugs, Viagra, you name it, which kept my head in a fog and my cock up like a pole the entire time, and when she wasn't riding me she was whipping me. This amazing whip, all thick handle and knotted tails. My butt was her target. She went for it, whipped until red welts came up. You look as astonished as I was. Everything that had shocked me in the house in Baker Street became, with her, the promise of heaven. I still hated Gustav for exposing me to all that debauchery, but it was one rule for him, quite another for me, and I don't care how twisted that sounds. It's how it was with me and Margot. I would have taken any kind of treatment from her because she was my saviour. My world.'

The waitress is standing there with two cocktails on a tray, and some tiny dishes of nuts. My God. How long has she been there? How much has she heard?

The cocktail is something called a Ginger Fig, and I realise as soon as I've taken a big swallow that it is even more powerful than the previous one.

Pierre's voice has gone very soft. 'Being kept prisoner became normal to me. No one else would understand that. Not even you. Not even the mates I have now. The more sophisticated ones like Tomas would never believe the power that woman had over first Gustav, then me.'

'Shit. I should have been ready for that. Why did you have to mention Tomas, of all people?' I lift my glass and take another sip to hide the blush scorching my face. It's a mistake, because the cocktail practically knocks me sideways. 'I'm not sure how sophisticated he is, anyway. But I could wipe the smile off his face if Gustav had him thrown out for revealing the secrets of the club.'

'Go ahead and try it.' Pierre smirks. 'I must say I'm surprised at Gustav, letting you dance like a slapper in front of a room full of stags. Although I'm told the striptease was your idea?'

There's that vision again, the guy with the golden curls, running his tongue up me.

'What's the point of being in a big bad city if you don't experiment with what's on offer?' I realised I was enjoying the expression of undisguised admiration on Pierre's face. 'Gustav is wiser than any of us because he knew that having dipped my toe in that particular murky pond I won't do it again.'

'Not what Tomas said. He reckons if Gustav hadn't come into that smoking den – well. They'd all pay a king's ransom to see you dance like that again.'

'Just one last question, Pierre. I have to get this clear. I have to understand five whole years of hostility. Didn't Margot's delight in whipping you, and you getting a taste for it yourself, tell you that Gustav wasn't the monster after all?' I say, trying to keep a handle on this conversation. 'It just proves that she likes to whip, and be whipped. End of.'

'And so do you, don't you? But Gustav didn't feature any more, because of what Margot had told me about the fire. And it was easy to believe her, easy to follow her, because once we'd left that house, that past life, he was gone, just like that.' Pierre flicks his fingers disdainfully. 'Margot was the only person, the only thing in the world that could reach me. Sometimes we'd re-enact what happened back at the house but once she'd initiated me, got me addicted to it just like Gustav before me, then she'd take it further, with handcuffs, or blindfolds. She'd pretend Gustav had burst into the hotel room and she'd conduct an imaginary conversation with him. And then one night she told me we were leaving. I wonder to this day if it's because Gustav had discovered where we were.'

I collapse back in my seat and unwittingly slump against his arm, which has slipped off the back of the seat and onto my shoulder.

'He would have been looking for you. Not for her.'

'Well, he was too late. We got to New York, and then she kept me in this apartment for another six months or so. I never left. I didn't want to.'

We stare at each other as the restrained hubbub flows round us. We are so close that I can see the bustling waitresses reflected in the pupils of his eyes.

I clear my throat. 'Like Stockholm syndrome?'

He shrugs, looking away from me at something, someone, who isn't there.

'If that's when you fall in love with your demon gaoler, then yes. It's every man's dream, isn't it? A beautiful, wicked older woman who can never, ever get enough.'

We both pause and look up. The waitress is there again.

'We shouldn't be seen together.'

'Oh, I love a good intrigue.' Pierre is halfway through drawing some dollar bills out of his wallet. 'Look. You asked me to tell you about Margot.'

I close my eyes to hide the hot tears that have sprung from nowhere. 'I know, but now I want you to stop.'

'Nearly finished now.' He reaches up and strokes at a tear that has escaped from my eyelid. 'One morning I woke up to find her wearing a tarty red leather dress. She'd cut all her lovely long hair into a horrible bob and dyed it porn-star yellow. She looked like a Latvian hooker. Totally unrecognisable. She started whispering all this poisonous stuff about having ruined me as well as Gustav, that I would never find satisfaction, never want another woman after her. That was her plan all along, and now she was done with me.'

'Why couldn't you and Gustav have seen a mile off how deranged she is? You were just another scalp for her belt.'

'I think he saw it loud and clear, and wanted her anyway.' Pierre grins. 'But my excuse is that I was too young to get the measure of her. I just wanted her. I still do, Serena. If Margot was here, I'd take her right now in front of you. I mean it. And she'd go with it. She doesn't care where, who, what, when.'

There's a long pause. My fingers are locked around my glass. Our kneecaps are touching, our half-drunk drinks hovering in front of our mouths.

'Then let us pray that she never comes back,' I say thickly, not moving. Everything is sliding like a movie through my mind. The triumphant woman in those destroyed sketches from the chalet in Lugano is right here again. I can't bear to imagine her with Gustav, but I can see her using and abusing this young stud, her brother-in-law, changing him forever.

'I was lying there for hours. She sent two cleaners in to find me. They giggled themselves stupid to find me still attached to the bedpost. They made a half-hearted attempt to unlock the handcuffs but, when they couldn't, they decided to sample the goods themselves. Yes, that's right. First one, then the other. I had two naked, slutty, gymnastic Mexican cleaners crawling all over me!'

Pierre tips his head back against the velvet sofa and exhales a kind of gasping laugh. 'My God, Serena. It was like every sexual fantasy rolled into one. No wonder I'm ruined, just as Margot intended. No wonder I go cherrypicking. I'm incapable of fidelity. All the girls in that theatre wouldn't be enough. I'm an absolute shit and Polly's well rid of me.'

His legs are slightly spread, one hand resting on the back of the sofa. For the first time since I've met him he looks spent. Exhausted.

'God knows how I'm going to explain this to Polly, but I'll try.' I stand up shakily, step round the coffee table, pick up my camera. 'You're still living in that apartment, aren't you? That's why you never invited Polly round. And that's how Margot will always know where you are.'

Pierre stands up, too. He takes my hand. I let him hold onto it, because I'm feeling unsteady on my feet and because I want an answer. But instead of shaking it and dismissing me, he lifts my hand and kisses it in a direct echo of his brother's charming gesture. I catch envious glances around the room and realise with a shafting pang of unease that we must look like a couple.

'I call it my love nest. But that's not your business, or

Polly's. I stayed there because I'm the addicted loser around here, Serena. Which means that no woman is safe. Not Margot.' He grins wolfishly, as if to say there's nothing he intends to do about it. 'Not even you.'

He brings his mouth down to mine, starts to brush it over my lips. I can feel the heat of him, the heaviness of his body, and for a moment my head swims with confusion and, oh, God, the dart of desire.

But then I twist away, furious at him. Furious at myself, the tell-tale blood burning my face. I clutch the velvet sofa for balance, stoop to collect my other things and realise, too late, that I've left everything except this one camera at the theatre. I don't know what to do. I need my equipment, but I need to get away from this man far more.

Pierre lets his hands drop to his sides as if, despite trying to kiss me, he couldn't give a damn if I stay or go. I propel myself round the table and bang him on the chest.

'That didn't happen, Pierre. OK? And another thing. You called me "sis" earlier. I let it go, in the spirit of friendship. But don't ever call me that again.'

Pierre lifts his hands in mock surrender. 'I called you "sis" in the spirit of friendship, because who knows? We might be related one day. If my brother has any sense, Serena, he'll keep you close.' He gives a military bow, cocks his head to study me. 'Because be warned. If I can't have the woman I want, I might just have to take someone else's.'

CHAPTER ELEVEN

I can't evict the two dark-eyed men who circle me in the night. One is slightly taller than the other, slightly slimmer, but otherwise they are indistinguishable. When I sit up in bed, shrugging off sleep, they are standing over by the window watching me wake as the sun climbs higher over New York. I open my eyes wider and they blur and merge, part and merge again, like a drunken lens trying to focus.

And then one of them pushes the other out of the way and comes towards me, unbuttoning his shirt. The only way I'm going to be able to tell the difference will be from the body beneath. If it's Gustav, I will wind my limbs around him and make him take me, right there in front of Pierre.

If it's Pierre, if there are those raised, gnarled scars under his shirt, I will have to sit up and face Gustav, and confess that his brother came on to me in the bar last night and I was too weak to stop it.

'You will say nothing,' one of the men says, but I can't tell which one because the sun is so bright behind them, reducing them to black silhouettes. They are both on the bed now. I can feel the weight of their bodies as they sit down, the mattress sagging further and further, the floor rising up to bump at my bones. The men are so heavy that the bed collapses and now they are both pulling back the duvet and I'm naked, the way Gustav likes me to sleep. The silk negligees that he gives me are hanging in a row on the wardrobe door like pastel corpses.

I try to hide myself, fold my arms across my breasts, pull up my knees, cringe back in the bed, and when one of them grabs my wrist to clip on the silver chain I realise I'm still dreaming.

I never thought I'd say this, but thank God for the Weinmeyers.

After my perilous evening with Pierre Levi and a sleepless night apparently shared with both brothers, I could weep with relief and a kind of resigned recognition when I rush, late, into the Central Park Boathouse and see Mr and Mrs Weinmeyer sitting by the lakeside window, sleek, pale, matching in cream cashmere, and waiting for me. Their assured, expensive air is so calming, and weirdly so comforting. If they weren't such a kinky pair of perverts beneath the pearls and pinstripes, I could even think of them as family.

Mr Weinmeyer lifts a heavy paw, glistening with gold hairs, in greeting. 'There she is. Our homing pigeon.'

'My goodness, sugar, what's up? You are gorgeous as ever, but you look a little – dishevelled today? Like you're running a fever! The Big Apple finally getting to you?'

I fall into Mrs Weinmeyer's scented embrace and hold on to her just a moment longer than necessary before sinking into my chair.

'I'm so sorry I'm late, but I've just been incredibly stupid and disorganised, that's all. I left my iPad and all my photographic equipment except my main camera at this theatre where I was shooting yesterday, but when I went to fetch it just now the place was locked. Deserted. No lights. No sound. No dancers or musicians lining up outside. And no one is answering their phone.'

229

I pick up the menu and realise my hands are shaking. Mr Weinmeyer lowers it so as to look into my eyes. He rests his hand on mine. On his little finger he wears a gold signet ring.

'Perhaps because it's Saturday. Even New Yorkers need a break sometimes?'

Mrs Weinmeyer lays her pretty white hand on top.

'Old-fashioned pen and paper will do for today, Serena. We just want to take you on a little journey away from all this madness. How about Venice? By the way we've gone ahead and ordered. Smoked fish platter for us.'

'I looked up the menu online. I'll have macaroni gratin.' My stomach rumbles. I am starving, as it happens. 'And I'm fine. I love New York. But I've a lot on my plate at the moment. As well as the macaroni.' I stitch a smile on and realise that the adage about smiling making you feel better seems to work. 'And I am really pleased to see you!'

'After what we tried to make you do last time?' Mrs Weinmeyer pours ice-cold Chablis into tall, inviting glasses.

I take my glass gratefully. 'Well, I've been behaving fairly outrageously myself since then, haven't I, Mr Weinmeyer?'

He taps his nose and grins. 'What goes on at the Club Crème stays right there.'

Mrs Weinmeyer sniffs a little jealously. 'I'm sure whatever she was doing was sensational. But today we wanted you to feel more at ease, that's why we chose this place to meet. Halfway. We couldn't trust ourselves to be alone with you at our house.'

I chuckle conspiratorially and twist my hair into a thick plait to maintain some kind of control over the ringlets and tangles that have taken over like Sleeping Beauty's forest in the night. The word 'trust' reverberates. Gustav trusts me. It's the most important word in his vocabulary. I suspect more important than 'love'. And yet what have I done as soon as he's out of town for five minutes? Got myself into a situation with his brother where he thought he could pounce on me, that's what.

I pray that Pierre doesn't tell him, either, somehow put the blame on me when all I was doing was trying to get everything clear in my head about Polly and Margot. And about Pierre himself. I suppose I can't get hold of him to warn him off, but surely he won't risk this fragile new relationship by telling Gustav he came on to me. Because Pierre must know, as surely as I do, that if he did lie about it, Gustav would throw him out of his life for good.

I lift my glass to them. 'You were trying to educate me and, although I declined, it was a privilege. And it's given me a lot to think about, if I'm honest.'

They nudge each other and nod in unison. 'Well, if you're prepared to risk more adventure and debauchery, we'd like you to go to Venice. We thought, after you admired our goblets, that you'd enjoy a visit to our glass supplier in Murano. You can stay at our palazzo both as our guest and as our in-house photographer, because this is the year we want a record of our infamous Carnevale ball. We'll even buy you a brand-new camera and iPad if you can't get back your other gear in time for the journey. So then what we want you to do once the ball begins is photograph it in your own inimitable, voyeuristic fashion, all the music and colour and food and debauchery, because there will be tons of that, but also we'd like to see you let your hair down, too. Your pretty little cheeks are going pink at the thought of it, sugar. You fancy it?'

And so by Monday afternoon, when Gustav is expected back from Toronto, I've calmed down a little. Even become so used to the solitude that I'm relishing it. I have barely been alone since I left Devon back in October.

All Gustav asks of me is that I love him, and be true. Not so much to ask, is it? And yet I can't shake off the feeling that if I'd let Pierre kiss me the other night, as well as betraying Gustav I might also have jeopardised the next most important thing in his life: his relationship with his brother.

The weekend has passed with no answer from Pierre's phone, or Polly's for that matter, so I have spent the Monday in my home-made studio to take my mind off the simmering unease. I have to keep working. Having my main camera means I have edited, printed and enlarged the best shots from the theatre shoot, and my favourites, the ones that stand out artistically, are drying on the floor. They are still a little slick from the printer, so they need to be laid out flat, but before Gustav arrives I'll select which ones I want him to see.

I tidy away the pizza boxes I ordered in last night, prepare a supper of salmon in tarragon sauce and my first attempt at New York raspberry cheesecake, and then step into the bathroom to make myself scented and beautiful for Gustav. I pour oils and salts into the Jacuzzi, submerge myself under the bubbling water, staring out at the amber sky turning peachy over in the west, and force down the restlessness. I have to make tonight special, because soon I am flying to Venice and I can't wait to tell him about the details of the Weinmeyers' amazing offer. I've always wanted to be there for the fiesta time that is Carnevale there. And I want to persuade Gustav to come with me so I can show him the sexiest city on earth and take pictures of him and all the other guests going crazy at the infamous Weinmeyer ball.

As the hot water washes my hair and the jets buff up my skin, I can't resist touching myself with the soap, teasing it over my stomach and down between my legs. I'm so impatient for Gustav, I need him inside me, and soon I'm floating on the water like the mermaid he called me, my fingers working to pleasure me beneath the bubbles, working to push away all the confusion in my head, draining me of thought and deed and worry, and when at last I come with a single whimper I am calm, and excited.

As I wrap a huge white towel round me I sense, rather than hear, his presence in the flat. He's early. I haven't finished my preparations, or cleared my things away properly. Quickly I check my reflection, comb my wet hair straight down my back, no time to dry it, and tie on a pale-violet kimono splashed with waterlilies, cut with a low V-neck and deep slashes to the thigh.

'Gustav! That you?'

His bags are by the door. His coat and red scarf are draped over the sofa. The fire has been stoked and the candles and lamps lit around the sitting room. He's even switched on the music, my favourite Miles Davis CD. He's picked up the mood and run with it. So why doesn't he answer?

I pad back into our bedroom but he's not there, and not in the bathroom. Then I hear the thick rustle of photographic paper from the studio, and he's in there kneeling on the floor, looking at the prints.

Holding the biggest enlargement up in both hands and studying it.

'You never cease to amaze me, Serena. The brilliance of your pictures. How you give so much of yourself away somehow.'

I freeze in the doorway. Surely I'm imagining that ring of steel in his voice.

'Aren't you going to say hello?'

Still holding the enlargement he turns, and his smile doesn't quite erase something going on in his eyes. Anxiety or displeasure, I can't tell which. Either way it's not the unadulterated delight and welcome I expected.

He lays the print down on the table and beckons me to come over to him.

233

We look down at the large, bold image of his brother. I have played with the shutter speeds and apertures so that while Pierre stands in the middle of the stage with his hands held out from his sides like a showman, looking directly into the camera and in perfect monochrome focus, the dancers whirl around him like a startled flock of birds in perpetual flight, a white blur of movement with flashes of scarlet from a feather or the slash of an open mouth, the hint of outstretched limb or curve of breast.

After what seems an age Gustav's arm comes out and pulls me to his side.

'He looks like a circus master, directing everyone around him. It's brilliant.'

I realise what it looks like. Why he sounded so curt just now. That Pierre Levi is the centre of the universe.

'Well, talking of circus masters, later, when we've had our supper, before we go to bed, there's something I want you to do.'

I take his face in his hands and kiss him, feel the soft give of his lips as he asks, 'What's that?'

'The film.' I whisper the first thing that comes into my head, anything to distract him from the awkward subject of his brother. I curl my arms and legs around him. 'I've been so bored and lonely while you've been away. I want to see it!'

'Whoa, what film?'

Gustav stands and guides me down the corridor into the vast sitting room.

'You secretly filmed me in London, remember? After we'd been to the house in Baker Street and you showed me all the kinky dominatrix films there. That night you took the little nun's whip to me and showed me how it could liberate me. I've been naughty. I want to see it, Gustav.'

He crosses to the other side of the room to fill a big glass of white wine, and as he turns and studies my wet hair, the kimono already coming open over my breasts, the way I'm breathing fast, his black eyes glitter approvingly.

Push his brother out of your mind, Serena.

'What's brought this on?'

His voice is still a little cold as he hands me the wine. I take a big gulp of it to calm my breathlessness.

'I did something at the theatre after you'd gone. It wasn't part of the job, actually, and now I'm nervous because I think I may have stepped over the boundaries.'

Gustav pushes my hair off my face. Runs his finger thoughtfully under the delicate chain that suspends the golden locket. He turns it over, as if there's a message on the other side.

'Back up a moment, Serena. Should I be worried? I've only been away a couple of days and already there's that feverish look in your eye. What have you done? Or what has someone else done?' He grips my arms tight. 'It's that brother of mine. He's upset you. Was it when you went for that drink together? What's Pierre been saying?'

Gustav's fingers are hurting me as they dig into the muscles in my upper arm, but I don't want to move. I meet his eyes calmly, tip my chin to make sure he keeps looking at me.

The whisper of unease becomes a roar as I recall Pierre's eyes burning with this same expression. I take a breath, lift my hands and lay them flat over Gustav's heart.

He starts to run his hands over my shoulders, my throat, down towards my breasts, which are jumping now with my own heartbeat. He cups them, stares down at them, moulds his fingers round them. My nipples prick up keenly beneath the flimsy kimono.

'Like I said, something happened at the theatre.' I keep it very quiet, very low. 'But also I'm upset because it's all over between Pierre and Polly.'

Gustav relaxes a little. Perhaps I know more about him than I realised. How to arouse him, how to distract him. How

235

to make him react the way I want, without realising he's giving in.

He lets go of me, leaving dents in my arms, and pours a glass for himself. He goes to stand by the window overlooking Central Park.

'And you think watching the whipping film will help you?'

Something tells me to stay where I am. Something in my eyes, if I get too close, will give me away. I go to sit on one of the sofas that face him.

'The conversation I had with Pierre. It got a bit heated. To explain why he didn't want to be with Polly, we wound up talking about Margot.' I decide to risk getting a little more personal. 'Pierre's a pretty unsettling person, Gustav. He's too scarily like you. When I'm with him all I want is to be with you.'

'Thank God, because all I ever want, wherever I am, whoever I'm with, is to be with you, Serena.'

He holds his arms out to me. I run to him on my bare feet and lean my forehead against his chest so I don't have to meet his eyes.

'So that's it, really. We talked about Margot, how he's like he is because she got him addicted to her kind of sexual power complex. And although she tossed him aside in the end, she told him she'd ruined him for any other woman, and that's why he's constantly searching for a woman who'll match up. He's off the scale, Gustav. You should see him with those dancers.'

'I did.'

'He takes a different one home with him every night. Polly hadn't a snowball's chance in hell.'

Gustav leans his chin on the top of my head. 'I'm glad you're associating with my brother. Getting on with him, even. But that was a pretty intimate chat.'

'I don't want to associate too closely, actually. Turns out it

236

was too intimate.' I realise my hands are in a praying position as I pull away to gaze up at him. 'I feel awkward about it. I wanted him to explain why he's dumped Polly and all he did was boast about his sex life.' I hear my voice rising into a kind of mew. Is that the sound of a lie being told? 'And when he said Margot had spoiled him, that other women would never match up, well, could it be the same for you, too?'

'Don't insult me, Serena.' Gustav frowns slightly. 'At first, maybe even for most of those five years, that may have been true. Until you walked into my life. But I don't want to talk about Margot. I'm more interested in hearing what else is bothering you. Why you want to see the whipping film.'

'I went behind your back.' I push my forehead against his chest. 'I stayed late at the theatre and these girls persuaded me to – I think I need punishing.'

He sighs and leads me across to the sofa.

'What have you done, Serena?'

Tell him. Tell him Pierre tried to kiss you. It was only a silly flirtation. If you don't tell him, someone else could paint a very different picture.

I reach up and touch his beautiful face. It's so solemn. So reined in, despite the bandit beard that shadows his cheeks. He knows how much I love it when he looks rough and ready. The palm of my hand lets the bristles prickle as I stroke him.

He catches my hand and kisses the palm, then he pulls me hard up against him. I settle myself onto his lap so that the kimono falls open and he can see that I'm naked underneath. Now there's no mistaking his arousal. The hardness pushes against me.

'I'm no good without you, Gustav. I do things, I lose things – Anyway, these two dancers. They frog-marched me into making this girlie film but they roped me into the action so in fact it was me they were playing with. I've got this on my camera and they're going to pay me with a dinner out one night. First I thought it could be a nice little welcome-home gift for you. You said you could handle the idea of me trying it with a girl, so long as you could watch. But now I'm worried because I went ahead without you being there.'

Before he can reply I load the DVD player with the film and hope this has deflected any more talk about Pierre.

The flat screen lights up his face and I watch his expression as he watches the film. His mouth relaxes into a smile as he sees me being kissed and fondled by those two gorgeous dancers. The wet sounds of the kissing, the wandering fingers and the growing moans sound very loud in the quiet apartment. I recognise the flush of arousal as he watches it to the end.

He rubs his eyes. 'I think you may have crossed a boundary we hadn't thought of here. This was in the theatre? On the stage? Where anyone could have seen you?'

I burn red, not sure what he's getting at. 'Well, yes.'

'So Pierre could have seen this going on?'

'He'd gone into a meeting. Something about a press release. The place was deserted. The girls were begging me!' Nevertheless I go cold. Pierre could well have seen the girls and me cavorting. Or he could have seen the video on my camera at the Gramercy when I was in the ladies.

'I hope you're right.' Gustav stares at the blank screen. 'Getting you closer to Pierre does *not* include him seeing you naked.'

'You see? This was supposed to be a gift for you, some kinky lesbian footage to turn you on, but it's backfired, hasn't it? I've been so reckless. That's why I need punishing, Gustav!'

Gustav stands up again, lets his fingers trail through my hair. His erection is pushing against his jeans. I reach for him, but there is still a stain of darkness across his eyes, in the sharp angle of his nose and jaw, the tightness returning to his mouth.

'A good spanking will sort you out, will it?'

I shrug, aware of how adolescent that looks. 'Maybe just watching the video will do the trick?'

Without another word he puts his glass down beside mine and marches out of the room. I perch on the edge of the seat, shivering with tension.

The darkness smothers the trees and lakes down in the park as I wait, leaving a backdrop of sparkling lights over on the East Side. And then Gustav is beside me again, sitting down on the sofa. He has the disc in his hands. And also the little whip.

'You sure about this, Serena?' He pulls my face towards him and kisses me very briefly on the lips, but enough to get my senses prickling up on red alert. 'You want to watch the film of me whipping you? Making red stripes on you?'

'I'd rather you showed it to me than it fell into someone else's hands. After that I want you to destroy it.' My voice is very quiet in return. 'And then we can go to bed and I can show you how much I love you.'

'My girl the voyeur. Now she wants to watch herself.' A flicker crosses his face. I tense up with fresh anxiety, but I see that he's biting back a slight smile. 'I certainly don't like it that Pierre and Polly's troubles are getting you all worked up like this. But I'll have to go along with what you demand and spank the worries out of you instead.'

He slots another disc into the machine. The screen flickers into life.

Gustav's voice on the screen murmurs, 'Are you ready?'

I'm the girl in the film, spread-eagled on the huge sofa in his drawing room in London. The girl lying there looks so young, what little I can see of her. Her dress is wrinkled up over her hips, laying her bare. It's a relief when Gustav drapes a white cloth over her face. I don't want to see her eyes. I knew nothing then. I barely knew him. All I had was my naivety, a dose of determination and my talent.

On the screen Gustav takes some pretty little glass and ceramic bottles and pops the corks from them. I remember how that felt, how every touch of those creams set me on fire. My stomach coils with sudden, unbidden fury. Are the ointments Gustav is using in the film the same as Margot used on him once upon a time? Gustav on the screen is smoothing cream over my thighs, into my bottom, up between my legs into all the hidden crevices. Cream that Margot may have swiped her fingers through to smear his body when he was her husband.

I wriggle on the seat as I watch. I have to get that image out of my head. Margot went with Pierre, remember. Margot and Gustav hate each other.

The remembered heat from the creams and the whips is already seeping through my skin, deep into my muscles, getting hotter the deeper it seeps. Gustav sits very close to me on the sofa. The only part of him touching me is the tip of his finger, running up and down my neck under my tangle of hair, hooking into the little chain holding my golden locket.

I have to get that image, Margot's fingers in the cream, on his body, out of my head.

'Can you remember how green you were that night? Yet you had already shown me, the world, that behind that cute freckled face was a hard-eyed voyeur. All you needed was to enact what you'd seen other people do. You loved it, you low-down little slut.'

I moan and press myself against him. The sounds on the screen are muted. No words. A whisper of music in the background. The flicker of candlelight. The clink of the ointment bottles.

The Gustav beside me pushes me down onto my stomach. 'Lie down, Serena. You're like a cat on tacks. You need calming down. These ointments will do the trick.'

With a low laugh he dangles the silver chain in front of

me, then clicks it onto my bracelet, winds it several times round both wrists. He is here with me now, and he's taking charge. Relieved excitement twists inside me as he attaches the chain to the end of the sofa. I allow my gaze to linger on his long legs. The hard bulge behind his zipper.

As on the screen, which I can just see if I twist my head, there's the pop of a bottle stopper here in the room, and Gustav's hands in the film are pushing my dress up, and in real life they are peeling away the kimono, and massaging sweet smelling oils into my legs. He's being gentle, but his hands move sensuously, his fingers lingering and probing, exploring and stroking, far more intimately and deeply than he did that first time. The lotion is setting me on fire. I can almost hear it sizzle, piercing the tender skin, but although I clench my bottom in pretend protest I keep quiet while the girl on the screen screeches out crossly, something about chilli.

'My beautiful girl. You really want me to slap you? Or shall I find some props to do it with? A slipper, perhaps? Or one of my ties?'

I try to twist round to see if he's serious.

'That's not in the script.'

'There is no script. Just what I tell you to do.' He pushes my face down into the cushions. Now I can only glimpse a corner of the screen. A pair of white legs. A young, plump bottom waiting to be striped with punishment.

Gustav pushes my legs open and goes on massaging the cream right in, up and in. Every sense is magnified. As well as the heat and scent of the creams soaking into my skin, there's the strong, almost sickly perfume filling the air. At last, thoughts of everyone else, his brother, his ex-wife, my cousin, they all fade and pop, like a trio of burst flash guns.

On the screen I've gone very still. I try to look at that girl dispassionately. But how can I, when the sight of her is turning on the voyeur in me? So much has happened to that other Serena since then but, I think with another wriggle of excitement, so much still is happening.

I try to focus on the film. I demanded he take it out of its hiding place, but a new and disturbing thought insinuates itself: if he showed this film to anyone else, or if someone discovered it, Pierre for instance, it could be dynamite. Serena Folkes as an installation. Whether that's a good thing, maybe for future publicity, remains to be seen. For now I want it just for me. This is my therapy. It worked before, when I wanted him to thrash memories of my miserable childhood out of me. Now it's thrashing away unwelcome thoughts of his brother.

But what exactly does *he* think he's teaching me?

As his long fingers swipe and wipe the cream until the whole area is alive and throbbing, I try to find the answer to that one. As before I'm feeling stoned and woozy, the heady scent of the cream curling up my nostrils into my brain, filling it with fog. The rest of my body feels floppy and weak. There's only one part of me aching and burning.

I wonder if I've dropped asleep, because nothing is happening. On screen there is vague movement. He's turned the sound right down now. My eyes are closing and Gustav seems to have wandered off.

But just as the arm on the screen rises silently so there's a rush of air in the here and now as Gustav's arm goes up. Here it comes, that delicious wasp sting as he slaps me hard on the butt, thrusting me forwards over the suede sofa with the force of it, making me squeal and squirm. He slaps me harder on the same spot and stinging heat from the blow sends a shaft of twisted pleasure through me.

That sharp whisk of air, then a handprint of fire on my buttock as it lands. The stinging goes deeper this time, radiates away from the original soreness, burns inside me, makes me twitch. I can feel myself closing up tightly. The tentacles

242

of pain touch me everywhere. I twitch and groan, unable to control my own reflexes now.

'I've got your little nun's whip right here, Serena. Ready to do this all over again?'

'Yes! Give it to me!' I struggle at the chain round my wrists, but that just makes it tighter, the silver chain biting into my wrists. 'I deserve it all!'

I hear him testing the whip on the palm of his hand for a moment. Then it comes down on my other buttock and the pain daggers straight up me.

He chuckles softly, whips me again, that quick, vicious whip lashing down. I am smarting with the lashes. I know I'll be striped with thin red welts. I strain at the silver chain binding my wrists, welcoming the nasty thrill releasing me, the hot darts of pleasure shooting through.

As I struggle, the golden locket gets caught in my hair so that, every time I move, my hair draws it tighter around my throat. I try to speak but the volume on the screen suddenly turns up to full, the voices and the gasping, the whipping and the background music all drowning out my gasping attempts to breathe.

I don't care any more. This is a different kind of stress. How complicated my life has become since October. Now I have genuine guilt and anxiety to add to the mix. Everything I've done and said with and without Gustav. Stepping way out of line talking so intimately to his brother. Letting Pierre think he can lean in and kiss me.

The spanking feels so good. I feel released. Confident in the man doling this out to me. Confident that I can ride any small storm I may have caused. Confident that maybe, just maybe, I am beginning to get this lovely man where I want him.

Another slap, stinging and hot on my rump, sizzling through me. I was waiting for it, I knew what was coming, the shock of the slap itself, the blood rushing to that one burning place, and the lovely afterglow. There will be the brand of five red fingers on me, and thin red lines from my little nun's whip smacking the naughtiness out of me.

Just as in the video Gustav is silent amidst the furore, he's behind me, above me. He smacks the other cheek hard until the heat prods and probes everywhere, fingers of fire and pleasure inside and out.

Just as in the film I lift my sore, tender bottom up in the air, and hear a low grunt of laughter.

'Such a naughty girl. This is for all you've done since we came to Manhattan. The Weinmeyers, the Robinsons, the Club Crème. Worst of all, going for intimate drinks in glamorous cocktail bars with other men. With my brother, just to rub salt into the wound.'

Every inch of my bottom is sore and tender. There are spasms inside me now, deep between my legs, hungry spasms of pleasure and wanting.

He doesn't know. Oh, Gustav doesn't know and I need to tell him. But now he's pushing my head into the cushion, snagging the golden locket even tighter around my throat, a glittering ligature, forcing me to take short gasps, loving the free, natural high from the lack of oxygen. I feel the dip of the cushions as he kneels on the sofa behind me and the lack of air is making me hallucinate now, reminding me of my drunken fantasies after my session at Club Crème and my dreams while Gustav was away, the two brothers coming to my bed, pressing on the mattress until it reaches the floor, pulling the duvet off me, unable to tell the difference, which one will it be, which one is going to take me in front of the other?

I squeal as someone, one of the brothers, lifts my bottom towards him, spreads open my legs. Through the noise and the music I hear the rip of his zip. His breath rasps hot, burning hot, on my neck. Who is it? Who is it? My pulse beats frantically as if hammering to get out. One of the brothers slides his mouth down under my ear, his lips dry at first, then getting wet as they linger over the spot. The tip of his tongue runs under the chain of the locket, touches my pulse, echoing the push of him between my legs, hitching my hips so that I bang up against him.

His fingers play over me, into all the slippery creamed soreness, feeling inside to open me, feeling the wetness, and then he's in there, which one is it, which brother is it, he's long and strong and hot and hard and pushing, pushing my face deep into the cushions, the golden locket a sharp little nub pressing against my throat, the silver chain snaking from my wrists across my back towards him, our mutual crescendo matching perfectly as he hammers the nonsense out of me and I cry out his name.

We lie there, panting crazily, my face still pressed into the cushions until he rolls me in a tangle of limbs to face him. Gustav hangs over me, unhooking strands of my hair from the golden locket. The metallic hidden object slides from side to side as he shakes it.

'What is in there, Gustav? I walk around with that little sound knocking against my clavicle all day. Why won't you tell me?'

'I will open it for you when the time is right. I like the thought that in the meantime it's driving you mad!'

He strokes my hair off my face. I lean up to kiss him, breathe him into me.

'Why not now?'

'You still have to earn the right to see what's inside.' His eyes crinkle slightly at the corners, his face shadowed in the candlelight as he opens his mouth to say something.

And then the door buzzer goes.

'Ignore it!' I screech, trying to sit up. Gustav frowns impatiently and releases my hair, but not my wrists. He holds me

245

down for a moment longer. The buzzer goes again and he stands up reluctantly and lazily zips himself up, leaving me sprawled in my half-open kimono, the golden locket half-strangling me, the silver chain still fastened.

There's a quiet murmur of voices and I give a silent sob of relief that it's not Pierre but one of the doormen, handing Gustav my camera cases and iPad. Gustav thanks the guy and turns to me, the door still open behind him, his eyebrows raised questioningly.

'He says your equipment was just delivered to reception. They didn't leave a name.' He hands me the iPad. 'But they said to be particularly careful with this. You lost your stuff? What is the matter with you?'

'I didn't lose it. I was going back to collect it.' I run my fingers round my sore wrists and take the iPad off him. 'But everything was delayed by that girlie video, and then the drink with Pierre. They locked up the theatre over the weekend with my things inside.'

The iPad must have been switched on all this time. The battery is dead. I carry it into the bedroom and plug it into the charger.

As I come back out into the salon the peace is shattered by a manic flapping in the doorway as if a bird has been trapped in the building. 'Where is she! Where's my beloved cousin?'

Polly's voice is high and reedy with anger as she pushes through the door that Gustav has not yet closed. She lurches through the hallway and into the sitting room. I pull my slippery kimono over my damp nakedness and take a faltering step towards her.

She looks even thinner and paler than before, not helped by the fact that instead of her usual neon colours she is dressed from top to toe in funereal, baggy black. She stops dead in the middle of the floor and is staring past me at the TV screen. Gustav has paused the film so that all there is in the centre

246

of the wide screen is my white bottom, striped with red, the fuzzy outline of a whip shivering down onto it.

'My God! It's even worse than I thought!' she gasps, her hands up over her white face. She looks like Oliver Twist in the oversized cap and baggy raincoat, her legs bare, her satin ballet pumps stained by the rain. 'You're all at it! All whipping the living daylights out of each other, and it's not just some kind of artistic illusion, either. You're all masochistic freaks!'

'Calm down, Polly,' says Gustav. 'You can't come in here shouting the odds. Pierre said you weren't with us at the Library Bar the other night because you were in Boston.' He comes up beside her and takes her arm. She stiffens, but she doesn't shake him off.

'Serena knows I never went to Boston, but you'd all love that, me out of town so you can all have a good laugh at me.' Her eyes slide from the screen to me, her face hectic with fury. 'Look at you, all ravished and undone. That the way Pierre left you after your night at the Gramercy Hotel?'

'What are you talking about?'

'You've ruined everything, Rena! He was the one. You saw us together at Halloween, all loved up. How could you come on to him?' She takes a step towards me, but her skinny legs give way so that she slumps down in the middle of the rug. 'I asked you to talk to him, not sleep with him! You should have seen them, Gustav, your long-lost brother plying your girlfriend with cocktails. Playing with her hair. Kissing her!'

'He didn't kiss me! And I was only doing what you asked me to do.' I slide across to crouch next to her on the floor, horribly aware of my brazenly skimpy kimono and the sticky scent wafting off my legs. 'You won't like what he had to say, though.'

I glance up at Gustav. That stony look on his face has crystallised. He closes the front door very slowly and comes to stand beside the fire. I notice him quickly unclipping the silver chain from the sofa, but it's still attached to me.

'Serena has told me they met for a drink to go through the day's shots. She's told me what they talked about.' His voice is deep, calming. 'Your cousin and I have learned through bitter experience not to have any secrets.'

I smile at him anxiously from my lowly position on the floor, keep my eyes on him, but he doesn't smile back. I rely on that voice to keep me grounded.

I turn back to Polly, stretch out my hand, but she flinches away from me. Her eyes are almost transparent with rage. Cold fingers crawl up my spine.

'What has Pierre been saying?' I ask her quietly, kneeling up, pushing myself at her, trying to flash a silent warning at her. 'Whatever it is, it's lies.'

'Nothing directly. We don't speak, thanks to you!' Polly snatches the hat off her head and throws it to the floor. With her hair shaved so close to her perfectly shaped head she looks like a chick just hatched. 'Because you kept putting off talking to him for me, I was reduced to skulking outside the theatre.' Polly shifts away from me, scrabbles in her big bag to bring out her phone. 'I saw the two of you sitting on the steps the other morning. I got inside, saw you both flirting up on the stage, you dressed up like a harlot, him prancing about like he owns the place—'

'But he does own the place,' Gustav remarks quietly. I so wish he was over here, next to me.

'No, he doesn't! He hasn't got any money! He doesn't even have his own chauffeur, like he pretended in London. He lives rent-free in a SoHo flat owned by Mrs Margot Levi. I've been doing some digging, you see – why didn't I do it before? – and that theatre was bought by some film people to use as a sound stage. He's a bit-part actor who buys dresses!'

'I've got this information down on my iPad from our briefing, Polly. There's a little more to it. He never said he owned it, though I admit he implied it to begin with. He may not have much money of his own but he's refurbishing the theatre for a production company. Designing it. Directing the show. Everything.'

Gustav clears his throat. He's stroking his chin, but his hand, the silver chain still wrapped around it, is trembling, making the metal glint in the fading light.

'Polly, you've misinterpreted some perfectly innocent situation. From what I can gather it's not Serena you should be yelling at, it's my brother. God knows he's got some answering to do when I get to him. He's misled us, even if he hasn't exactly lied. He's obviously not as successful and influential as he made out. That's why he keeps insinuating that he needs money. And what's he doing living in Margot's flat?'

'He told me that, too.' I close my eyes, horribly aware how cosy that sounds. 'That's where they lived when they first arrived in New York, and that's where Margot left him. As far as I know she's never reappeared, but he said staying there was all part of the hold she had over him. Maybe she still has?'

'I know the flat. I gave it to her. That's why I am living at the opposite end of Manhattan now.'

Gustav and I stare at each other across the vast empty space. He said 'I', not 'we'.

'Forget about fucking Margot! What about little Rena and your brother?' snaps Polly, hectic flushes streaking her cheeks.

'Stop it, Polly!' I reach out and shake her. Her eyes are huge and blank and unseeing as if she's drugged. 'If you've been staking out the theatre, you'll know he takes his pick from a bevy of girls, a different one every night.'

'Or so he says!' she screeches. 'He never wanted to do it half the time! Even when things were going great I thought it was because of me, so to comfort myself I put it down to those awful scars he kept hidden away. But this is all far more messed up than I realised. I'm pretty certain now there were always other tarts on the side, but then you, Gustav, came into the picture and now, whoops, there's Serena, who's ruined everything!'

I fling my hands in the air helplessly. 'Stop stalking him. Walk away with your head held high. Don't let a bastard like that come between us, for God's sake.'

She curls herself into a ball and bangs her forehead on her bony knees.

'I may as well show you the evidence, then you can both decide what to do.' Polly jumps to her feet and rushes at Gustav as if he is trying to escape, waving her phone in the air. 'Look at these pictures. How about this for having no secrets, Gustav! Not only were they kissing at that hotel, for all I know they got a room, but did you know that Pierre and Serena are sloping off to Venice for a cosy jaunt? Did you know that your brother is planning to steal your girlfriend?'

I'm too late to stop her. She has pushed her phone under his nose, and Gustav is staring in horror at it, his face hollowed by the light cast from the screen.

'Is this why you've been so cagey and strange ever since I got back, Serena?'

I shake my head with a strangled cry and try to get up, but I only get as far as my knees. I look like a nun, praying for forgiveness. Gustav slowly turns the phone towards me. It's a blurred close-up of Pierre's dark head bent over mine in the Gramercy Bar three nights ago. Gustav scrolls along the next one. A close-up of Pierre's lips on mine.

I have to say something, quick. 'It's not how it looks. He was fixing my scarf round my neck, and he went to kiss me goodbye, and he misfired, that's all.'

Gustav's face goes deadly white. He hands the phone back

to Polly and opens the door. She averts her head haughtily and marches out onto the landing as if throwing this little tantrum has given her some long-needed strength.

'The camera never lies, Serena,' she shoots back at me. 'You of all people should know that, no matter how clever you are with an image or how many tricks you pull. I'm not a photographer. I just aimed my phone at you and took the pictures, right while it was going on. You weren't trying to talk to Pierre about me, or get him to come back to me. You were kissing him! How tacky does it get?'

'Polly, come back! Why are you doing this? I'm your family, for God's sake! Your cousin!'

She pushes the button on the lift outside, her oversized coat wrapped like a great batwing around her frail body.

'You were a foundling, remember? You're not my real cousin!' She shouts as the lift doors open. 'You are nothing to me!'

The words punch all the air out of me. I crumple down onto the floor, where she was sitting just now, but she is gone. Those are the very words I heard over and over again when I was a child. I thought they could never hurt me again.

I manage to heave myself onto the sofa, pull the kimono round me. My nakedness feels shameful. But it might just melt him. I'm shivering, even though it's warm in here. Gustav steps towards me, and I look up eagerly, but he's looking at me, just like Polly did, as if he's never seen me before, or worse, as if what he sees he detests.

I grab his hands, but they are dead in mine. *Think, Serena, think*.

'Margot is in Pierre's head, making mischief. That's all this is. But I don't give a damn about his twisted motives. He did give me a rather close kiss, but I pushed him off! I was trying to help Polly and I thought it would help you, too.'

'You said yourself, we can't trace every bad thing that happens back to Margot.'

251

'And we can't let one grainy, misinterpreted photograph destroy everything either.'

Gustav lifts my wrist and I think he is going to sit beside me, and put his arm around me. But instead he unclips the silver chain, winds it quickly round his knuckles and goes to pick up his coat which is still lying across the sofa.

'I should have known he'd got to you when I saw that magnificent photograph of Pierre, standing on the stage like the king of the world. Something has been wrong with you ever since I got back this evening and it takes your poor troubled cousin, who you were supposed to be helping, to show me the light. How could you, Serena? With my brother, of all people!'

I curl up in a ball, my head in my hands. 'It's just a picture, Gustav. They're all just pictures. It's my job, remember?'

I hear him shake out the red scarf. I look up. His head is bent as he starts to wind it round his neck. His aquiline nose, his profile so fine. So hard and unreachable.

'A job which you have started doing just a little too well. I wonder if it's affecting your judgement. The all-seeing, all-knowing eye behind the lens.' He draws the knot tight around his neck and moves towards the door, picking up his coat and dragging it behind him.

'I'm just capturing people, and moments. But if it upsets you, I'll stop!' I kneel up again. 'I'll cancel the commissions, all those portraits and family groups and Club Crèmes and threesomes and voyeurs' delights, and I'll concentrate on my personal project. "Windows and Doors" I was going to call it, remember? I've had it planned ever since the London exhibition opened. I'll do anything to stop one picture jeopardising what you and Pierre have.'

'Stop avoiding the subject, Serena! Ironic that this all stems from the one picture you didn't take yourself!' He opens the door as if it weighs a ton. Everything is happening in slow motion, yet much much too quickly. 'Pierre and I have all the time in the world to sort out our differences. We are brothers, so there's always hope. What's jeopardised here is you and me.'

Turn around, Gustav. Stop talking crap. Turn around and make this all go away.

All I can see of him is the back of his head. His strong shoulders. His shirt, one tail sticking out of his dark-blue jeans. He pulls on the coat slowly, as if it's hurting him. Pushes his black hair out of the collar. His lovely hands, resting for a moment on his ears as if to blot everything out.

'I don't know what to think any more. I've got nothing to say to you.'

'Nothing to say? How about coming out with it and saying sorry, Serena, for all my grand words I don't really trust you? That I didn't mean a word of it when I said I wanted to set you free? That's what you should be saying. Not turning your back on me just because my demented cousin thought she saw me kissing your brother! Don't you see how ridiculous that notion is? Haven't I told you enough times how much I love you and want to make you proud of me?'

Gustav's hands hang lifelessly in the air as if they've somehow betrayed him, too. 'Can you hear yourself? You sound just like him. This is hurting me, it's just like our own vile version of that stand-up row in the gallery in London. Accusation and counter-accusation, and all shrouded in uncertainty. I can't take it, Serena. I won't take it.'

I stand and start to walk away from him towards the bedroom. Then I stop and wheel round again, burning with fury.

'This is nothing *like* that showdown with Pierre! That was you and him rehearsing years of resentment and misunderstanding fuelled by an evil bitch whose main aim in life is to harm everyone in it. I stood beside you in that gallery and told Pierre that every word spewing out of his mouth was wrong and twisted, and it wasn't hard for me to do that, because I love you, and I'll do anything to show the world what a fantastic man you are.'

'A man who never learns who he can trust.' His face remains expressionless as granite. His black eyes slide away from me as he shakes his head. I take a step towards him, across the echoing poured-concrete floor of our home.

'But you can trust me! We've moved way beyond all that!' I wave my hand at the door where Polly has just rushed out like a bat out of hell. 'This is me, Gustav. You, me and a pathetic photograph of a bungled conversation and a clumsy goodbye in a bar, taken by a girl who's been rejected and is beside herself with jealousy. You knew I was meeting your brother for a drink. You encouraged it! And yet you still believe I went behind your back and kissed him?'

When he still doesn't reply something shuts down, goes numb and cold inside me. The same feeling I had as a child when nobody, ever, would listen. The world is suddenly bleached of colour. The maelstrom of the past few weeks has halted like a broken clock. If Gustav is telling me that one apparent error of judgement, one drink with one man, has cost me everything, that he can shut me out that easily, then whatever I say won't sway him.

I leave the door open for Gustav to come into the bedroom and take it all back. I have nothing to apologise for. I spent the first half of my life wishing those closest to me would love me, and the second half knowing they never would. I'm not going to stand here and beg him to trust me when I've done everything I can to show I'm solid.

Meanwhile it feels wrong being half-naked. I pull on some clean clothes. I can't stand this hostile atmosphere a minute longer. We need distance. How far, how long, I have no idea. Maybe a day. Maybe forever. I start throwing some other clothes into a bag.

I glance out of the window, over the skyline that I will always associate with our brief life together. But it all looks fake now. Precarious, like a painted backdrop. How did I ever think this magnificent palace could be my home?

I have to get out of here. It's one thing observing Gustav's fight with his brother. It's quite another having him turn his anger onto me. If he'd listened to anything I've said about my childhood he'd know that I'm not a coward, but I won't stand and be attacked either.

Individual thoughts rise to the surface like cream curdling. All I've done in the last three months is dance to his tune. All I've done since Christmas is try to help bring him closer to Pierre. As for Polly – I can't even think about her.

I catch sight of myself in the mirror. My hair is still damp. My face is scrubbed and unmade-up from the bath. The only things adorning me are the silver bracelet and the golden locket. I yank at them, try to break both the chains, but of course they are unbreakable. Only the best, strongest metals for Gustav Levi.

Then I hear the heavy clunk of the front door, and silence. He really has gone out and left me.

I fasten my bag with the theatrical zip that always heralds a dramatic exit in the movies, my heart hammering with despair and fury, and as if in response my iPad, still plugged into the charger but buried under the rumpled duvet, makes the swooshing, clicking sound that announces that it is coming to life.

The screen is so bright it shines right through the Egyptian cotton sheet. I pick it up. It's an email. And the sender's name is Margot.

I should delete it. Whatever hateful nonsense this is, I should delete it. But instead I open the message and a face fills the screen. It's the woman from the theatre, painted to look like a swan, eyes decorated with the white lace mask,

255

holding a bouquet of edelweiss. She pushes her nose into the flowers, gazes up through heavy, oriental lids. In the background there is some kind of church music. A wedding march. The arrival of the Queen of Sheba.

'Hello, Serena. I would have sent this direct to Gustav but then, well, you really shouldn't leave your devices lying around backstage. It was too tempting to make a little mischief. I know this will get to him as soon as you've opened it, anyway. You share everything, no? So this is for you, Gustav darling,' says the woman in a deep, smoker's voice. 'Remember these pretty bridal flowers? Remember this wedding music? Remember me?'

I can't tear my eyes away. The woman is pulling the mask off with one hand, glancing down, picking up a big wad of cotton wool, and wiping it across her eyes. She smudges the black birdlike maquillage into a horrible mess over her cheeks and forehead, then she takes another pad and carefully wipes first one eye, then the other, keeps wiping until all the make-up is gone.

The face is still dead white, the lips bright cerise pink, but the black oriental eyes are the same, staring at me just as they did from those sketches Gustav made in Lugano. The mouth keeps moving, but I can't hear the words because the organ music fills the air. I back away into the living room, still clutching it.

'I've had enough! Take him!' I scream like a madwoman at the gloating screen. 'You're welcome to him. You've won! You're welcome to the lot of them!'

I drop the iPad from my scorched fingers, grab my bags, and run from the apartment – leaving it, still talking, the screen refusing to fade, on Gustav's favourite sofa.

CHAPTER TWELVE

I'm standing in front of a giant furnace, blazing out heat like a scene from Dante's *Inferno,* complete with doomed souls. In the glowing embers I see a burning old building in Paris and a young man carrying his baby brother from the flames.

The people around me shuffle their feet on the concrete floor that sparkles with shards of glass, and I force myself back to the present. Even though this is a pleasure trip I still raise my camera. Even though my hands are shaking with fatigue I wait to capture the performance that is about to begin. The gaping maw of the fire's grate is for my 'Windows and Doors' exhibition. The light and shade is perfect for a moody, typically Venetian composition.

Even in here the sea breeze reaches us, cutting viciously off the iron-grey lagoon separating this little island from the domes and spires of the watery city that rises like a herbaceous border on the horizon.

I lean against the wall and watch as a young guy saunters out from a back room, unbuttoning a loose white shirt. There's no fanfare except a muttered commentary from the tour guide in charge of the tourist group beside me. I try to listen in, but she's speaking in a language I don't recognise and in any case I'm distracted by the long hard stare I'm getting from the guy as he strips to the waist.

The flirtatious glance is all part of the show, a trick to improve sales, and it must have the desired effect. The other tourists all clap enthusiastically as the shirt comes off. The guy picks up a long metal pipe and plunges it without further ado into the bubbling furnace. The back of his head, spine and legs are painted with darkness, the outline of his face, chest and arms thrown into relief by the roaring light.

The muscles in his shoulders and arms flex as the glass blower grasps the pipe. His ribs jab through his skin. All that intense heat must knock the breath out of you.

'I'll have him washed and brought to my room,' one of the other tourists mutters.

My stomach tightens. The cold air has brought tears to my eyes. Not just the cold air. I feel so alone here. And stupid. I am missing Gustav as badly as if someone has chopped off one of my limbs.

I'm standing in the one place I've dreamed about revisiting, but what's obsessing me is the mess I've left behind me. Gustav slamming the door of the flat without another word. Me left alone to zip up my bags, enraged by his distrust and scared shitless by that iPad message. A very quiet voice inside me, constantly being squashed down by all the other arguments, wonders if I was too hasty running off like that. But if I'd stayed, would he have come back? Was that one of his midnight flits, as Pierre called them? Would he have listened even if I'd wanted to talk?

I can't hold on to this kind of anger for long. All I know now is that the oceans I've put between us may have calmed me down a little, but they have solved nothing, just made me realise that the one man I want by my side isn't here.

A wedge of muscle thickens down each side of his back as the young man manipulates his iron pipe, dipping it into

258

the furnace again. I know from my researches into glass-making that the furnace is called the glory hole. When I read that, lying in the First Class cabin the Weinmeyers had booked for me, my first instinct was to text something obscene to Polly, because I could hear her reaction: *He can poke my glory hole any time!*

But Polly and I are not on speaking terms. In fact, I don't even know where she is. My darling cousin has taken leave of her senses. She's decided that I've stolen her boyfriend and trashed her life, and Gustav thinks the same thing.

The glass blower scoops out a sort of jelly and dances across the cold workshop to a slab of marble where he rolls and flips it, constantly lifting and twisting and swinging his pipe. Then he lowers his mouth and his cheeks pull in as he starts to suck. There's a muted collective gasp around me.

For the millionth time I wrestle with the temptation to make that call. Swallow my pride and sort this out. I need to know how Gustav has reacted to that iPad video. Why the hell did I leave it there? If Margot and Pierre filmed that together, then they are even more evil than I thought. They are finding their way back to Gustav.

The glass blower rotates and twists his pipe as his cheeks blow life into the red-hot globule gathered at the end and coax it into shape. As the embryonic glass elongates at the end of that pipe it swells and grows, unmistakably resembling a hard-on.

A frantic, hopeless desire grips me. My body, my heart, arguing with my head. I can't switch this off. Gustav is on the other side of the world, but who am I kidding? It felt right to jump on the first flight out here. Remember, Gustav was very quick to believe that I had let his brother kiss me. But that could have been part of Pierre's plan. And I was starting to warm to Pierre. Part of the plan, too. He was working some of that sinister magic on me.

But Gustav has hurt me by believing Polly's stupid photograph rather than me. That injustice will keep me in Venice, and away from him. Let him get on with his life without me by his side, and deal with his poisonous brother on his own.

The glass blower sketches another *pas de deux* with his instrument, coaxing the elegant line of metal as he breathes air down the tube, and look how the globular mass responds, fading from garish tangerine to a rosy hue and forming into a lovely oval.

If this was the last moment of my life I would discard everything else. I would want Gustav's hands running over me, coaxing my body into amazing shapes. No words. Just a mind-blowing reunion.

The ballet slows as the glass blower, still swinging his pipe to keep the momentum, rolls the dark-pink mass onto another slab and then suddenly, with his free hand, pinches the neck of the glass, which has stretched into a column, and decapitates it. Then it's over. The shapeless, molten mass has turned into a unique ruby-red glass vase.

And everything will be all right, because I have work to do, and a life to get on with.

There is a deep hush inside the workshop. Everyone here seems reluctant to break the spell. But then the tourists start whispering, and gradually my scattered thoughts rearrange themselves into a pattern, like the multicoloured particles in a mosaic.

I approach the workbench. I study the vase closely, adjust the lighting over it, take some pictures of it with both my camera and my phone.

'Please gift-wrap this and ship it to this address in Manhattan. The smaller one can be delivered direct to the Palazzo Weinmeyer. From me. Serena Folkes.'

I hear the cool authority in my voice and this time I catch a look of genuine admiration in the guy's face. He looks me up and down, the expensive clothes, the quick slick of lipstick, the contrasting wild russet hair. He nods obsequiously and retreats to the back office to fetch the shipping documents.

I straighten my duck-egg-blue and white spotted silk scarf as I wait. I close my eyes, crumple the ends of the scarf up to my nose to sniff the slight remaining traces of Gustav's tang from when he last wound it round my neck.

I walk slowly round the workshop. I finger the delicate glass ornaments, vases, bottles and bowls. I recognise the bulbous red goblets sitting on the equally delicate shelving. The Weinmeyers filled one of these with wine in their house on the Upper East Side and tried to seduce me. Spotlights are cleverly angled to make the glass objects glow, red, orange, green, blue. Seahorses, budding flowers, plain dishes, fragile glasses, all set out here for the discerning buyer.

The man emerges from the back office attired now in shirt and jacket, a pair of cool glasses on his nose. He hands me some forms and a pen. The guide ushers the tourists out of the workshop like a bunch of school kids.

'*Grazie*,' I murmur to the young glass blower and owner of the factory as I sign the forms with a flourish. 'Signora Weinmeyer is going to love it.'

The first part of my mission has been accomplished. The Weinmeyers sent me to Venice ahead of them to check up on some rare black Murano glass chandeliers that are being made for the New York mansion, but actually they recognised that the sea air might do me some good. They have been so kind to me over the last couple of days, revealing a genuinely nurturing side to their flamboyant personalities, and I want to treat them to something.

I follow the straggle of tourists along the main street of pastel-coloured houses, past other closing workshops fronted by their little outlets. Every window glitters with glass trinkets.

A low green canal runs along the centre of the street, boats bobbing listlessly.

A cold wet wind blows off the lagoon, slapping some life into me as I stare out over the water. It's good to be travelling again, the best possible therapy, especially as this time I've got money, decent clothes, some clients eager for my expertise, and leisure to gather material for my next exhibition. After only a few days in Venice I can already feel myself loosening, at least physically. If only Gustav was here, if somehow we had made up, this would be perfect.

I falter as I reach the *vaporetto* stop to wait for the water bus. All very well thinking about my next exhibition, but that was going to be in New York, with Gustav's help and patronage. If I'm on my own again I'm going to have to go back to the drawing board, comb through every new contact and client, and stage it myself.

The watery city is low-slung, balancing on its jigsaw of islands. Above the red-tiled roofs the apricot finger of the campanile beside San Marco Cathedral points up into a heavy sky laden with rain, and other bell towers rise here and there over the city as if answering a call.

Now the *vaporetto* has reached us and is churning up the water as it heaves round to reverse against the quay. The rattle of the barrier, the rumble and vibration of the engine beneath my feet as the boat strikes out across the lagoon are so familiar from when I was here last summer. Although speed limits were introduced years ago to try to reduce the damaging effects of the motorised wake of the *moto ondoso*, the streamlined wooden taxis passing us still look like racehorses straining at the gates.

The water bus drops me at Riva degli Schiavoni, the strip of pavement that passes outside my hotel, edging the south side of the city. A few yards further along is the Bridge of Sighs and the pink and white wedding-cake façade of the

Doge's Palace. I can hear the thud of music coming from the Piazza San Marco. They're setting up stages and sound systems for the famous annual Carnevale, which starts in a few days' time and will stretch itself out for as many days and nights as it can justify. It is always held in February, when Venice is at its coldest, but the Carnevale always co-incides with Valentine's Day, too, which adds to its magic. With the masks and costumes and noise and flares and baroque atmosphere, it is like a romantic version of Halloween.

For everyone except me, that is. What kind of Valentine's Day is this going to be, with no lover? No Gustav?

There's already an unmistakable vibration of excitement throbbing through the city as the big party approaches. There are lamps and stars and streamers decorating the buildings, the costume shops are bursting with even more colour and texture than usual, their windows crammed with spooky eyeless masks adorned with sequins and feathers. Some are full face, to be worn beneath the traditional tricorn hats. Others are just intended to hide the eyes.

Already I've seen groups of children darting out of the paved alleyways, which are filled-in erstwhile waterways and are known as *calli*. The kids cross my path, dressed as clowns, devils or princesses. Halloween back in London is like a dressing-up box full of auntie's cast-offs compared with this finery, where the entire population enters into the spirit.

I am jostled off the lumbering hull of the *vaporetto* by the other tourists, baying now for pasta and beer. I stand aside to let them pass, and stare up at the rusty red façade of my hotel.

Despite the encroaching sea fog and constant threat of rain, I'm a film star compared to the urchin who was in Venice last year with no money, no family, no friends, just one little camera and, later, a little whip for company. Last year I stumbled off a train in the middle of the night. This time I got off the plane at Marco Polo airport and was whisked into the Weinmeyers' private boat, a wooden craft with white leather upholstery that looked just like the Riva boats I'd seen moored away for the winter in boathouses at Lake Lugano.

At my destination a couple of liveried bellboys handed me out of the boat and into the hotel, and that's when I missed Gustav the most, not because I needed him carrying my bags, but because of the admiration and respect that follow him wherever he goes. Well, now it's up to me to attract some respect of my own.

I push through the revolving doors of the Hotel Danieli. When I was in Venice last time I used to walk past this place on my way to my pensione in the Castello area just behind San Marco. I'd peer in at the rich guests floating down the majestic staircase to take aperitifs in the cocktail bar to the left of the foyer, with its potted palms and the grand piano tinkling out show tunes. Even now I half expect a snooty concierge to take me by the scruff of the neck and chuck me out.

Now I'm the rich guest here on business, floating up the stairs to her palatial bedroom with its double bed and rich carpets, ornate furniture and Murano glass chandeliers, the walls hung with watery silk.

I walk straight across the room and fling open the shutters to take in the view over the lagoon, the boats and gondolas rocking on the water striped with lights from the hotel and other buildings lining the *fondamenta* below me. I gaze at the grand façade of Santa Maria della Salute glowing orange in the sunset, the lights from the opulent hotel Cipriani just beyond.

'Why the big sigh, Serena?'

I spin round and, to my complete shock, there is Crystal, gliding out from the marble bathroom holding a hairdryer and a pair of tongs. I gape like a gargoyle and then burst into tears.

'Crys, what a fantastic surprise!' I gulp noisily. 'You come all this way to do my hair?'

'Crystal. And it's a good thing too. Those tresses are a disgrace! All wet and windblown. You need constant grooming and, since Gustav had already booked me to come over here to assist the pair of you on this trip, he reckoned that you'd still need looking after. I'm sorry to see that you appear to have mislaid him somewhere along the way.'

'We've split up, Crystal. Did he also mention that?'

'He said you were here alone. That is all.' Crystal snaps the hairdryer into the socket as if clapping it in irons. 'I don't believe you've split up. It would kill him.'

'Those Levis are too much trouble.' My voice strangles with more tears. I take one of the thick curtains in my fingers, draw it across me and start to stroke the velvety, sound-proofing brocade. I used to hide behind the curtains when I was a child. 'But it's killing me too.'

Crystal waggles the tongs plugged into the wonky socket then licks her finger on the wand to test the heat. 'Nevertheless, love like that only comes once in a lifetime. Gustav will never let you go.'

I push the curtain away from me. 'Crystal, I love you, but be honest here. Gustav may have finished with me, but he still needs to control me. So he sent you to keep an eye.'

'And admit this, young lady. You wouldn't have him any other way. I'm here because what fool would turn down a large sum of money to come to Venice? Especially at Carnevale, when this city is full of dark people in dark corners, doing dark deeds. Beautiful young women on their own have to be very, very careful.' Her aubergine lips rise at the corners in her version of a smile. 'More pertinently, I gather it's your cousin you've fallen out with?'

'She grabbed the wrong end of the stick and banged me over the head with it. She thinks I'm after Pierre!' Hot tears rush up into my eyes. I turn back to the window, untie the scarf and wind it round my fingers so tight the blood stops coursing. 'And Gustav believed her.'

Crystal comes round behind me, takes off my coat and brushes the shoulders before hanging it on a padded hanger. She is dressed in a tight-fitting black polo-neck sweater and pencil skirt, her hair combed tightly back in a bun at the nape of her neck as if she's an off-duty flamenco dancer.

'Did he actually say that?'

I stare at her, comb my tired mind. 'He didn't want me anywhere near him.'

'That's not the same, and you know it. From where I'm standing, Polly Folkes is the real reason you're here. It's not Gustav who wants you gone. He's treading on eggshells to get this right with his brother, he saw you stamping all over them, and he lost it. I told you Pierre was his Achilles heel. He never sees, until it's too late, how Pierre's *raison d'être* in life is to ruffle feathers.'

I allow her to push me down on the padded stool. She unwinds the scarf from my knuckles, rolls it up to prevent creases, and starts to brush my hair, dragging my head backwards briskly as she does so. I close my eyes, exhausted.

'Wise owl. You always hit the nail on the head, Crystal. Although it's more than feathers this time. More like applying dynamite to a skyscraper. Because then there was Margot.'

Crystal's hairbrush pauses halfway down. 'She's finally reared her ugly head?'

'On my iPad, yes. She must be in New York, because I saw a woman looking just like her at the theatre where I was working last week. She was like this prima ballerina, dancing with Pierre. When I later remarked that she looked like Margot, Pierre said I was imagining things, but I didn't imagine this message on my iPad, Crystal! It's a film of Margot plastered in the same theatrical make-up and holding her wedding flowers. It was a nasty little warning intended for Gustav via me.'

'Have you never heard of webcams or media messages? She could have been delivering her message from anywhere in the world. Melbourne. Moscow. Or Marrakesh.'

'Which means Pierre may not have filmed it or known she was sending it. But at the very least he gave her my email address, or showed her my iPad when I left it at the theatre. And even if she's somewhere else now, she was definitely in New York last week.'

The hairbrush snags on my hair. 'Where is this iPad now?'

'In the apartment. On the sofa. I dropped it and left it there. It's got all my notes on it but I didn't want to touch it or see it again, Crystal.'

'Reckless and foolhardy to leave it there, Serena, but it means Gustav will have found it by now.' She starts brushing my hair again, hard, so that my head jerks back against her stomach. 'Have trust in him, Serena. He will deal with this. Meanwhile, you are here, which is the best place to be, and you have work to do. Gustav will come for you when he's ready.'

We regard each other in the mirror as her words sink in. She continues brushing my hair until I'm calm, twists it into a loose ponytail and then lays a simple black sheath dress on the bed. I reckon it would suit her better than me, but it's beautiful and once I put it on I will be dressed to kill.

'The Weinmeyers have finally arrived at their palazzo from New York and you are invited to dinner. They want you to stay with them, but I did explain that you had booked yourself in here for the whole week. I will also be dressing you for their infamous Valentine's ball, the highlight of Carnevale. I understand you will be treading a fine line between working

267

girl taking photographs of the festivities and honoured guest enjoying herself, and I am here to make sure you stand out from the crowd.' She brushes imaginary fluff off the dress, and arranges the vertiginous Louboutins to stand side by side. 'So I'm here for as long as you need me. Hair, make-up, wardrobe. Apart from that I'll be invisible.'

I touch her as she moves to open the door. 'It'll be no fun going alone to the ball, Crystal. Gustav should be here.'

'*Mademoiselle*, I will bet my priceless collection of voodoo dolls that Gustav Levi is yearning, even as we speak, to be here with you. And if you want my opinion that message from Margot, if he finds it, and if it's authentic, will spur him on, but first he'll need to get to the bottom of it. He'll drag an explanation out of Pierre, too, if Pierre is to blame for playing with fire like this.But he won't come for you before everything is clear in his head. And no, you shouldn't call him. So spread your wings and get on with your work until one of you makes the first move.' She taps my hand where it rests on her thin arm. 'You look worn out, but what a transformation from that tangle-haired kid who wandered into his life on Halloween night. Really. Even jet-lagged you are sleek, elegant, clear-eyed. And beautiful.'

I bow my head gratefully. 'That was Gustav's influence. He treated me so well, Crystal. Wardrobes full of clothes. Meals out in all the best restaurants. This lovely little locket that I can't undo.'

Crystal's eyes gleam like a blackbird's as she fingers the golden locket, runs her long fingernail over the little rim of pearls and the hidden embossed 'S'.

'You are good for him, too. Your chaotic, youthful exuberance has breathed new life into him. So stop speaking in the past tense. Get a proper sleep tonight. Tomorrow you focus on what you do best: watching, observing, with your camera in hand. "Windows and Doors", wasn't it? The title of your next show? It's time for you to get back to work.'

The *acqua alta* has flooded the Piazza San Marco the next morning. Venice is in peril, they say, from the elements, which are determined to return the city to its watery foundations. Nature is laughing at mankind thinking he can build houses, churches and museums on stilts and then wonder why it's permanently in danger of sinking. But what it means is that this early in the morning there are few people about, because everyone is waiting for the waters to recede.

When I open my bedroom door after taking my breakfast of warm pastries and heart-joltingly strong coffee, I see a pair of Hunter wellies that Crystal must have put there. I pull them on, shove my new Breton beret low over my forehead to keep my hair somewhat in check, then steal down some back stairs and out of a door near the hotel kitchens to start my safari through the city.

Crystal has also provided some soft ballet pumps to put in my bag in case I decide to enter an establishment that might not welcome the sight of ungainly boots. But I have no intention of entering any establishment. Windows and doors by their very nature are the apertures to an invisible world within. The observer remains outside. All I want to do is wander like I did when I was last here, round corners, through alleyways, over bridges, until I'm far away from the Ciprianis and the Harry's Bars and the increasing activity and pounding music in the piazza.

I step across the raised wooden duckboards forming walkways across the cold grey water that has flowed in from the lagoon, flooded the piazza and streamed through the alleyways that branch off the main square until it's halted by steps or a bridge.

'Windows and Doors'. I tried to get started on my

collection in Manhattan as soon as we arrived, zooming in on various windows up at sky level, trying to catch the life going on inside, but being up close and personal with my portrait subjects I haven't had the time in the last month to give my voyeur instinct free rein. Walking around at street level now, what's intriguing are the intimate characteristics of a door or window when it's firmly closed.

Here in Venice I almost feel I should be recording the smells and sounds, too. Unlike other cities, there is little traffic noise to deafen you, so when you see a pair of pale-green peeling shutters, a hand edging through a lace curtain to pinch off a petal from a long wooden box of red geraniums, you can also hear the snap of a bed sheet, the sudden flurry of an argument or a baby's cry, a few scales on a piano or the crash of cooking utensils on a tiled kitchen floor. And always the smell of pizza dough, oregano, coffee, brandy and custard, and further north, the salty tang of the sea and of shellfish being hauled out of the brine.

I wander through the cold, quiet morning until I am lost, and that's the way I like it. My head is heavy and aching slightly after too much rich food and copious wine with the Weinmeyers and their Italian friends last night. It was a hugely entertaining evening despite having to constantly swerve the topic of Gustav, and then politely insist at the end on returning to, and paying for, the Hotel Danieli. I wanted privacy. I didn't want to lie down in the admittedly adorable tapestried chamber that they had prepared in the attics of their palazzo, with its ornate Romeo and Juliet stone balcony overlooking a side canal. I didn't want to wait for the tap on the door.

'We will get our hands on that lovely body of yours one day, sugar,' complained Mrs Weinmeyer as they handed me into their private boat. 'We haven't flown you all the way over to Europe just to look at your pretty face.'

'We can always corner her at the ball, Ingrid, or get one of our guests to warm her up for us, especially as she's flying solo!' said Mr Weinmeyer with a chuckle as he laid his hand on his wife's ass. 'Anything can happen at one of our balls.'

'One day you'll have me,' I said, smiling. 'I promise.'

I suddenly felt very old, and very weary, and envious of the tight bond joining those two. They were like a couple of lovesick teenagers as they waved me off from the jetty leading into the arched salons of their grand palazzo.

I've been up to the Fondamenta Nuove, the deserted, more industrial north-eastern edge of the city. I've sat on a bollard on the quayside and taken pictures of steamed-up little trattorias full of sea-swept men shucking their lunch straight from the shell. I've walked back through Cannaregio and the old Ghetto area, studded with apartment buildings with their additional storeys. They had to build up, rather than out, when yet another diaspora brought the Jewish people flooding in.

I follow the Fondamenta della Misericordia. The pavement of pity. It's a wide walkway beside a canal parked with small craft, unlike the bulky barges that do the business of trucks and trains on the mainland, delivering produce and moving furniture around the canals. These look like private boats. I wonder who owns them, who has just thrown that rope over the mooring ring, still dripping with water, and entered a peeling building with nothing but a small number to indicate the address. What was he or she doing out on the lagoon, who is he or she greeting now as they enter their stone-tiled home?

I quicken my pace past the mostly closed pizzerias with metal chairs piled up against the doors. In the summer this *fondamenta* would be buzzing with colour and voices, the hot smells of tomato and basil, of hot sugar and dripping raspberry gelati. I take a picture of a restaurant door hung with a red and white ribboned curtain to keep out the flies in the summer – and what, or who, in the winter? The garish over-tinted photographs of the pizzas and sweets offered within could not be less appetising if they tried.

I walk over a bridge, my feet vaguely directing me towards the Rialto area and then home. Although I'm loving being back here, breathing the old, cold, slightly dank air, although I like to think of my feet making their own faint permanent print on these ancient stones, I miss Manhattan. In the month or so that I've been there, I've got used to being a city girl, used to being up high looking down, pushing my way along the busy sidewalks, being buffeted by the wind that slices round the corners and whistles up and down those ruled, reined-in streets.

And I've got used to coming home to Gustav every night. Watching his face melt from its accustomed wariness when he sees that it's me who's come back to him.

How cold that face was, refusing even to look at me when he walked out of the apartment.

Now I've come to a halt and I'm sitting on an old well in the middle of a pink- and apricot-painted campo, eating ciabatta stuffed with avocado and Bel Paese cheese. And then I hear them. The bells. All over the city the churches start tolling their bells. Always reminiscent of Italy, even if I hear one tolling in England. The Italian bells have a richer tone. Deeper, holier, somehow. Maybe this is something to do with the Carnevale.

I must be right under a bell tower, because the curls inside my ears and even my bones seem to be ringing. I glance around me. I can't see any church here. The *campo* is a tiny square of quiet, shuttered houses, paved now, once green and planted. The only movement is coming from the inquisitive pecking of pigeons at my ciabatta crumbs, but in the far corner is an alleyway. I glance up above it, and a block or two away there's a bell tower with a massive iron cross on top.

I know that tower. That cross. The sound of that bell. I scurry down the pitch-dark alleyway, a *sottoportego*, which is more of a tunnel with a very low ceiling, bowed from the building above.

My heart jumps about in my chest as I venture down this tunnel now.

Yet again I think about Gustav. What he's doing. Who he's talking to. What expression would have been on his face when he returned to the empty apartment after his angry exit, maybe ready to say sorry to me, instead finding not me but my abandoned iPad lying on the sofa with his ex-wife dominating the screen.

Yet again, thank God for the Weinmeyers. When I left the apartment I headed straight across Central Park like a homing pigeon. I was half-expecting to run into Gustav in the park, actually, but his long legs had taken him far away from me by then. So when I got to their mansion I told them that something had gone very wrong between me and Gustav, a terrible misunderstanding about his brother, and I begged them to get me on the first plane out to Venice. They invited me to stay the night while they organised the flight, astonishingly laid not one finger on me (other than a very long, very scented hug from Mrs Weinmyer), and the next day they had their driver take me to the airport and out of New York.

There's no barrier at the other end of the alley so that I nearly slide over the slimy stretch of paving and straight into the khaki waters of an unexpected canal. A few feet along to my left is a dead end, barred only by a little stone bridge with no balustrade. This is where I first saw that little nun, Sister Perpetua, on that boiling summer night. This is where I tried to ask her for directions, and she saw me, and her hands flew up in fright as if I had startled a rabbit from its nest. She ran away, and I followed her.

I run my hand along the crumbling walls as I try to retrace those steps. They say you will find your way out of a maze if you keep your right hand on the topiary at all times, but only a skein of thread would work in this labyrinth. I have a really strong, desperate urge to find that convent again. The photographs I took here last summer were the bulk of my first exhibition, and the images of those nuns whipping themselves in penance in their lonely cells helped to launch me as the voyeur photographer. Maybe this time I should get permission to come in and take some photographs, rather than skulking round the staircases and corridors like a thief in the night.

I pause as I come to a crossroads. I can't remember which way to go.

A bell chimes softly but it seems further away now. I start walking again, fumble my way along the wall, looking for the little gate that the nun led me through that other time. I'm certain I can even smell the sharp prick of lemon from the little trees that stood about in the hidden courtyard.

But the convent has gone. Perhaps it was never there. My fingers run along the length of the wall without finding any lemon tree, nor any gate.

'You don't understand. The silver chain joins us. It's physical, as if it's right here, tugging me back to him.' I stop and bend over, clutching my stomach. I jab my finger at the exact spot in my navel.

Crystal regards me wordlessly for a moment, holds up the leaflet as if she's about to deliver a lecture and studies the map the hotel receptionist gave her this morning. Then she stops on the little bridge and points across to the next one. 'This is it. Campo San Barnaba. And see, at the base of that bridge is the costume shop where according to this information we will find the ball dress of your dreams.'

I shake my arm from her digging fingers. 'I'm not in the mood for a ball.'

'You want to cancel your commissions? Lose the most influential clients you're ever likely to have?'

Crystal glides on down the bridge, glancing at the oversized vegetables heaped on the hefty barge moored there and surrounded by equally hefty housewives. Amongst the shapeless coats and head scarves she looks as if she's just landed in a spaceship. Tall, skinny and wearing enormous sunglasses, she's also wearing a dark-purple jumpsuit that suits her frame perfectly, topped with a boxy mahogany fake-fur jacket. She's given up the struggle of persuading me to look suitably businesslike so I'm wearing my favourite dark-green leather jacket and indigo jeans.

She pauses halfway along the *fondamenta* running between the two bridges. 'We have to get your gown for the ball and I want to surprise the Weinmeyers with something sensational.'

I let her walk on ahead of me. I glance down and notice two stone footprints. I'm standing on the Ponte dei Pugni, the bridge of fists. This was one of the official spots where warring factions were directed to meet and fight, placing their feet in the demarcated spots before throwing each other into the canal.

I allow myself a tight grimace. I would love to throw someone off this bridge. Since my solitary walk yesterday my sorrow seems to have turned into the restless anger I haven't felt since I was an adolescent in Devon with no horizon but the view from the cliffs. I'm cut adrift in this confusing city, which is what I wanted. But how can you be free on the one hand and yearn to be securely rooted on the other?

Crystal is gesticulating at me. I raise my camera and take a picture of her. In the shop window behind her a jumbled display of scary faces crowds forwards, the visages sporting various expressions ranging from mirthless hilarity to fathomless doom. The reflection of the grey sky with its desultory smattering of clouds muddles the glass, making the faces look as if they are grinning and winking with a life of their own.

Crystal waits, because she knows that I will come to her. Her mouth is a thin line stained the same purple as her jumpsuit, as if she's been eating crushed blackberries. Her button eyes are hidden by the shades. But she reaches out her leather glove and gives my thick plait of hair a sharp tug before we turn towards the shop.

A little bell on the door jingles as we enter, setting the bevy of masks dancing manically on their ribbons, eyeless faces lunging at us, long-nosed ones pecking at our shoulders like birds. Crystal runs her hand along a rail of heavy brocade dresses with square lace-trimmed Marie Antoinette necklines.

I take a few steps further into the dark shop where the costumes seem to loom out of the shadows as if inhabited by long-dead bodies. Crystal is busy trying to lift a very heavy powdered wig off a polystyrene head.

A small woman dressed in a flowing gold kaftan and matching turban appears from the back of the shop and spreads her hands in welcome. Crystal raises one finger to keep the woman waiting, and comes back to me.

'Your mission is to be the belle of the Weinmeyers' ball, Serena. Take the photographs, fulfil your commission, then you can go back to New York, or London, or wherever you want to go. Until then you remain ambassador for the Levi/Folkes brand whether you like it or not.'

Crystal picks up a huge Japanese fan decorated with a

picture of Mount Fuji painted in black brush-strokes. She flicks it open, sending a spray of silk poppies adorning a particularly enormous headdress bouncing and nodding. When I don't respond, she tweaks my beret.

'I might stay here.' I sit heavily on a vast carved chair that the woman in the kaftan has just vacated. 'Just go and choose whatever you think is suitable.'

Crystal pats me on the cheek, and the lady beckons us to enter an Aladdin's cave of Venetian costumes and jewellery. As soon as we enter I am reminded of Pierre's theatre, the dancers, the music, the burlesque dance. What a perfect source this would be for his costume business. I remember Polly declaring her discoveries about the business and the apartment he lived in, as if they proved he was a fraud, but he'd already told me and Gustav that his London business was failing and he'd told me that he didn't own the theatre in Manhattan and was still living in Margot's flat. He's a loudmouth costume supplier with delusions of grandeur but with undeniable talent as a designer. There was no faking the respect he commanded from everyone in that theatre. Just like a Levi. But what will bring him down in the end is that he's a liar, and what liars do is compound their lies and make everyone else think they are going mad, and what everyone else should do is step away.

I came so close to liking him when we talked in the Gramercy Bar about the scars we both carry. But no sooner do you warm to him then the next lie pops up, this time on my iPad. Margot *was* in the theatre. I didn't imagine it.

Oh, why did I run off like that? Half of me wants to confront Pierre, demand answers, warn Gustav that he is not to be trusted. The other half wants to drag Gustav away so that neither of us ever sees or hears from Pierre Levi ever again.

Crystal and the lady pull me inside the changing rooms. The lady makes a beeline for an outfit already laid out and

I stand there like a dummy while the two women fuss and flutter.

'Why was kaftan lady so insistent that I wear this costume? Why did she go on and on about having to wear exactly five feathers in my hair?' I remark as, an hour later, we emerge with a grand dress complete with wig, headdress, cloak and mask, all sealed inside a kind of bodybag. 'How did she even know I was coming?'

'I get the impression someone might take a back-hander for directing visitors to her select little shop. Who knows? There's probably some significance in five feathers, too. A secret emblem so you can be recognised amongst the masks? Anyway, we'll have fun making you up as the Principessa Serena. But now we're going to cross the Grand Canal like true Venetians.'

Crystal hooks my spoils carefully over her arm as we find our way via a *cicchetti* bar where we stand and eat fried calamari, tuna balls and slices of eggplant and mozzarella. A curious calm comes over me as I let her order my food. We each down a couple of shots of sambuca, then Crystal leads me on, lecturing me calmly on the surrounding architecture, churches and *scuole* until we reach the nearest *traghetto* stop. To our left is the soaring hump of the Rialto Bridge with its market and infinite river of sightseers. To our right the wide canal curves towards the brighter light of the lagoon, lined with the pink and white palazzi with their Gothic arched windows, fluttering now with bunting and flags.

'Think of all the lovers who have lived here,' Crystal remarks as we stand on the scooped-out gondola and the ferrymen row us silently to the other side. 'Casanova, who had two sisters on the go at once, both nuns. His favourite he called *elle-même*. One of Lord Byron's mistresses threw herself out of a window just like the ones overlooking us now. Georges Sand stayed in your very room at the Hotel Danieli, you know. I think her lover was sick and she went off with the handsome young doctor who came to tend to him.'

'I can't be without Gustav, Crys.' I drag my feet as she stalks through the streets as if she was born here. 'I need to speak to him.'

'Have patience. And dignity.' She slaps my arm. 'If he wants you, he'll come to you.'

The city snaps into electric light as dusk falls. Lamps in windows, fairy lights round colonnades, dazzling arc lights rigged up beside loudspeakers pumping disco, jazz or rock from the corners of the busier streets and squares as the city revs up for tonight's festivities.

'Well, you know what they say. If you can't be with the one you love,' I remark glumly, ready to be sucked into the hustle of Piazza San Marco.

Crystal blows me a playful kiss.

'Love the one you're with.'

CHAPTER THIRTEEN

It's dark now, or at least as dark as a city can get when it's alight with flame and music.

I turn on my narrow embroidered kitten heels to wave at Crystal as the hotel taxi backs away from the quay to drop its other guests at their own parties, but already she's been swallowed up by the traffic on the canal. I hoped she was coming with me to this ball, but she has dressed me, bewigged me, made me up and perfumed me, and now she's abandoned me.

She's also been tanking me up with some very strong gin-based cocktails while transforming me from ragamuffin to royalty in a silk brocade ball gown in the same emerald green as my eyes and set off by the five peacock plumes pinned to my powdered pompadour wig. The plunging neckline squeezes my breasts and pushes them to bulge over the bodice. My three-quarter-length sleeves are trimmed with creamy lace and a pair of emerald satin gloves cover my little bracelet. The only other jewellery is the golden locket, nestling at the base of my throat, another permanent reminder of Gustav, and some amazing dangling green glass earrings that Mrs Weinmeyer gave me earlier, insisting that I wear them tonight.

Over the ensemble Crystal has tied a green velvet hooded

cloak, which is sewn onto the back of my dress like a weight to stop me floating to the surface.

'Cinderella,' Crystal murmured earlier in the water taxi as it joined the flotilla of other boats, gondolas and *vaporetti* taking guests all over the city. 'Just make sure you don't lose your glass slipper.'

'Sans Prince Charming,' I mumbled. The taxi thrust its gears into reverse as we came alongside the Palazzo Weinmeyer's private jetty furnished with a golden canopy and carpeted in rich matching gold, lit by beacons the height of grown men, throwing flames into the air. Footmen stood to attention in golden frogged tailcoats and breeches.

'These Weinmeyers sure know how to go to town!' I whispered, glancing round at all the gilded accoutrements. 'They have a Midas complex.'

'Or Goldfinger,' Crystal whispered back.

'So am I the only person who isn't painted like an Oscar statuette?'

'No. There will be every colour of the rainbow in there. Now, before you enter the ball like a conquering heroine, hold still. I need to take a picture of you before you are ravaged by the festivities.'

The other guests on the boat, a motley mixture of devils and angels, virgins and executioners, had all stopped talking and were nodding and smiling at me.

'Hold your mask by the edge here. Hide the ribbon for a moment,' she urged as she held the phone up and illuminated me with the flash. 'And look as if you own the place.'

Now she's gone, taking the phone with her. Glowing away inside that phone's memory is a vision in emerald green glittering with gold sequins, my mask half lowered like a yashmak so that it covers my mouth, my eyes wide and staring and sparkling with heavy make-up and unshed tears. Behind me looms the superb rose-ochre backdrop of the Palazzo

281

Weinmeyer draped in gold flags, the striped mooring posts standing proud in the water, and a seething blur of humanity parading along the corniche above the landing stage.

What would Gustav think if he could see me now? What if he could see me through his telescope, far away in Europe? Is he worrying about me, what I'm doing, who I'm with? Or is that why he's sent Crystal to watch over me? Is he regretting turning on me like that? Is he subsiding onto his favourite suede sofa in front of the window overlooking Central Park, remembering the feel of my lips on his, my mouth sliding down his chest, over his stomach, curling my tongue around him to pull him into my mouth? Will his hand go down to take hold of the hardness growing there, and will he wish that I was there, ready for him to come inside?

'Welcome to Palazzo Weinmeyer!'

A matching pair of animated gold statues take my invitation and escort me into the marbled hallway and up a wide flight of stone stairs flanked by more flaming beacons throwing elongated and exaggerated shadows onto the gloomy oil paintings. I am ushered through an arch into a ballroom on the *piano nobile* which I wasn't shown when I came here for dinner. The room extends along the entire width of the building, the Gothic-arched windows framing views of the Grand Canal crammed with flotillas of water craft bearing revellers.

My invitation is handed to two figures sitting on huge golden thrones who are also painted gold but swathed in white and gold togas and crowned with gold laurel leaves. My curtsy feels curiously natural in the whalebone corset and wide hooped crinoline of my dress. Crystal and I practised this in my bedroom earlier, and my hosts incline their heads in approval.

I search for some kind of friendly signal from this king and queen as they nod and tap my cheeks and shoulders in a kind of papal blessing, but the Weinmeyers are keeping up the act and like every other person in the city they are totally unrecognisable, their golden faces pocked with diamonds, their movements, like everyone else's, stiff as marionettes'.

The long wall opposite the French windows is entirely mirrored, and the walls at either end are hung with thick, ornate tapestries. It's not as large as the kind of ballroom you would find if you were visiting a stately home, and the two or three hundred people who are filing in make the room feel crowded and hot. The masked guests move slowly about in their costumes. The majority are dressed in the traditional eighteenth-century style, the women gliding in their long dresses, the men stepping self-consciously in their unaccustomed breeches, but there are plenty of more outrageous disguises here too, such as devils or animals. As the room fills to bursting point people have to turn stiffly sideways to make way for one another.

I am helped to my feet and given a large black goblet full of a spicy punch. I drink it down very quickly and programme my camera. I can feel my senses popping, goosebumps rising on my skin. There has to be some kind of amphetamine or opiate in the viscous liquid, maybe a weird mixture of both, because, as I press the camera to my eye, everything I see through the slightly steamed-up viewfinder starts to look as if it's been outlined with thick marker pen. All the figures round me become clear and stark. Movement and sound are slower than seems normal, as if I've stumbled into a jungle where half-seen dinosaurs or mythical creatures lumber and flit in the shadows cast by creepers and trees.

I pan round the ballroom in video mode, holding the camera away from me, which not only stops it pressing the mask painfully into my eyes but makes it clear that I am working. I want to capture this as a dream-state where everyone is moving in slow motion in that shy, awkward early stage of a party before they are loosened up with drink, when they don't know each other. Except they will never know each other, because tonight everyone remains a stranger.

When the music begins in earnest I can zoom in on individuals under cover of the dancing. As I pan back to the starting point I realise I must be hallucinating because the door where I came in seems to have been sealed up. It's like being shut inside one of those jewellery boxes containing a tin ballerina spinning arthritically to ghostly wind-up music.

I move from my position by the wall and start to circulate, switching my camera back into still mode. Yet again I'm reminded of Pierre's burlesque show, because this is not like a random party but a rehearsed play. It's impossible to tell behind these masks, but everyone seems to be acting like friends rather than being genuinely acquainted.

All seems pretty tame so far. Nothing like the orgy the Weinmeyers told me to expect. I relax into my stride. I'm right at home. All I have to do is what I'm best at. Watching. I can take part if I like, but not until I've recorded what goes down at a madcap Weinmeyer ball. It's all presented like a readymade painting.

I shoot and sway and mingle with the crowd, zooming in on the tilt of a chin or the courtly wave of an arm, the clacking of a painted mouth, a tight red smile, the unintentionally amusing sight of one person addressing another who is not listening.

A harpsichord begins to twang out some perfect period pieces. The chandeliers start to spin like glitter-balls. They must be on some kind of electronic circuit connected to the amplifiers. The effect is making a shifting kaleidoscope out of the sedate masked figures on the polished sprung dance floor, as they move like puppets into position and start to sketch the stylised steps of the waltz and the minuet. The third piece I recognise as the cotillion, another antiquated mating ritual disguised as a dance that Crystal and I practised earlier, odd couple that we are.

'Cotillion comes from an old French word meaning petticoat,' she puffed as she marked out the places in the middle of my bedroom. 'It was a four-sided dance, precursor to the quadrille, and it was particularly popular at dances to showcase young girls coming of age. You lift your skirt, like this, and show your ankles. Very daring for the time.'

I wish she was here. Apart from anything else she could have held my camera for me when I was trying to have a drink. I'm already very hot. Perhaps she could have dressed as a man, in matching emerald green, and escorted me here? Why didn't we think of that? What on earth is she doing now, anyway? Rocking on a chair outside my room, waiting and knitting, like a *tricoteuse* by the guillotine?

A heady perfume hovers across the mirrored ceiling, so that when I look up all the powdered or hooded heads nod and twirl as if they're exotic birds making formations through cirrus clouds.

As well as the moving statues and the odd angel or goblin, most of the guests are in costumes like mine, exaggeratedly sexy versions of Casanova-era clothing. These would be absolutely perfect for Pierre's purposes – whatever they are. Stop it! Stop it! I try to push thoughts of him and his brother out of my head, but the combination of the cumbersome headdress, the heat in this ballroom, the wine and the effort of steadying and focusing my camera is already wearing me out.

I scroll quickly through the catalogue of false faces, hands, gloves, fans, breasts, chins, legs, feathers, feet, until I'm dizzy. If someone could loop those images together, together with any video footage, this would be a sensational montage. Or the backdrop to a burlesque show . . .

I put the camera back into video mode and push myself across the polished parquet, using it to search through the sedately dancing crowd and the chattering people around the edges for someone familiar. But apart from Mr and Mrs Weinmeyer these are all strangers. Even if I did know them, I would never recognise them, because many of the masks have a mesh across the eye holes to conceal even that slight flicker of familiarity. All the faces are either masked or plastered in thick theatrical make-up.

The Weinmeyers' wide-ranging dress code, which they outlined to me the other night, has been adhered to to the very last stitch. Although, from what they've told me about past balls, they seem determined that every last stitch will eventually be unpicked. They wanted people to arrive at this ball ready to discard all inhibitions, and partners, at the door. An even more extravagant, outrageous version of the Club Crème, in other words.

I continue to mingle, shooting and watching as breasts and chests begin to heave for breath, and feet occasionally trip as the dancers start to tire. The impression is that these are all statues, come to life. No human foibles or weaknesses or sins to worry about here. No manipulation, or persuasion, or sorrow, or happiness, because there is no emotion on these blank faces. They are automatons. Maybe the dress code should have been 'sex toys'. Anyway they are coming to life now. A hidden switch has been thrown to send them into debauched mode until someone switches them off at the end of the night.

Some dresses are so low cut that breasts rest heavily upon the whalebone of the tight bodice, the red nipples exposed and positioned like cherries stuck onto white scones. The full skirts of the dresses are slashed at intervals and totally see-through when the wearer stands in front of the light.

The low murmuring of voices goes quiet as the harpsichord trails off. The room is jam-packed now. I'm squeezed among blank-faced swordsmen, duchesses, gladiators and wenches, all playing musical statues. They are waiting for the next dance, heads tilted expectantly, beribboned wig-tails bouncing with an invisible pulse, painted mouths curved in patient smiles. Gloved fingers resting on chins as if waiting for a signal.

A violin tests its strings, followed by the discordant screech of tuning up, and then the members of the little orchestra, who have been sitting blank-faced on tiny gilt chairs, raise their bows and wind and brass, and swing the music into a mad, galloping polka.

I try to sidle to the side of the room as everyone is urged to follow the pace of the dance. Because the room is so full there is no sense of formation, and although some pairs manage to get hold of each other it's becoming more a group dance, or a Scottish reel. It's impossible to tell if some of the guests are male or female, but the form seems to be that those who are obviously women wait their turn, swinging their hips, clapping their hands and stamping their feet, while the men rush around in a kind of circling dance, first face to face with the nearest partner, then turning their backs to face a new one.

Suddenly I'm grabbed and spun round relentlessly with all the other women until we are dizzy and breathless. This is becoming more like the Weinmeyers' stated plan for the night. I manage to sling my camera on its strap over my shoulder and try to open the little purse Crystal gave me, so that I can put the camera in and keep it from banging against my hip. All I can do is enter into the spirit of it until the dance is over and retreat to my position on the sidelines.

The madness is infecting everyone. The Weinmeyers' trick is fairly simple, but has to be flawlessly stage-managed. Stir willing guests, potent wine, glittering costumes, beautiful lights and rousing soundtrack together to produce an atmosphere of wonderful abandon. And right on cue the music shifts with a great swooping crescendo from the fast waltzes and polkas into what I can only describe as an almost tribal dervish dance, complete with the thumping of a drum to replicate an increasing heartbeat.

It is so loud in this contained jewel-box of a ballroom that people have abandoned any attempt at polite conversation and are starting to sing and whoop along with the wailing strings and hooting trumpets.

Without being able to view this through my camera, and with my mask partly obscuring everything, I can't focus on the figures cavorting around me, and I am still as safely anonymous as they are. My mask only covers my eyes, but my face is painted chalk-white, which obliterates any real expression or individuality. My lips are dark red, and Crystal has daubed a large black beauty spot on my cheek. I am the same as everyone else except for one thing. I'm the only person dressed in this sensational emerald green and I want to kiss the kaftan lady for kitting me out in the perfect costume.

I could be anyone. The lady in green. That realisation makes me exhilarated, and high. It's exactly what I need after everything that's been happening. The thoughts are only half formed, the faces of Gustav and Pierre faint and flickering in the distance, but the feeling inside me, here and now, is real. I'm free, and flying. For the next few minutes I'm free from everybody and everything. I'm part of this great big messy scenario and that's exactly the way I want it.

I fling myself backwards out of the circle I'm in and rush back to the side of the room. My hands are shaking when I get my camera out again. I glance around to see if Mr and Mrs Weinmeyer are observing me. I want to show them I'm getting this right. I need to make this a sensational record, just like any other job.

My viewfinder is showing me Act 2. The scene, although in the same setting and inhabited by the same figures, is totally different from my initial shots. Guests are no longer sedate, artificial figures stepping through the traditional dances. Now the increasingly mad music has injected them with a hypersexual serum. I'm not zooming in on smiles and delicate waves of fans and fingers. I'm seeing mouths open wide in laughter, arms spread wide, feet kicking wildly, skirts raised, coats flung sideways, shirts and breeches clinging with sweat to thin, fat, muscular, flabby bodies.

And now it's happening to me, too. I keep my eyes on my screen and film for as long as possible, so I can't see clearly what's happening around me, but as I'm dragged back into the fray there is no doubting the touching, the gloved paws starting to reach out for me as I am spun round and round. Despite waving my camera at people to warn them off, there's no stopping the velvet fingers poking under my dress, plucking at the bloomers that the lady in the shop admitted were not made of authentic linen but of a flimsy muslin designed for easy access.

Through my mask I can see that the women are being flung about like tasty morsels at an anarchic picnic. Some of them when they land on the floor lift their gowns coquettishly, offering a glimpse of what's beneath, and sashay within an ogling circle of men and other women. I am sweating now, too. A new impatience goads me. I'm wondering how soon before something really outrageous happens, just as the Weinmeyers promised.

People spread their arms, toss their heads with unholy laughter as they offer themselves to be grabbed and fondled. I film the increasingly daring antics, dresses being pulled down, gloves grappling at crotches, but always, always the masks in place.

But then someone grabs my arms from behind, making my camera fall out of my hands to dangle on its strap, and in front of me a man in a blackbird mask, which jerks and pecks like a magpie, waggles his white gloved magician's hands then scoops one of my breasts out of my bodice and squeezes it.

I can hear my own squeal of shock, but nobody else can. I'm powerless to pull away or kick him off. This is probably what the Weinmeyers meant by me enjoying myself as well as working. Except the original plan was for Gustav to be here with me.

The arms behind are holding me like a vice, and gradually a kind of melting helplessness overwhelms me. I wrestle with anxiety that I will lose my camera and a shameful sense of pleasure at the feel of these random, anonymous hands feeling and squeezing my body at will. There's probably a mischievous attempt to stop the camera woman working, or perhaps it's my unique green costume, my sparkling sequins, my huge plume of peacock feathers waving from my *fontange* head-dress, that attract them, because others suddenly start to elbow the magician out of the way in a feeding frenzy. Someone hoists the other breast out, holding both treats for inspection, and pinching the red nipples I secretly painted with lipstick when Crystal was out of the room.

Just as suddenly I'm flung aside, and I stagger against the wall, every part of me tingling and urging me to get back in there, forget the filming, just have more of those fingers on me.

But on the other side of the room things have degenerated even further. I can see a woman in a white dress trimmed with gold lace, her expressionless gold mask covering her eyes and nose, her yellow ringletted hair falling over her bared shoulders as she is stretched out between two men dressed in striped cat costumes. One is thrusting his face into her cleavage and drawing out one nipple between very sharp teeth.

I zoom in close so that I can see the nipple reddening as he bites it. Meanwhile the other cat man is lifting up her long skirt and crawling between her legs, pulling down her bloomers, tossing them with an exaggerated flourish into the applauding crowd, and oh, God, a third man, also dressed as a cat but in such a black costume that I can't even see the glitter of his eyes or the wetness of his mouth, has approached and very calmly unzips his black leggings and lowers himself over the woman's face, prises open her big, laughing mouth, and pushes himself into it so that she is forced to suck him while the others poke and prod and bite. She arches her big, artificially firm breasts at them as if feeding kittens, and she wriggles and writhes with obvious pleasure.

As I raise my camera to take a shot of the trio, the lady turns her head, still sucking, directly towards me as if she's deliberately posing for me.

I'm not being held now, and I spin of my own accord, stumble here and there, my cloak occasionally wrapping itself round my legs to trip me. Even the king and queen on their thrones are being kissed and groped by a bevy of white-robed courtiers.

My whole body is burning and fizzing with filthy excitement, nerves and senses on high alert in the midst of this Roman-style orgy. I am a mass of sensation, vision and sound. There's not a single rational thought or word finding its way through my brain. I needed this obliteration. Badly.

I am dizzy with the drink, horny as hell, high on the intoxicating atmosphere. I want whatever's going, whatever anyone can give me. The drug or whatever was in that punch has dragged me up to an unbearable pitch of arousal, and I find myself in the centre of the room, spreading open my arms and legs wide to say *come and get me*.

More hands smother me as I dance. A man covered in blue and yellow feathers and with an orange crest like a parakeet lifts my skirt and squeezes my buttocks. His fingers scrabble at me. I jerk with delighted shock and curl my leg round his to keep hold of him and maintain my balance, but then he vanishes and another figure in a flashing top hat like a magician spins me and rocks me from behind, pushing his erection into the bustle of my dress and bundling my breasts into his hands.

The crowd starts to whoop and clap, even sing. Hard bodies push against me, encased in velvet and Lycra and leather. I'm aching with excitement now, electricity darting all over my body.

'*La putana inglese!*'

Or at least that's what I think I hear in the brouhaha. Then the emperor Weinmeyer appears, all in white, stalking stiffly, holding out his arms to me. I hold my arms out to him. Suddenly I want someone to claim me. I like the fact that he and Mrs Weinmeyer are the only people in this room who have a clue who I am, and even then they only know me because I'm the lady with the green earrings wielding the camera.

As the white and gold statue reaches me, he bows briefly then turns me so that I'm wedged up against his white costume and something thick and hard nudges at my bottom. My breasts are still tumbling out and my knees start to buckle as Mr Weinmeyer's gloved hand fans out on my stomach to bend me so that he can raise my skirt and push at me more easily. I know it's him, because through his gloves I can feel the dig of his signet ring. So let him do what he wants. He's the boss, after all.

All around us, featureless revellers elbow each other and gesticulate, unable to speak in the now deafening music. All pretence of period chivalry has vanished. The people around us start to clap as our host lifts my skirt higher for all to see.

Everyone is in a state of insanity. Those who aren't watching are doing it themselves. On the dais I can see Mrs Weinmeyer in her white flowing gown, lying on her back, one slim leg hooked round the arm of her throne as a man in clinging snakeskin swipes his narrow pelvis at her.

The sight of her, of all the others enjoying this orgy, the

escapism, the madness, suddenly blinds me like a flash of lightning and I pull away from Mr Weinmeyer. I stagger away from him. Before I pick up my camera I need to cover myself. My bodice feels tighter than ever, making it difficult to breathe now. As I try to stuff my breasts into some kind of order they push and squeeze, only half encased, ready to bounce out again. I flick my fan at Mr Weinmeyer and give a deep curtsy as if letting him have his fondle and then teasing him like this was all part of the pretence. Even in my tripped-out state I know I mustn't anger him.

What did he call me? *Putana*. That means 'slut' or 'whore', if I'm not mistaken. Well, that means I'm playing my role perfectly. But still I have to work.

To my relief Mr Weinmeyer sweeps a low bow in return, and hands me over to a newcomer who I realise has been hovering on the edge of the circle as if biding his time. All the costumes are padded to exaggerate people's contours, so that women's breasts and hips look huge, men's shoulders and groins are massive. This new participant wears a tricorn hat which casts a deep triangular shadow over his fully masked face, a glorious green velvet coat and tight-fitting breeches and a white ruffled shirt. His muscular calves are encased in green stockings and he's wearing traditional black buckled shoes.

Topping the ensemble of the newcomer is a single long, petrol-blue peacock-tail feather, complete with the round, staring evil eye, the same as the five feathers Crystal has pinned into my powdered headdress.

We are a perfect match.

My suitor sweeps me into a sedate, swan-necked waltz, spinning me so fast that the lights and the watching faces become a nauseous blur. Everyone falls away as if they, too, know who he is. Mr Weinmeyer knew. He's handed me over. I belong to the newcomer because he's the only person dressed

293

in the same emerald green as me. He's my soul mate, come all the way from New York to find me.

With a relief unlike anything I have ever felt, I realise that it is Gustav. I press up against his firm, warm body, feel the hardness already nudging inside his breeches. I wish I could rip his costume off right here. I want to yank off the full-face mask to see that hidden mouth, biting down to hide the waiting smile. His hands, one on my waist, the other guiding my hand through the dance, are holding me like he never wants to let me go.

I keep my eyes on him to anchor me through the endless spinning.

'Gustav! Oh, God, this is brilliant! You came after me! Come on, let's get the hell out of this madhouse! The Weinmeyers will understand.'

Gustav pauses in the middle of the dance, holding my hand up above my head as I spin beneath his finger. But he doesn't speak. A mask can't emote, but a body can, and there's something alert and watchful in his body language. Did he hear me? Is he considering his answer? Is he still angry at what passed between us, or relieved that he's found me? Does he want to kiss me or yell at me? Is that a slight tilt of his head in a yes? Or is that sharp shake, making the peacock feather jump over his hat, to indicate a no?

'You look so gorgeous in that green costume. You're even wearing a peacock feather like mine!'

I raise my hand to touch the feather, lower it to pull off his mask, but he snatches my hands and keeps them trapped inside his highwayman's gloves.

He pulls me close up against him, so close that the big gold buttons on his coat dig into the fleshy tops of my breasts where they bulge out of my overworked bodice. Has he just arrived, or has he seen everything that's been going on? The people groping me? Mr Weinmeyer trying to take me from behind? Gustav's hard-on, packed inside his breeches, barges against my stomach. Well, whatever he's seen has turned him on. My body quivers in delirious response.

I stand on tiptoe, start to yell his name again. But he still doesn't speak. I must have broken some kind of ballroom etiquette calling his name. I wish I could wrench our masks off and get out of here, but he's following the anonymous code to the letter, because abruptly he kicks his shoes together at the heel and lifts his hand in farewell. As he backs away through the frenzied crowd I try to push my way after him but I am grabbed by someone to stop me.

I punch out and realise that it's the woman in white who was being ravaged by the two men earlier. Her yellow wig has slipped slightly to reveal a raven curl in front of her small, neat ear, slightly pricked. I'm seeing things now. Did he also spot the similarity? Has the sight of a Margot looka-like spooked Gustav and chased him away? Or is he playing some other cruel game?

I run round the room looking for him. He's not there, but he can't have gone far because there don't appear to be any doors into or out of this room. Perhaps he's escaped another way. I push through one of the tall open windows and hang over the balustrade draped with flags and heralds, searching up and down the quayside below. I lift my mask to see better. But there's no sign. No emerald-green coat or peacock feather.

I put my hand over my mouth to stop me screaming with frustration. I have to find him. The cold, salty air is like nectar as I take great gulping breaths. Gustav is playing with me. He must be waiting for me somewhere, or if he's still testing me he'll have taken the more straightforward route and gone back to the hotel so we can talk properly without masked madmen capering all around us. Or is he disgusted, after all his efforts to fly over here to get me, to find me having the time of my life with a bunch of stoned strangers and about to be ravished by Mr Weinmeyer? But surely he also saw me pulling away? I've done nothing wrong tonight. Nothing.

Yet more explanations. At least I know he's made the first move. If he wants me to grovel he can sweat for a little longer. I'll find my own way back.

I grab one of the golden flags draped by the window, hitch myself over the balcony and slither down onto the gold carpet below which is now deserted. I notice a *calle* crossing at the end of the private walkway. My vague reckoning is that it must lead towards the Rialto, in which case if I can get to that bridge I can make my way back, albeit in a roundabout way, to the Hotel Danieli and the safety of Crystal's unemotional wisdom before Gustav gets there.

I realise too late that not only have I again rejected the advances of my host but I've forgotten my manners and failed to say farewell. Well, I'll make sure they're pleased with what I've done. This assignment has been a gift. I've got some fantastic pictures and film here. I peel off my gloves and wrap them round the camera to keep it safe inside the little purse. I'll call on my patrons tomorrow, make it up to them.

Just as I reach the street I collide with a wall of jostling, dancing people. On the other side, the way I want to go, I think I see the peacock feather. I try to push through, but instead I'm grabbed and pulled into the swelling tide of masked people and dragged away from where I want to go. Some are gliding silently, some batter my senses with violent revelry, banging drums, tootling tuneless trumpets, some are jerking like puppets or deathly as corpses, but all of them seem to turn their heads to stare through me as they parade beside the water and over the grand arch of the Rialto Bridge.

Noise and colour echo off the surrounding buildings. My feet barely touch the ground as I am swept along, everyone drawn like magnets along the narrow alleyways on the other side of the Rialto where they are forced to pause to let other parties pass.

I try to kick and punch my way out of the group, desperate now to get back to Gustav, but my struggles and screams are drowned in the torrent of noise. We flood on through the city until I recognise the colonnades at the west end of Piazza San Marco, and then we plunge straight into the glare and music and colour.

Floodlights are suspended from the corners of the cathedral and the Doge's Palace and they spin and change colour, bouncing light off the walls and windows and shops, making the kaleidoscope of masked figures already twirling like dervishes in the centre all the more confusing. At least I know where I am now. I just have to make my way down the edge, past Caffe Florian, out towards the lagoon, and I'll be home. Please God, let him find his way there.

But it's not so simple. Even the orchestra playing outside the famous Caffe are dressed as vampires, blood running down their chins as they scrape away at their violins like those brave souls who played on the *Titanic* until it went down. There's no escaping this crowd. Gustav will be as caught up and lost in it as I am. Panic swells inside me. I have no choice but to give myself up to the pushing and pulling of the other masked revellers. Suddenly, flickering amongst the multicoloured costumes, I think I can see the woman in the gold mask who tried to stop me earlier, her gold wig fallen off completely now, coils of black hair flying round her bare shoulders.

She isn't watching me, but this is still becoming like a horror film. I need to get a grip. It can't be the same woman. If it was, how could she possibly find and follow me in this crowd?

The dancers move round each other in spirograph circles and the woman is extinguished. I make a mental note to ask the Weinmeyers who she was and what the hell was in their drink before I'm lifted right off my feet and tossed across the sea of bodies toward the corner of the square where it opens up to the sea, and as I land into a net of hands I see my peacock-feathered highwayman again, leaning against the final pillar watching. He raises his hand and beckons me.

The clapping and stamping crowd throws me towards him. Flamenco music clashes with hip-hop, the strings outside the Caffe Florian battle with a heavy-metal thudding from over by the lagoon, and I am hurled out of the crowd into the space beyond.

Gustav catches me like a wedding bouquet, drops me to my feet and runs with me, but instead of heading for the hotel on the Riva della Schiavoni he drags me towards Harry's Bar.

'I thought I'd lost you, Gustav! Why did you leave the ball?'

He presses a gloved finger hard on my painted mouth. That's our special gesture. All my despair has evaporated. Gustav is here, and that's all that matters. How could I have doubted that he'd see sense and come for me?

'OK. I'll go along with the silent treatment, if that's what turns you on. We have all the time in the world to talk. But can't we just go home?'

Gustav shakes his head and I let him lead me away until the music becomes muffled by distance, and after a while we reach a slimy walkway edged by elegant barley-sugar pillars beside a tiny canal where a collection of empty, somewhat funereal gondolas are corralled, bobbing and fidgeting like wild horses.

I glance up at the brightly lit windows across this canal, silhouettes of partygoers jerking behind the billowing curtains of other palazzi. We are alone together in this madness. No one will come looking for us.

Gustav tightens his grip on me and steps onto the first of the parked gondolas. It tilts violently. He pauses, gets his footing in the elaborate buckled shoes, slips slightly on the elevated heel, then steps across to the next gondola and the others tethered in a row until we reach the last one, which has a big black canopy of thick velvet curtains, its floor strewn with black and gold cushions.

'Can't you talk to me now we're alone?' I whisper, but he just chucks me unceremoniously onto the thick pile of cushions. The brute force of it, the suppressed anger, or perhaps the impatience to have me, turns me on. He grabs the mooring rope and lashes one of my hands to the bench seat.

'Where's the silver chain?' I ask, tugging on the rope, but he grabs a gondolier's pole, pushes us off, and soon we are rocking gently in the middle of the canal. He's expert at this. Another of Gustav's many secret skills.

Gustav keeps his head averted, as if I'm a cargo of stolen booty. His tricorn hat and green spangled mask with the long, hooked bird's nose make a strange profile as he punts us up another dark, dank canal, dips under bridges where occasional costumed revellers still trail, their voices and feet echoing dully, slowed by too much partying.

I watch the bend of his leg, the ripple of muscle working in his strong thigh and calf as he balances on the stern of the boat. He looks gorgeous and muscular in the costume. The tight breeches are like the jodhpurs he wore when we went riding in Lugano.

I wriggle with frustration as well as cold. The drugged wine is beginning to wear off now, but in its place is a fresh, ferocious lust. I lie back in the cushions, feeling the dip and sway of the boat as we drift through the city. I try to pull the cumbersome headdress off but Crystal has pinned it on too tight. My hair feels matted and damp beneath it and my head is aching. A cold drizzle is falling outside now, but sweat is itching between my breasts.

The gondola bumps up against the side and Gustav flings another rope round a post. I can't see where we are because he pulls the curtains closed, but there seems to be more noise here than before. Then he crawls across the cushions, flicking his green frock-coat out of the way to get at the tiny mother-of-pearl buttons that are straining to contain the swell under his green velvet fly. I squirm with wicked, renewed, impatient desire. We have been apart for too long. I will never let this happen again. He unpicks each button. The corner of his white shirt pokes through the opening.

I watch, and wait.

He leaves the breeches unbuttoned, puts his glove back on, then pushes my legs open so that he can kneel between them. He raises my dress up over the rumpled silk bloomers, settles the lovely fabric round me as if to frame the sight, then yanks down the bloomers and throws them into a corner. A demented giggle bubbles inside me. I've lost count of the knickers I've lost over the last few weeks. But Crystal chose these especially from the little dress shop, and if I lose them she will be furious.

I slide down the cushion so that I am underneath him.

'Couldn't we undo this now?' I whisper, wrenching at the rope. 'It's hurting me.'

He starts to loosen it, and there's a bit of give round my sore wrist, but then he shakes his head. He wants to keep it there, the alternative to our silver chain. Why didn't he bring it with him? Surely tonight would have been the perfect occasion to tether me once again? The leather fingers of his gauntlets are rough and catch on my skin as he pushes my legs further apart. I'm squashed down in the cushions now, and he is heavy on me.

The water slaps beneath the underside of the boat. It could almost be slapping my bare buttocks, spread open on the cushions. Presumably in Casanova's day they wore delicate lace drawers, I think drowsily. Or perhaps Casanova's conquests came to him well prepared, sans culottes. Just the way Gustav likes it.

My dress rips slightly as Gustav's gloves rove up my stomach, over the swell of my breasts. This strong, silent treatment is incredibly horny. Through the meshed slits in his green mask he can see me laid out beneath him, pale and semi-naked on the black cushions. The green velvet fly falls open and there it is, already hard, standing thick and tall like a church candle in the moonlight. I'm loose in every sense, awash with desire as the sensations tangle and build inside me. My skirt is a cloud around us. He lowers himself over me, his invisible eyes searching my face, pushing me into the cushions. He holds himself tight within the grasp of his leather gauntlet, running his fingers up and down thoughtfully for a moment.

'Don't stop now, Gustav!'

There's a sudden roar as a motorboat slows down beside us, its wash banging the side of the gondola despite the speed limits imposed on the city. Raucous singing and shouting come from the crowd on board, and the boat hoots several times. They are just the other side of our canopy, as if they're waiting for us to come out and join them. Or explain ourselves. A searchlight moves over the closed canopy of curtains as if they know we're in here.

Could it be Crystal, alerted that I'm missing?

Gustav and I freeze like criminals on the run. He turns towards the searchlight, still holding himself like a baton, then slowly looks back at me. Something's not right. The wash of the boat has opened the curtains slightly. Surely the idea of being caught, seen, should be kinky and fun. But it isn't. It feels degenerate, and dangerous, especially when his hand slams down on my mouth.

I scrabble at him to try to get upright, but he's holding me down too hard. He's hurting me and I can't breathe. I grab hold of his shirt and it comes out of the breeches. My fingers scratch slivers of cool skin.

A large troop of revellers runs over the bridge above us, whooping and shrieking. I peer upwards. Through the gap of the curtains I think I recognise the bridge and the buildings around us. The flowing tide of pageantry slows as people notice our rocking gondola. I can only see their feet pausing, some bare, some booted, some buckled. The noise seems to rouse Gustav, too, because he lifts my legs and hooks them over his shoulders.

As he moves me and I realise the people up on the bridge can see, I reach round his back to pull him closer and my nails catch not on Gustav's smooth, muscled back but on a ridge of bumpy, jagged scars. Too late he jerks back violently and knocks my hand away.

I try to scream, but his hand is still smothering me. *This isn't Gustav, you stupid, stupid girl.* These are burn scars, all over his stomach and back! I kick furiously but he tries to push himself harder at me, aiming himself deep between my legs. He starts to thrust at me, and somehow I find the knot in the rope round my wrist and as I pull it loose I raise my knee and shove it, hard, into his groin, then kick him again, right in the balls this time, with the one sharp-heeled shoe that I'm still wearing, so that he rolls away from me, yelping, as I crawl out of the enveloping cushions.

I've hurt him badly but he still finds the strength to grasp at my ankles to stop me getting away. I kick his hand away and stamp on it. That will hurt, too. All Pierre Levi will have of me is one slipper. Just like Cinderella.

I scramble out of the gondola. Hands haul me up onto the slippery stones of the quayside. I stand there shivering helplessly, tugging at my tattered headdress, folding myself inside my cloak. I realise I'm home, after all. This is the Ponte del Vin, right beside my hotel.

Some people gesticulate merrily towards the gondola, some even pushing me towards the edge as if my disarray is all

302

part of the show and I might want to get back in to continue my ravishment, but when I turn to check that Pierre Levi isn't coming after me the gondola has already slipped its moorings and is disappearing up the Rio del Vin, into the fog.

Tears start pouring down my cheeks as I gasp for air through my bruised mouth. The people nudge each other and melt away from this dishevelled creature. I don't know where to go, what to do. Who to tell! How can I tell them Pierre Levi was here? He has followed me all the way to Venice like a man possessed. And he nearly had me.

I've done exactly what Gustav warned me not to do when we talked about setting me free to explore darker pleasures, so long as it was within certain boundaries. I've disobeyed him, unwittingly, but will he ever believe me?

You'll know if you've gone too far when the time comes. Because it will either feel right or it will feel very, very wrong.

Suddenly, someone is peeling away my mask, lifting my headdress off my aching head, combing kind fingers through my damp hair.

'Crystal, thank God!' I sob, tripping on my one shoe into her arms. 'Get me away from him!'

But it's not Crystal. It's the real thing. Gustav. The one person in all the world I want to see. Tall and dark as he pulls me out of the shadows and into the warm light cast onto the *fondamente* from the hotel. The strong black bristles are starting to push through his jaw. The black eyes are gazing at me, full of things he wants to say, the love burning there totally unmasked. He's the only man in the whole of Venice dressed in twenty-first-century clothes.

'Get you away from who? Hey, hey, I'm not letting you get away from me again!' Gustav kisses my wet eyes, the tip of my nose, pushes the hair out of my face as we stop outside the hotel. 'Look at you! All this revelry has undone you! Thank God I waited for you here. I thought looking for you in this crazy city would be like finding a needle in a haystack! What are the chances, eh?'

'Oh Gustav, I can't believe it's really you this time!' I frame his face with my hands, try to stay calm even though I'm trembling. 'Before you say anything more, I've done something terrible.'

'It was all a disastrous misunderstanding. My fault, as usual.' He captures my hands in his. 'And Pierre's, for backing you into a corner like that. But he has explained everything.'

'He's here?' I scream, and stare round wildly, expecting his green-clad brother to steer the black gondola back down the canal and reappear below us. 'What do you mean, he's explained? What has he told you?'

'He was waiting in the apartment when I got back. Oh, God, you will never know how much I regret storming off like that. I should have locked you in or something! Bloody stupid blind idiot that I am. Pierre came round while I was still out, to check you got your camera equipment back safely, but when I saw him standing there looking at your things calm as you like I thought you'd invited him in and was about to punch him. But it was obvious that you had vanished and then we were beside ourselves with worry.'

'Pierre was worrying about me, was he? So where is he now?' I'm nearly screaming again.

Gustav puts his fingers on my mouth to hush me and pulls me closer. 'Why do you keep asking that? Honey, you were in such a state when you left the apartment that you left the door wide open! Where did you go?'

I can't focus on him. I keep looking up and down that black canal for an approaching gondola.

'Serena! Speak to me!'

I stare at Gustav wildly. 'I went across Central Park to the Weinmeyers. I couldn't think where else to go. I was so furious with you! With all of you!'

He nods again and again, his eyes burning so intensely, as if he has found me like treasure in the dust. 'I know that, too, *cara*. The Weinmeyers called me, not till you were safely on the plane, mind, and they told me to stop being such a bloody arrogant fool and either let you go for good or do everything in my power to get you back.'

I keep staring at him as if he might melt away. My head is thumping painfully. It's like threading thoughts together one by one on frayed string. 'The door – I thought I'd banged it shut! I'd had such a shock–' Spots spark and pop in front of my eyes. I curl my fingers round his hands to stop me fainting clean away. 'My iPad. Did you find that?'

Gustav nods. 'That's what really sent me into a spin. You'd left that behind on the sofa, apparently. Pierre had already found it and switched it off. I've brought it with me. It's here, in your hotel room.' Gustav wraps the cloak round me like a parcel. 'I was frantic thinking you'd even left that behind, with all your notes and commission details. Making sure you got that back was my excuse for coming after you.'

My teeth are chattering. 'You don't need an excuse. I'm just so happy you're here. That you forgive me.'

'I can't forgive myself. You need to forgive *me* for going off the deep end, because as soon as I saw Pierre standing in our apartment I laid into him about Polly's photograph of the two of you, and to be fair he didn't deny what happened at the Gramercy Hotel. You got to him, he said. He loved your photographs of the burlesque show, but he resented your interference in this business with Polly. You were pricking at what little conscience he has. So even though you were being a pain he found you irresistible. Captivating, in fact. His words, not mine. Which led to the brotherly kiss that misfired. Which I recall were exactly your words and I should have listened.'

305

I push my hands on his mouth to try to stop him. 'But this time I *have* done something awful, Gustav!'

He holds me even tighter. 'He treated you like one of his conquests, and he's sorry. And that's why I'm here, too. To say sorry.'

I stand very still, tears like boulders in my throat. 'Pierre came with you to Venice?'

Gustav gently kisses me. 'My confused girl. Pierre is not here. He was called over to California.'

I pull away from him and walk to the water's edge. The city is gradually going to sleep, but I can see the odd fizz and spray of fireworks up the Grand Canal and over on the Giudecca Island. I feel like throwing myself headlong into the black, choppy lagoon.

Lie after lie.

Gustav pulls me away from the edge. 'I'm just a jealous guy. Isn't that what John Lennon said? I have so much to say to you, Serena Folkes. But those Weinmeyers have run you into the ground. So no more now. Sleep. Tomorrow I'm going to prove how special you are to me.'

The sweet relief and happiness in Gustav's face are breaking my heart all over again. How can I ever tell him that the lying cheat Pierre Levi is not in California at all, but somewhere in this very city?

'But first we have to get rid of this hideous thing. What was Crystal thinking of?'

He holds up my discarded headdress, which looks like hairy roadkill, and tosses it into the murky water. 'I would never wear a peacock feather, and nor should you. Didn't you know? They bring bad luck.'

I fall back against his warm body as we watch the head-dress float out towards the lagoon, feathers spread open like five fingers releasing a secret, and then start to sink.

CHAPTER FOURTEEN

As sleep slithers off me I hear the swish and pelt of heavy rain against the window. Every winter morning Venice gives itself up to the sea, but the sky above is drenching us as well, tipping its load relentlessly over the red-tiled roofs and pink and apricot palazzi, washing away all the signs of the Carnevale last night.

I am lying in an amazing canopied gold four-poster bed in the ornate bedroom of one of the most iconic hotels in the world, next to the man who has stolen my heart. But as soon as the grey daylight permeates my eyelids, what separates itself from the maelstrom of my mind is not Gustav but the looming figure of his brother.

I lie staring at the watery play of light on the ceiling. The situation is as clear as if he was standing in front of me, confessing all. He ingratiated himself with Gustav. Then came here. Then bribed the hotel receptionist to direct Crystal and me to the correct costume shop. He must even have bribed the kaftan lady to supply us with that exact outfit.

Pierre must have known, after their touching conversation back in New York, that Gustav would come after me. His video of Margot didn't hit the intended target, so he tried a different tack, came after me as well, made sure he got here first, delayed Gustav, and steered the gondola right to the hotel in the hope that Gustav would catch us. He's out to break me and Gustav. But why? Either he wants Gustav for himself. Or he wants me.

Pierre is still in Venice. Any minute he could walk up the majestic stairs, if he doesn't already have a room in our hotel. He'll knock on our door, and when Gustav welcomes him in he'll reveal exactly how close he was to detonating our happiness.

I roll over on the satin-soft sheet and push my face down into the mattress. The pillow is still warm but Gustav isn't beside me. The sound of rushing water isn't the rain after all. It's coming from the shower.

I jump out of bed, kick my way past my green dress and cloak, which are draped over the carpet and chair like the skins of hunted wildlife. I snatch up the iPad. I didn't dare look at it last night. I switch it on and click through the folders and emails. The Pierre folder is there, complete with the neat bullet points that I'd made when he was briefing me about the story-board for the burlesque show.

The Margot email, the film, the wedding march are erased. Deleted. Or imagined?

I push my way into the steamed-up bathroom. I must get close to Gustav.

His body is gleaming like a dolphin's. I stand and stare at his broad shoulders, the winged jut of his shoulder blades, the regular bumps of his spine, his muscular, rounded butt. His hair is plastered black and wet against his head, outlining the fine shape of his skull. He's already shaved and is lifting his face to the jet of hot water, his long eyelashes stuck together, his mouth half-open as he sings something softly under his breath.

I have the power to make him happy. I also have the power to shatter him.

I sidle into the shower behind Gustav, shiver with pleasure as the water sprays over my sleep-warm skin and pricks it into life. I wrap my arms around him from behind, rub my tight nipples against his back. He turns his face so that I can plant a kiss on his cheek, grins broadly, then continues casually with his washing ritual as if he's not to be interrupted. I hesitate. I'm not going to be dismissed. I've got work to do here. I must remind him that we are unbreakable.

I squirt perfumed gel from the glass dispenser on the wall, rub it between my palms until it foams up into a thick meringue of soap, and then reach round and take his length in my hands, feeling it jump in eager greeting. He continues shampooing his hair as he waits to see what I'll do next.

I start to soap him, tuck the still soft end of him into one hand and swipe with the other, watching it quiver and rise. I begin to relax. It's extending from his lovely flat stomach just like his beloved telescope, smoothing out the velvety skin, ironing out any wrinkles until it is straight and smooth and emerges strong and proud and ready in its blanket of pale-pink bubbles.

A ball of nausea rises in my throat as I remember the sight of Pierre's thick, tall erection, standing proud of his velvet breeches and intended for me.

I pull Gustav more roughly, lather the soft balls, watch his head roll back as the sensations start to weaken him. I'm weak, too, with shame and with love for him so fierce it hurts.

He falls against the shower wall. He doesn't touch me. He's letting me make all the running. The smile stops playing as my hands play faster up and down the long, hard shaft, working the soap into a luxurious lather. I feel him flinch and grow under my touch.

With my other hand I cup his balls and then try something I've never done before. My finger travels further back, up between his gleaming buttocks, darts straight into his tight butt, forcing a groan of surprise from him. I feel his balls retract with his mounting excitement and I chuckle softly as my finger pokes higher, reaching for the moment when he will become helpless.

He groans again, grapples for me blindly and grabs my hips, spins me round, jams me up against him, his hands squeezing my breasts. My feet slip on the marble tiles and I grab the chrome shower pipe as the needles of water continue to stimulate my skin. I can just make out his blurred reflection in the steamed-up shower panel.

He lifts me so that my feet rest on the little step running round the base of the shower tray, and then he cups one large hand and parts me, thrusting his fingers inside, the water and soap mingling with my own juices. How did this happen? How does he always end up in control? My body is contracting wildly to take in his long fingers, but he pulls them out again and parts my legs until I rise right off my toes.

I will learn one day to take total control, but for now I give in yet again to my role as living doll. My stomach kicks with desire as his familiar hands manipulate me into the position he has chosen. I am practically swinging off the shower rail now, balancing on the tops of his legs which are slightly bent as he grapples me from behind. As he lowers himself I rise to meet him and then I feel the tip of it, ready and waiting.

I rest my cheek against the panel, ecstatic to feel him there, wanting the moment of anticipation to go on forever while the water shoots down onto us, steadily reducing in temperature. I shiver as I balance against the panel, feel him solid and strong behind me, flexed and ready, and then I slide down onto him, inch after glorious inch, descending slowly and triumphantly until my buttocks are squashed up against his stomach.

I let go for a moment and then he tilts so that we both start to fall. I let out a shriek as we land on hands and knees half in, half out of the shower. I start to crawl forwards – perhaps we can finish this in the comfort of our big expensive bed – but he yanks me back inside the cubicle so that the water, now really cold, keeps showering onto our backs, and the cold seems to make him even more rigid.

My nipples are stiff as my skin shrinks against the cold water, tingling now with tension as he starts again, slowly pushing, not pulling out at all, so that I am manhandled across the slippery floor with whatever rhythm he chooses, my hands and knees squeaking with the friction, his hands holding me, not needing to do anything more to stimulate me, just letting my body tighten and welcome him, engulf his familiar hardness so that we are welded together, the beast with two backs, rocking back and forth on the hard wet floor of the bathroom.

The water runs colder, Gustav pumps faster, and I'm shuddering both from the cold and from uncontrollable excitement as he accelerates, muttering into my neck, kissing, licking, now biting, jamming me against him as he lifts me off the floor with the force of his coming and I squeeze for more friction and then yield into an explosive climax that flows and mingles with the freezing water and the ebbing bubbles.

There's a harsh rapping at the door and my heart stops. I can't move. I scrabble for a towel, teeth chattering again as Gustav flings on a bathrobe to answer the door. I try to form the sentences that will explain it all.

'Room service!'

I remain in a huddle as Gustav murmurs to the waiter. I pluck at the towel as I try to compose myself.

'Breakfast is served, my love!' he cries, uncovering with a flourish the huge silver tray of food laid out on the table in front of the window. Coffee, orange juice, fruit, eggs, prosciutto, pastries. 'Just look at this view, Serena. Santa Maria della Salute and over there Giudecca. Did you know that from above the map of Venice is shaped like a fish?'

'I did, yes.' I smile and cup my cold hands round the coffee pot. 'How appropriate is that for a watery city? You notice the Grand Canal is its gullet?'

'We could go to the Accademia, walk towards the Zattere. There's a fascinating workshop on the other side of the Ponte del Accademia where they make gondolas. Or how about a trip over to the Lido?'

I reach out for my cream silk negligee to drop it over my still wet, shivering body, then get up and walk across the thick rug towards him. I let him pull out a chair as if he was a waiter. He throws a huge white napkin over my lap, pours strong coffee and into it a generous dollop of cream just as I like it. Then he sits down opposite me and bites noisily into a large, buttery croissant, scattering crumbs comically all over his still wet chest.

'How did you know it was me wandering about on the bridge last night?' Too late I regret prising open this possible can of worms.

He frowns with his knife poised in the air, smeared with butter. His eyes are narrowed against the white light slicing in from the lagoon. He looks as if he should be modelling for a Tom Ford advert.

'Crystal sent me a picture from your phone to cheer me up, thinking I was in New York. Cunning little matchmaker. But my flight to Venice was delayed. The plan I'd made with the Weinmeyers was for you to set off for the ball and for me to follow you and surprise you. I was desperate, you looked so stunning in the picture, so perfectly the part. The Weinmeyers told me to get straight to the ball from here and they'd kit me out in a costume but I landed long after the ball had begun and before I could get out of the airport my bloody brother phoned me.'

A fist reaches inside and clenches my ribcage. I try to hide it by cutting a half moon slice of melon. 'Pierre? Couldn't he have left us alone for five minutes after the trouble he's caused?'

'You kept asking about him last night, Serena. Darling, you must stop feeling guilty!' He dips bread into runny egg yolk, gulps down coffee as if it's his last meal on earth. 'He rang to tell me about LA. He wanted to apologise again. And to ask after you. Anyhow, by the time we'd finished talking it was far too late to find you. All I could do was sit here and wait.'

Gustav puts his cup down. Wipes his mouth with the snowy napkin.

'Actually if I hadn't come out for a walk and found you on the bridge last night my intention was to surprise you this morning and grovel until you forgave me. But there's another reason I came.'

I bite my tongue. Feel the blood rushing to my head as I pull my knees up to my chin. All my acting skills fly out of the window to join the pigeons down in Piazza San Marco.

'You couldn't live without me for another minute?'

'Something like that. *Chérie*, anything could have happened to you at that ball. All that strong liquor, illegal substances, tight corsets. I know I had no right to worry, but I did. I do! I always will. I know I said I want to set you free, within limits, but how can I when the minute you're out of my sight I can't bear the thought of it either? I know those Weinmeyers have taken you under their wing, but they're still not to be trusted when they get into one of their orgies.' He half sighs, half chuckles. I wind lacy fronds of prosciutto around the melon. 'Masks, swords, fire-eaters, it's like one big production of *Phantom of the Opera*.'

'It was just a party, Gustav. Not some kind of cannibalistic ritual.' I shrug, curl my tongue around the sweet melon and salty ham. 'So you came flying over here to rescue me from some nonexistent danger?'

Gustav puts his cup neatly down on the plate and goes to stand by the window. His hand reaches up and strokes the heavy velvet curtain.

'I came over here to apologise and tell you I love you. But the danger wasn't entirely nonexistent, was it? You were in a state when you got back here, and so was Crystal, because she disobeyed my orders and lost track of you.'

I work my way carefully through the melon. If I don't tell him what happened, Pierre will.

'That was my fault for leaving the ball without telling anyone. Gustav, let's just be happy that you came. Venice doesn't feel right without you.'

He opens the window. Cold sea air blasts into the room, knocking over the little glass vase of tiny rosebuds on the breakfast tray.

'I'm a fool, I know. I should have trusted you to look after yourself. You're my feisty mare, after all. But I can't help it, Serena. You're my treasured possession. The more I watch you grow and blossom, the more I want to be near you, taking care of you.'

'You sent Crystal to do that instead.' I push my plate away. 'And I'm grateful, Gustav. You don't have to worry about me, but it was lovely to find her here. Where is she, by the way?'

'I sent her back to London. Rather abruptly, I'm afraid.'

'Crystal's my friend, Gustav. Not my bodyguard.' I close my eyes, grope about in the fruit bowl and find a peach. I lift it to my lips and bite into it. 'And I'm sure the Weinmeyers wouldn't have let anything bad happen.'

I let the peach juice swirl over my tongue. That's if they'd known where I was. I'd put myself into that danger by running off in search of the man in green.

Gustav nods. 'They wouldn't let anything harm their latest protégée. They adore you, Serena, and no wonder! Already

314

they've sent out invitations to a party to view your boudoir portraits of them in their house. No doubt the ballroom montage will be another glittering Weinmeyer exhibition, too, when that's edited.'

Gustav scoops my ball gown off the floor with his toe and lifts it to sniff the sweat and perfume on the fabric. His black hair is drying now, falling into his eyes as he squints against the light. He doesn't notice that the robe is falling open, baring his muscled stomach and the dark shadow between his thighs. I spit out the peach stone with a clatter onto my little plate.

'So? You said there was another reason you came here?'

Gustav hooks the gown on a hanger over the door of the wardrobe. Stroking the green silk with his long, strong fingers. 'A little promenade, I think, and then I want to show you something.'

We have a few more hours before our night flight out of Venice. We mustn't waste it. I walk slowly through the city. For the first time in days I have something of the old spring in my step. That's having Gustav within reach, of course, but I'm also basking in the genuine delight of the Weinmeyers just now, when we went through the stills and film of their Carnevale ball.

I smile as I remember the scene that greeted me at Palazzo Weinmeyer. Most of the party detritus had been cleared away, but I still spotted a couple of masks hanging from an oil painting and some cut-out scarlet knickers adorning the head of a marble statue before the exhausted and hungover pair greeted me in their little salon.

'You left the ball without saying goodbye. Not always safe to do that. Anything could have happened to you on a night like Carnevale,' chided Mrs Weinmeyer, resting a cool cloth against her head. 'But you'd fulfilled your brief, so we'll let

315

you off. I daresay that stranger in the emerald green had something to do with your flitting away like Cinderella?'

My face flooded with red as I packed away my camera. 'I needed to get back. I was tired, that's all.'

'You and Prince Charming had a lot of catching up to do, I'm sure.' Mrs Weinmeyer winked at her husband. 'That was our doing, you know. We persuaded Gustav to come hotfoot from New York and claim you at the ball. We had no idea he'd be clever enough to find the very costume to match yours, though! Even we didn't know what you were going to be wearing that night, did we?'

'Mrs Weinmeyer, Mr Weinmeyer, I have to tell you something in total confidence.' My hands stop fiddling with my camera case. I look up, and they are listening intently. 'The man in green wasn't Gustav. How I wish it had been! He just vanished into the crowd, I didn't see him again, but I think Gustav would be happier not hearing about him, especially as he's so furious he didn't get here in time to come to the ball!' I laughed shakily to hide the guilt and the pleading note in my voice as they tried to pay attention like a pair of tired birds, their heads on one side and resting against their armchairs.

Mr Weinmeyer lifted a silver bell and tinkled it to summon the butler to let me out. 'What happens at the Weinmeyer ball, Serena—'

I laughed quietly. 'And that's why I have to get going now. Gustav's waiting for me down near the Giudecca Canal and he's whisking me back home first thing tomorrow morning. As you say, we have lots of catching up to do! See you back in the Big Apple!'

'You certainly will, sugar,' crooned Mrs Weinmeyer. 'You owe us a little private fun.'

As I ran down the wide marble staircase I caught sight of a buckled shoe discarded in the corner of a balcony.

316

Now I walk on through the white afternoon to meet my lover. The few sightseers who pass me are bedraggled after last night's excesses. The city is still quiet, restored for a day or two to its inhabitants and their secret lives behind the chipped arched windows and freshly planted red geraniums.

One pair of buckled shoes nearly destroyed me. Pierre wore them to lend him the extra height that made him look more like Gustav. And now I can feel the sway of the gondola again, the pressing of my body into those cushions with Pierre's weight on me, his hands and lips, every part of him trying to take me away from Gustav. Nausea swirls in my stomach as I see again the fly of his breeches opening to show me what he had in store, the deep kick of excitement and readiness in my response.

No wonder I can't shake off the fear that eyes are watching me. Pierre could be anywhere. When I see him again he will be unmasked, with such a story, and I wonder if I will ever be free of the fear that he will tell it.

I walk south down the side of the gallery and across Campo Sant'Agnese, empty today save for a clutch of pigeons and a waiter emerging from a small corner trattoria and optimistically putting out metal chairs and tables even though this wind is Arctic. A bent old lady wearing a black coat, with a black mantilla draped over her sparse white hair, edges her way round the piazza with her back pressed against the walls, eyes darting from side to side as if she is poised any minute to surrender to a hail of gunfire, like a very old Bonnie who has lost her Clyde.

I take out my camera, my automatic reaction whenever my imagination starts to work overtime. In my viewfinder she shrinks into a batty old woman who wants to feed the birds, tuppence a bag. But like all of us she has a history. She could once have been a great beauty, had a great voice, was a famous dressmaker or explorer or pastry cook, had been a maestro's mistress, enjoyed great passion. And now she'll be forever old and frozen inside my box of tricks.

I scan the square, into the windows, up to the roofs. Pierre is like a sniper, taking aim. I lower my camera and keep walking. Last night's encounter, even though it didn't come to fruition, is a ticking time-bomb if I don't find a way to defuse it. All I can hope is that Pierre won't say anything because if he tells my boyfriend he tried to fuck me in a gondola he will lose his brother all over again, with me as collateral damage.

But if he does decide to tell Gustav some hideous story, I have no option but to tell the truth. That I thought he was Gustav. That it was a case of mistaken identity. But until then there's the horrible feeling that I am Pierre's hostage. I become more absorbed, foraging material for my 'Windows and Doors' show as I pass a scattering of closed shops and bars, and then I'm on the wide southern pavement of the Fondamenta Zattere. Every evening last summer this was where the colourful *passeggiata* of artists and residents took place, away from the central areas, watched over by the melancholy Isola della Giudecca. Now I'm almost knocked backwards by the wind slicing up the Giudecca Canal in the wake of an obscenely enormous white cruise ship that is taller than most of the buildings. It looks crude and false, superimposed, as if the city is a green screen and the gigantic cruiser is the harbinger of a disaster movie. The engines throb like a sore thumb, their underwater vibrations trying to prise up the old stones beneath my feet.

Venice has cobwebbed around me like a network of arteries and veins. I can't envisage this city collapsing into the waves, like the special effects in the closing scenes of James Bond's *Casino Royale*.

The only other person out here is a shabby bearded painter in a drooping trilby and an overcoat. He is huddled over his easel, a stack of blank canvases beside him. His paintbrush is poised like a dart as he ignores the stout backside of the retreating cruise liner and instead stares eastwards towards Chiesa San Giorgio Maggiore and the lagoon. On the paper clipped to his board are the first few strokes of a dreamy watercolour, so understated that all I can see is a tangerine haze, so he must have been here since sunrise. Sunsets here are coral. Spires and people are ghostly smudges on the page, designed to play tricks on the eye until interrupted by the curved black prow of a gondola entering the picture from the edge.

I wonder if he realises that a blob of terracotta watercolour paint in the top corner has elongated into a tear drop and is now a rusty stream piercing the delicate outlines of his work.

I continue until I'm able to take a surreptitious picture of the artist as he bends to look at his paper. He notices the spillage and absently traces the stream of paint with his finger.

I see Gustav before he sees me. Through the big open doors of a *squero*, a small shipyard on the Rio di San Trovaso, where the carcases of broken gondolas and the embryos of new ones hang from the rafters, he is squatting on the floor amongst curled shavings, listening intently to a grizzled geezer as he planes dark wood. Gustav is stroking the rib of a half-formed gondola with the tip of his finger, and I stand on the other side of the canal watching him, a shiver of desire going through me as I look at his big warm hands. When he's not punishing me he strokes me just like that.

Right now the boat looks like the bleached skeleton of a long fish. I come up behind the two men and scuffle my feet in the sawdust. Gustav half-turns and waggles his fingers over his shoulder but I'm not to interrupt. I squat close to him, dying to ferret my nose into his black hair just where it falls on to his red scarf. It would be rude to start licking his neck in front of this old gondola-maker, but I want to breathe him in.

'Did you know, there are seven different kinds of wood going into this gondola? Two hundred and eighty pieces in the hull alone,' Gustav remarks after a moment. The old man nods at me, a gold tooth glinting, then gets back to work.

I raise my camera and start to shoot.

'He uses oak for the flanks, fir for the bottom of the hull because apparently it's light. The stern is made from cherry, and the bow is mahogany. He has to make it asymmetrical. The left side has a greater curve to balance the lateral action of the oar. It's a work of art. He'll take out all the nails and do it again if it's a millimetre out of line.'

Gustav stands up and bids farewell to the gondola-maker in fluent Italian.

'Is that what you wanted to show me today?'

'No, but it's fascinating nevertheless. Maybe we should plant all those trees in the garden we are going to have one day, Serena. In England. Italy. Wherever. Wood for these beautiful boats. It's just a shame they're so overpriced now, once the gondoliers reel in the tourists.' Gustav seems deep in thought as he puts his arm round me. 'Like streetwalkers tarted up for business.'

We walk back along the Zattere and push open the door of a warm lino-floored pizzeria noisy with the clatter of pans and cutlery. The rustic walls are adorned with misty paintings of the city.

We spend a long afternoon drinking beer and eating pizzas the size of wagon wheels slathered in melted mozzarella and sprinkled with bright green basil before leaving reluctantly and making our way slowly back over the slim Accademia Bridge. We stop in the middle, taking in the curve of the Grand Canal.

'La Serenissima. Venice the serene and beautiful. They named this town after you, Serena.'

I smile and lean against him. 'You know this bridge was intended to be temporary when it was built? They were supposed to be finding a suitable permanent design but they seem to have forgotten, and this spindly wooden one is still here.'

We watch the parade of finished gondolas slide under our feet, all painted and varnished and lacquered and gliding nimbly amongst the businesslike *vaporetti*. A trio of heavy *peate* lumbers down the centre of the channel with several grand pianos lashed to their hulls.

'A bit like the London Eye. That was only supposed to be for the millenium, wasn't it?'

'And how different this watery thoroughfare is from the Thames.'

I close my eyes and see the giant wheel turning on the South Bank, how it caught my eye every time I looked out of the window of the Levi gallery during my first-ever exhibition in London. I remember the quiet circuit Gustav and I made on it that day just before Christmas when he asked me to go to New York with him. How thrilled I was.

And yet at this moment the last place I want to be is New York.

The couples below us who have paid a king's ransom for the privilege of being propelled in a gondola look faintly ridiculous as they rub mottled violet hands and try to arrange their legs elegantly on their cushions, exclaiming and taking pictures while the bored gondolier whistles soundlessly above them.

'I've got something here to perk up those shrivelled-looking honeymooners. Don't they know there are other ways to enjoy a gondola?'

Gustav chuckles quietly and pulls the silver chain out of his pocket. It has been rolled up so that it looks like a tennis ball made of metallic wool, something a kitten would toy with. It's tied all round so that it won't unravel.

'Gustav? What are you doing?'

He waits for the gondola to slide under the bridge and then tosses the ball straight down into the gondola, making the couple jump and wonder.

Gustav kisses my hair. 'It'll take them a while to work out what it is for. But I hope they enjoy it. We don't need it any more. You're free.'

'You came to Venice to set me free?' I rub my wrist, where the silver bracelet still glistens. This explains his serious expression. He came to tell me that it's over. 'I don't want to be free. I want to be glued to you forever!'

'And you are. You will be. But we don't need the silver chain to bind us. However long a leash I attach to you, you will always stretch it further. It's a symbol that has run its course, because I trust, I *know*, that you'll always come back to me, even when you run away as far as Venice. So I think we need something new to symbolise what we have.'

We stare from the bridge down the Grand Canal flanked by Gothic palazzi towards San Marco, my hotel, and the wide expanse of light from the lagoon beyond. The coral sunset is beginning to stain the sky. Beneath us a boat churns up green foam. Gustav presses his hand on the rail to make me stay put, and dashes down the bridge the way we came. He darts into a little bar beneath the Hotel Galleria and comes out again with two tall glasses of prosecco.

I take a sip from my glass. It's delicious and light, but the bubbles aren't inside me yet.

'You know the strangest thing, Gustav? I've done a lot of walking while I've been here. I went looking for the convent where I photographed those nuns last summer, but I couldn't find it. It was as if it had never existed. But then the other morning I passed the Ospedale della Pietà, not far from the hotel actually. Historically it was the church where the fallen women of the city left their babies, nearly always girls, to be brought up. And Vivaldi trained many of them to sing like angels in his choirs.'

My eyes spring with hot tears as I look over in that direction.

'We can always come back here again, Serena. How about a tour of Italy next year? We can find a lovely villa, in Tuscany maybe, that will only be ours.'

I don't really register what he's saying. I lean my head on his shoulder. 'The foundlings were given the surname Trovato, did you know that? It means 'found'. Maybe I could do that. Discard my own false history once and for all. Make myself a new one. I could change my name to Trovato. What do you think, Gustav?'

Gustav doesn't respond. I'm not sure he's heard me. The wind whistles past us. The buildings of Venice crowd round us as the light fades.

Then he turns me to face him. My heart starts thumping, knocking the golden locket against the bone. He lifts the locket, snaps it open with a little key no bigger than his little fingernail, shakes out into his hand whatever has been rattling in there for the last seven weeks. Now his face has gone white, anxious, unsure, and that makes it suddenly youthful. His black hair whips into his sparking black eyes as he kneels down like a gallant knight bowing to his queen.

The soundtrack to this moment in my life drowns out all those worries, wipes away all the shadows trying to scare us. A crescendo of violins washes around us. Gustav's black hair blows back from his face so the love shining in his black eyes is clear and absolute.

He opens his hand. What I've been carrying around with me all this time, knocking quietly against my throat in the golden locket, is a beautiful diamond ring.

'I've a better idea. How about changing your name to Levi?'

323

CHAPTER FIFTEEN

A different stretch of water now, far away across the Atlantic, flowing through a gritty urban landscape of skyscrapers and apartments. I am standing on an old freight railway line thirty feet above the ground, being buffeted by the wind off the Hudson River.

I have an hour to spare after having spent an extravagant afternoon browsing in the boutiques of Gansevoort Street and shopping in Diane von Fürstenberg's flagship store. I'm now shamelessly weighed down by bags full of dresses with names like Wanda and Zarita, which make me feel like a fortune-teller but also high-maintenance and super-sexy, all long legs and curves. I know my purchases will please Gustav, who likes me in jeans but loves me in dresses. In fact I'm wearing the pretty Wanda dress in midnight-blue lace now but I also have on my biker boots to walk along as much of the High Line as I can before it gets dark. Plus I'm going commando.

Now I am turning back, because soon it's time to meet my fiancé.

I spread out the fingers of my left hand. The princess-cut diamond set in platinum catches the light. The engagement ring has given me a new place in the world. It hasn't replaced all the worries. But there's a fresh, clean start, a new life for me. Soon I will be Levi, not Folkes.

We're only just into March, but there are one or two spring-like shoots sprouting in the greenery they've planted up here. It's a cool leafy site in the midst of all this concrete. I am alone and it's not long before the space will be closed. What would happen if they locked all the staircases before I had a chance to get to the ground? What would it be like spending the night up on the High Line?

It would be fun in the summer. Disastrous in the winter. I quicken my pace along the reclaimed railway sleepers, passing over the Meatpacking District with its old roller-skating parks and basketball courts, rusting fire escapes zigzagging their treads across brick façades, traffic lights swinging on cables in front of huge billboards displaying monochrome six-pack male torsos.

I've completed the material for my 'Windows and Doors' exhibition. In fact the images are printed and framed already. But I'll always be a voyeur at heart. Every so often I stop and use my new extra-powerful Leica zoom lens to pry through windows at the ragged signs of human life, the flickering of a TV screen, cutlery placed like the hands of a clock across the messy circles of abandoned plates, a solitary dress dangling like a cadaver off a hanger.

I train my lens like a marksman on one apartment in particular. It's level with where I am but attracts my attention because it's like a glass cube balanced like an afterthought on top of an old warehouse on the other side of a litter-blown car lot where Coke cans clatter like the shoes of ceilidh dancers. Inside the loft I can clearly see that it's like a movie set, all poured concrete and exposed bricks. It's furnished with battered old car seats for sofas and wood burners and iron girders. Huge leaded windows open onto a flat roof with a barbecue and cane loungers and nothing but a low parapet to stop a several-storey drop.

Despite the bright lights burning in there, I can see no signs of life. Not surprising, really. The inhabitants are probably out at work or shopping, like I have been. I'm about to wind in my digital eye when over against the graffiti-splashed far wall of the apartment the lifeless hump in the unmade bed suddenly erupts into movement. Some naked bumster will jump out in a minute no doubt, late for a date, and hurtle into the shower that I guess is concealed behind that wall of glass bricks. But although a long arm flicks aside the sheet, revealing two sleepers for the price of one, they don't get out of bed. Quite the reverse. There's a flailing of youthful limbs, elbows and knees and chins tangled so that I can't tell where one person starts and another ends. But then they separate and arrange themselves into an intricate pose so perfectly choreographed that I realise, too late, that it really *is* a movie set, complete with studio lights and other unwinking cinematic eyes just like mine.

A dark-skinned girl rises out of the snowy mound of bedclothes and flicks a mane of very long, messy black hair off her face and down her sinuous dancer's back. She is sideways on so I can see the curve of her back and the soft heavy drop of her big breasts over a man's chest. She hangs over him, lifting her bottom and thumping it down onto his groin. Then looking away into an unseen corner of the room she starts to speak. The gloss on her lips glistens even from where I'm standing. Studio make-up. Perhaps it's a romantic comedy they're making, or the love scene from one of those street-dancing movies. Or porn.

Still speaking to an unseen observer or director, the girl starts to gyrate, a fluid wave moving up from her hips through her spine to her shoulders and back again. A pair of hands comes up from beneath her and cups both breasts, and she leans lower so that her nipples dip onto the man's mouth. Still her lips are moving. Is she reciting lines, or poetry, or is she singing?

The railway sleepers shake a little beneath my feet. Someone else must be up on the High Line taking a sunset walk. I really ought to tear myself away.

I am about to stop filming – because I am on video mode now – when I realise with a twist in my gullet that if this is a sex scene it may not be simulated. The man's mouth is right on the girl's breasts now. I can see the muscles in his cheeks draw in as he sucks on her nipples. Mine sharpen in response. The girl is flinging her head back, pushing her nipples hard into his mouth. Her little bottom lifts up, showing me the shaft of him going right into her; no way is that simulated. She lifts right to the tip then plunges down on him, and they both lift off the bed, ramming faster at each other, his fingers digging furrows into her breasts. She leans back to angle him into the small of her back and he's throwing her off the mattress as her mouth opens in a silent scream. She freezes mid-climax.

I'm breathing fast, leaning against the railings of the High Line, my legs knocking with the cold, my bare thighs clamped tight against the wetness springing there.

My face, Gustav's face, our bodies superimposed on the action going on over there. All my voyeur instincts and responses kicking in. I want him now. As soon as I get him on his own I'm going to make Gustav do that to me. I'm going to get him on his back, push my nipples into his mouth and ride him like a cowgirl. We can make our own sweet music together, and this time he will be starring in the video alongside me.

I can hear footsteps approaching. Rather than drop my camera as if I'm guilty I allow myself another few seconds, long enough to get the shock of my life because the girl in the movie turns slowly as if she knows I'm there. She looks straight down my zoom lens, beckons to the crew. They mooch towards her, a scruffy bunch in combats and baseball hats, obviously asking what she's seen. Then they all turn to the window, see me over here watching. The voyeur on the High Line. One frowns. One turns his zoom on me. The others wave and make crude fisting gestures. And the dark gypsy girl, still straddling her fictional lover, sends me a huge, dirty smile.

The watcher watched.

Our eyes lock for a few seconds. I'm tight with desire. Everyone is invisible except her. She's gorgeous. Huge sexy lips. I want that girl, badly.

I waggle my fingers at her, and she waggles back. My God, this girlie fantasy won't go away. It keeps nipping at my ankles when I'm least expecting it. Mrs Weinmeyer, Emilia Robinson, a sexy film star. Now that life is looking so good, I might run the idea past Gustav.

Time to go. I walk quickly under the Standard Hotel, vaguely aware of someone wearing a scarlet beanie hat leaning on the rail near the staircase that will take me down to street level. I can't see if the figure is a man or a woman as I fiddle with my glove to check my new Piaget watch. I'm late, and I've still got to find the venue where I'm meeting Gustav.

'You look bloody pleased with yourself, young lady.'

The person blocking my path and dressed all in red is my cousin Polly. I gulp and stare at her for a long, tense moment. Her voice has a kind of deadness to it. I have no idea if she wants to kiss me or kick me. Then she holds her arms out. I drop my bags and walk uncertainly towards her. And pause. I can't forget the terrible thing she said. And I can't handle another row.

'My God, Pol! It's so good to see you, but how did you find me? Who told you I was here of all places?'

'I come in peace, Rena. I hope you do, too.' She pulls me

slowly into a hug, and when I don't resist she tightens her arms around me. 'You can thank Gustav for this. He found me, not the other way round.'

I rest my face against hers. 'So What's been going on? I've tried to call you since I got back from Venice. I hoped we could talk. Where have you been since that awful row? It's been at least six weeks.'

'I'm so sorry, Rena. I was a total bitch to you. What I said was unforgivable.'

I rest my chin on her shoulder, looking between the buildings out to the river beyond us. 'You really hurt me, Polly. You know you got it all wrong.'

The tension in her relaxes but she keeps her arms around me. 'I was directing my angst at the wrong person. You were the soft target, and I'm sorry.' Her skin is soft against my cheek. Her flowery perfume is achingly familiar. 'Gustav got my agent's number out of Pierre. Only useful thing that bastard has ever done. Anyway, my agent told Gustav that I was in London for a while. We had a long chat on the phone. He told me that although Pierre's ashamed of the way he treated me there was no going back and I was best out of the relationship. Of course he's right. We'll have to come to some kind of uneasy truce one day, as we're going to be linked by the two of you getting married. I don't know how that's going to work. I only agreed to come this evening because Gustav told me Pierre is in LA.'

'Typical Gustav, trying to line up all the ducks in one phone call. But I'm sorry too, for being such a gullible klutz.' I cling to her even tighter. I can't tell her, ever, any of them, what that bastard tried to do to me in the gondola. 'The brothers at least are still talking. Pierre seems to have persuaded Gustav that he's sorry for any damage he's caused. But I'm no keener to spend time with him than you are, even though he's apparently fallen on his sword.'

'Pity his sword didn't do him some serious damage. Sorry. Sorry. He's apologised to Gustav, maybe. But he's never had the guts to say sorry to me. You and I know he's a shit-stirrer, Rena. So just steer clear.'

I pull away and look at her. Once I would have told her everything. The ball. The gondola. Pierre's velvet breeches, opening in the darkness, ready to take me. The scars on his back that gave him away. The woman who looks like Margot appearing yet again. Margot herself on my iPad. The gondola sliding noiselessly away into the fog.

Now? It's a poisonous secret I have to keep locked away.

Polly unpeels herself and fusses over the bags I've dropped on the ground. 'So. Look at all this. DVF bags. Beautiful leather jacket. New camera. That *ring*. You've got it made, hon.'

I decide to keep schtum about the VIP area in the boutique I was invited down to as soon as I mentioned the magic words Gustav Levi. It sounds so trivial. I scrabble to pick up the bags. 'None of it means a toss without you to share it. Come with me, and we'll talk on the way.'

She takes a couple of the bags and we clatter down the staircase. 'I can't stop long, Rena. I'm leaving New York tonight.'

I get to the bottom of the metal staircase, my heart sinking. 'So you are still pissed with me.'

'Serena, it's not about you. I need help. Therapy, detox, that kind of thing. I've burned the candle at both ends for long enough. Taken too many illegal substances. I've always been hyper but Pierre Levi was like the worst kind of drug. That's why I fled back to London. I'm a bit dopey now because of the pills. Anyway, I'm going to a spiritual meditation place in Morocco. Like a retreat.'

'Just when we've found each other again, Polly? Oh, honey, of course you must do whatever it takes to get you feeling

330

better. I want my own Polly back. But really? Another country? Where? When exactly?'

'Soon. Tonight.' She hooks her arm through mine and leads me up a wide, apparently deserted street flanked by low-level metal-shuttered warehouses. 'I'm not doing too well, Rena. I really need you to understand. This isn't an overnight thing. It's been brewing since Christmas, maybe even longer. Therapists call what I had with him a toxic relationship. Whatever. Ironic, eh? You're the one who had such a lousy start in life, and I'm the one falling to pieces. I can't be on the same continent as Pierre Levi at the moment.'

'There are things – I still need you.' I hitch the bags up to look at my map of where to go. 'Isn't LA far enough away?'

She shakes her head, gives my arm a playful pinch. I punch her back. Thank God she's put on a bit of weight.

'I'll get over Pierre in time. I hope I'll just be able to put it down to bad choices. But it's not easy being around you, either. It's a kind of role reversal. You're so darn happy, but I need to be on my own. I'll be back like a bad penny when the dust settles.'

'And you'll be my maid of honour when we get married?'

'Already arranged! I'm designing your wedding dress and definitely hair and make-up as well!' She smiles. 'But you won't even notice I'm gone. You'll be far too busy running this place.'

She stops in front of the wide, brightly lit window of an art gallery. Its pale-green painted façade is angled disdainfully away from the wind blasting off the Hudson River and it doesn't appear to have a name. It is empty, but as I start to walk past I suddenly notice, mounted on the whitewashed wall of the gallery, an enlarged photograph of a green shuttered arched window. A bright red row of geraniums are planted in a box below it, and a thin white hand is reaching into the flowers to pinch off a dead petal.

'You take that photograph, Rena?' Polly asks, draping an arm around my neck. 'Looks just your style.'

'How did that get there?' My breath makes steam on the window.

Polly opens the door of the gallery and pushes me inside. Other windows and doors from my travels are hanging on the walls. And walking towards me, tall, dark, gorgeous in an aubergine cashmere sweater and holding out a flute of champagne, is my Gustav.

'Come in from the cold, my betrothed.' Gustav kisses me on the mouth. I close my eyes and rest against him, alone in our private bubble for a moment, breathing in his sharp clean scent, rubbing my lips along the very slightly rough surface of the skin on his chin and jaw.

He laughs to see Polly miming a vomit behind us.

'This gallery is my engagement present to you, Serena. You want to be independent, and so you shall be here. You can show your own work whenever you want, but I think you're ready to start sniffing out new talent, too. This is your domain. You can commute here every day or if you get wanderlust you can employ trusty assistants to run it for you.'

'I'll get Crystal on speed dial now that you've forgiven the poor woman for losing me in Venice.' I pull my beret and jacket off and spin round to take in the photographs that already are bringing back memories. 'But what are we going to call my new venture?'

'Ingrid? Ernst?' Gustav cups his hands round his mouth in a stage whisper. 'You can come out now!'

Mr and Mrs Weinmeyer come through the door at the back of the gallery holding between them a large square parcel wrapped in brown paper. They are dressed identically in elegant tweed suits and narrow woollen neck ties, their Aryan heads sleek and blond under the spotlights of the gallery.

332

'This is a small gift to thank you for the stunning Murano glass you bought for us, Serena, and of course a token of our appreciation for your beautiful portraits and those sizzling Carnevale photographs.'

'But you've already paid me handsomely in filthy lucre!'

'Always happy to invest more if it's something worthwhile, and we think this venture is going places!' Mr Weinmeyer laughs. 'And we haven't forgotten the little promise you made us in Venice.'

Mrs Weinmeyer pats her shining helmet of yellow hair with a wink over at Gustav and lays the parcel down on a glass table. She beckons me over, snaking her arm round my waist to pull me closer. 'You look beautiful in that dress, sugar. You're turning into one classy dame. Those amazing legs.'

Mr Weinmeyer produces a large pair of scissors and indicates that I should cut the string of the parcel.

'And of course we hope we can entice you to our humble abode for another, ah, get-together before too long. Our friends are so keen to meet you.'

I glance at Gustav who strokes his chin thoughtfully. I catch a gleam in his eyes as they travel over the short lace dress, the diaphanous sleeves, the deceptively prim neckline.

'Who are these guys?' Polly hisses. 'They look as if they'd like to gobble you up for breakfast. If they haven't already!'

'I'll tell you later, Pol.'

'Open it!' cries Mrs Weinmeyer, scratching at the brown paper with her red talons.

I tear off the paper, and inside is a sign painted with the word *Serenissima*.

'The name of the gallery? I love it. Thank you.'

Everyone claps and clinks glasses. Polly pulls me aside.

'I have to go, hon. Just remember you are more than my

cousin. You're my sister. I should have known you'd never do anything to hurt me, or to hurt Gustav for that matter.'

I cling to her, stand in front of the door to bar her way. 'Right now? Don't go, Polly!'

'You're stuck with me, doll. I'm still the only family you've got. Me, and your lovely fiancé in there. As for the rest of his family?' She pushes me gently aside and goes out into the cold night. 'Just be careful, Rena.'

At last they've all departed. The sign is already hanging in the window to announce the new name of my establishment. I walk round switching off the lights. I am the proprietress of a glittering new modern art gallery in Manhattan, and in a minute my fiancé and I are going out to celebrate.

Gustav comes out of the office, holding the phone.

'Pierre wants to say congratulations on the new gallery!' he says. 'He also wants us to go to LA to see what's happening with this pilot show.'

I take the phone and stare at it, as if a viper's tongue might flicker out. The absence of Pierre since we returned from Venice has been such a relief. There's no question ever of telling Gustav what nearly happened in Venice, and Pierre obviously feels the same. For now. Every time he opens his mouth I will always dread what's going to come out. Reluctantly I put the phone to my ear and wait for him to speak.

'It's congratulations on your engagement, actually!' Pierre says quietly at the other end of the phone. 'Gustav and Polly aren't the only family you have now, see? I knew that one day I'd be calling you sis.'

'We will work this out as we go along.' I turn away from Gustav to hide the fact that I'm trembling. 'But I will never be your sister, or have anything more to do with you.'

'We are inextricably linked whether you like it or not, sis. How are you going to explain why you don't want me around

334

unless, hmm. Unless you leave Gustav? I've made sure he and I are solid now.' Pierre pauses. I can hear him swallowing. 'Tricking you like that was clumsy and unfair and I'm sorry. But you have only yourself to blame for being so goddamn desirable. Something clicked between us in the Gramercy Hotel bar when we were talking. Don't deny it. I wanted you, Serena. So I had to come after you, find out if it was real. And it felt real in that gondola, didn't it?'

Across the room Gustav lifts his mobile to indicate he has to make a call. I blow him a kiss to hide the angry flush in my face, and turn away again. 'Just one thing, Levi. How did you know it was me at the ball?'

He chuckles. 'Impersonated my brother. I know, wicked, isn't it? Found out from the Weinmeyers where you were, asked the hotel to direct you to the correct shop and then told the lady in the shop to hire you the ball gown I had selected from the internet, and deliver to me the men's version.'

Nausea rises in me. To think I was prancing around in a dress Pierre Levi had chosen. 'Well, your sick plan didn't work.'

'And I got a bruised scrotum for my pains! I'm keeping my distance for now, because I can't trust myself around you.' Pierre's voice descends to a whisper. 'So now it's your turn.'

Coldness rushes down through my body and I put my hand up on the wall to steady myself.

'To do what? Listen to me, Pierre. If you try any more of your tricks, I'll tell Gustav everything.'

'It will be your turn to choose, Serena. I'm back in Gustav's life for good. If you don't want to have any more to do with me, you know where the door is.'

I stare round at the photographs in my new gallery. My new domain.

'I am going nowhere. I'm staying right here, and if you

threaten me again I'll tell Gustav you tried to fuck me in Venice. And I'll tell him about the Margot video you sent to my iPad, intended for him!'

'Now you really are getting paranoid. What video? I don't know about any–'

I can hear some kind of spluttering at the other end but I hang up. I put the phone down very gingerly on the desk. What am I thinking, talking like some sort of gangster?

Trying to hide the tremble in my hand, I walk slowly across my miniature empire with its images of windows and doors hanging on the walls, mostly Venetian but some taken in Paris and London and some taken with my voyeur's zoom lens here in New York, the bird's-eye view. The latest image is still in my camera, the girl straddling her lover in a rumpled bed in a loft apartment.

I turn all the lights off, even the spotlight over the main photograph. I have never come so close to wanting to kill someone. If Pierre Levi wants a fight, he's got one. War is declared.

Gustav walks out of the office and turns to switch off the lights. 'I've made a reservation at La Lanterna, Serenissima. They have the best pesto lasagne and the coolest jazz in town, and a gorgeous conservatory at the back.'

I call softly across the darkened gallery. 'Then you'll have to be quick.'

I'm sitting on the low-slung lounger by the window in ersatz Christine Keeler pose, legs spread, hands dangling between my thighs. My new short designer dress is hitched up. The leather is cool under my bottom. My hair is loose around my shoulders. The images I've spied and photographed are still scrolling through my mind, images from the last few weeks, from the last hour, fuelling my desire.

This is my moment. No-one is going to ruin it. I feel strong and sexy sitting in the dark, waiting for my lover.

Gustav's brogues tap on the polished wooden floor of the gallery as he comes to tower above me, tangling his fingers in my hair. He yanks my head back so I'm looking up at him.

'Do you remember the first time we were in the gallery in London? Talking about my exhibition. About the contract? How young I was then, how wet behind the ears?'

I run my hands up his legs, over his bottom, and then with no preamble I start to unbutton his jeans. This is my man. No one is taking me away from him.

'And how you'd dressed up that morning to impress me, even though I had already made my mind up about you? I'll never forget a moment of our time together.' His fingers tighten in my hair, the roots tugging gently at my scalp.

'I'd made up my mind about you, too, but you were still the sophisticated tycoon and I was the chaotic country girl. I had a lot of catching up to do, but you know I'm a very quick and willing learner.' I open his jeans and take him into my hand, run my fingers up the ready stiffness. 'But in a few short months I no longer feel junior to you. In fact I reckon we're partners. You're my assistant, remember? You carry my gear and come when I call. You watch, I do whatever I want. So what do you reckon? Maybe I've even overtaken you?'

I flick my tongue out, like a snake's, feel him push against me. I run my tongue round the very tip, enough to feel it jump and harden against my teeth. These are my weapons. My tongue. My teeth. My mouth. My hands. And the sexy core of me, where Gustav will always want to go.

'You have blossomed before my very eyes, Serena, and I'm so proud of you. But I'm still watching you, and getting one hell of a kick out it.' His voice is hoarse with lust. 'Our life is just going to get better and better.'

I smile quietly, hold his buttocks and feel them clench as

337

I suck a little harder, nibble down to the base as he starts to buck gently, but I want more. I pull him down beside me on the seat then as I start to kiss him I push him down onto his back. I pull his jeans down a little so that he rears up in the dim light from the street.

'See how beautiful it is,' I croon as I encircle it with my fingers. 'See how well it's going to fit.'

I kneel up, work him under my dress, between my legs, then pause with him resting against me while I lean over him.

'What's going on with you, Serena? You're very low down and dirty tonight.'

His dark eyes are deep and gleaming in the semi-darkness. His hands rest on my bare hips, tweaking at the lacy dress, and as I move slightly he pushes in.

'Just horny, honey. You make me so horny I want to try things,' I murmur, flicking my hair back then pulling the dress up over my head, tossing it carefully aside and unclipping my bra. 'And now you're going to do it just the way I want it.'

His fingers dig into my skin, trying to push me down on to him, but I resist, the muscles in my thighs keeping me kneeling up so that only the tip of him is inside me. I lean so that the golden locket swings and taps. I lift one of his big hands and place it on a swollen breast, make him feel the way my hard nipple pokes against his palm. My head falls back. I spread my knees, balance more comfortably on the leather seat so that my spine is arched and my breasts are pushing at him, jumping up with each heartbeat.

He grins at me, shaking his head slightly at my cheekiness. We're both breathing fast as he brings his other hand up. My breasts are enfolded in his strong fingers and he starts to squeeze. I'm supposed to be in charge, but it's his strength I'm after, and ultimately his power. In fact I'm melting already, my legs shaking as my breasts throb and swell under his touch. I want to subside, open myself to him, but I want to watch his face, too. I try to delay it as long as possible.

The fluttering in my stomach tightens into a clump of desire. His fingers dig into my breasts, wander across them and mould them, press them together. I push them into his face. His tongue flicks across first one nipple, then the other. His hands squeeze until my breasts sing with delicious pain. Then his lips nibble, his tongue lapping round, and he draws the burning bud into his mouth.

I could stay like this forever. I glance over his head, across the street, at the traffic lights changing colour, the shop displays, the restaurant signs, the outlines of people walking along the pavement. At my own reflection in the window, the arch of my spine, my hair tumbling down to my waist, I'm an actress in a sexy film, my lover's pulling at me, making me ache and pulse with longing as I strain towards him, fall onto him, electricity streaking through the emptiness.

He is biting and licking and I have no more control over the urge for selfish satisfaction as my body engulfs his. He releases my nipples and his fingers twine in my hair to pull my face down so that he can kiss me. Really kiss me.

Outside, heels click past on the pavement.

We are both groaning but I can hear laughter. I try to slow down. There are voices outside. Is that the glass door rattling in the sharp wind? I pause altogether, let the hovering orgasm recede. I can't concentrate. I don't want to miss this golden moment by coming too soon.

Just passers-by. I rise on my knees like the girl in the loft did, sliding right to the tip so that I can see the extent of his hardness. I let it rest there then I slide down again, smiling at the way his eyes are glazing over, his hands still resting on my breasts, my bottom tilted in the air. I watch his face and gasp deliciously as I'm filled a little more, the tension is ecstasy, but I can't hold on to it for much longer, and slowly, luxuriously, I slide all the way to the hilt.

It is tempting to ram it but I work into a slow rhythm, ease down again, moaning quietly, and the next time he is with me, pulling his hips back, waiting when I wait. Perfectly in tune. But we do have an audience.

Gustav knows it, too. His eyes are still on mine but as I sigh with delight a low-slung grey car, a Porsche or a Jaguar, purrs up the street and stops outside, its engine idling.

'Someone's watching us,' he whispers as he grins up at me. 'What do you think, Serena? Want to be the first live installation in The Serenissima Gallery?'

I glare at the car, and gasp again. A female figure gets out of the driver's seat, leaves the door open and stands on the deserted pavement. She is wearing a black belted trench coat and a black beret, just like mine. It looks like the girl from the loft I saw earlier except that now she's wearing dark glasses. Maybe she's more famous than I thought, hiding from the paparazzi. Tendrils of black hair coil on her shoulder. That luscious mouth is painted red, grinning.

'Yes, I want her to see,' I puff, barely able to speak. 'Go on. Let's do it.'

'The famous photographer and gallery owner at work!'

Gustav chuckles and taking advantage of my distraction he thrusts inside me. The woman doesn't move as Gustav takes over, driving me on to spikes of pleasure.

'No bells and whistles. No clamps or dildos or even our silver chain. Just us, *au naturel*,' I gasp triumphantly.

She can see it all. Is she turned on by my white thighs parted like some tart in an alleyway, breasts bare and bouncing, my lover flat on his back, taking me rapidly? My thoughts scatter and I start to come, arching my back in a beautiful, perfect pose for her benefit, shaking and moaning as Gustav finishes.

Gustav holds me against him. Juice trickles down my legs as we lie there. I close my eyes. I hear a footstep, and the discordant clatter of the post box. Then the car door shuts, and it purrs away down the street.

'You are very, very wicked, Serena.' Gustav wraps his arms around me as I start to shiver with the cold. 'A voyeur and an exhibitionist, all wrapped up in one naughty package.'

I pull my clothes on again. While Gustav goes to check the lights and the alarm, I pick up the long white envelope that my sexy actress dropped on the doormat. The windows rattle with a sudden blast of wind charging down the street.

The envelope feels so light that it must be empty. Gustav's name, not mine, is printed in the same Bodoni font that he uses for all his Levi literature.

'Talking of packages, what have you got there, *cara*?'

Gustav comes up behind me, soft as a lynx, and busies himself arranging my beret and my scarf. He hands me my gloves and I give him the envelope.

His black eyes rest easily on me, still soft with lust, yet alive with excitement at everything we have in store for us. He pokes inside the envelope and pulls something out.

'No note. No letter. Why have I been sent this?'

My heart goes dead in my chest as we both stare at the single long, petrol-blue peacock-tail feather, complete with the round, staring evil eye.

END OF BOOK TWO

Can't wait to see how it ends?
Read *The Diamond Ring*, the dramatic
finale of the Unbreakable Trilogy when it
hits the shelves in May 2014.

Missed the first instalment in the
Unbreakable Trilogy?

Bound by passion, she was powerless
to resist . . .